PRAISE FOR THE GODSERFS SERIES

"*Silent Hall* is very nearly a perfect novel. I wish my first book had been anywhere near as inventive and challenging to the norm."

James A Moore, author of The Last Sacrifice

"Epic fantasy at its most divine."

Sean Grigsby, author of Smoke Eaters

"Love this story."

H D Lynn, author of The Corner Store Witch

"A great, mythological sort of story that brings all of high fantasy's good stuff to the table."

Jasmine Gower, author of Moonshine

"I am constantly surprised how a new author can bring a creative world into the light of the written word and unfold a competent and entertaining novel. Really astounding, as it reads like an accomplished author that has been writing for many years. GET THIS!"

Koeur's Book Reviews

"N S Dolkart has achieved an epic tale with an intimate feel because despite the vast geographical and co... cters' needs,

"T

Morpheus Tales

BY THE SAME AUTHOR

GODSERFS
Silent Hall
Among the Fallen

N S DOLKART

A Breach in the Heavens

GODSERFS BOOK III

ANGRY ROBOT

ANGRY ROBOT
An imprint of Watkins Media Ltd

20 Fletcher Gate,
Nottingham,
NG1 2FZ
UK

angryrobotbooks.com
twitter.com/angryrobotbooks
Never a moment's peace

An Angry Robot paperback original 2018

Cover art by Andreas Rocha
Set in Meridien by Argh! Nottingham

Distributed in the United States by Penguin Random House, Inc.,
New York.

ISBN 978 0 85766 740 3
Ebook ISBN 978 0 85766 741 0

Printed in the United States of America

9 8 7 6 5 4 3 2 1

To my daughter Leila, eleven days old when I started this series and six years old next week.

Let he who was fatherless find his true sire
And he with no wishes fulfill his desire
Let she who is dark bring light to the people
And she with no church raise skyward her steeple
For I see the end now to all things once planned
When he who was murderer rescues the damned

PROPHECY OF THE DRAGON KNIGHT

1
PSANDER

Psander hated feeling nervous. She'd hated it ever since she was a girl, trying to work up the courage to ask her wealthy uncle to take her on as his apprentice. He'd been a master glass-blower in one of the coastal towns between Parakas and Atuna; his work had graced the halls of nobles. Psander could still remember the heat of his workshop and the smell of melting sand. How wonderstruck she'd been, that a thing as plain and gritty as sand could be transformed into such incredible beauty. She had longed to wield her uncle's power and learn his art, to turn the stuff of the ocean floor into a glowing orb so hot and dangerous that children were forbidden from even being near it. The final product had never interested her as much as that orb, that moment of perilous transformation. She had longed for her uncle's skills with such passion that she had been afraid to ask him, afraid that he might reject her and equally afraid that he might not. She had actually been sick over it.

And after all that, he had turned her down. A girl her size couldn't even hold the rod properly, let alone use it. He had made her feel like such a fool, not only for her desires but for that accursed nervousness that had made her voice shake when she asked him to teach her.

She was too ambitious, he had said. Why yearn for a man's job when a woman's work was equally valuable?

Because she had *wanted* it, that was why. Psander had always been a stubborn one, and a contrarian too. When her uncle told her that she was too ambitious, she had taken it to mean that she had not been ambitious enough. If he wouldn't teach her his art, she would find an even better art and learn it from a more worthwhile teacher – and she would never again let her desires make her weak and nervous. From that moment on, Psander vowed that she would walk through the world as if all of it was hers to manipulate, hers to heat and melt and transform as she pleased.

And until now, she had stuck to that plan. When a messenger had come to her uncle from the wizard Pelamon, asking him to produce a hand-sized decorative dragon, Psander had abandoned her parents without a second thought and tracked the messenger back to the outskirts of Parakas. There she had pounded on the wizard's door until he opened it, and demanded that he teach her magic. Pelamon had been about her uncle's age, and she had expected him to show similar resistance to the idea of teaching a girl. She had prepared herself to stand at his door for hours after he first turned her down, slamming her fists into it until they were raw and bloody and he had to let her in just to stop the noise. But the wizard hadn't been reluctant to teach her at all. He had only looked her over in an appraising sort of way and told her that she would have to prove her aptitude.

So she had. When the wizard gave her a task, she performed it. When he gave her a scroll without explaining what it was for, she studied it until she could recite it back to him word for word. When he sent her to assist the mages at Gateway for a time, she did so without question. She assaulted each task as if it were the last, smallest obstacle between her and glorious victory, and she didn't stop after Pelamon officially accepted her as his student. Why should she? She had no interest in being some competent practitioner, for her uncle was much more than that in his own field, and she meant to surpass him. She meant to be a master.

Of course, even a master wizard had much to fear. Unlike her mentor, who had made dragons the focus of his studies, Psander had gravitated toward the study of the Gods. She had primarily been interested in the way They marked Their domains and Their territories in the human world, but it did not take long for her to realize the danger They posed to the entire academic community. A riot here, an unexplained smiting there... the details varied with time and place, but the pattern was clear: the Gods had decided that academic wizardry must end.

But she had braved even that revelation without feeling nervous. Fearful, yes. Angry, yes. How dare the Gods try to take this beautiful thing from humanity? What had she or her colleagues done to deserve Their persecution? It was frightening, and it was infuriating, but she had survived it. She had protected what knowledge she could and brought it with her to this place that the Gods had long ago forsaken, this place where They would not follow. And she had done it all without ever succumbing to that weakness and insecurity, that dreadful anticipation.

But now Psander was nervous. The queen of the Goodweather elves and the prince of the Illweathers would be arriving within the hour. And it was necessary, of course it was, but she still almost regretted inviting them.

A wave of heat rose through her chest, growing into that familiar, intolerable flame. She was sweating now, naturally. Just when she needed her poise the most, Psander's body seemed bent on sabotaging her efforts.

She wiped her reddening face and checked her wards again. Would they function sufficiently? They'd better. The elves had an incredible mastery of their world – the very air obeyed their commands – so she had consecrated her fortress to the absent Gods, reminding the stone walls and everything within them that they were not of this world at all, and need not respond as such. It was undeniably ridiculous that she should have spent half a lifetime warding the Gods away only to turn around and claim Their ownership now, but Psander wasn't bothered by such ironies. She was bothered by the possibility that it might not work.

The brutal truth was that there was likely no ward that could put Psander on an equal footing with those she had invited. Their magic wasn't like hers, based on endless reflections and refractions of others' power. It was innate and pure. Academic magic was endlessly clever, but in any direct confrontation, purer forms were bound to prevail.

It would be no better should this meeting come to combat. She had chosen Hunter and his best pupil Tritika to guard the door of the meeting chamber opposite the elves' trusted captains, but Hunter had warned her not to rely on them as a safeguard. Though he and Tritika had defeated other elves in the past, the raider captains were extraordinary in their martial skill.

"I've watched them fight each other," he had said. "Even

two against one, we couldn't take either one of them."

Psander had assured him that his role and Tritika's would be ceremonial. At least she hoped it would.

The Illweather prince arrived first, wearing a flowing green robe that glowed with a silver sheen. His captain was a severe-looking elfwoman who held her sickle in one hand with casual ease. Hunter shuddered at the sight of her – there was a history there. Perhaps Psander would learn it from him later, but for now she sent him downstairs to greet her guests. She needed someone level-headed for that task, and Tritika was still too young to be trusted.

She turned back to the window. It was broad daylight, so in the contrary way of their kind, both elves' skin had turned black as night. Over the years, Psander had had the chance to inspect a captured elf or two, but she had yet to discover the mechanism or, for that matter, the purpose behind these complexion changes. Whatever the reason, it was unsettling. In the dark, elves shone like the moon; in the light, they were so dark that they seemed to suck all the brightness out of the air and swallow it completely. Elves in daylight were not black like islanders – they were black like death.

The prince and his bodyguard swept toward the gate of Silent Hall, where Hunter met them with a bow and led them into the fortress and out of sight. Psander had set aside an antechamber where they could wait until the Goodweather queen arrived – she had no intention of meeting with them separately. The elves' wariness and mistrust of each other might well be the best safeguard she had against their turning violent.

Psander didn't have to wait long for the queen of the Goodweather elves to arrive. She and her captain came riding on a pair of soulless elvish horses, trotting to the gate as if on a casual jaunt through the woods. The queen wore a magnificent saffron-yellow dress that set off her daylight coloration gloriously; her raider captain wore a brown so drab it might have been burlap. They slid off their horses without bothering to tie them to anything – elvish horses never wandered, after all – and were met at the gate by Tritika. After that, Psander left the window for the chamber where she intended to meet her guests.

She had elected to use her laboratory, a room with significance because it had once held a captured elf, and she still remembered his pain. She had cleared most of the books and implements but left the saw with which she had eventually opened the elf's skull. Its presence was not an attempt at intimidation, for she did not believe that the elven rulers would know or care about the saw's significance. It was, rather, a focal point for the room's wards, a reminder to the fortress that within its walls Psander was the only master. She hoped those wards would hold.

There were not many chairs in Psander's fortress, so she had had to bring three in from her library. She chose the largest of these and sat down to wait. At least the heat beneath her skin had now abated, so she had the chance to compose herself. Soon the queen and prince would join her, and then would come the hard part: asking for their help.

One thing at a time. Were the wards set? Of course they were. Was she prepared to rebuff attempts at mind-reading? Always. Why did she have to feel so nervous again, after all this time? How she hated it.

At long last, the door opened. The two elves entered and unpleasant pleasantries were exchanged. At this proximity, the elves' power was palpable. Psander could feel her wards straining to contain it, to keep the stone and air and flesh within her walls from obeying these creatures' whims. Her mental wards too, forced to resist not one but two elven monarchs, felt as if they might crumble before too long. The wizard smiled through her introductions anyway – since the wards were holding for now, the elves could not feel her struggle. If she kept the strain out of her demeanor, they would not know how taxing this was for her.

The queen of Castle Goodweather held out her hand, fingers down as if waiting to be kissed. In the dimmer light of Psander's candles, her skin had turned that eerie white again, but her fingernails were black. They were long and pointed and very delicately filed – unless they somehow grew that way naturally? Psander had never cared enough about her appearance to do any more than cut her own nails and hurriedly file the jagged edges – for her colleagues, beauty had been a distraction; for the lay public, she had favored illusion.

The queen's gesture demanded some response, and as Psander had no intention of kissing her hand she took advantage of her own mild curiosity instead. She gently lifted the queen's fingers with her palm as if admiring its beauty and said, "Your nails are magnificent."

"I am entirely magnificent," the elf queen said. Then she laughed. "You godserfs are a shadow of us, wizard. Your masters were too afraid to make you more than that."

Psander considered countering that shadows could grow larger than those who cast them, but battles of verbal wit had never been her strength, and she suspected that she would lose if she went down that path. So instead she said, "If I am somebody's shadow, elf queen, I don't believe I'm yours."

The Illweather prince sneered. "We did not beg to come here, wizard, it was you who begged us. Say whatever you mean to say."

"I *advised* you to come here," Psander answered, "because I am no longer capable of acting on my own. My apprentice Phaedra has done all that she can in the other world, but without some further intervention both our worlds will soon end."

The prince glowered. "Explain yourself."

"Naturally."

Psander wondered at his demand. Could it be that he didn't know? Didn't suspect what was happening? What did he *think* all those skyquakes meant?

"Perhaps," she said, "I should begin with the mesh. I don't know what you call it here, but mesh is the term academic wizards use for the barrier between the worlds. You might be aware that the mesh is double-sided – that is, that the layer holding us in this world corresponds to another layer on the opposite side. This is why every opening of a gate produces not one but two physical manifestations: your nets, and a mist."

The Illweather prince looked scornful. "You godserfs are children. Your knowledge is simplistic."

"Well," Psander countered, matching the coldness in his voice, "if your kind wasn't so bent on eating us, we might have had discussions such as these long ago. Then I would have a better understanding of what you do and don't know, and I wouldn't have to waste any time on simplistic explanations. As it is, you will forgive me while I establish where our common understanding *does* lie."

"Continue with your point," said the Goodweather queen, waving her on.

"My point is this: the two worlds may seem as if they abut each other, but on some esoteric level they do not. There is distance between them, metaphysically speaking, and each world has its own mesh. The gateways are places where the two sides *do* connect and where the mesh on both sides has been rubbed thin."

"They *were* such places," the queen said, "until you wicked children closed them. There were no raids last year, as I am sure you know."

"I am not unaware," Psander said with some satisfaction. "But surely you must realize why I had my apprentice seal them. Twelve years ago, when Castle Goodweather's seed was introduced into my world and encouraged to grow there, it created a new gateway from my home here to the island of Tarphae on the other side. That new gateway bound our worlds closer together and ended the equilibrium that had existed for millenia. The skyquakes we have experienced are a result of the way your older, smaller world has been destabilized. Put bluntly, we are being drawn ever closer to the world I came from, and our eventual landing will be anything but soft. My best guess is that the meshes of our worlds will either compress upon themselves or overlap altogether – either way, the result is that all of reality in both worlds will be shredded. Phaedra's purpose in sealing the gates was to cut a few tethers, to release some of the tension and restore equilibrium."

The queen rapped those long nails of hers against the table. "But the skyquakes persist."

"I've noticed that, yes."

The prince was scornful. "You godserfs lack the strength

to do anything meaningful."

Psander almost rolled her eyes, but restrained herself. "My apprentice Phaedra has sealed your gates – is that not meaningful? Even from that alone, we have already gained much. When she began her work, the skyquakes were not only gaining in frequency and intensity but gaining in frequency and intensity *faster than they are now.* That is to say, the periods between the quakes may still be shortening, but they have been shortening a good deal slower than they were before."

Illweather's prince dismissed this point with a wave of his arm. "Meaningless. I hope for your sake that you have more to offer than this."

"You hope for all our sakes," Psander corrected him. "Don't pretend that you will be exempt from the destruction."

The queen clicked her nails against the table again. "Enough. We hope for *our* sakes that you're less of a fool than you sound. So far, it seems to me that you have contributed nothing."

"My dear queen," Psander said, "if it seems that way to you, then you haven't been listening. Sealing the gates has had a definite, calculable effect. By my estimate, if Phaedra hadn't so diligently loosened those tethers, our worlds would have *already collided.* Three and a half years ago, to be precise."

"But now all the gates are gone except for this one," the prince said, "and this one cannot be sealed. Goodweather and its offspring are holding it open, thanks to you and your apprentice. If your latest efforts have only delayed our doom by a few years, do not expect the Illweather elves to be grateful for it."

"I'm not asking you to be grateful," Psander snapped. "I'm asking for your help. Phaedra's efforts have bought us time, but I have found no permanent solution to our problem. I don't expect to find one today, or possibly ever, but if a possibility *does* arise before it's too late, the power of the elves may be required. My question to you is simple: can we make common cause in the interest of self-preservation, or must I split my efforts between saving our worlds from destruction and saving my people from myopic child-eaters?"

The Goodweather queen laughed at this for far too long. "Not to worry," she said at last. "We will let you focus on one danger at a time."

2
HUNTER

Hunter stood with Tritika across from the elvish captains, trying to keep his mind blank. The fairies could read minds, and he didn't like to give them any advantage. Luckily, he was no stranger to calming his thoughts. He gazed upon his foes and counterparts, imagining the scrape of sword against whetstone, the comfort of repetitive motion and that marvelous sound, undoubtedly irritating and yet so satisfying, like scratching an itch. His friend Narky couldn't stand it, but the sound had always been a balm to Hunter's nerves.

His eyes remained alert. He knew these elf captains well enough to know that any attack would be blinding in its speed and viciousness. He had seen them fight each other once, watched as they exchanged perfectly matched blows until the sudden end when the Illweather captain had removed her opponent's arm and head. The Goodweather captain had taken it well at the time, and he didn't seem much the worse for wear now. There was just the hint of a scar on his neck where the blade had sliced through. Hunter wondered what magic had put the elf's body back together, but then he managed to focus once more on the sound of the whetstone and pull his mind back from speculation.

The Goodweather captain smirked. Did he find Hunter's meditations amusing? Or had Tritika somehow revealed something inadvertently, something that he would soon report to his queen? There was no way to know, not yet. He concentrated on the sound.

"I have sympathy for your friend's point of view," the Illweather captain said. "It is an unpleasant noise."

"I'm enjoying it, myself," her counterpart replied, his smile growing wider.

"You Goodweathers have always had poor taste."

Hunter chanced a look at Tritika. The young woman was a decade his junior and very, very quick, and her fervor in training for battle had always been unmatched among his students. She was one of the few villagers who had mastered his elf-fighting technique of mental misdirection. Psander had not needed his recommendation to choose her for a second bodyguard: Tritika had already proven herself last year by fighting off a pair of elven scouts and making it home to safety. Hunter was quite proud of her.

Tritika had a look of intense concentration on her face, no doubt focusing on keeping her own thoughts blank. She was very earnest. But of course, Phaedra would have said the same about him.

He could not think about Phaedra, not now. Afterwards, yes, when the elves were gone and no lives depended on his concentration. This brief conversation was a feint, a distraction designed to keep him from staying sharp.

The Illweather captain was smiling mischievously at him now. "What are their majesties discussing, do you suppose?"

"I don't know."

"Perhaps your wizard is negotiating an exchange," the Goodweather captain suggested. "Selling some of you in return for our rulers' help."

"Help with what?" Tritika asked, taking the bait.

"The skyquakes, I believe. Your Psander created them herself, but they have gotten out of hand. Like your Gods before you, you godserfs have difficulty controlling your creations."

Hunter went back to honing the sword in his mind. If he knew more than the elves did on this matter, he ought to let it stay that way. He could explain what Phaedra had told him later, when the danger was gone.

Hunter missed his actual sword. It was bittersweet to focus his memories on the experience of sharpening it when the sword itself had broken long ago. There was no blacksmith in Psander's fortress and certainly no iron mines – Gods knew where the elves had procured the steel for their sickles – so the only weapons he had now were those he could make or loot. Today he held an elvish sickle, chosen both for the dominance it signaled and because his preferred spear was too long for such close quarters. Would he need to put it to use?

An hour dragged by, slowed by Hunter's need to remain alert at every moment. His arms were getting tired of holding the sickle, his eyes of glancing back and forth between the captains, watching for early signs of hostile motion. His muscles ached with tension. The fairies could tell, of course, but still they had not attacked. Hunter suspected they had never meant to, but it was too dangerous for him to make such assumptions. If he let his guard down...

Finally, the door opened and the Illweather prince swept out, followed closely by the Goodweather queen. "Come," the queen said to her captain. "Castle Goodweather must be informed. Its help may soon be needed."

Hunter gave Tritika a glance and they fell in behind the elves, escorting them back to the gate. Then at last the enemy was gone, the threat over.

Tritika collapsed against a wall. "I thought that would never end!"

"It was long," Hunter agreed, "and you did well. If they had learned much from us, I think they'd have said so."

Tritika nodded. "They do love taunting."

As they made their way back upstairs, Hunter finally let his mind wander. His first thought, as always, was of Phaedra, so brilliant and so beautiful and so far away. It had been eleven long years since he had seen her, years that had felt empty in her absence. The older villagers kept urging him to forget about her, to marry and have children and behave like a man with blood in his veins, but he could no more forget Phaedra than he could forget to breathe. If there was any chance that she would have him when she came back, he could wait forever.

She loved him too, or at least she had said so, but her work had been far too important for her to abandon it and make a life with Hunter. It was more than that too: she didn't want to marry him, because marriage so often led to children. She didn't dislike little ones, he thought, but her study of magic was more important to her, and it would *always* be more important. She could risk no distractions.

Hunter could accept that, but he didn't think he would ever truly understand it. He had himself lived an undistracted life once, and come to regret it. He knew now that only *people* were worth dedicating one's life to. He hoped she would give him the opportunity to devote his life to her.

What was taking her so long? He asked himself that question nearly every day. She had sealed all the gates besides Psander's one – he was sure of that. The elves had gone wild when the gates would not open for their raids and had come storming up to Silent Hall to demand that Psander let them through. Psander had laughed and the villagers had thrown stones at them until they left. So if the work was done, why had Phaedra not returned?

Perhaps Mura was to blame. The pirate sorcerer had set up his camp on the island of Tarphae, where Psander's gate led, so returning was probably easier said than done. But Phaedra was adept at travel magic, so Psander said. If she couldn't find some way to clear them off the island, couldn't she at least evade them? She had managed once before.

But there was always that worst possibility, the one that Hunter refused to believe: that Phaedra had tried to come back to him and failed. That she was dead. It was a horrible thought and he always pushed it aside when it came to mind, but for how long could he keep this up? How many years before he would have to consider her lost?

When Hunter and Tritika got upstairs, they found Psander still sitting in her workshop, apparently lost in thought. "Did the meeting go well?" Tritika asked.

Psander didn't even look up. "As well as might have been expected," she said.

"What does that mean?"

"It means," Psander answered, "that if we're very, very lucky, we may all survive the year."

3

DELIKA

Criton was agitated. He always got like this before a visit from Goodweather, his eldest daughter. He would stalk about for days, clenching and unclenching his hands and being generally useless while his wives managed their children, washed the clothes, herded and milked and sheared the sheep, cooked the meals... in short, while they did everything. The older three rolled their eyes and labored on; only Delika found his nervousness endearing.

"Delika, what did you like to do when you were twelve?"

They were in Delika's bedroom; she was mending clothes while he paced in front of her.

"You don't remember?" she asked, folding her arms and pouting at him. "You were there, you know."

But he didn't answer, just looked miserable and desperate. Delika took pity on him.

"I liked being with you," she said.

He smiled weakly at her. "You're no help."

"That's what she's coming here for."

"I should show her something she's never seen before. Did I bring her to the citron groves last visit?"

"Yes. But there weren't any fruits yet. I bet she'd like them better now. It smells so nice there."

He came over and sat down beside her on the bed. "Do you think she'll be angry about us? You two are like sisters."

She wanted to soothe him, to deny that Goodweather would care that they had gotten married, but she couldn't bring herself to. Of *course* Goodweather would care. She and Delika were best friends, despite the distance and the infrequent visits. Delika didn't know what she'd think of this new arrangement, but she was bound to have strong feelings. Would she hate Delika for what she'd done?

Criton didn't even wait for an answer. "I'm going to find Horda," he said, standing up again. "Goodweather loves her lamb with the carob paste."

That was the one problem with marrying Criton: Delika still had to share him.

She wished she didn't have to. Though she was his newest wife, Delika had known Criton longer than the other three. Not much longer, she had to admit that. Maybe a year. But what a year that had been.

Criton had rescued Delika twice when she was five years old, first from elves she could not remember and then from the grasping ocean God, Mayar. He had found her a family near Ardis, since she had not known where her own was, but a few months later she had run away from those not-parents and found him again. After that, he had given up on sending her away. When his first wife had left him for another woman, taking her baby with her, she hadn't even considered bringing Delika: Delika was his. She had always been his.

But then, a few weeks later, his cousin Belkos had killed

him. The two-and-more months that followed were still
the worst in Delika's life. Kilion Highservant, who was
now high priest, had taken her in, and she supposed he
and his family had been kind to her. She didn't really
remember how they had treated her, to be honest – all she
remembered was the pain.

It was almost funny, in retrospect, that the Highservants
had been the ones to watch over her after the assassination.
Their own daughter Vella was that very same girl who
had run off with Criton's first wife, Bandu. She was now
Goodweather's second mother, so in a strange way they
were *almost* all related. But back then, the Highservants
had only been grieving parents with a missing daughter,
and Delika had only been a little girl with no parents at all.

Things were better now, so much better, and Delika
had Bandu to thank for that. Bandu had traveled to the
underworld with her strange magic and brought Criton
back from the dead, so for all Delika's jealousy, for all that
she wished Criton didn't have that longing look in his eyes
whenever he asked Goodweather how her mother was
faring, Delika did her best to be grateful. When that ugly
feeling rose, she reminded herself that without Bandu
there would have been no Criton for her to marry.

Delika had always wanted to marry Criton, though
her reasons had changed over the years. When she was
little, she had thought that if you loved someone you were
supposed to marry them, and it was as simple as that. Then
it had been the overwhelming need to stay with him, the
fear of having to part from him when she got older. Her
awakening had come late, only a couple of years ago. She
had never been boy-crazy, but all of a sudden she was *him*-
crazy, so much that it frightened her.

It still frightened her, really. It wasn't until this year that she had overcome her fears and asked, demanded, *begged* him to marry her, because she hadn't been wrong when she was five and she hadn't been wrong when she was ten and she still felt the same at fifteen, so it wasn't going away. It had taken persistence and courage to make him see her as anything other than a child, but she had managed it in the end. Now he was hers, really hers, and it was her greatest accomplishment.

Naturally, the other wives resented her for it. Three wives should have been more than enough for any man, even Delika couldn't deny that, but their marriages were all political, not love marriages like hers. Criton had taken two wives among the plainsfolk and one Dragon Touched widow, all in order to bring his people together. The young city of Salemica was thriving on the peace he had wrought, and these other wives and children were very much a part of that. But Delika had cemented no alliance for Criton, bought him no peace treaty. It was obvious that if he had married her, he must love her more than the rest of them.

Horda was the nicest about it. She had been the first to marry Criton after his return from the dead, and though she clearly still thought of Delika as a sort of stepchild, she had never treated her like a threat. She had borne Criton four children: Torgos, Galanea, Aegypa, and baby Salemis, who had been named after the dragon. They were all so much younger than Delika – all the children were – that taking care of them had been her primary chore for years. Horda had greeted Delika's marriage with dismay and even horror, but she hadn't taken it out on Criton's newest, youngest wife. She was a good woman. Delika didn't exactly *like* her, but she tried to appreciate her.

Papira was Criton's second wife, if you didn't count Bandu. Her jealousy was obvious, as was everything else about her – frankly, Delika found her boring. She didn't talk much, but when she did, she may as well not have. Her one redeeming quality was that she was too much of a coward to really cause trouble for anyone. That was a relief, but also not remotely interesting. Papira's motivations and opinions were completely standard, her insights uninsightful – even her face was dull.

Criton would never have married such a boring person if not for the politics of the thing, Delika was sure of it. But when she had said so to Criton's third wife, Iashri – a mistake in itself, talking to *her* about anything – Iashri had smiled wryly and said that those three children hadn't seeded themselves.

Iashri was Criton's only Dragon Touched wife, and she was the one who really bothered Delika. She always acted as if she knew so much more of the world than Delika did, and this knowledge inevitably involved some critique of Delika's happiness. If Delika liked Goodweather's visits, it was because the two of them were so frivolous together. If she thought Criton loved her, it was because she didn't understand men. If she enjoyed Horda's cooking, she was eating too much.

Delika had almost, *almost* managed to hold her tongue and let Iashri's comment slide, but instead she had muttered, "Lord knows how he managed with *you*," and of course Iashri had heard her. Delika's big mouth was always getting her in trouble.

It had been that way ever since she was little, and she didn't know if it would ever get better. A part of her hoped it wouldn't. She knew the other wives thought her impetuousness came from youth and immaturity and she didn't want them to be right, even if it would mean trouble her whole life. Whatever they thought, Delika was happy with who she was.

It was Iashri, really, who didn't have any confidence in herself – that was why she kept trying to make Delika feel the same way. Delika might have been younger than her, but she wasn't stupid. Iashri's favorite phrase had once been, "When you get married, you'll see," but now that she couldn't use that anymore, it had been replaced by, "When you have children." That was still safe for now, since Delika was the only wife with no children of her own. Horda had her four, Papira three, and Iashri was pregnant with her second.

"Wait until you have your own," Iashri had told Delika a month ago. "You think you love Criton more than we do because we don't worship him; well, wait until you have a screaming baby and Criton disappears."

Delika hadn't had a good response for that one. It was undeniable that Criton wasn't as helpful with his children as he might have been. He played with them often and showered them with love in a most endearing way, but when they cried or whined or made demands he would leave them to their mothers or to Delika and disappear. Still, Delika didn't think it was right to blame him for it, because it was when Criton tried to deal with the situation himself that he most often ended up in one of his rages.

He had to be careful about these things, because when he was tense Criton became prone to fits of rage. There was no predicting their timing: they would strike suddenly in the midst of some otherwise unexceptional argument or conversation, and when they did it was terrifying.

He would shout, slam his fists against the furniture, and breathe sparks, and that wasn't even the scariest part: the really frightening thing was that it was all so undeliberate, so sudden and disproportionate and sometimes even nonsensical, that anybody watching him could see that *he couldn't stop himself*. And that meant that if it ever *did* turn to physical violence…

Well, it hadn't yet, and everyone was alive and well.

Criton did always apologize after an outburst, but even Delika had to admit that it wasn't good enough. What good was a heartfelt apology if he had so little control over himself? He couldn't promise never to do it again, because he hadn't meant to do it to begin with.

She did wonder sometimes if it had been the outbursts that chased Bandu away. Delika could remember times when the two of them seemed to do nothing but argue. On the other hand, she couldn't remember any rages from those days, so perhaps there hadn't been any. Maybe it had only started after she left him, or after he had died and come back; maybe there had been instances that she didn't know about, before she had come to live with them. After all, Delika had only spent a few months with them before Bandu left Criton, and his rages weren't all that common. Even now, with his life a good deal more complicated than it had been back then, he didn't lose control more than a few times a year.

In any case, avoiding frustration was clearly the only way he knew to avoid an outburst. Surely the other wives ought to forgive him for that – he was doing his best for all of them.

At least he wasn't frustrated right now, just anxious. Goodweather visited only twice a year, when she and her stepmother came to Salemica for a few weeks to visit their respective relatives, and more than anything, Criton was afraid of disappointing her. He desperately wanted her to enjoy her visits and spoke openly about how happy he was that she and Delika were friends.

They really were the best of friends. Goodweather was just the right age where they could pretend they were sisters, even though Criton's daughter was brown-skinned and Dragon Touched, and Delika was neither. They were barely six years apart – not quite that, even. Delika was not yet eighteen, after all, and Goodweather was already twelve.

The thing Delika adored most about Goodweather was the way the younger girl looked up to her. Goodweather was enthusiastic about being with her, unlike the other wives' children who saw her as a caretaker. She made Delika feel clever and wise, not like some foolish child who didn't deserve Criton's attention. With Goodweather, Delika could be the elder who was admired, without having to aspire to any dubious higher maturity.

Goodweather was very much her mother's daughter – at least, that was what Criton always said. She was quick to judge people, for good or ill, and she had a tremendous amount of confidence in herself. Delika did too, so they got along splendidly – dangerously, even. They had a tendency to encourage each other a bit too much and had nearly drowned once, when Delika had tried to wade across the river with Goodweather on her shoulders. A few visits back, Delika had taught her how to make a reed flute and how to play one – though to tell the truth, neither of them was very good at it. Goodweather, in return, had tried to teach her some magic to alter her body, but either Delika was incapable of magic or else Goodweather's instructions had simply been too garbled and childlike to follow.

Hopefully this visit would go well. Hopefully Goodweather would forgive Delika for marrying her father.

Delika finished sewing a torn bedsheet and picked up another item from the pile: one of Papira's lighter dresses. Sewing was one of her least favorite chores, but it did beat working in the hot sun.

A sudden thunderclap made her prick her thumb on the needle and drop her work. It was soon followed by a second, near and loud enough that instead of sucking on her bleeding thumb, Delika brought both hands up to cover her ears. How could there be thunder when the sun was shining so bright?

She turned to look out the window just as the wind slammed the shutters closed. She rose and went to push on them, but at that moment the wind changed direction and tore them away from her, nearly causing her to fall out. Delika reeled and grabbed hold of the sill to steady herself. Then she looked up, shrieked, and backed away from the window.

4
VELLA

Vella hated these visits almost as much as she loved them. She loved her parents and her brother, and it was nice to be treated as an exalted guest nowadays, especially after the first visits had been so fraught. That had mostly been Grandma's fault: despite loving her granddaughter, Grandma Hessina had felt that her position required her to punish Vella as an aberrant adulteress. Several times she had openly considered having her granddaughter lashed or beaten, but Vella's parents had always been able to talk her down. Now Grandma – may her memory be a blessing – was gone, and since the high priesthood had passed to Father there had been no more talk of punishment.

Father's permissiveness had had a wondrous effect on the people of Salemica. The last time Vella had visited her parents, a man had stopped her at the market and thanked her for what she had done. She had stood there, blinking, as he told her of how her influence on her father had allowed him and others to live as themselves, without fear of a religious mob. Kilion's blessing was seen as a mark of God Most High's will, and so, simply by marrying Bandu and retaining her father's love and protection, Vella had set a hidden people free.

But it was no longer the threat of violence that led Vella to hate these visits. No, she hated them because they inevitably brought her face-to-face with Criton.

Vella despised Criton. His spirit had hung over her relationship with Bandu since the very beginning, when she had feared that Bandu might return to him. That danger was long gone, but Criton was slowly stealing Bandu away anyhow: she was giving her life to him, year after year.

Eleven years ago, Criton had been killed before he could finish arranging a peace treaty between the Dragon Touched and Ardis. To save Vella's people, to make the world a safer place for Goodweather, Bandu had journeyed all the way to the underworld, to the sea of the dead, to retrieve him. The price was that for every year Criton gained, Bandu lost one of her own.

Bandu and Vella had both been teenagers when they first met. Now the first of Bandu's hairs were turning gray. How long before they all went? How long before her strong, beautiful body began to grow weak?

At first, the differences had been subtle. Bandu was not as scrawny as she had once been, but then, neither was Vella. But with each passing year it became more pronounced. Anyone could see now that the two of them weren't the same age anymore, though Goodweather was still too young to think anything of it. That would change too, sooner or later.

Vella hated Criton for taking these years from Bandu. She hated the way he asked after her longingly, as if he hadn't already taken too much of her precious time for himself. He was a selfish man, and the worst part was that he didn't realize it.

She knew these visits were good for her daughter, though. Goodweather loved her father, and she was close friends with Delika, the girl he had raised to worship him. For all Vella's distaste and for all her resentment, she couldn't begrudge her daughter's happiness. Let Goodweather grow out of these people on her own, if she ever would.

Goodweather was growing giddy as they neared Salemica, bounding toward the city like a puppy. She was so cute; always had been. She reminded Vella of all the things she loved most about Bandu: her confidence, her unapologetic vigor. She was so full of life, it was a wonder she didn't burst.

Salemica had come into view a mile back, rising out of the plains. It was a striking city, its wall of dark Ardisian stone standing in such contrast to the wheat fields surrounding it. The dry months were a good time to visit, when there was less fieldwork to be done and Vella could leave Bandu to tend the garden without help from her or Goodweather. Bandu had been a forager in her youth, not one to cultivate her own vegetables, but Vella had taught her and over the years it had more than paid off. Bandu had a knack for making plants grow. She would talk to them whenever she was in the garden, and whether this was a form of magic or only a way to pass the time, it worked wonders. Bandu could bring the puniest seedling back from the brink of death and make it yield the finest fruit.

The dry season wasn't without work, of course. There were plenty of people out in the fields and orchards even now, herding their animals or gathering the figs and apricots of summer, but come harvest time Vella and Goodweather would journey back through fields swarming with workers. There would be tents here then, so that the men and women of Salemica could save themselves the time that it took to go from their houses to the fields. Nearly the entire city emptied out at harvest time.

But not Vella's family. Her father was high priest now, and was not permitted by the old laws to own land. Instead, the townsfolk brought all their sacrifices to him, from which his family was allotted a portion. Vella's parents ate well.

Goodweather was bounding ahead again. "Slow down," Vella called to her.

She turned around, their beautiful girl, her face radiant. Goodweather had inherited her simple, joyful smile from her father, along with her nose and forehead and, of course, her scales. Those golden scales and her dark brown skin complemented each other perfectly, so much better than Vella's did. She kept her hair short like her mother's, but it was still long enough that Vella could braid it tightly to her head in narrow plaits. Bandu's friend Phaedra had taught Vella that style some years ago, before her voyage east. Perhaps it was a mother's bias, but Goodweather was a joy to behold.

Goodweather caught her mother's expression and sighed. "What?" she said.

Vella never got the chance to answer. Before she could even open her mouth, there was a deafening crack from above and the whole sky began to shake.

Winds assaulted Vella from every direction at once; passing clouds cracked and burst open; even the sun jiggled dizzyingly. Rain and hail fell from blue skies in confused patches, as if slipping through cracks in a ceiling. A vulture, king of birds, was torn to pieces overhead, showering Vella and her daughter in blood and feathers. Vella fell to her knees, too stunned even to pray. It didn't matter that the ground was perfectly still – it was impossible to keep her balance with the heavens shuddering above her. She covered her ears with her hands, trying to blot out that terrible sound of the sky apparently *grinding against* something. The earth felt firm and stable beneath her, but that only made the jerky movements of the sun and clouds more nauseating. More birds kept falling out of the sky, some broken and some intact, all buffeted this way and that throughout their descents.

Vella squeezed her eyes shut, waiting for it all to end, drawing strength from the earth's stability. The vertigo eventually receded, though the ringing in her ears remained. When the wind died down, and its direction became steady once more, Vella opened her eyes. She looked first to Goodweather and was relieved to see the girl sitting up already, looking sick and frightened, but uninjured.

"Thank God," Vella muttered to herself, and found that she could not hear her own words. Oh God Above, would she be permanently deaf? That impossibly long thunder, the grinding, must have damaged her sense of hearing. Would it ever recover?

All she could do was hope.

She gave Goodweather a hug, thankful that her daughter was apparently no worse than shaken. The birds that had survived their falls were now recovering and taking flight, but other effects of the bizarre quake remained: the few clouds had somehow shattered into pieces, their jagged edges only now beginning to soften and fray. How could a cloud break? What *was* this thing that had happened?

Father would know. He must know. God Most High was too merciful to keep His high priest in the dark about something like this.

"Let's hurry," Vella said, and was relieved to hear herself this time, muffled though her words sounded.

They raced through the fields toward the gray walls of Salemica, Goodweather keeping pace with her mother – she was growing into quite the runner, that girl. They were joined in their hurry by every farmer in sight, all headed for the same place: the temple of God Most High.

Through the gates and into the heart of the city they went, passing wooden houses and plots of vegetables, the former beginning to encroach on the latter. Salemica was a young city, and every time they visited they found it bigger than before. There was a thriving market that had arisen in response to the influx of gold tribute from the south, and a community of artisans had built itself around the needs of the temple. And yet even last year, before this terrible and frightening omen, there had been a rising tension here. The fifteen-year treaty with Ardis was entering its twelfth year – soon the shipments of stone and gold would end, and Salemica would have to stand on its own feet or else go to war again in the hopes of a more lasting victory. To his credit, Criton would not entertain that second option. To their detriment, the rest of his people already had.

There was an unmistakable buildup of arms in the city. Spears were common as walking sticks, and there was a beautifully painted shield outside the cooper's door showing off his handiwork. Just seeing it there put Vella on edge.

By the time they reached the temple of God Most High, the crowd was almost too thick for them to push through. The whole city was crying out for answers. Vella held tightly onto Goodweather, claw to claw, and pulled her toward the house of their God, which was also Vella's father's house.

The temple of God Most High was made not of wood or stone, but of enormous bricks dried from the clay pits west of the city with straw from the first harvest after the city's founding. Vella's grandma Hessina had insisted that only worshippers of God Most High could be involved in building His temple, so stone from Ardis was forbidden. Therefore, where the rest of the city was gray stone and brown wood, the temple of God Most High was red.

It was also huge. Long steps led up to a base half an acre in size, and in the center of this foundation stood a second building, the core rooms of the temple housed within it. But at the edge, right before the steps, stood the altar, and atop the altar, shoeless, stood Vella's father.

A hush went through the crowd. Kilion's voice had never been loud, though he spoke clearly and precisely, so the ears of the multitude had to strain to hear him.

"I have seen what you have seen," Vella's father said. "A time of judgment is upon us, possibly the last. God Most High is judging the heavens above and us below, and this omen is His warning. We must all fast tonight, and tomorrow, and the next day. Do not feed your animals, or work them in the fields, only pray with me that our God will be merciful as He always has before and choose to spare us. Tomorrow morning, each clan should bring an offering to be raised to God Most High."

From there, he led the people in a set of familiar prayers

to the might and glory of their God, urging Him to take their side against all enemies. Vella was pleased to see Goodweather joining in despite her visible disappointment. In the past, Criton had always feasted his eldest daughter's arrival. Goodweather had been looking forward to this ritual, and now it would be ruined by a fast. Vella felt sorry for her.

She felt sorry, but she also knew what she had witnessed. Things might *seem* like they were back to normal, but to believe in that normality would be ridiculous. Vella had heard the grinding from above and seen the sky shake; she had watched clouds and birds get torn to jagged pieces – these things were decidedly *not* normal. There was something horribly, fundamentally wrong with the world right now, and she desperately hoped that God Most High would put it to rights.

When the prayers were finally over and the crowd began to disperse, Vella and Goodweather climbed the temple steps toward Vella's father. He gazed down upon them, joyful at their arrival despite his obvious weariness.

"You are safe," he said, when they were almost at the top. "You saw the quake on your way here?"

"Yes," Goodweather said. "It was really scary. But couldn't the fast wait until tomorrow? We've been walking and walking, and I'm hungry!"

Kilion gazed down at his only granddaughter with sympathy. "I'm sorry, Goodweather. You're of age this year. We cannot exempt our own."

"Criton usually feasts her," Vella said.

"He does, yes. Well, your feast will have to be postponed, sweet one, but I'm sure it won't be abandoned altogether. Your father loves and misses you too much to cancel a celebration of your presence. Would you come in for a bit while you wait for him?"

They accepted the invitation and followed him into the temple, where Mother was waiting with open arms and, behind her, Malkon sat polishing the formal silver breastplate and the various implements of sacrifice that Father would be using tomorrow.

"Uncle Malkon!" Goodweather cried, leaping into his arms almost before he could put down his work. Vella's brother laughed delightedly and rose, carrying Goodweather with him.

"She grows bigger every year," Mother said to Vella.

Vella sighed. "It's true."

Malkon was swinging his niece around now, while she shrieked with feigned terror. At last he put her down and said, "You're getting heavy there, girl. What have your mothers been feeding you?"

"Food," Goodweather said. "But I eat more here, except when there's a fast."

Malkon rolled his eyes. "You kids eat *more* when there's a fast, just to make up for the rest of us. Come here, Vella."

Vella gave her brother the hug and kiss he was expecting and fluffed his hair for good measure. "Goodweather's twelve now, fuzzy head. She'll be fasting with the rest of us."

"Oh ho!" Malkon cried cheerfully. "Welcome to grown-up life, you big grown-up! And how about you Vella, how have *you* been? Everything all right with you and your hermit wife?"

"It's all right," Vella answered, feeling only half truthful. She had never been able to bring herself to talk about Bandu's aging curse – the curse that was Criton's continued life. Bandu probably wouldn't have minded – she had told her friend Phaedra about it, after all – but Vella had always felt nonetheless that it was not her story to tell. And, up until recently, one might not even have noticed how Bandu's age was outpacing Vella's. But with each passing year it became more obvious. Even happy, oblivious Goodweather would notice sooner or later, and Vella dreaded the day when her daughter would have to be told the truth.

It didn't matter that Vella despised Criton. Goodweather adored her father, and she deserved to be able to love him without complication or guilt. Vella felt she owed her that much.

Malkon eyed his sister skeptically. "You don't seem happy."

"I am happy," Vella answered. "We're happy together. But how about you? Shouldn't you be finding someone for yourself soon, you old man?"

Malkon smiled wryly. "An old man of twenty-four. No, I haven't made any progress there. Maybe I should let *them* choose for me, since they have such strong opinions. He wouldn't let me marry a plainswoman a couple months ago because of the priestly traditions."

"Our traditions were the least of her problems," Mother broke in. "Don't go blaming the purity rules when the real trouble was that the girl was *unpleasant*."

"She was very pleasant to me," Malkon said, and their mother snorted so loudly that Vella couldn't help but laugh. "Oh, don't you take their side," he retorted.

"I'm not taking anybody's side," Vella said. "I don't even know this person."

"Do you think my father knows I'm here?" Goodweather

asked.

"If he doesn't," Malkon answered, "he will soon. He's probably just busy making sure all his wives and children are accounted for."

There was a brief pause, during which Vella caught the look that her parents were sharing. There was some news about Criton's family that they hadn't told her yet, something they found vaguely unpleasant. Vella chose not to ask. She was sure she'd find out soon enough.

Her stomach rumbled. This would be a long fast.

"This'll be a good visit," she said, a bit defiantly. "It's good to be home."

5

NARKY

This month had been miserable enough before the quake, but now it was truly hellish. Everyone wanted Narky's personal assurances that the world was not coming to an end, but that was more than he could be sure of himself. He had holed himself up in his chambers in the temple, supposedly meditating and communing with his God, but so far Ravennis had been no help at all. Narky's dreams over the past few nights, if at all prophetic, had been too confused and too easily forgotten to be of any help. With his God silent on the matter – or effectively so, anyway – Narky didn't even know what to tell the other priests. So far, he had gotten by with the words, "Ravennis is our lord, and He will watch over us," but he could only be evasive for so long. After all, it did not take much thought to realize that Ravennis would watch over everyone if they died too.

He wished he still had Mother Dinendra to advise him. The former High Priestess of Elkinar had been indispensable in the early years of the unified church, convincing her followers to embrace the notion that their God and Ravennis were one and the same. It was Mother

Dinendra who had helped Narky memorize passages of the Elkinaran holy book *The Second Cycle*, who had spent countless hours teaching him how to better fulfill the duties of a high priest. When her bitter second-in-command Father Sephas had rebelled against the unified church and begun his own nihilistic sect, it was she who had held the region of Hagardis together with her leadership. Sephas still had his little cult of followers, but thanks to Mother Dinendra, his theology had had little chance to spread.

The Sephans refused to believe that Ravennis and Elkinar had ever been the same God. Sephas preached instead that Elkinar had been betrayed and murdered by Ravennis, and he led his followers in acts of sabotage and revenge against those they deemed to be their aggressors. They operated in secret, since in both Ardis and Anardis membership in the Sephan cult was punishable by death. Sephas himself had fled to Atuna, and there was perennially talk of bargaining for his extradition.

The talk never amounted to anything. King Mageris did not prioritize the religion as his father Magerion had, so Sephas' status was always left out of trade agreements in favor of some other concession. To the first king, for whom the Ravennian religion had been an extension of his city's power and influence, Sephas had been the last great piece of unfinished business. With Mageris, it seemed that the matter was settled – he simply hadn't said so aloud yet.

Mageris was more sentimental and less ruthless than his father had been – the trouble was that he was sentimental about the days when High Priest Bestillos had ruled in the name of Magor. As a consequence, he had never looked kindly on Narky, the man who had killed his idol with a cowardly shot to the back. If not for the shadow of his father's expectations and the degree to which Narky and Ptera had entrenched their religion in the city, Narky suspected that Mageris would have ordered his death within minutes of taking power. He still worried that it might happen someday.

Narky had never had more to live for. He and Ptera had a beautiful son, eight years old and sweeter than any child of Narky's had a right to be. Grace had been a surprise to them both, born despite Ptera's believed infertility. They had named him after the Graceful Servant, the first high priestess of Ravennis as Lord Below, who had also brought the two of them together.

It was a happy pairing, despite its origins – the marriage had been arranged entirely by Ptera and the Graceful Servant, and more or less forced on Narky. This remained a sore spot between them, though Narky had still endorsed Grace's name wholeheartedly when Ptera suggested it. It was the Graceful Servant who had elevated him and named him as her successor, after all, and besides, the name fit their son perfectly. He was a graceful child.

At that age, Narky had been clumsy and unloved by anyone but his father. At that age, his mother had left him to chase after that ironmonger. It made Narky nervous, wondering if his God of Fate would be unkind enough to mirror that abandonment somehow. There was no particular reason to think Ravennis would be so cruel, except that Narky never expected kindness when fate was involved.

Would Ptera leave him? It seemed preposterous given how happy she appeared to be with their life together, but every little argument, every period of silence or pensive glance made his mind run wild with visions of some other

man stealing her affections. When he confessed such
thoughts to her, she only laughed and asked what kind of
a man could possibly lure her away from her handsome
young high priest. And he'd smile sheepishly and joke,
"One with two eyes."

It didn't have to be a love affair that broke them – there
were plenty of other, worse possibilities. Ravennis might
choose to take one of them by illness or freak accident;
He might inspire some lesser priest to murder Narky
and take his place; He might turn Mageris against the
priesthood. Every time someone in the family coughed,
every time a supplicant asked him a question he could
not answer, Narky felt a momentary panic. Was *this* the
thing that would lead to Grace's abandonment? No? How
about *this* one?

He felt, somehow, that if Grace could reach his ninth
birthday without disaster striking, things would be all
right. He just needed everything to hold out until then.

And then, the skyquake. Nothing in the world could
make a high priest more vulnerable than a disaster he
couldn't explain. Such a thing could only lead to panic. It
had certainly led to *his* panic – he was supposed to have an
answer, a confident explanation, and what did he have?
Nothing.

He had hoped, the first day or two, that Ravennis might
deign to give him some hint as to the skyquake's origins
and meaning, but by now he had more or less given up
on that. If Ravennis did not speak to him, he would just
have to make something up. Others were doing so already:
there were prophets on every corner these days, making
contradictory claims and sowing distrust in the priesthood.
Narky hated to put words in his God's mouth – it was a

mortal risk every time – but Ravennis wasn't leaving him much of a choice. The time to act had really been two weeks ago, when the quake struck. He had waited too long as it was.

At least he had Ptera to talk to about these things. She was the only member of the priesthood he knew he could trust, the only one who viewed his position as a personal accomplishment and never as an obstacle. Narky was undoubtedly respected by his peers, and his qualifications were unimpeachable, but there was no doubt that several priestly functions were beyond the reach of his talents. True theologians could run circles around him intellectually, and the pastoral functions of tending to the sick, comforting mourners, and so on, were best kept away from him. Narky was known and valued as a prophet, a tool of his God, but he did not have a light touch. Sooner or later, everyone found in him *something* to be frustrated by.

"What am I going to do?" Narky asked his wife. They were between services, and she had joined him in their room. Grace was elsewhere being tutored by a junior priest, and preparations for the day's sacrifices were being overseen by a more junior one still.

"I don't like lying, Ptera. How can I satisfy them all without lying?"

"Ravennis hasn't abandoned you," Ptera said. She was reclining on their bed, looking up at him patiently as he paced back and forth. "The last time we were in a crisis like this, He spoke through you to unify the church. You just haven't needed Him like this in so long, you've lost your trust that He'll see you through."

"How do you know it wasn't a fluke when He spoke through me? And anyway, I can't lose a trust I never had.

I didn't *expect* Ravennis to speak through me, you know."

Ptera smiled. "Listen to yourself, sweetheart. After all the Lord Below has done for you and all that you've done for Him, you're telling me you think His support might have been a *fluke*?"

"No," Narky sighed. "No, I guess that *is* pretty ridiculous-sounding. It's just that I've been waiting way too long for Him to show me what He wants, and I've gotten nothing. It's like Ravennis hasn't decided what to do yet either! Like I'm waiting for Him to tell me what to do, and He's just waiting for me!"

She lay her head down on her arm. "He'll guide you, Narky. He already has."

"All right," Narky said, "but *when*? I've run out of time – you see that, right? If I let this go on any longer, nobody will be listening to me by the time I *do* have something to say."

"So what'll you do?"

"I guess I'll tell the people that Ravennis is testing us. You know, testing our faith in Him. I'll say that as long as we make our sacrifices and worship the Lord Below with all our hearts, He won't send another one of those quakes; but that if we don't, He will. That way no one can really say I was wrong, no matter what happens."

Ptera frowned, half rising again. "That's not much, after two weeks of hiding back here. Let's hope He chooses to speak through you instead."

"Well, if He does," Narky snapped, "it won't really matter what I was planning to say, will it? I'll just open my mouth and His words will be there. The only reason I need a plan at all is that He probably *won't* speak through me. This'll do, right?"

"It'll do."

She didn't look remotely satisfied, but just then someone knocked on the door so Ptera let the conversation end there. "Come in," she said, sitting up.

A senior priest, Lepidos, entered. "Sorry to interrupt, Your Eminence, but I thought you would want to see this."

He was holding a scroll of cheap Atunaean reed paper with shaking hands. Narky could not read, but he knew a Sephan tract when he saw one. Sephas was constantly producing these treatises and manifestos calling on the former priests of Elkinar to turn against their new leaders and return to the old faith in defiance of Ravennis. They were always well-argued, for those who could even understand them, but though each one caused its own new controversy within Narky's church, they had never yet succeeded at their insurrectionist goal. Sephas may have a brilliant analytical mind, but he had yet to accept the one basic truth that kept him in exile and Narky in the Great Temple: there was more power in the unified church than there had ever been in the separate ones.

When Narky had first come to the mountainous region of Hagardis, Elkinar had been only one of two major Gods there. He had been the foremost God of Anardis, and the secondary God of Ardis. Since the latter city had been dominant over the former, Elkinar's status had been inherently inferior. Now there was only one God and one religion for all of Hagardis: no matter which city or town one visited, Ravennis-Elkinar was supreme. All theology aside, there was no reason for Elkinar's priests to yearn for the old days.

Father Lepidos himself was one such priest. Formerly the senior Elkinaran priest in Ardis, he had followed

Mother Dinendra into the unified church without hesitation. Now that Mother Dinendra was gone, he and Ptera were Narky's closest advisers.

Most helpfully, he could read. Neither Narky nor Ptera could, so they waited patiently while Lepidos gathered himself and read them the latest sedition out of Atuna.

"In the halls of God Most High kneels His servant, the lowly Ravennis. 'Why have You called me here, my eternal Master? Have I offended your children, the Dragon Touched? Beat me a hundred thousand times if so, for they are more beloved to You.'

"'Fear not, Ravennis, I have not called you here to punish you. But I am always jealous, and you have made Me more jealous than ever before. How has your following grown larger than Mine, when you are but My servant in the underworld and I am Lord Above All?'

"'Why,' says the lowly Ravennis, 'do You not know? Have You spent so long in these heavens of Yours that only I, lowly servant, know Your children's hearts? Listen, then, and I will tell you. Your children are so terrified of their mortality that they will always prize an afterlife above all else. If You make them choose between worshipping their true Creator and worshipping the one who will guard their souls after death, precious few will choose the Creator. They would rather lose their lives securing a better place in my realm.'"

Narky interrupted the priest's reading. "What is this we're listening to? It's nothing like Sephas' usual stuff."

"No," Father Lepidos agreed. "This is new to him, this blasphemous satire. It's not in his usual style."

"Are we sure it *is* him? Could it be someone else?"

"Certainly," the priest acknowledged, "but who?"

"Whoever wrote it," Ptera said, "they don't just hate Ravennis, they have contempt for His followers and for God Most High too. If it's not Sephas, it's probably one of his followers."

"Right," said Narky. "That's got to be it: not Sephas, but one of his people."

"It's disgusting," Ptera added.

Narky waved the priest on. "Read the rest of it."

"'They would rather lose their lives securing their places in my realm,'" Lepidos repeated, finding his place. "'That is the way of humanity.'

"The Dotard On High rises from His throne in anger. 'You think these creatures would give up their only lives in the world they know, all for the dubious hope that you will favor them in an afterlife they have never seen? It is absurd, Ravennis.'

"Ravennis answers, 'I know them better than You, Lord, for they are like me: greedy and insatiable creatures. Just as I am always reaching for more than is my share, a single life will never be enough for them. They will do anything for more.'

"But God Most High, slow of action and of thought, does not punish insatiable Ravennis for his greed. He only says, 'I must see this for Myself, if it is true. Watch, Ravennis. I will test this unearned faith in your afterlife, and We shall see if a few precious moments of life do not outweigh it.'"

Lepidos stopped there and rolled up the scroll, holding it with just the tips of his fingers like some filthy item that he wished he could drop.

"That's it?" Narky asked. "It ends just like that?"

"Yes, that's the end of it."

A test of faith. Oh, Gods. The scroll was undoubtedly

blasphemous, but what if there was still truth to it? Had Sephas or one of his followers been divinely inspired?

"When did this start going around?" Narky asked. "It didn't come straight to us from the author, obviously. How far has it spread, do you think? And was it written before the quake or after?"

The priest shook his head. "It doesn't seem to have spread very far yet – this copy came to us from Father Corvus in Atuna, which is where I assume it was written either just before the quake or just after. After, I should think, based on the way it ends."

"I hope so."

Ptera saw what Narky was thinking and said, "It's not prophetic, Narky. It's blasphemous and vulgar and *Sephan*."

"But Sephas didn't write it. It sounds nothing like him."

"It's his premise though," Father Lepidos said. "The notion that Ravennis is a usurper and God Most High a fool sounds very much like Sephas, even if he has never written satires before. He doesn't see that he is fighting against his own living God, not avenging a dead one."

"Is it so hard to believe that he's recruited a second writer to his side?" Ptera asked Narky. "Atuna is full of playwrights and people like that."

She was right, that was the most likely explanation. The trouble was that Narky had always secretly believed in the Sephan premise of Ravennis as usurper. Ptera knew it, and she was trying to protect him.

"True," he said, after a moment's hesitation. "It's just the timing, right around when the quake hit… the Gods are definitely watching our response. This 'test' thing doesn't seem so far off, and if some God is feeding Sephas prophetic knowledge, it could be a very, *very* big problem.

It's bad enough that he's being sheltered by the Atunaeans. If he's also getting help from Atun, say, we could be in for another war."

Lepidos raised his eyebrows. "Over a text like this, the Dragon Touched might well join our cause."

"They really might," Narky admitted. "And if they did, it would be our best chance to end the Sephan heresy for good. I'll bring it up with the king. Thanks, Lepidos. I'll take that scroll."

When the priest had gone, Narky sat down beside his wife. "I'll have to talk to Criton about this. The king first, but then Criton."

He couldn't keep the reluctance out of his voice. Ptera put a hand on his thigh and asked him what was wrong. "Criton is your friend, and it's been ages since we saw him. What's the matter? Did he do something to offend you?"

"He married Delika. I can't even think about him anymore without feeling dirty."

She withdrew her hand in surprise. "Because he married her?"

"You don't find it disgusting?"

"Why should I? He's as close as the Dragon Touched have to a king – let him marry whoever he likes, especially someone who loves him."

Narky had to suppress a wave of nausea. How could his brilliant wife not see? It must be her Ardisian upbringing. Growing up worshipping the God of the Wild must have prepared her to accept all kinds of barbarism.

Ptera saw the expression on his face, and still pressed on. "Don't look like that, Narky, their age difference isn't unreasonable."

"Of course it is."

Now she glared at him. Narky realized too late that this argument wasn't just about Criton and his new wife – it was about him and Ptera too. Oh, Lord Below. How ridiculous. Sure, there were some eight and a half years between Narky and Ptera, but there was a difference.

"It's not like with us," he said.

"Oh, is that so? You were seventeen too, when we got married."

"That was different. You hadn't known me since I was a child."

"Sure, it's different. She's loved him for years."

Narky winced. He wished he hadn't begun this conversation. Ptera had never quite forgiven him for his initial reluctance to marry her, nor for that matter had he exactly forgiven her for arranging the marriage without his knowledge. Happy as they had been together these eleven years, it was a sore spot between them. And here he was, treading on it.

"When you met me," he said carefully, "I was independent. I'd killed two men – no, three. I'd said goodbye to my only friends. I'd loved, sort of, and I was about to be named the Graceful Servant's successor. But Delika's only had Criton, since she was young enough to need his help bathing. She loves him because he *raised* her that way! He's never given her the chance to love someone else, or to be someone without him. She was his little girl, and now she's his wife. I think it's disgusting because it is; don't make this about us."

"What do you think he should have done, then? She's loved him as long as I've known them – you think he should have abandoned her once she came of age? Or married her off to some other man against her will? What would you have him do?"

Narky couldn't even tell if she took her argument seriously, or if she was just defensive and lashing out. "I think if you adopt someone as your daughter," he said, "it's your job to treat her like she's really your daughter. Even if she wanted to marry him, which I don't know, he shouldn't have done it. I don't care how much she loves him. Grace loves *you* more than anyone, that doesn't mean you'd marry him if he wanted you to."

"So, Criton's taken care of her since she was young – he was young too, and things have changed. She's *not* his daughter – he's not even old enough to have sired her. It's just not as unreasonable as you think it is."

"Well, if I can't convince you, I can't convince you. But you asked."

Thankfully, that at least ended the argument. Ptera took a deep breath and said, "You're protective, and that's not a bad thing. It makes you a good father."

Narky smiled at that. He loved being a father, a fact that he could never have guessed at when he was younger. Somehow the cries of his son had never irritated him the way that Goodweather's cries had, and the older Grace became, the better Narky liked him. Already at eight he had gained Narky's admiration by doing what neither of his parents ever had: he had learned to read. That junior priest Erebid had taught him, and now they were studying sacred texts together.

Erebid was another of the former priests of Elkinar in Ardis. The Elkinaran priests had been a studious bunch; most of them knew how to read at least a little. But Erebid wasn't only a good reader, he was an excellent teacher too, and Grace always came back from his lessons excited to show Narky what he had learned. Which, for the most part, Narky was unable to follow. But that was what it was like, he thought, if you did your job well. Your children would surpass you.

Narky had surpassed his own father, without a doubt. His father had been a farmer, and a famously cowardly one at that. He had feared the sea, and wolves, and his neighbors, and even fairy stories. Narky had been ashamed of him as a child and a teen, but time and experience had cured him of that shame. The Gods that Pa had feared had indeed killed him in the end, and having met several fairies, they were every bit as real and terrifying as Pa had believed. Narky had lost an eye to them, and he was lucky not to have lost much more. The longer he lived, the wiser and more reasonable his father seemed.

Fatherhood had taught Narky a lot too. He had seen some horrifying things in his twenty-eight years, and been absolutely terrified of most of them, but in retrospect he had not known fear until he became a father. The night Grace was born, Narky had stayed up until dawn while Ptera screamed and pushed and bled – bled so much more than he had known to expect – and his heart had been so filled with panic that even after the bleeding and screaming had ended and the baby was safely sleeping on its mother's chest, Narky could not breathe for fear. He had dreamt that fitful morning that he had somehow killed them both by breathing the wrong way, and when he awoke, well past noon, he could not be sure whether he had escaped a dream into blessed reality or escaped horrid reality into a blessed dream.

Narky had thought once that nothing could be worse than being slain by his God. Now he knew better. The fear of losing his wife and child was worse than that – it was so paralyzing that it could strike him dumb in mid-sentence just to think of it. Now that he had a community, he knew men and women who had felt that staggering loss. That they lived still, that their losses had not physically slain them, still surprised and intimidated him. People who had experiences like that without being destroyed must be far stronger than Narky, or else they must be remorseless monsters who could feel no pain. The latter was sometimes a comforting thought to him – it let him pretend that the pain he imagined for them wasn't real. But he didn't believe for a moment that it was true.

Even so, Narky was a good father, and there was some comfort in that. Whatever his weaknesses as a human being – and there were many – he had his son's love and admiration, and he never abused that sacred trust. The very fact of Grace's admiration was a holy thing to him: Pa had not been a source of pride for Narky growing up, so it was infinitely gratifying that his own son felt no shame about his ancestry. And really, why should he? As far as Grace was concerned, Narky had *always* been the respected High Priest of Ravennis, and Ptera had always been a senior priestess. What was there to be ashamed of?

Narky was a lucky man. Suspiciously, almost unbearably lucky. His most disturbing conviction was that sooner or later, all this luck would run out.

But oh please, let it be later.

6

PHAEDRA

Phaedra was in the gardens when the skyquake struck, spreading its terror across the skies and among those beneath it. And though she had never experienced such a thing before, she instantly knew what it meant. It meant that she had failed.

Eleven years. She'd been at this eleven years, Gods help her, traveled west over the mountains and east over the sea, sealed every gate to the elves' world save the one, and it hadn't been good enough. The final gate *couldn't* be sealed, not with the Yarek holding it open, so what was there left to do? If the skyquakes hadn't stopped but had in fact grown so strong that they were spreading now to her world too, there must not be much time left. Her sinking heart told her there was nothing she could do – that her best efforts had failed, and the worlds would be ending with or without her approval. Her head said she had to see Psander.

If there was anyone who could devise a final way to avoid this disaster, it would be Phaedra's mentor. Phaedra had learned much through experience and practice, but Psander was more experienced, easily as intelligent, and almost infinitely better read. The weeks Phaedra had spent learning from her and reading in Psander's library could hardly make up for the decades the older wizard had spent in study. It was time to go back.

She had to find Kvati and her brother, Tnachti, to give her farewells and beg for a ship to take her back home. They would want to see her anyway – she was the only wizard on the continent, the only wizard left in this world. Essisha, this beautiful continent from which her distant ancestors had sailed, had exterminated its wizards more than a hundred years before the west had followed suit.

So far, that had done her more good than harm. It had rendered her less viscerally threatening to the local powers, who had treated her presence not as dangerous blasphemy but as a curiosity, a throwback. They had passed her from court to court like a prized historical artifact until she had found her way to Ksado, the land of the final gate. Ksado's prince, Tnachti, had been as indulgent as the rest of them. He had been thrilled to learn that a gateway to the elves' world lay in his territory, and when she told him she intended to close it, he had made it a grand affair, inviting courtiers and noblemen from multiple courts to witness the spectacle. It had made her work difficult and awkward – people kept interrupting or getting in her way, and they had been universally disappointed by her lack of showmanship. But the gate was closed now, and that was what mattered.

Tnachti's sister was different. Kvati was like no one Phaedra had ever known: as formidable as Psander, but with all the warmth of the sun. It was because of Kvati that Phaedra had stayed here so long, nearly two years beyond what it had taken her to seal the gate. The co-reigning duchess had showered her with gifts and attention, but not as the other nobles had. Kvati had sought a genuine connection, and she had found it. It was rare for Phaedra to meet someone so willing to discuss taxation and poetry, philosophy and fashion, and all of it thoughtfully. They had spent many an enlightening evening together after dinner, to the point where Kvati had laughingly proclaimed her husband jealous – and hadn't changed her habits a whit.

It didn't matter. Kvati's husband and teenage children treated her like a Goddess – everyone did. Her belly laugh was contagious, her embraces bone-crushing, and if she disapproved of someone, heavens help them. Her mere expression could have flattened mountains.

The duchess and her brother were in the flowered gazebo when Phaedra found them, deep in conversation with their favorite teacher. Teacher Zakai wore the white garb of his calling, Tnachti his peacock robe, and Kvati blazed in orange. Her magnificent hair, never cut, had been recently made to resemble a tree, its vertical trunk spiraling up to splayed branches. When she looked up and waved Phaedra over, the branches seemed to do the same.

"Oh, there you are," she said, as if she had sent for Phaedra ages ago. "What do you make of all this?"

Phaedra hesitated. Her Estic was nearly fluent by now, but how could she translate a word like "skyquake?" Should she even try to explain its implications? If yes, how? She had never even learned the Estic word for earthquake.

"I've heard of these," she said, "but I haven't seen one before. They've are – no, sorry, they've *been* – common in the elves' world for some time. I was hoping you could–"

Tnachti interrupted her. "Teacher Zakai says they are a

sign that the Godly Conflict is escalating. He suggests that we cease efforts to convert the worshippers of Karassa and pray to Her and Kgini to make peace before Their struggle causes any further harm."

Phaedra looked over at Zakai and was glad to see his expression open and curious. There was a reason Kvati liked him best. "Peace between the Gods is a worthy goal," she said, "but the elves' world is cut off from Theirs. The... wall... between that world and the heavens is stronger."

"A storm breaks the stronger trees first," Teacher Zakai replied. "What else could shake the heavens besides divine conflict?"

Phaedra paused to consider her answer. That was one advantage of being a foreigner here, of occasionally struggling with the Estic language: she could think long and hard about her answers, and nobody found her pauses suspicious.

So far, she had only told people she wanted to seal the elven gates to protect the world from the fairies themselves. She had told no one about the Yarek. After all, she had had a hand in planting it – she did not want the Essishans to know that she, this quaint foreign wizard, had endangered the world.

If she told them of her true mission now, of how Psander had sent her specifically to close gates and prevent further skyquakes, Kvati and her brother would be more than willing to help get her home. They might even give her a war fleet to wipe the pirates off Tarphae and clear her path to the last gateway. On the face of it, that seemed like the easiest solution.

But on second thought, it would be a mistake. A fleet would raise alarms all across the continental coast. Atuna and Parakas would ally against the foreign threat, and then Phaedra would have started a naval war she had no guarantee of winning. The continental fleet might even make common cause with the pirates, if it came to that.

What's more, Mura had a special connection with the Goddess Karassa, and Her presence was far stronger in the eastern seas than in the west, where Tarphae had been Her furthest outpost. At home, Karassa had the rival Sea God Mayar to contend with, and Atun the heavenly sailor, but out here She was the lone Sea Goddess. It was too dangerous to send an Essishan fleet across Her seas with the stated purpose of defeating Her servants. Better for Phaedra to slip back westward alone, warding herself against Karassa's notice, and attack the problem from a different direction.

They were still waiting for a response. Phaedra apologized for her delay, and said, "You may be right, Teacher. I do not know. I would like to talk to my own teacher about it, if I can. There are going to be more of these, these, um, shakes? Sky-shakings? But there might be something I can do about them, if you will let me return to my home and consult with my teacher. I will be sorry to leave you."

Kvati stared at her disapprovingly. She was not the sort to let go of people she liked.

But Tnachti nodded. "Of course."

"Might I have a ship to take me as far as Antaka? Even passage on a merchant ship…"

"We will arrange it."

"I am gratified," Phaedra said. "I'll leave you with Teacher Zakai."

She withdrew and went to pack her things, her heart

heavy. She had stayed here well beyond any reasonable claim to necessity, having become enamored of the Ksadan culture. She loved Estic with its chained consonants, loved the fried delicacies of the various Essishan courts and the magnificent structured clothing of their courtiers, loved the poetic decadence that a few decades of peace and prosperity had wrought. Gods, she would miss it here.

She scanned her wardrobe, choosing what to keep and what to leave behind. Kvati had gifted her with over a dozen dresses in varying degrees of formality, the least of which might have dazzled the socialites of Phaedra's youth. Current Ksadan fashion revolved around evoking plants and animals, as Kvati's hair and Tnachti's peacock robe had done. There were heavy, bone-fortified dresses with wings that rose from their backs and shoulders, dresses with slithering fishtails that never touched the ground, reptilian dresses layered with flaps of golden-brown cloth that reminded Phaedra of nothing so much as the scaled armor Hunter had worn so long ago. Many were impossible to fold or roll, disqualifying them. Most were poorly suited to travel. But she couldn't leave that gorgeous blue fish behind, or that lovely headdress, and the butterfly yellow dress with the purple highlights was terribly flattering and not at all impractical...

At last, she was ready. The entirety of her life in Essisha was packed into a single satchel: clothes, a silken coin purse, a bottle of perfumed hair oil, a few combs in varying sizes. The bracelets she could wear, but the rest of her jewelry she left behind. There was too much of it, and it was too heavy. She could not rely on others to carry her things for her.

Lastly, she took up her staff. It was the one item from

home that she would never have disposed of, no matter how many substitutes the Essishan courts had presented her with. She had long ago carved a story into its wood, the only written record of Bandu's journey to the underworld. The most she would let the Essishans do with it was to fill the carved letters with golden lacquer so that they would be easier to read.

When she left the capital, nearly the whole Ksadan court came to wish her farewell. She had become friends with many of them, for all that they had seen her as a historical artifact, and the farewells took longer than she had expected. The one person she did not part with yet was Kvati. It was a two-day journey to the seaport, but Kvati chose to escort her the whole way there.

Phaedra did not object to her friend's company. It was a touching gesture, and Kvati's forceful presence and bustling attendants kept the panic at bay. She needed that. Her panic wasn't even about what had happened, really. Whether or not she and Psander could devise a solution to the skyquakes, what she dreaded most was seeing Hunter again.

Eleven years ago, Hunter had proposed to marry her. She had turned him down, though not for lack of love. That would have made it all so much easier, but no, it had been the risk of pregnancy that forced her hand. Pregnancy affected magic in unpredictable ways – she had seen as much with Bandu – and at least back then, the world could not afford for her to take a year off from saving it.

Even if it could have, it wouldn't have mattered: Phaedra didn't *want* children. The very thought of giving up magic to raise a family filled her with resentment. Her life belonged to her, not to some future generation; she hadn't pursued academic magic just to abandon it for the second-hand greatness her parents had aspired to. If that meant she had to wait for her childbearing years to pass before she could pursue a romance, so be it. If Psander had taught her anything, it was that a woman did not need a child to have a legacy.

That wouldn't make it any easier to see him again.

He would be married by now, with the children she knew he wanted. It would do no good to pretend otherwise. He was a beautiful man, and she had told him she would never marry him – the villagers of Silent Hall would have been sure to match him up with one of their own by now. He may have put them off for a time, nursing the heartache she'd given him – he *was* the brooding sort, after all – but they'd have gotten to him eventually. It was a fundamental truth about Hunter that he allowed himself to be guided by others.

Whom had he married? That Atella girl?

She felt silly even worrying about such personal troubles. Hunter's private life was hardly the greatest of her concerns now – or at least it *shouldn't* be. And yet, somehow every thought of visiting Psander came back to that. The wife, the family. Even the potential end of the world came back to that. How profoundly ridiculous.

Maybe she should have gone back sooner, instead of drawing her pain out like this. It had taken nine years to seal all the gates, so naturally she had dallied for another two and made it worse. This was how she had always been, she supposed – she used her curiosity as an excuse to put things off. She had learned many fascinating things that way, but apparently not her lesson.

Kvati interrupted her thoughts. "You're worried," she

said. "You know more about this trouble with the sky than you've let on, and it worries you."

"Lots of things worry me."

"Tell me."

Phaedra shook her head. "Your teachers in Ksado are wise and capable. Look to them, and I'll look to mine."

The older woman regarded her sternly. "You trust him more than you trust me."

"My teacher is a woman."

Kvati erupted in that great belly laugh of hers, and Phaedra couldn't help but smile.

"A wise choice, I'm sure," Kvati said. "Better than mine, I suspect."

Phaedra shrugged and said nothing. She barely had words to describe Psander in her own language, let alone Estic.

She also found it hard to convey just how deeply she respected Ksado's "teachers." They were the closest thing the Ksadans had to priests, but there were no hierarchies in the Essishan religions she had come across – only collegial study and endless, endless debate. Even their various rivalries were couched within a collaborative framework.

But most impressively, the teachers had turned their people entirely away from animal sacrifice, replacing it with language-offerings that were little more than rote, if effusive, praise. It was a jarring difference from western religion, and an impressive one. The eastern Gods must appreciate mere words better than the western ones did.

Phaedra wondered if God Most High would be amenable to such a change. She had high hopes. If the Essishan Gods were happy enough without ritualized slaughter, shouldn't the Creator God be equally willing to see the practice ended? The trouble was working up the courage to find out.

The substitution of prayer for sacrifice was hardly the only difference between east and west. Even nations out here were arranged differently, with giant bureaucratic empires that spanned multiple cities and huge swaths of territory. The bureaucracy in Ksado had impressed her no end. The formulae involved in calculating the nation's taxes were a true technical marvel. Kvati and her brother had been much amused by Phaedra's interest in such things, which had only encouraged her to further pursue the details.

The vastness of the eastern empires encouraged large navies and a substantial shipping trade, but the voyage from Essishan shores to the western archipelago was long and tumultuous enough, even with Karassa's favor, that trade with the west remained limited. Phaedra was gratified that Kvati had found her a merchant ship on such short notice to take her to Antaka, the archipelago's easternmost island. But there it was, waiting for her.

"I'm sorry to say goodbye," Phaedra said. "I... ah... want you farewell."

Kvati nodded, and her hair-branches danced with the motion. "I wish you farewell also, but listen to me: do not stay away for too long. I have grown fond of you, Phaedra, and I would see you again."

"I hope so."

Phaedra embarked on the ship and gave her friend and benefactor a wave. She did hope she would see Kvati again someday, though a part of her worried that there would be no solution to the skyquakes awaiting her at Silent Hall, that there would be no time to come back here before the end. But all she could do on that front was to hope. Whatever the future held, for her and for the world, it was time to go home.

7
GOODWEATHER

By the time Father came to take Goodweather home, she was seething. She had overheard Grandma's whispered news and spotted the worried, sympathetic looks cast her way. Criton had married Delika. First Goodweather's feast had been replaced by a fast, and now her father had stolen her best friend.

It wasn't fair. He had three wives already; what did he need Delika for? On previous visits, she and Goodweather had shared a bed and spent whole nights giggling over nonsense, pretending to snore, poking each other awake just because they could. Now all that was over, for the worst and most grown-up of reasons. Whatever anyone said, growing up was awful.

Take this fast. Last year, Goodweather would have been too young to participate, and she would have been allowed to partake of her intended feast. Now she envied her younger half-siblings, who were encouraged to eat double portions of *her* welcome meal so that less of the food would go to waste. Watching them eat was depressing. So was helping Horda scrape all the remaining lamb, sticky-sweet with carob and honey, into the fire.

Delika tried to make it easier on her, but there was an unwelcome distance between them now. They had been the two eldest daughters, once – or at least, that had been the way Goodweather thought of them. Now they were daughter and wife, *stepdaughter* and wife, and their relationship could never be the same again. Goodweather hated it; she *hated* it. Sometimes anger overwhelmed her sadness and sometimes sadness overwhelmed her anger.

She did her best to act normal. She helped her father's other wives with chores, she watched over her half-siblings and played with the younger ones, but she avoided Delika because every time she saw her, standing there and struggling with that awkward new distance that had grown between them, it made her want to scream.

The fast made it that much harder to control the tears. Goodweather had never fasted a full day before, let alone three, and it made her head feel light. Midway through the second day, Grandpa announced that pregnant and nursing mothers must begin eating and drinking once more, but everyone else was only newly permitted to drink. So naturally Goodweather drank too much water at once and ended up heaving it all out again. She thought that God Most High might be personally invested in making her miserable.

Goodweather never quite knew where she stood with God Most High, or for that matter, where He stood with her. Her mother Vella, whom she had called Myma since her toddling days, always spoke of Him much the same way she did of Grandpa: as a powerful, loving figure who lived too far away. Myma's prayers were personal and yearning, like she wished God would visit more often, and that was how Goodweather prayed too, but she didn't have the same certainty that her messages would be heard. That was probably Ma's fault.

Goodweather's Ma, Bandu, did not pray. She rarely spoke of the Gods, but when she did it was almost always in the plural. Goodweather got the sense that her Ma thought the Gods were all the same, or at least all equally indifferent to her desires and needs. She sometimes scoffed when Myma prayed, though less now than when Goodweather was younger. Myma had scolded her about it many times, and she was trying.

When Goodweather was younger, she had worried that God Most High would notice Ma's defiance and smite her for it, but He never had. Did that mean He really was indifferent? Myma said He heard but forgave, knowing all that Ma had done for Him and His people. That made sense, but it was hard to live with Ma's casual scorn for long without starting to wonder if their God was really paying that much attention.

Had He noticed that His people were fasting and praying to Him? That they were begging Him to save them, to turn away from whatever judgment had caused Him to shake the sky?

Would He notice if Goodweather secretly broke the fast?

By the third day, Goodweather was incapable of doing chores or even playing with her little half-siblings. She spent most of the day lying down, feeling faint. Many of the grown-ups were doing the same, so at least nobody expected better of her. When she did try to stand, the blood drained from her head and she fell back down on the pillow-bed that Papira had prepared for her in the Children's Room. The odd thing was that by then, she almost didn't mind the dizziness. The fast had done strange things to her.

They broke the fast together, with bread, soft sheep's cheese, and dates. It tasted good, but by that time the taste was irrelevant: it was the sustenance she craved, not the flavor. Just to chew her food and swallow it seemed like the most satisfying thing she had done in years. She burped loudly, and automatically glanced toward Delika to share a conspiratorial smile – they had once competed over who could burp the loudest. Her new stepmother was right there, grinning back at her. She did not burp out a response – she had to keep up her new, dignified façade – but that was all right because Goodweather could tell that she was considering it. Delika had won the competition last time; it was enough to know that she was tempted to defend her victory. Whatever their new circumstances, Father hadn't actually swallowed Delika up – she could still be Goodweather's friend. She had changed, but not *that* much.

The younger children picked at their meal. Having not fasted, they met the grown-ups' hunger with boredom and frustration. They were not allowed to leave the long table until everyone was finished; it was their job to clean up afterwards. So the half-siblings sat glumly staring as the adults, Goodweather newly among them, ate nearly without end. At another time, their stares might have put Goodweather off her food. Not this time.

The one benefit of being old enough to fast was that Goodweather wasn't expected to help the younger ones clean. Instead, when the meal had concluded, Delika offered to take her for a walk out to the fields. Pa nodded and told them to be home before dark, so they set off without another word, abandoning the envious littler ones.

Goodweather didn't know what to say, and neither did Delika. It wasn't the same as before. They walked in silence until Delika pointed and said, "I'll race you to the gate."

"What?" Goodweather responded, and then bolted away before Delika could repeat herself. She was fast for her age, with her father's long legs and Ma's endless stamina, but she still needed every advantage she could steal against the older girl. Delika won in the end, though it was very close and Goodweather was able to take pride in how heavily Delika panted afterward. As they collapsed against the gate, their eyes met and they both began to laugh – or, rather, to wheeze with the intention of laughing.

"It's all right, isn't it?" Delika asked when they could breathe again. "You're not angry at me anymore?"

Goodweather shook her head. "Why did you do it?"

"Because I love him, Goodweather. I always have."

"Not always."

"Always," Delika insisted. "Since I was a little girl. You know how I found him; everyone knows. People used to call me his blood-daughter. I'll bet they call me his blood-wife now. Everyone thinks they know what happened, but all they know are the stupid, obvious things. I didn't save myself from burning, the way they think I did. God Most High saved me. He's the one who showed me the vat and kept the smoke out of my lungs even when the air above me was full of it, and He only did it because I was looking for Criton. That's what people don't realize. I was *meant* to find Criton, so his God saved me. It was loving him that kept me alive."

Goodweather couldn't help but recoil from Delika's

weird, passionate speech. There was fire in her eyes, a
fire Goodweather didn't understand. Maybe she was too
young – that was something Myma said fairly often – but
the passion behind Delika's outburst was so foreign that
she found it downright unsettling.

Her contention was bizarre too, even by Myma's
standards of personal worship. Sure, people prayed
for God Most High to intervene on their behalf, and of
course thanked Him when things went well, but it was
outrageous to *assume* that He had stepped in just for you.
God Most High had sat back and watched His dragons get
exterminated. He had watched silently when the Ardismen
nearly wiped out the Dragon Touched. How could anyone,
even Delika, believe that this same God would intervene
just so that she could become Pa's fourth wife? That took a
special kind of delusion, and it was frightening to see such
madness in her eyes.

She would have liked to be diplomatic anyway, but
she was her Ma's girl. The most she could manage was to
answer, "If you say so."

They continued their walk, the conversation turning to
safer territory. They spoke about the fast and how relieved
they were at its end. They speculated about the quake,
what had caused it and whether there would be another
one. Goodweather hoped not; Delika oddly disagreed.

"Sometimes I feel like this world *needs* shaking up," she
claimed, probably just for the sake of conversation. "It's
too settled."

"You live here," Goodweather said. "And anyway, I
thought your life was perfect now that you're married to
my Pa."

"Oh, it is," Delika answered airily. But her eyes changed

their focus and she went quiet.

Goodweather studied her friend. Delika was definitely happy now, probably happier than Goodweather had ever seen her, but she wasn't carefree anymore the way Goodweather remembered her. That was the real barrier between them. More than the fact that she had married Pa, it was that new grown-up worry that separated her from Goodweather's world.

What were these mysterious worries? Why was Delika so restless now, when she had what she'd supposedly wanted forever? Goodweather often felt like she was cut off from grown-up logic. Myma always said that she'd understand when she was older, but Goodweather had her doubts. Myma had been saying that for years, and she still didn't understand.

They finished their stroll outside the gates and walked back home as the sun set. Pa's house was enormous, one room for each of his wives and one for all the children, a hall with a separate kitchen, and a latrine out back just for the family. It was built out of Ardisian stone with a roof of sturdy wood, and it stood impressively against the other houses nearby. It was as close as Salemica came to having a palace, because Pa was as close as the Dragon Touched came to having a king.

The Dragon Touched had no king but their God, officially speaking. People called Pa "Criton," and in theory his word was advice and not law, but at some point this distinction stopped mattering. God Most High had decreed once, when Goodweather was just a baby, that Criton should be the leader of the Dragon Touched in matters of war and peace. With a broad enough interpretation, practically everything fell under his purview except for the interpretation of God's will, which was left to the High Priest. It was Pa who met with messengers from Ardis and other cities, who decided which merchants to welcome and which to exclude, and who levied taxes and oversaw the construction of everything from the city walls to the irrigation ditches. In theory, he was just another citizen of Salemica. In reality, everyone knew that was nonsense.

It was no wonder, then, that everyone treated Goodweather like a princess. A descendant in one way or another of both the city's ruler and its high priest, and of a famous witch besides, she was able to go wherever she pleased in the city without fear of harm. Merchants and citizens gave her gifts sometimes, which would have been much more effective for gaining Criton's attention if Goodweather had had a good memory for names. Her father's wives never ordered her to do anything, as they did often enough with each other's children, but actually thanked her when she played with her half-siblings or helped with chores. Goodweather knew she got special treatment in Salemica, and she reveled in it. It might have grown tiring if she had ever stayed for long, but as it was, it was a nice break from home.

At home there was always work to be done. Either Goodweather had to help Myma with the weaving or the cooking or the cleaning or any number of other indoor chores, or else she was helping Ma tend the garden, or forage for mushrooms and berries, or train dogs or hunt with them. Ma refused to keep dogs of her own – there was a history there that Goodweather did not quite understand – but she trained them for others in exchange for a share of the hunt. Goodweather loved working with them, and wished she could keep one for herself, but she knew she would have to wait until she was old enough to leave her parents' house. It was a happy life anyhow. She loved it. But it certainly wasn't easy like her visits to Salemica.

She stood outside the house with Delika as the world grew darker, entering only when they were sure there could be no chores left. Her mothers would have been horrified at how lazy Goodweather was here, but she felt only faintly guilty as she and Delika slipped through the door and made for their respective beds. Surely it was no crime to enjoy every moment she could with her friend, especially now that Pa would be making more demands on Delika's time. Even her mothers couldn't have objected, not that they'd ever find out.

She spent the next day at the temple. Her grandparents were at least as doting as Pa, even though she wasn't technically of their flesh and blood. They gave her sweet wine and carob candies, and asked her about her life at home. Grandma asked again whether she was meeting any other youths her age, which Myma tried to answer for her, since the answer was essentially no. It was a familiar conversation: Grandma asked this question every time they visited Salemica, and Myma always got defensive. They were doing their best, Mother! Plenty of good people lived in remote areas! It wasn't like the Dragon Touched had to marry their daughters off early anymore, so what was the problem? And so on.

Goodweather didn't think their house was so remote. It was only a few miles to the nearest village, a perfectly walkable distance even with a wheelbarrow. Myma was right that Grandma had no cause for concern. Goodweather was plenty friendly with her peers there, even if it was only to play a few games of Rock Harvest before she left again.

Rock Harvest was a one-handed game of gathering stones off the ground while a tossed one was still in the air, and all the children of the plains played some version of it. There was much controversy among Dragon Touched children as to whether claws were an advantage in this game or should be turned into fleshy hands instead. Goodweather had tried both ways plenty of times, but it didn't seem to make much difference: either way, she was about average at the game.

It was easy for Goodweather to let her mind wander while Myma and Grandma kept up their low-level argument, following the same old ruts left by previous ones. Myma loved her mother, but she took every little comment about Goodweather's upbringing as an attack, which turned her every response into a counterattack. Grandma, in the meantime, did her best to soften the blow by always prefacing her critiques with phrases like, "Of course, you know best," but everyone knew these words weren't meant to be taken literally. That was why she so obviously found it dismaying when Myma would turn those phrases back on her and say, "Of course you're right, I know what's best for my daughter."

Grandpa Kilion, as always, spent the time trying to engage Goodweather in side conversation while casting the occasional dismayed look at his wife and daughter. The argument never got so heated or uncivil that he actually intervened, but he seemed to be eternally considering it.

Yet these arguments were nothing next to the day Pa and his wives joined them at the temple for the afternoon meal, their eight children in tow. The temple had a dining hall where the priests usually ate together, but Grandpa had sent most of them north across the plains to reassure the populace that God Most High was with them. Their absences left enough room for Pa's big family, but no matter how much space there was, it felt too crowded. It felt like they didn't belong.

Even with the din of so many people talking and eating, the tension in the air was so strong you could have strung a bow with it. There was tension between Pa's wives and tension between Myma and Grandma, but the worst of it was between Myma and Pa. They usually avoided each other, but today it was worse: Myma glared at Pa every time he spoke, almost as if the quake that was the main topic of discussion was somehow his fault. For the first time, Goodweather realized how much Myma hated Pa. They had never gotten along – there was too much jealousy on both sides over Ma – but this was more than jealousy. Myma *hated* him.

Was it because Ma had brought him back from the dead? Goodweather had long wondered if this was the source of Myma's jealousy, but whenever she had asked her about it – mostly at a younger, less polite age – Myma had spoken glowingly of how Ma had brought Pa back in order to bring peace to the nations. In Myma's words, she had "saved us all." But if that wasn't her complaint with Pa, why did she also seem to blame him for everything that went wrong? She blamed him whenever Ma felt achy, whenever another of her hairs turned white – it was frankly ridiculous. He and Ma had spent less than two years together, and that was more than a decade ago! How much damage could he possibly have done?

Goodweather just wished her three parents could sort out their differences and leave the rest of the family out of it. As far as she could tell, Pa didn't have anywhere near the kind of loathing for Myma that she had for him. He seemed, if anything, bewildered by the way she was glaring. Couldn't they just make up somehow? What if Pa apologized for whatever it was that he had done? Or if it wasn't the kind of thing you apologized for, couldn't Myma just forgive him already?

Pa cleared his throat. "I hear from Goodweather that Bandu is training dogs now? How many do you have?"

"None."

Myma's curtness brought him up short, but Goodweather jumped in to ease the awful tension. "We don't train them for *ourselves*, people pay us to train them. Ma and I do it."

Pa frowned. "She's so stubborn. She'll never find a true replacement for Four-foot, so she won't even keep a dog? She'd be happier if she'd only–"

"She had a chance to bring Four-foot back," Myma snapped. "She wanted to. But she chose you instead."

Goodweather winced almost as much as her father did. The words were hurtful enough on their own, but the savage conviction with which Myma had wielded them was enough to tear someone apart. Goodweather hoped her mother would never turn on *her* like that. Even watching her do it to someone else was enough to shake her to the bone.

Goodweather had heard of Four-foot, Ma's legendary wolf friend. Pa had told her of how the wolf had come to his rescue and how it had died, how Ma had loved it, and how it was Four-foot's death that had cleared the way for her to love a human being. Ma always spoke of Four-foot with such longing that Goodweather had no trouble believing Pa's assessment. And Myma wasn't a person who just made things up: if she said that Ma had had the chance to bring Four-foot back instead of Pa, then it was probably something Ma had told her.

But Myma had always spoken with pride of the way Ma had brought Goodweather's father back, since it was Pa who had really made the peace between the Dragon Touched and their southern neighbors in Ardis. How could she now suggest that Ma should have chosen Four-foot instead?

Something had filled her with rage, something that Goodweather did not quite understand. It frightened her.

Pa was dumbstruck. "What are you saying?" seemed to be the best he could muster, in a voice whose anger couldn't mask its shock. Everyone was staring at Myma now: Criton, his four wives, Grandma and Grandpa, and all the children old enough to understand even a portion of what was going on.

But Myma didn't wilt. "Bandu made a sacrifice, a *heavy* sacrifice to bring you back, and not because she wanted to. She sold part of her life away so that you could save all the people who depended on you, so what do you do? You make people depend on you *more*. More wives, more children. You're disgusting and ungrateful. That's what I think."

"She never told me about a sacrifice," Pa said quietly. "She just hid herself away with you and disappeared."

"As she had every right to do. She doesn't owe you anything, Criton, *you* owe *her*. You've been leeching off her for eleven years now – that isn't enough for you?"

Pa sat silent, his expression roiling with anger and guilt and confusion. Not a word was spoken – even the children went quiet, looking from their father to Myma and back again. At last Grandpa rose, coughing awkwardly. "It's getting late. I think maybe we should..."

He trailed off as two people entered the room. The first, bowing his head respectfully, was that night's watchman at the gate, a curly haired plainsman with a cleft chin. "We tried Criton's house first," he murmured, "but I see you're all here."

The second person was Ma.

8

BANDU

Her first priority after the quake was to make sure Vella and Goodweather were safe. She sent the dogs running back to their owners, packed what food she could, and began walking toward Salemica, not even planning for what to do once she arrived. The important thing was to see how her wife and daughter were faring, to protect them if they needed it.

She didn't know what had caused the quake, but she knew whom she could ask. The Yarek, whose great body stretched from the heavens to the underworld, would know what was happening.

Whether it chose to answer was another question entirely. It had fulfilled its obligation to her the day it had led her down to the underworld on a staircase of roots. Now that it owed her no favors, she would have to rely on its kindness, insofar as it had any. Castle Goodweather had been kind to her as a child, but the Yarek was more than just the product of Goodweather's seed. It was its own massive entity, raised on the rich soil of this world in the shadow of the Gods it had once threatened. Close as it was to Them, maybe it couldn't afford to be too kind.

Even if that was true, Bandu had no doubt that she had been right to insist on bringing only Goodweather's seed to this world. Even if this new Yarek wasn't exactly kind, it was certainly a good deal kinder than Illweather had been. Just the thought of bringing home a seed from the plant beast's cruel half was enough to make Bandu glad of her decision.

So she would ask the Yarek, once she knew that Goodweather and Vella were safe. She had seen trees crack and birds get torn apart when the sky shook – what if her family had been inside a building when it happened? Would the roof fall on them? Salemica's buildings were tall, especially the temple where Vella's parents lived. If the shaking sky could break tall trees, that temple was worth worrying about.

She hadn't been to Salemica in years. Once Goodweather had grown old enough to tramp alongside her Myma, Bandu had been glad to let the two of them travel here alone. Salemica was Criton's city; she had never liked being there. Anyway, it was far enough away, and there was always enough to be done at home in her wife and daughter's absence. The weeks alone cleared Bandu's head, and made her appreciate them better when they returned.

She certainly liked solitude better than she liked the idea of seeing Criton again. She didn't hate him, didn't get angry about him anymore the way Vella did, but she had nothing she needed to say to him and nothing she wanted to hear him say either. Vella gave her reports each time she came home, and that was more than enough. It had been easy to let the years slide past without visiting again.

Let Goodweather love her father – she deserved as

much, and so did he – but Bandu could admit her mistakes, and loving him had been one of them. It had been an easy mistake to make, back when they were both too young to know better and had so recently lost the ones they loved, but she and Criton had never been well-suited to each other. She doubted he was well-suited to anyone, really. There were things he was good at, and love was not one of them.

The two greatest joys Criton had given her, he had given by accident. The first was Goodweather. Criton had wanted to mate with Bandu, he could not pretend otherwise, but her pregnancy had come as a shock to him. A shock, as if he somehow hadn't understood the way young were made. Then again, perhaps he hadn't. She hadn't considered back then how little he understood, how he had never seen a pregnancy or even watched animals mate. She may have come to him with too many assumptions, just as he had with her.

Either way, he had given her Goodweather by mistake. Fatherhood had been something that *happened* to him, and from what she heard it was still happening to him fairly regularly. Bandu was grateful for Goodweather's existence, but she didn't give her former husband more credit for her than he deserved.

The second joy Criton had given her was even more accidental than the first. Bandu had followed him to his people and lived among them for several long and miserable months while they waged war on their northern neighbors on the way to waging war on their southern ones. She had made few friends among his people while guiding them toward their victories, but one of those few had been Vella.

Vella had come to her as a friend of Dessa, who was the daughter of Criton's cousin, and confessed her attraction to Bandu one day while helping her with Goodweather. Bandu had taken her along when she left Criton, a choice that was selfish and cruel and for which she had been unfairly rewarded with over a decade of love and support. Bandu was profoundly grateful for Vella. Their marriage had horrified Criton when she told him about it, but it still could not have happened without him.

Now Bandu would be seeing him again, whether she liked it or not. There were uncomfortable conversations ahead of her. Bandu had given half her life to bring Criton back from the dead, but she had never told him so. Well, it would be obvious enough now.

She could still remember the pain in his face when she had said she would not be returning. Vella would have called his pain selfish and ungrateful, and she was right, but it was also true that he had known nothing of Bandu's sacrifice. All he had known was that she would not be staying, and at the time it must have seemed to him that she had brought him back to a world without love. If that had been true, he would have had no reason to be grateful.

But it wasn't true. There was plenty of love in the world, of all different kinds. For one thing, Bandu had left him with their adopted daughter Delika. He had always been better with her than with Goodweather anyway. And whether he had found any love with a mate since then, he had clearly found new wives without difficulty.

She arrived in Salemica shortly before dusk. The lands were so fertile she could feel it in her toes: the great river she had followed flooded in the rainy season. Salemica stood on an incline too gentle to be called a hill, but high enough to spare it from the waters, at least most years. She thought that a major downpour must reach and breach its walls, but maybe that was the point. Criton's city could only stand so long as his God protected it.

Not for the first time, she shook her head at this foolishness. God-worshippers had a perverse inclination to put themselves in these positions, as if the Gods would reward them for their trust. Bandu would never understand it, especially not with God Most High. It didn't matter if He was more powerful than the rest, because He was also the most inattentive.

She marched to the gate and told the men there that she wanted to see her wife and daughter. The guards at the gate were young, but not so young that they failed to recognize Bandu. She saw the flicker of confusion and reevaluation on their faces as they tried to reconcile the way she looked now with their memories of her. Hadn't she been of an age with Criton and Vella, more or less? But if she had been a teenager eleven years ago, and in her twenties a few years later, how could she now be verging on middle age?

"I am here for Vella and Goodweather," she said again. "Where are they?"

They mostly stared. "I can show you Criton's house," a guard offered.

Bandu nodded at him. "Good."

Inside the gate, Bandu marveled at the city's growth. Salemica was an unusual city, in that the walls had been built well before there was town enough to fill them. Now there were houses everywhere, with little alleys running between them. The further she walked into the city, the larger the streets and houses grew, as if each wave of people who settled here had thought there couldn't be too many more behind them. As each group had been proven wrong, the newcomers built smaller houses to make sure there would be space.

The streets, which began as those narrow alleyways near the gate, ran together like rivers as she neared the city's center. Already from several streets away she could see the Great Temple, rising mountainlike above even these larger houses. Within minutes she and the guard had passed into the widest road, bustling with merchants and other vendors, which led to the great road-lake into which all rivers flowed.

In other cities Bandu had seen, temple squares all contained more than one temple. Here, though, the house of God Most High stood alone. It had been the first house built, the one Criton's people had erected before any people had made their own homes in the city. God Most High had moved here first.

The temple was massive, giant blocks of red brick piled on top of one another so that the priests of God Most High could live and do their work closer to the sky. Bandu thought that if mountains had been designed by people, they would look very much like this: all bricks and stairs and right angles. There were no more doors on the ground level than there would have been in the side of a mountain, only stairs to the huge platform on top. There, a great altar stood before the house where Vella's family lived, and where they spoke to their God.

"This way," the guard said, leading Bandu along the edge of the square to a sprawling building that stood across from the temple steps. Criton's house.

His house disgusted her, even from the outside. It was

the same size as that abbey she and her friends had visited long ago, a building that had easily housed not only its five guests but a half dozen grown men besides. The house was made of stone, just like that abbey, with wooden shutters and two chimneys. Even with Criton's three wives and many children, there would be more than enough room, and that meant that whoever had designed it had assumed there would be more wives and children on the way. That might have been the most obscene part of it all.

The chimneys weren't smoking, so Bandu told the guard to check whether Goodweather and Vella were there. She didn't want to set foot in that house if she didn't need to.

The guard returned promptly; there was nobody at home. "They might be at the temple," he suggested.

They pushed their way through the crowd and began their climb. Bandu was glad to be going to the temple, despite all the steps. The building had a better feeling to it than Criton's house. For one thing, its size made more sense. Gods were big and vain and would probably start killing people if They didn't get big grand houses that showed off how much people feared Them. What was Criton's excuse?

The funny thing about building your God a big house was that it didn't matter if the God actually lived there, because the important part was the respect. It was Vella's family that *lived* in the temple, but everyone knew it wasn't the Highservants' house, because they weren't the ones who had to be appeased with big red buildings that towered above a city.

Bandu's legs grew tired as she neared the top. There were so many steps to be climbed before she could pass the altar and enter the dwelling. The base of the building had taken a great deal more labor to build than the actual house, and its only purpose was to make the temple taller: closer to the heavens and easy to see from any of the streets below. The house on top, tall and square and grand, was still smaller than Criton's house.

The guard led her inside to the place where the priests ate. As Bandu walked, Vella's voice came from up ahead, raised and angry. She was yelling at someone. The guard looked at Bandu with awkward curiosity, but she ignored him and passed through the archway to the dining room. Sure enough, there they all were: Vella and Goodweather, Kilion Highservant and his wife Chara, Criton and his whole family. Though Vella had clearly been yelling at Criton, it was Kilion who was standing, trying to make peace. He would likely succeed, Bandu thought: there was nobody Vella respected more than her father.

Once Bandu had stepped into the room, though, Kilion's peacemaking efforts became moot as all focus shifted to her. Everyone went quiet and stared, which Bandu found uncomfortable. Except for Vella and Goodweather, who were only surprised to see her, all the other adults were going through the same reevaluation as the men at the gate. How could she have aged so much in so few years? Bandu wished people would stop doing that.

Criton spoke first. "Bandu," he said. "You're here." He looked like he wanted to leap across the table towards her. Was he really so eager for this meeting?

He had changed since the last time she'd seen him, though not nearly as much as she had. He looked much as she remembered him, tall and handsome though no longer as thin as he'd once been. There were no holes in his clothes, of course, and no dirt rubbed into his skin; he no longer had the look of a man who lost sleep at night. The years had been good to him. *Her* years had been good to him.

"The sky shakes," Bandu answered. "I need to see Vella and Goodweather are alive."

"We're alive," Vella assured her. "Everyone is fine."

"So come home with me."

"You're not going to leave already?" Criton cried, sounding altogether desperate. "Goodweather's been here such a short time, and I haven't seen you in ages!"

Bandu frowned at him. "This is not home for us. We go."

"Tomorrow, maybe," Chara interjected. "It's too late to be leaving now, and Malkon will be up north until tomorrow or the next day – he should at least have the chance to say goodbye to his sister."

Vella looked at Bandu with that hopeful face, and she never had the chance to argue. "We wait for him," she said. "You let us sleep here?"

"Of course," Kilion said. "You can stay here for as long as you like."

As long as she liked! Bandu didn't want to stay at all. This was a God's house. Still, it would be better than sleeping in Criton's house. God or no, she felt safer here.

Goodweather did not feel the same way, and asked if she could stay in her father's house that night. Bandu and Vella looked at each other and quickly agreed. Time alone with each other was precious, and they knew Goodweather liked to spend time with Delika.

Looking around now, Bandu was shocked when she finally noticed Delika. She had changed so much since the last time Bandu had seen her, and she barely even resembled the girl Bandu watched alongside Goodweather while Criton led his people to war. She had been a little girl then. Now she was grown, about the same age Bandu had been when Goodweather was born. She was sitting next to Criton with a calming hand on his arm, looking more like another wife than an adopted daughter. The sight disturbed Bandu.

Delika caught her glance and stared back at her defiantly. It hadn't been her imagination: the two of them were really mating. That sealed it. Bandu had long ago soured on Criton, but she hadn't thought he would do *this*. If he could claim Delika as a wife and place her beside him with pride, was even Goodweather safe?

"You must be hungry," Chara said, making room for Bandu at the table. "I'm finished here – you sit and eat."

Bandu really was hungry, so she swallowed her disgust and did as she was told. The others went back to their food too and soon the room was noisy again. "I'm glad you came," Vella said.

"I'm glad you are safe," Bandu answered. "The sky shouldn't shake."

"No, it shouldn't."

"Do you have some idea what caused it?" Criton asked. He respected her magic, anyway.

"I ask the Yarek later. It's so strong now, I think it hears me in our trees."

The mealtime sounds ceased. Everyone was staring at Bandu again. Of course. The Yarek was God Most High's ancient enemy. To sit in His temple and suggest talking to it was what people called sacrilege. They were right, too – Bandu had made a terrible mistake. Gods killed people over this sort of thing. The God of the Dragon Touched hadn't killed her yet, so that was a good start, but she couldn't pretend it meant He didn't mind. If He was letting her live now, it was probably because she was still useful to Him.

That was a problem too. What could Vella's God – what could *Criton's* God – possibly still need her for? Hadn't she given enough of herself to His causes already?

Bandu hated being a part of the Gods' plans. She had spent a very happy decade without Them steering her toward anything, and she wished it would stay that way. Life was easier when They kept Their distance.

These *had* been happy years, despite her unnatural aging. Vella was a good mate and partner, and they were raising Goodweather well. They were teaching her everything she needed to know, but most importantly they were raising her happy. It almost hurt Bandu's heart to see how happy and carefree her daughter was when she herself had never known such a life. Goodweather didn't have to worry about her next meal, didn't have to worry about getting eaten, had never had to fend for herself without a parent in easy shouting distance. There were times when Bandu worried that all the happiness and support were making Goodweather fragile, but she still thought it was worth the risk. Being strong wasn't as good as being happy, and anyway, even strong things would break in the end.

How long until Bandu herself broke? For now, her body was in perfectly fine condition; the difficulty lay more in knowing how quickly the years would pass than in feeling the effects physically. Still, how many more good years did she have? Fifteen? Twenty? Assuming Criton's God didn't kill her first.

She shouldn't have said that about talking to the Yarek. Not here.

"Do what you must," Vella said, careful with her words. They all knew that Bandu's idea hadn't been a bad one, it just wasn't safe to say so out loud. Even Kilion was nodding approvingly at how his daughter had phrased her agreement.

Vella had always been good with words. It was a skill she had in common with Phaedra, a skill Bandu admired but would never have. Bandu's wife had the best things in common with her friends: she had Hunter's loyalty and protectiveness, Narky's honesty, Phaedra's way with words. She was also stubborn like Criton, which was not something Bandu liked, but Vella put it to better use than he did. Criton's stubbornness had endangered his friends' lives and dragged Bandu halfway across the continent. Vella had just taught her to read.

She was patient, that was the thing. It was easier to love somebody patient, and Vella was easy to love. If Bandu did or said something wrong, Vella always told her, but she didn't expect her to change right away. She would just keep coming back and coming back to it until Bandu caught up. It was what she had done with Bandu's reading, and it was also what she had done with love.

Vella had loved Bandu first, after all, and Bandu had used that love against her. She had used Vella to pry herself away from Criton, without any thought of what it would mean for Vella herself. That had been typical for her. Bandu had always been too hasty with those sorts of decisions, not least when she had taken Criton for her own. She was lucky it had turned out so much better the second time.

It had taken all of Vella's patience and skill with words to make Bandu understand how selfish she had been. Bandu had been afraid to admit how right Vella was, and that was after it had taken her far too long to figure out what the other girl was talking about. Yet despite all of Bandu's language troubles and all of her defensiveness, Vella had never given up on her. That might be the best thing about her: no matter how long it took, she insisted on being understood.

To judge from Criton's expression as he glanced between them, Vella had been making herself *very* well understood when Bandu walked in. At least she had been fighting for Bandu this time, and not with her. Bandu's deal with Ravennis for Criton's life was still the greatest source of tension between them. It was always lurking in the background, ready to come out anytime Vella was worried or angry about anything.

Bandu agreed with her, of course. It wasn't right to trade away years that should have belonged to her and Vella for the sake of a man who had never even been good to her. No matter how much it had made sense at the time, no matter how important it had been to end the war between Criton's people and Ardis, it still wasn't fair. For Bandu, it was enough to know how unfair it was, to mourn the lost years and try to enjoy the ones she still had. But Vella believed in a just God, and if her God was just and kind, that meant some *person* had to be responsible for this injustice. Sometimes that person was Bandu; sometimes it was Criton; sometimes it was Vella's late grandma, or the cousin who had murdered Criton and made the whole thing necessary; but it was always *someone*.

Luckily, the meal concluded without any more fights. Criton and his pack went home, taking Goodweather with them, and Bandu and Vella were left with Vella's parents.

"I know," Vella said, before Bandu could form her thoughts into words. "I'm sorry. I shouldn't let him anger me the way he does. He just has so little self-awareness, it's maddening. He's blind to everything he doesn't want to believe in."

Kilion frowned. "I hope you're not expecting me to take sides. This is not a good time for me and Criton to be having public disagreements. Even rumored ones are best avoided."

"I know," Vella said, bowing her head. "I'm sorry."

"Delika is his wife now?" Bandu asked.

"This spring," Chara confirmed.

"You find that disgusting too, right?" Vella asked, turning on her mother.

Chara grimaced. "She seems happy enough about it, and it's not technically against our laws. My interest ends there."

"But God Most High is angry for something," Bandu said. "Maybe that."

"No," Vella said. "He wouldn't punish us all for something Criton did."

"When I leave Tarphae, Karassa kills the whole island because She is angry at king."

"Well," Vella replied, "God Most High isn't Karassa, and Criton isn't our king."

Bandu thought her wife could see the skepticism on her face well enough.

Kilion leaned back in his chair. "We've had reports that the sky shook in Ardis too, and in other places beyond our borders. If this is a punishment for Criton's behavior, it's awfully diffuse."

He was probably right. It was too much to hope for Criton's God to punish him over something like this. It was too human a problem – it didn't insult any Gods, only people. And as disproportionate as the Gods could be, it *did* seem unlikely that Criton's God would shake the sky over something as irrelevant as his sex life.

They got up, and Vella showed her where they would be sleeping. It was a small room for a temple this big, with just enough space for a bed and a wooden shelf for clothes. But it had a door that closed, which was more than could be said for some of the other rooms here, and the bed was comfortable enough. The window was so high on the wall that Bandu couldn't look out unless she stood on the bed and leaned over toward it, but that was by design: the windows here were for looking up to the heavens, not for surveying the land.

"I hate the way Criton looks at me," Vella said as they were getting undressed. "Like I'm a rival for your affections, and if he could get me out of the way he might have you back."

"He never gets me back."

"*I* know that, but he doesn't seem to. He still acts like I'm in his way."

Bandu put a hand on her shoulder. "You want me to do something?"

Vella sighed. "No, I just want you to know about it. I don't want to be alone with this."

"You're never alone."

"Good."

They sat there for a time, until Bandu decided they must be finished talking and unwrapped her skirt.

"I'm glad you've decided to do what you have," Vella said. "My father is a holy man, but you can tell he doesn't know why God made the sky quake like that. Anything that gets us closer to the answer has to be a good thing."

"Maybe your God thinks so too. He doesn't punish me yet."

"My God is merciful, Bandu. He doesn't punish people over every little thing. You spoke out of turn, but you didn't mean any disrespect by it."

"Maybe. Or maybe He wants me to do something again. Criton is not enough for Him from me. Maybe He wants me to fix the sky too."

The weariness in her voice must have showed, because Vella gave her a kiss and hugged her tight. "Or maybe He just wants me to be happy."

Bandu stroked her wavy hair, pulled it back gently so she could see Vella's face. "That's nice. Maybe you are right."

They kissed, and this time Vella refused to let go. She was breathing heavier, and now she was stroking Bandu's upper leg. Bandu smiled and pressed her closer. Vella liked having privacy – it was more important to her than it was to Bandu. Sometimes that was frustrating, but right now it was very very nice.

She liked Vella's idea that maybe God Most High really was done with her, that for once He was letting her live just because she and Vella deserved it. It meant she was free to live like this until her time ran out, and it made sense too: not everything was about her. There were plenty of others who could serve Him if He needed it.

Good. That all made sense. She would pretend it was true.

9

PHAEDRA

Phaedra stood on the ship's deck, watching the waves roll by underneath. She couldn't wait for this voyage to be over. From Ksado to Antaka, from Antaka to Theris, from Therisport to Belinphae – port after port, ship after ship, each one bringing her closer to her goal. The very indirectness of her path was a shield against Karassa's vision, better than any of the wards she had placed on herself or, secretly, her ships. Let her be yet another itinerant traveler, making her slow way to Atuna. In the past, God Most High had protected her from stormy seas and angry Gods, but that did not give her an excuse to take unnecessary chances. To put trust in a God was a holy thing; to force one's hand, blasphemous.

That was also why she meant to overshoot her homeland and sail for Atuna instead. It might have been possible to convince some poor fool to take her to Tarphae directly, but delivering herself over to Karassa and Her servants on the assumption that God Most High would protect her would have been so arrogant that the thought of it made her shudder.

This was a better plan. She would convince the

Atunaean High Council to help her eliminate the pirates entirely, lessening the burden on God Most High to keep her safe.

Phaedra had confidence in her persuasive skills, but she also knew the power of a strong entry. When at long last her ship arrived and she disembarked, she slammed her staff on the dock and, as loudly as possible, hired a young girl to show her to the High Council building. At her pace, there would be several minutes for the council to learn of her impending arrival before she actually got there. It would be just long enough to wonder about her intent and to discuss admitting her, but not long enough to actually reach a consensus, and, as a result, there was less chance that she would be turned away. At least, so she hoped.

She received plenty of stares as she followed the girl through the city, but Phaedra had grown used to these. A wizard could expect no less, and anyway, she had always received attention. In her teens, it had been for her beauty and grace. Then it had been for her status as one of the five cursed refugees of Tarphae, the wanderers who brought ill luck wherever they went. Now it was for the magic.

Phaedra loved her staff for these purposes. It drew attention away from her limp and toward her power, and better, it made people think that the two were somehow connected. The golden letters spiraling from top to bottom made her wizardry clear, even to those who hadn't realized wizards still existed. Nobody questioned her with her staff: they only feared and respected her.

A crowd was gathering behind her as she walked, murmuring its curiosity. She didn't turn, but upon her arrival at the council building lifted a hand and said,

"Thank you for accompanying me. You may go home now."

The murmurs only grew louder, of course, as people began to wonder whether it was her magic and not their curiosity that had drawn them in. Was she really so powerful? It was a good thing for them to wonder.

The Atunaean High Council Building was as grand as any temple, rows of orderly pillars leading up its steps to the double door in front of which statesmen spoke to their citizens often throughout their tenure. The doors were closed now. Phaedra climbed the steps anyway.

They opened before she reached them. A broad man with a spear and short sword stood in the doorway, watching her progress. "State your business," he said flatly.

"I bring word of Mura's pirates," she answered, "and the solution to piracy in your waters. The council would be wise to hear what I know."

His eyebrows shot up. Whatever he had expected, this was not it. "I'll ask the council," he said, and closed the door.

Phaedra stood outside, trying to be patient. They would let her in – they *had* to let her in. The crowd was watching. It made her want to give them a display of something besides her patience, but she knew it wasn't a wise instinct. She had the power to open this door by magic, but that could only insult the council. No, she must stand here and look as patient as a statue until that guard came back.

Was it just her, or was the crowd growing quieter? Were they dispersing? She did not risk a glance behind her, lest it betray her weakness. In other lands, where kings and noblemen ruled, the opinion of a crowd was only relevant when someone was stoking it to violence;

but here in Atuna, it was the mob that ruled the city. The council sought to please *them*, not the other way around. The guard had seen them all below when he opened the door to question Phaedra; their presence would be one of the factors that convinced the council to see her, if indeed they could be convinced. In any case, Phaedra could not afford to lose the crowd. They were her key through this door.

Her wait seemed interminable, but eventually the guard returned with another dressed and armed in the same way, and bade her enter. The council would see her after all.

Through a small antechamber the meeting hall was bright and airy, with large shutterless windows every few feet. During elections and at other times of great controversy, the heads of the city's many families would crowd into this space while others stood outside, making their voices heard despite the barriers between them and the chambers. Phaedra had read of one man who had leapt through one of these windows and charged a councilman he opposed – he had been restrained by his neighbors but allowed to speak. Now that she was inside, Phaedra suspected that a few intrepid citizens would climb the stairs after her so that they could eavesdrop on her meeting. Maybe the girl she had paid would do it. Gods knew, it was what *she* would have done.

There were twelve councilmen in Atuna, but only nine were present today. That was still too large a group for Phaedra to know whom to look at when she spoke, so she swept her eyes over them all as she waited for one to speak.

All the councilmen were dressed in the garb they had earned at their election: the stylized servant's tunic with its patterned gold lace and red dyed thread on a background of white. If she remembered correctly, both colors officially represented Atun the Sun God's blessing, not wealth or blood. But she was sure the colloquial meaning was different.

"You told Platana that you were here to talk of piracy," a balding shorter man said. "We would hear you speak."

Phaedra nodded, calling up the appropriate term for addressing the council. It had been a long time since her father had spoken to her of his trade meetings in Atuna. Even so, etiquette was one of the things she rarely had trouble remembering.

"Esteemed Citizens," she said, "the piracy problem has grown worse over the last decade, to the point where no merchant feels safe. I have heard the rumors as I traveled, of how pirates have snatched ships right out of port, how they've overtaken them at sea. Nobody knows where they disappear to. The seas, which had been so safe after the Treaty of Belinport, have become treacherous once again."

"You sum up the problem nicely," another of the councilmen commented. "Go on."

"Thank you," Phaedra said. "Esteemed Citizens, I know these pirates intimately. They captured me once, and I was barely able to escape them. I know where they have made their home, and how they have evaded the Atunaean navy up until now. I know how to eliminate them, and I want to help you do just that. I only ask that I be allowed aboard the flagship that brings them to justice."

The councilmen glanced at each other, looking far less skeptical than Phaedra had feared.

"Tell us everything you know," said the first.

"The leader is a man named Mura, a sorcerer who has

used his terrible magic to command complete authority both among his own men and the many slaves he has captured. I say this as a practitioner of magic myself: this man is inhuman, and his magic is no less so. He has made his base on Tarphae, my former homeland, and bought his safety there with human sacrifice. Karassa has a new people, and they are all pirates."

There were audible gasps. "I see," said one of the councilmen, perhaps the oldest. Unlike the others, he was seated on a stool, a cane at his side. "The people of Tarphae were formidable back when Karassa still favored them. With Her favor, these pirates will be no less so."

"I agree," Phaedra said. "I am from Tarphae myself, and the favor I saw the Goddess bestow upon Mura I had never seen before. The priests of my youth did not have the kind of connection with their Goddess that this sorcerer has. Defeating these pirates will not be some simple naval operation. So long as Mura retains Karassa's favor, the Goddess will try to protect him. There may well be storms when Atuna's ships sail for the island, and who knows what else She and Her servants will throw in our way. That's why I want to go with the flotilla, so that my magic might counter Mura's and my God may counter his."

"Oh?" asked the old councilman. "And who would that be?"

"God Most High, the God of Dragons and God of the Dragon Touched, He who created the first world out of the Yarek's carcass and made room for the second with barriers of sky. It was He who protected me from Karassa when I was trapped on Her island eleven years ago, and He who protected me again when I sailed east from Mayar's territory into Hers. With God Most High on its side, Atun's navy has nothing to fear from Karassa even in Her own domain."

She could see how her words were impressing them, and it made her feel giddy. This couldn't have gone better – she had chosen the right course.

"We will confer in private," the balding councilman said. "Where will you be staying, so that we may call you when we've made our decision?"

Phaedra made a quick calculation. Should she stay at an inn, knowing the exposure she would have there? Was it safer to remove herself from society, despite her yearning for a good bed?

"I will be back tomorrow morning," she said. "You can tell me your decision then."

As she left the council building, Phaedra took one of the square Ksadan coins out of her pocket and rubbed it against her temple. The coin carried her disorientation at being in a new land, passed jovially from one court to the next; it carried her old unfamiliarity with the Estic language and the foreign sights and smells of Essisha's many ports. Stopping on the steps, she stuck the coin between the toes of her left foot. "Confound my pursuers," she whispered to it in Estic.

There were still the remnants of a crowd when she descended, but they parted for her, and despite their best efforts could not follow. Those who tried kept peeling off with vague looks on their faces, heading away toward their homes or the fish market before stopping in confusion and trying to remember what they were doing there. Phaedra's progress was slow, so the process kept repeating itself with new onlookers, but eventually she escaped the bounds of the city and found herself a flat spot in the woods in which to rest until dawn. She hadn't eaten since that morning, but she was too nervous to eat anyway: soon enough she would confront Mura, and if her God was good, she would defeat him and return to Psander. She put the coin back in her pocket, warded her resting spot against dew and rain, and lay down.

The sky was already beginning to brighten when she finally fell asleep, and the sun had barely risen when she woke again. She rose and stretched uncomfortably, but soon she was on her way back to the city.

Atuna's walls were vestigial things, buried more than halfway into the city. Its seven gates were always left open, though theoretically a bad enough military loss could force them shut if the city's core was ever in need of protection. Phaedra passed through one of these gates on her way to the council building, trying to look commanding rather than aching and sleepy. A crowd was waiting for her at the base of the council building, staring at the Tarphaean wizard who wanted to invade Tarphae. The nine councilmen stood at the top of the steps, joined by a tenth man who was dressed not as a councilman, but in a sea captain's formalwear. Phaedra was only halfway up the steps when the tallest councilman spoke, his voice booming.

"We have conferred regarding your request and have one last question. Merchant Kespha asked it at our evening meeting, and it deserves an answer before we can entrust our ships to your God's protection. If your God is as powerful as you say, tell us: is He also responsible for the shaking of the sky? We presume that as a wizard you have knowledge beyond the realms of men."

For a moment, Phaedra panicked. There was no way

to answer his question without betraying her lack of knowledge and losing face before the crowd. She was asking the city to entrust its warships to a foreigner who openly admitted to wizardry – persuasion depended upon her ability to project power and knowledge. She was about to fail.

She thought of Psander, of how disgusted she would be if she knew how her student was flailing at this most crucial of moments. The wizard would probably say something terse and devastating about lowering her expectations for Phaedra.

Wait, that was it! Psander never oversold her abilities, she used her natural terseness to her advantage and made anything beyond what she could provide seem impossible. It was a technique worth mimicking.

"You presume too much," Phaedra answered the council and the crowd, trying to speak just as Psander would have. "Wizards can do many things, but we aren't prophets. I mean to go to Tarphae precisely because I *don't* know why the sky shook, because I believe the answer lies somewhere on the island. Help me get there and you help yourselves. Turn me down, and we may never know the reason for the skyquakes until it's too late. The piracy will continue, and the next quake might tear the world in two for all I know."

She put a hand on her heart. "I respect the people of Atuna and the council they chose, and I am sure you'll make the right decision. The choice is yours."

The crowd went silent, watching the council quietly deliberate. The tall one turned back to Phaedra. "Shipping is the lifeblood of our city," he said. "Piracy harms us all. We will do as you say."

Phaedra couldn't help but smile. "Thank you, people of Atuna. You have done a great thing today. My God will not forget."

10
DESSA

Sooner or later, everything washed up in Atuna. Dessa certainly hadn't meant to end up here when she'd run away from home so many years ago. She had meant to find Vella and Bandu, wherever they had gone off to, and learn how to do magic the way Bandu did it. But she had never found them and could still barely do more with her magic than when she was a child. Instead she had spent a decade lost among beggars and thieves, always a meal or two from starvation and one piece of bad luck away from violence.

She had come to Atuna with a friend – it was always safer to do anything with a friend. But the friend had gotten himself killed breaking into a storehouse, so now she was back to the dangerous work of finding a new friend. She had been too trusting in the past and had scars to prove it. Choosing poorly was worse than having no friend at all.

If only she had found Bandu and learnt magic from her, Dessa's life would have been different. With the power to raise people from the dead, to make houses weep and force people to take her seriously, she would not have had all these troubles with dangerous men. She still lived with the hope that she might someday find Bandu, though deep down she knew it was a false hope. Dessa was no less determined at twenty-two than she'd been at eleven, but she knew now that determination wasn't everything. You needed luck too, and Dessa had precious little of it.

She should never have run away from home. Bandu and Vella couldn't have gone far – if she'd only stayed and waited for news instead of wandering off on her own, she might have found them years ago. She often wished she could go back and shake some sense into herself. How far could two teenagers and a baby really have gone? But once she had left home, once she had gotten herself involved with the sorts of people she had met along the way, it was impossible to go back. What could she say to her mother? To face the pain on Mother's face when she saw what a mess Dessa had made of her life – no, she just couldn't. Anything would be better than that.

Dessa had left Mother with so little. A dead, disgraced husband; an angry, confused, slowly dying mother; a missing daughter. The decision to leave home at eleven hadn't just been ill-advised, it had been unspeakably selfish. That was why she could never go home. As hard as the last ten-plus years had been, they'd been easier for Dessa than facing all the pain she'd caused Mother. Better to stay away, to be the mysterious lost daughter forever.

She'd had dreams once of returning home with her father in tow, having rescued him from death just as Bandu had rescued Criton. She understood now how ridiculous a dream it had been. Father wasn't a hero like Criton, he was a murderer. Nobody wanted him back but Dessa.

But even if she couldn't have that dream, she could still aspire to Bandu's magic. Nobody cared what kind of life a witch had had, or what mistakes she'd made in her youth. People like Bandu were mysterious, distant figures that people admired and feared. Nobody came close enough to see their flaws.

Dessa was sitting in a corner in the main room of a sailor's hostel, thinking about Bandu and her invisible flaws, when a man came over and offered her some honey wine. That was one good thing about Atuna: the best wines came through its port. Sailors were not the sort of people who saved up for things – they would arrive in some harbor with more money than expenses and no more responsibility than they had sense, and a few good drinks and trinkets later they were off to sea again. This particular sailor was toting two undersized bottles made of yellow glass, which must have been extremely expensive and come from far beyond the sea. Dessa knew the beers and wines of the continent all too well, and *nobody* out here put their wine in glass bottles. The bottle would have been ten times as expensive as its contents.

"What's the occasion?" she asked, handing him her cup.

"Been away for three years and come back to find my wife hasn't been pregnant since I left! This other bottle's just for her."

Dessa smiled despite herself. "You didn't have that good news when you bought it, though."

"No, but there's always special occasions. Here, drink it! You've never tasted anything like it."

He was right. She had expected something sweet and cloying, but instead her tongue met with an incredible subtlety of flavor that made her wish she'd taken a smaller sip. This wine was too good to drink quickly.

"Where did you get this?"

"Antaka. It's an island halfway to the other continent. This is an Essishan wine."

His names meant nothing to her, but she tried to look impressed. "It's amazing."

"Drink of kings," he said. "I'm going to treat her like a queen. She usually likes them sweeter, but you can't beat Essishan honey wine."

"Well if she doesn't like it, you know where to find me. What ship did you come in on?"

"The *Sunbeam*. Good Atunaean ship. Same one that brought that witch here."

Dessa had to put her cup down so it wouldn't spill while she coughed out the wine she'd inhaled. "What witch?"

"Called herself Phaedra. You hadn't heard? She made a big scene when she got here about going to meet the High Council."

It wasn't Bandu, then, but the name Phaedra did have a familiar ring to it. Besides, a witch was a witch. Dessa wasn't picky who she learned from, just so long as she got to learn.

"What does she look like? How do I find her?"

The sailor looked a bit surprised at her urgency, but he didn't say anything rude about it. "I don't know. She can't be at the council building anymore, that was hours ago."

"You don't know what she looks like either?"

"Oh, I know what she looks like. About this tall, real dark skin, almost black. An islander, or maybe even Essishan herself, though the name isn't eastern. Real beauty though. If she wasn't a witch they'd have all been cramming into her cabin. Talks like a councilman, with big long words. She's hard to miss, really."

"Thanks," Dessa said, rising to her feet and almost

forgetting her honey wine. She made a quick decision and drained her cup, not swallowing until she absolutely had to. He hadn't given her too much, but she still felt like she'd wasted it. She raced to the door and away from the hostel, ignoring the stares. She didn't even know where the council building was, but she imagined it was further from the docks than this. She'd ask on her way.

She knew where she'd heard the name Phaedra now – the description had been all she needed. Phaedra was dark-skinned like Bandu or Criton because she was their kinswoman, a Tarphaean islander. Dessa had seen her just the once, the day they had stoned Father. She'd had no idea Phaedra was a witch, but she had been there when it happened, and afterward she was gone.

Dessa couldn't let her disappear this time. She raced through the city, her head pounding, stopping often to ask how to get to the council building but only able to follow the directions of people's pointing fingers. She was drunker than she'd realized when sitting there in the hostel. It was very noticeable, to judge from people's reactions, but she didn't mind the embarrassment; she minded that it was making it harder to find the council building on the one day in her life when she really needed to be somewhere in a hurry.

By the time she got there, the witch had gone. Dessa was nearly sober now, but it didn't help much because everyone she asked about Phaedra acted as if they themselves were drunk. Nobody seemed to know where she had gone or even how long ago. Dessa's questioning only got her half-answers and vacant stares, which were so much worse than the judgmental stares she'd grown used to. Had anyone tried to follow Phaedra when she left?

Oh yes, definitely. Some of those Dessa asked had tried it themselves. But not one knew where she'd gone in the end, and every one of them pointed Dessa in a different direction. It was maddening.

Dessa couldn't believe that it was a coincidence. She had asked six different people in the vicinity of the council building, and *none* of them agreed with each other. It had to be a confounding spell. For whatever reason, Phaedra didn't want to be found.

Well, that was unacceptable. Dessa didn't care what Phaedra wanted. It didn't matter whether she was covering her tracks to avoid an enemy or intentionally persecuting Dessa for some reason, which was certainly what it felt like. The important thing was that Dessa would *not* let her slip away, not when they were in the same godsforsaken city! One way or another, she'd find her and make her reveal her secrets.

One way or another. If only she knew how.

That was the trouble with Dessa's life: she was all determination and no plan. She had always believed in herself, believed that if she just threw herself at a problem without reservation, it would yield to her. So far, it hadn't really worked that way. Too often she had confused her faith in herself for the protection of her God, and too often she had been disappointed.

God Most High had yet to intervene on her behalf, no matter how scary things got. She'd spent years on the road searching for Bandu and all she had to show for it was a decade's worth of bad experiences, a handful of Atunaean coins, and a taste for wine.

Everything would get better after she found Phaedra. It had to. There was nothing that magic couldn't fix once she knew the trick of it. Bandu had proven that much.

For an hour Dessa wandered around the city, asking after Phaedra and going in whatever direction people suggested. It wasn't a logical plan: the city was too large and the trail too cold. But it didn't get in the way of devising a better plan, it just gave her feet and mouth something to do that didn't feel as useless as pacing and mumbling to herself.

Next, she tried the marketplace and the temple square. They were likely enough places to find someone who'd recently disembarked from a long voyage, but if Phaedra had ever stopped there, she wasn't there anymore.

For the next few hours, Dessa checked every inn and hostel in the city, from the fanciest ambassador-worthy places to the least reputable sailors' hostels. At the former she was lucky to get a polite "no" before some private guard escorted her to the door; at the latter she only got the usual propositions. She feared – but rejected – the possibility that Phaedra had already left the city. If she had stopped to speak with the Atunaean High Council upon her arrival, she couldn't possibly have moved on already. Yet here it was growing dark, and nobody knew where she had gone. The woman had completely disappeared.

Dessa cursed that sailor for not having told her about Phaedra sooner. Maybe if she had left a few minutes earlier the trail would have been warmer and this search wouldn't be so fruitless. She doubted it, but it did help to be angry at someone, and the sailor was a convenient target. She hoped his wife spat out her wine.

She hated the way people stared at her while she roamed around the twilit city, as if looking unkempt and frustrated made her less human. She had half a mind to bring out her claws and give them something to really stare at, but there was no sense endangering herself over a few nasty looks. A dirty madwoman was distasteful; a dirty madwoman with claws was a public menace.

She couldn't let the stares go unanswered though, so instead of going back to the hostel, she spent some of her savings from the storehouse robbery – the one she'd lost her big friend to – and stayed at one of the nicer inns she could afford. The food was better, and they had baths.

It was the best night's sleep she'd had in ages. She dreamt that her mother was welcoming her home with tears and kisses, and that Father was thanking her profusely for what she had done. Vella was there too, saying how proud she was and calling Dessa her sister. She awoke with a smile on her face, enjoying the sunshine from her window, hanging onto the last remnants of her dream before she had to go back to her womanhunt. It wouldn't hurt to spend a few extra moments in bed – after all, rushing hadn't helped her yesterday. She'd probably do better if she spent less time running and more time thinking. Plus, she'd miraculously escaped a hangover, so the sleep was definitely worth it.

Her clothes were still a bit damp when she put them on – she had washed them in the bath the night before, after she had finished bathing. The wet cloth was rough against her skin, but it would dry in the sun, and at least her clothes were clean. She couldn't remember the last time she'd washed them. If she *did* find Phaedra today, she wanted to make a good impression. She ate a satisfying meal that was more lunch than breakfast, parting with some of her last Atunaean coins. When she finally left the inn, it was well past noon.

Her plan was to go back to the council building and see if Phaedra had returned, but that proved unnecessary. It was hard to miss the sheer bulk of armament being carried toward the docks, and when Dessa asked for an explanation, she was told that the Tarphaean witch was leading a fleet to rid her homeland of pirates.

Dessa raced for the docks, hoping to find some excuse for boarding the same ship as Phaedra. She didn't have any skills that would be useful on a ship – she had never sailed; never fought in a battle; couldn't even cook well. Could she just lie about that? She didn't think so. They'd know she was no sailor within seconds.

She reached the docks still with no plan, so she began by asking which ship Phaedra was on. *Atun's Favor* was the biggest warship in the Atunaean navy, too large to be anchored at the quay except when loading or unloading. Naturally it was fully manned already, waiting out in the harbor for the rest of the fleet. Dessa could almost have screamed. It felt like God Most High was throwing obstacles in her way on purpose. Why was He doing this to her?

Some of the smaller ships were still loading up for the expedition – she could try her luck with those. Dessa ran over to the place where a few armed citizens were boarding a dinghy. They wore no armor, so they must have been volunteers.

"Please," she begged the man who was directing them onto the boat, "take me too."

The man shook his head. He was tall and handsome, with a gold ring in the left side of his nose. "Boat's full, but I'll be back. The *Glimmering Sea's* not a ferry, though. If you can't fight or sail, we don't need you."

"I can fight," Dessa lied. Determination or no, everyone

else had a weapon and she didn't.

"No, you can't. Get out of here."

They shoved off, and Dessa watched them row to the ship. Time to try a different boat. But at each one, the reaction was the same. They were not taking unarmed women with no sailing experience. The fleet would leave without her.

She could wait until they returned, but knowing her luck Phaedra would come to shore in the middle of the night and be off before Dessa could even learn of her arrival. On the other hand, that dinghy was coming back for one more trip. Anything that got her onto it would be well worth the risk.

"You again," the man on the dinghy said when he looked up from his rowing and saw her waiting. "I thought I told you, we've got no room for useless passengers."

Dessa could feel the stares of the people around her. "I'm not useless," she said. "I could be very helpful."

"Oh yeah? How?"

She took a deep breath. "I'm Dragon Touched."

Slowly, she let herself transform. Her hands and feet turned into claws, losing their extra digits. She had spent so long in hiding, she'd almost forgotten how much more comfortable it was this way, when she wasn't stretching her hands to make that last little finger or forcing her scales down below the skin. She had always preferred it this way, but had learned the risks of being openly Dragon Touched outside her people's territory. She hoped this time she'd get a more favorable reaction.

The sailor only recoiled slightly, which was better than it might have been. The others waiting to get on his boat backed away to give her more room, their fear and distaste palpable.

"What good is that?" the sailor asked. "We don't need you gouging our planks."

"I won't gouge your planks," Dessa said, trying to keep the desperation from her voice. "You said I'd be no good against the pirates, but I can surprise them. I can breathe fire too, when I need to."

"That's dangerous on a ship, I don't want you–"

"I can control it," she snapped. "I haven't breathed fire on you yet, have I? But I could do it at the pirates' ships."

Well, he didn't look dismissive, so that was something. He didn't look enthusiastic either, though. "I can ask the captain..."

"If you take her, I'm staying here."

Dessa turned to glare at the man who had spoken. He wasn't anything impressive to look at, and the weapon he carried was just a board with some nails in it. She could hardly wait for the sailor to ask, "Who cares?"

But he didn't. Instead he just turned back to her and said, "Sorry, it's an interesting idea and all, but we can't have people saying they want to go back to shore because of you. It's not worth the trouble."

Dessa stood, her mouth agape, not knowing what to say. The other people boarded the dinghy, and all she could do was to choke out, "Wait, please wait," as they rowed it away. A few minutes later, the ships began to leave the harbor. What remained were only the usual fishing boats and merchantmen, going about their business as if nothing had happened, as if nobody's dreams had been dashed after getting so tantalizingly close to fulfillment.

Dessa sat on the dock and cried.

11
PHAEDRA

The Atunaean flagship was enormous, with three masts and two banks of oars, showcasing the latest and best in naval technology. There were giant crossbows built on the Parakese model except on a much grander scale, with cables attached to their projectiles for retrieval or for towing their unlucky targets. The sails could be raised and lowered using an ingenious system of pulleys, saving time and probably lives too, since it reduced the duration sailors spent climbing the rigging. The biggest problem was that the *Atun's Favor* had too deep a draft to reach the docks at smaller seaports. The harbor at Karsanye, the former capital of Phaedra's homeland, was good and deep, but she couldn't remember if the pirates had rebuilt the piers far enough into it. She thought so, but her memory wasn't perfect. Hunter would have known.

The admiral of the Atunaean navy was a curt, frankly unpleasant man named Sett, who had been appointed after the execution of his predecessor. In the fifty years since the overthrow of Atuna's monarchy, four of its admirals had already been executed for being too popular with their men. Atuna's standing navy was its greatest power, but that made it especially dangerous to the High Council, which feared the rise of a new king. The rise of Magerion in Ardis, which had swept aside the Ardisian Council of Generals, had prompted them to be especially cautious. Given Atunaean supremacy over the seas, a popular admiral was considered a far greater threat than an incompetent one.

Sett was a good combination, from what Phaedra had heard: neither incompetent nor particularly well-liked. He had a tendency to do the Council's work for them, rooting out his most popular captains and forcing them to retire. It did not win him any accolades, but it had kept him in his position. He had earned his post seven years ago, and there were no indications that he would be replaced anytime soon.

He did not look with favor upon Phaedra. She got the sense that he tolerated her existence only insofar as she had a job to do and he expected her to do it. To be fair, that seemed to be his attitude toward everyone. It was no wonder he had remained safely unpopular.

There was no doubt that Phaedra *did* have a job to do, and she was already doing it. While the sailors hurried about their work and the soldiers readied themselves for battle, Phaedra borrowed a sailor's knife and moved about the ship, scratching wards into the wood. She had done the same already with the other ships in the fleet, but had saved the flagship for last since she knew she would have more time there than elsewhere.

She wanted to be thorough since this was her last chance to prepare before the Atunaean fleet came up against Mura and his patron Goddess. Phaedra and the Atunaeans had the element of surprise on their side, but of course that would not be enough. Karassa was a Sea Goddess, after all, and it was easier to sink a ship than to preserve one.

There were obvious wards to use – keeping water away from the hatches, lightning away from the masts, fire away from the sails – but having used them already on nearly a dozen other ships, Phaedra began to doubt their effectiveness. They were *so* standard, *so* obvious, that a Goddess like Karassa would cast them aside with ease. Maybe Psander's magic was strong enough to stand against the Gods, but these wards of Phaedra's? No, she was starting to think she would need something stronger.

At one time, Phaedra might have carved prayers to God Most High into the ship's hull, but that was before Psander had stressed to her the risks of demanding a God's attention, especially after the Gods had sought to exterminate academic wizardry. Mura used prayer magic exclusively, and apparently it hadn't killed him yet, but he was also Karassa's only finger this far west. God Most High had a city now, and a great temple full of priests. Phaedra was expendable.

No, it was wiser to take Psander's approach and to try to mask her ship instead, to make it harder for Karassa to see. Phaedra hadn't ever studied Psander's wards specifically, but she thought she might be able to reverse-engineer them at least to some degree. Invisibility was too much to hope for – she would have to settle for misdirection. So while the Atunaean fleet sped toward her homeland, she carved sigils into the planks beneath her, identifying the *Atun's Favor* as driftwood. She started near the central mast, choosing it as the poetic heart of the ship, and moved outward from there, standing after each sigil to let the rolling of the waves direct her movements. To move in a more orderly manner would be very un-driftwood-like and might well cancel her spell's effect.

She could have sworn she felt the air tingle as she etched the first symbols into the boards. She suspected it was a sign of Godly attention, but she couldn't have said which God it came from. She hoped it wasn't Atun expressing His anger with her: whatever her intentions, it was undoubtedly an insult to suggest that a ship called the *Atun's Favor* was mere driftwood. She had preferred that to the alternative, letting Karassa get a clear view of Her enemies' forces, but of course Atun wasn't obligated to care about Phaedra's calculations.

When she finally rose to survey her handiwork, well after the island of Tarphae had come into sight, she allowed herself a sigh of satisfaction. She thought Psander would have been proud of her. Still, she wished she had thought to do the same for the other ships before they left port. Instinct and experience told her there was no substitute for completing another full spell on each ship, but she did what she could and hastily carved an addendum to her spell naming the entire armada "flotsam." That the *Atun's Favor* was the flagship did suggest the possibility that magic performed on it might extend to the whole fleet. In any case, it was the best she could do at this point. She cursed the oversight that had led her to such half-measures. It was not enough; it could not be enough. How many men would die?

Twelve ships had left Atuna on this mission. The *Atun's Favor* was the largest and least maneuverable, so despite its impressive speed Admiral Sett had chosen to slow its

approach as they neared the island to let some of the smaller
ships pass it. They approached the harbor of Karsanye in
two rows of six, an arrangement that obscured Phaedra's
vision as she made her way toward the prow, and made
her fail to notice the enemy until the ship in front of hers,
the *Glimmering Sea*, came about.

The harbor mouth was full of boats. Not ships, but
dinghies and longboats and other small vessels, clogging
up the path to the docks. The men aboard were rowing
them toward the Atunaean fleet, making slow progress
against the tide. Phaedra rushed to the admiral's side,
wanting the chance to advise him but also plainly curious
about how he would respond. He gave her one irritated
glance and ordered all the boats sunk.

"They're probably full of slaves," Phaedra said. "Mura
captured sailors too, not just ships. He had us reclaiming a
farm last time I was here. These boats are a distraction – he
must have dozens of ships by now."

The admiral sneered at her. "You think he's sending
these boats at us while his ships hide on the other side of
the island. Me too. I'm not an idiot. But you never know
what the enemy's thinking – maybe it's the ships that
are the distraction, and all the pirates are on the boats. I
don't honestly care. While the enemy's on just one flank,
destroy him. You go to war with me, you don't get to keep
your baubles."

Phaedra held her tongue. Admiral Sett wouldn't have
listened anyway, so it didn't matter how much she wanted
to yell at him that those boats were full of people, not
baubles. His reasoning was tactically sound, whatever
his morals: it would be reckless to let this fleet of boats
anywhere near boarding range. Just because Phaedra

thought they were mostly slaves and not pirates didn't mean she was right.

So she stood silently and watched as Sett's fleet drove toward the armada of little boats, loosing round after round of arrows until all the rowers were dead. She looked over the side of the *Atun's Favor* as the great ship neared one of the doomed longboats and saw all she needed to see: the rowers' ankles had been shackled to the hull. Along the boat's prow, someone had painted a message in blood: *Karassa, accept our sacrifice.*

Phaedra's stomach clenched.

"Sails!" cried the lookout. "Ships to starboard!"

"Turn to face them," Admiral Sett commanded. "Oars!"

The captain repeated Sett's message and the sailors sprang into action once more, furling the sails and lowering the oars into the water. There were two rows of them, one on the upper deck and one on the lower, strong enough to power through even the worst headwinds. They'd be needed today: the southerly wind was an advantage to the pirates, who were rounding the Southern Crags and speeding toward the Atunaean fleet. Phaedra counted five ships, then seven, eight, ten... she lost count sometime after the fourteenth ship slipped past the crags and into view.

But the *Atun's Favor* wasn't turning.

"Oars!" the admiral cried again, rushing back to yell at the rowers himself. "Come about! What's taking so long?"

"Something's caught them, admiral!" one of the rowers answered. "They're not moving!"

Admiral Sett turned his wrath on Phaedra. "Witchery," he said. "Fix it."

Phaedra leaned over the side of the ship and looked back

toward the oars. The water was full of round translucent shapes bobbing on the waves. Jellyfish. Karassa's sacred animal. As Phaedra watched, a few rows of oarsmen managed to lift their oars out of the water. They were covered in thick knots of seaweed and clusters of heavy starfish, and even a few of the jellies had managed to end up atop the flats of the oars, their tentacles drooping on either side down to the sea.

"Witch!" the admiral cried. "You were supposed to protect us from this!"

"I'm on it," Phaedra answered, glad that this was one of the contingencies she had prepared for. She climbed down to the main deck and made her way toward one of the oversized crossbows, pulling an ink bottle from the pocket she had tied around her neck and cutting the wax seal with her knife. Out came the quill pen and soon she was drawing symbols on the huge loaded bolt, marking it as the centerpiece of Atun's forces, the pride of the Atunaean navy.

"Loose this thing," she told the men who had watched her work. "Send it into the sea."

They untied the end of the bolt from its towing cable and did as she said. Phaedra watched it fly out across the waves in a glorious arc, slicing into the water easily a hundred yards away.

The effects were immediate. No sooner had the bolt touched the water than the jellies were yanked toward it almost as if they had been tethered to the end. The huge clumps of sealife that had impeded the oarsmen now unwrapped themselves from the oars and disappeared into the water, leading to cries of relief from the crew. Soon the *Atun's Favor* came about, and it wasn't alone: the whole fleet had come untangled.

Phaedra received no praise, but she hardly expected it; everyone was too busy either barking orders or responding to them. The lookout called down his count of the enemy's ships – twenty-two in total – and the admiral answered with the exact sequence of flags to raise for the rest of his fleet to coordinate their response. The pirate ships were many, but they were merchant ships not equipped with the Atunaean fleet's sophisticated weapons, nor were they swarming with a full invasion force of soldiers. With Phaedra's magic now a proven match for her opponent's, Sett was planning a board-and-sweep operation to reclaim as many of the ships as possible.

He must be less disappointed in her efficacy than she was. The fact that she had not warded the oars against entanglement was only a tiny piece of a much larger problem: Mura had known they were coming, and he had prepared for it better than Phaedra had. So far, all he had lost were things he didn't value: slaves; dinghies; the handful of illiterate lackies who had kept all those slaves rowing. He had lost these things, and nearly brought down the entire opposing fleet. If Phaedra hadn't been sharp, the battle might be over already.

She shuddered at Mura's lack of qualms. He had probably told his men that he was writing sigils of protection on their boats, when in fact he'd been sacrificing them. That ruthlessness was a major advantage – for all that Phaedra's God was more powerful, she would never be willing to sacrifice her allies to Him. Unless the Essishans were right and sacrifice was greatly overrated, Mura would be more effective in wielding Karassa's favor than Phaedra could be at literally anything.

She hoped the Essishans were right.

As the pirate fleet drew nearer, Phaedra prayed to God Most High to protect her and the Atunaeans from whatever trick Mura had prepared next. She didn't dare augment the prayer with magic, but there was still hope her God might hear and answer it.

"You have protected me from Karassa since I was young," she whispered. "Protect me now, and the people who have followed me. When the tempest came for me, You kept the clouds at bay. When the road was long and death was at my heels, You shortened my path and brought me safely to my destination. Don't cast me aside now."

If God Most High heard her prayer, He gave no indication. The fleets met across from the Southern Crags, the pirates keeping their distance in their more maneuverable vessels while flaming arrows flew back and forth. Phaedra was gratified to see that her wards against both arrows and flames were functioning as planned, but the situation was much the same on the pirates' side.

"Enough of this," Admiral Sett growled. "Captain, you see that one? I want you to ram it."

The captain blinked at him, but quickly recovered. "Aye, admiral."

The *Atun's Favor* had a ram built into its prow, but crashing one's ship into *anything* was an inherently dangerous proposition, ram or no. If Atuna's famous shipwrights had made even the slightest miscalculation, if there was perhaps an unexpected flaw in the guardian wood the ship was made of, then using that ram would be disastrous.

But battles were won and lost on such leaps of faith, and if Phaedra's strengthening spells had any power at all, they ought to protect the ship's integrity even through this. It was time to embolden the Atunaean fleet and strike fear into the pirates' hearts.

At the captain's command, the oarsmen accelerated their rowing to a furious pace. The *Atun's Favor* sped toward its target too quickly to be evaded, for all that the pirates did their best to maneuver their ship out of the way. A slight shift to port was all it took to make the collision inevitable.

All around Phaedra, the crew braced for impact. Only Phaedra stood tall in the ship's prow, bracing herself with magic so that she could maintain her visibility and make her own impact on Mura's pirates. She planted her feet and staff firmly on the ship's deck, growing metaphysical roots and sending invisible tendrils to the front and back for added stability. She knew she would be visible to at least some of the pirates, and she wanted to terrify them. They should not think that Mura's power was unopposed. They shouldn't think that it was enough to save them.

The initial jolt barely moved her, anchored as she was, though she felt it all the way to her bones. After that came a viscerally satisfying *crunch* as the *Atun's Favor* tore its way through the enemy ship, casting pirates and debris in all directions. A mast fell toward Phaedra and she swept it aside with a well-timed redirection spell, avoiding even the oars to drop it sideways into the water. Her wards against arrows sent splinters of deck ricocheting off to the sides, surreally beautiful in their flight. When the crew recovered enough to reverse their course and row backward, the pirate ship peeled off the *Atun's Favor* with an unnatural ease and quickly foundered.

After that, Phaedra allowed herself some confidence in her wards.

The ramming maneuver changed the battle immediately. The Atunaean fleet quickly closed the distance with the enemy, making clear the advantage that oars provided against opponents who could not retreat against the wind. Soon oars were being pulled back and grapples thrown, and soldiers stormed from one ship to another, slaughtering the men in their paths. The *Atun's Favor*, freed of its first target, maneuvered to do the same.

But Mura, wherever he was, hadn't been defeated quite yet. As Phaedra looked on, one of the many as-yet unmolested pirate ships suddenly burst into flames. She let out a low moan and tried to brace herself for whatever was to come. She had seen these spontaneous fires before, though on a much smaller scale, and she knew what they meant: Karassa had accepted another sacrifice.

The ocean heaved. Giant, angry waves rose up all around, driving toward the shoreline. It felt as if an earthquake had happened somewhere far below, but the waves moved in only one direction. The unexpected tremors caught both fleets off-guard and sailors scrambled to adjust to the raging waters, turning their ships where they could to avoid being wrecked. With a sickening jolt, the *Atun's Favor* was swept up and carried aloft, plummeting down the side of the first wave only to rise swiftly up a second. Braced as she still was, Phaedra avoided being thrown overboard, but she did not avoid getting seasick: the nausea was nearly overpowering.

Her vantage point was almost too good – she couldn't avoid the sights all around her as the sea carried her up and down, up and down. Karassa was gobbling up as much of both fleets as She could, capsizing some ships and hurling others against the Southern Crags. The *Glimmering*

Sea had been grappled to a pirate ship when the waves rose and now both ships were wrecks, foundering while still half-tied together.

"God Most High!" Phaedra screamed into the howling wind. "Protect us from Your enemy! Don't let Your servants perish here!"

Once again, she added no magic to her words – if her God refused to hear her now, forcing His attention could only make things worse. As she had feared, it looked like her masking spell had only been strong enough for this one vessel, a major failure of her planning. Now ship after ship was being swept toward the cliffs while the *Atun's Favor* rode the waves like so much driftwood, its progress stagnant.

Both fleets were being destroyed. Had Mura meant for this calamity to happen, or had he miscalculated? Even if he was safely ashore, it was hard to believe that he had meant for *all* his ships to be wrecked along with his enemies. Mura was no shipwright; if he lost his fleet, he would be trapped on the island for good.

Prayer magic was too dangerous, Psandcr had said. Once the Gods got involved, there was no way to get Them uninvolved. Phaedra hoped Mura was learning his lesson, wherever he was.

He was probably on the crags, she realized with a jolt. From the cliffside he would have been able to signal both to his rowboats in the harbor and his ships in the southeast, and he would have a vantage point for watching the entire battle unfold. The ship's motion was too dizzying for Phaedra to spot him, but she knew he was up there. There was nowhere else he could be.

Twelve years ago, Tarphae's king had stood on those very crags, threatening to jump off if Phaedra and her friends came too near. The islanders had convinced him to abandon his plan and to come with them, but Karassa had done Her best to stop them. They had barely gotten the king halfway down when part of the cliffside had collapsed into the ocean. Phaedra had the image seared in her mind, an image of terror and calamity. But now it was more than that. Now it was precedent.

Phaedra fixed her eyes on the cliffside, adjusting to the rise and fall of the waves. She did her best to project Kestan's ragged image onto those far-off rocks, remembering how he had stood in his dirty robes looking more like a madman than a king.

"Let Your anger burn, Karassa," she murmured, drawing symbols of waves and mountains onto her skin with the dry quill. "Remember Your rage when I came here to rescue Your prisoner, how You made the earth shake and the moutains tremble, how You tried to hurl us into the abyss. Past and present mean nothing to Gods – what matters is that I am here, as always, to take what rightfully belongs to You. That's me up there, casting my spells and ruining Your plans as if this island were mine and not Yours. My legs are unsteady, like King Kestan's were – can you feel how unsteady they are? – but still I taunt you from atop Your cliffs."

At first it was hard to tell if her spell had taken effect. The ocean was already tossing her ship about, and her vision was too shaky to tell if the island was moving too, or if it was just her. But dark clouds were gathering above the cliffs with implausible speed, and soon Phaedra could hear the rumbling all around her.

"Rage, Karassa," she kept repeating. "I stand on these cliffs to defy You. Rage on; do Your worst."

She could feel the Goddess respond to her goading, searching for the source of her spell. Would Karassa find her, or would She be fooled? Phaedra did her best to imagine herself on the cliffs, to forget herself in the spell and confuse her own location. The ship dissolved around her as her concentration intensified. Of *course* she was up there on the cliffs. All the world was up there.

Lightning struck. With a crack, a great sheet of rock separated from the cliff face and slid into the sea below. Phaedra exhaled. Were there human figures up there, falling among all the boulders? Phaedra couldn't tell, at least not at first, but then came all the confirmation she needed: the sea went calm. The *Atun's Favor* plunged down one last wave and found no new one waiting for it on the other side. Soon even the clouds had dispersed.

Had Mura's death driven Karassa entirely off the island? Had Atun or God Most High taken up the fight and slain the Goddess in the heavens? Phaedra didn't know; all she knew was that the battle was over.

To her great relief, not all her ships had been lost after all. Three other Atunaean vessels had managed to stay afloat far enough from the crags to avoid being crushed, and one desolate pirate ship was drifting mastless and forlorn nearby. The soldiers and sailors of the *Atun's Favor* were too rattled to cheer, and simply stared back and forth at each other like lost men. But Admiral Sett had recovered at least enough to march up to Phaedra and demand an explanation.

"What the hell was that?"

"That was us winning the battle," Phaedra said. "The one here, and more importantly the one in heaven. I do believe Karassa has been banished from these seas for good. She lost Her last western finger just now."

"If you say so. I say we lost eight good ships and hundreds of good men."

"I know. Let's go ashore. There will be some last pirates left there, and their prisoners too. We should free them."

The pirates' farming operation had expanded since Phaedra had been here last. What had started as a single farmhouse was now a whole thriving farm town with fields as verdant as they were awash in the misery of their workers. Under Sett's direction, the last pirates were rounded up and executed and the slaves freed. A few chose to stay to tend their farms, but most chose to return to the ships. With a newly empty pirate ship left to tow back to Atuna, there was plenty of room for them.

But when Phaedra told him she was staying, Sett raised his eyebrows at her.

"You want me to leave you here on this rock."

"If you could leave a small sailing boat, I would be most grateful. But yes."

He looked like he was about to say something scornful, but apparently he thought better of it. Instead he just said, "I'll arrange it."

Phaedra thanked him and gathered food for herself from the farmhouses before making her way into the forest. With magic to guide her, she found her way to the fairy gate by sunset and went about her preparations for opening it. As she had suspected, the mesh was far thinner than it had been last time. It probably helped that she was here at twilight, but most likely she could have opened this gate at any time now, with no need to even count her hours by elevens. The worlds were coming dangerously close together.

Psander would know how to fix it. Surely she would. Phaedra opened the gate and stepped through.

12
HUNTER

Hunter knew what that fog meant, and he was terrified. There could be only one reason for Psander's gate to open, and he wasn't ready. He'd been waiting over a decade for this moment and he still wasn't ready.

Phaedra was coming back. All the words he had rehearsed were useless. He couldn't even remember them as he rushed down the stairs toward the courtyard, hoping to be the first to greet her but knowing he wouldn't be. It was too late, just after dawn, and most everyone would be up by now.

Sure enough, there was a crowd by the tower door when he got there, all waiting to get out. Even though Hunter knew and loved these people, it was all he could do not to start shoving them aside. Yes, they were already hurrying to see what was going on, but *he needed to get through*. The whole world seemed too slow right now, like in one of those dreams where he ran and ran but didn't move.

By the time Hunter got outside, Phaedra was already there, talking to Atella and a few others. She held a staff carved with spiraling runes, and her clothes were of some unfamiliar foreign design, at once practical and extremely flattering. Her hair was sheathed in a glorious headdress of multilayered cloth, rising like a crown from her head. All he could do at first was gape: she was just as beautiful as he remembered. Maybe more so. Her expressions were as lively as they had always been, her movements so graceful they made him ache. She always gestured as she talked, and right now she was telling Atella of some naval battle she had witnessed or perhaps been a part of. He had caught enough of her story to understand that much, but then Phaedra saw him and trailed off. Hunter froze under her gaze, his legs rooted to the ground.

"Hunter," Phaedra breathed. She rushed over, throwing her arms around him in an embrace that caught him off-guard. He couldn't move, couldn't hug back, couldn't believe she was finally here in the flesh. At last she took a step back from his stiff body and said, "I missed you."

"Me too," he said, embarrassed not to have returned her embrace. "I'm sorry if I... could we...?"

Phaedra nodded her beautiful head. "I need to talk to Psander first, about what's happening. There was a skyquake back in our world."

"Of course," Hunter said. "That's much more important – I can wait."

"You should come too," Phaedra said. "I want you to know–"

"I shouldn't know," he told her. "Psander's had talks with the elves, and there'll be more soon enough. Trust me; I was guarding the door. The more I know, the more they'll learn just by proximity."

Phaedra's face betrayed her shock. "Psander's negotiating with the elves."

"They've got more power than we have," Hunter said, marveling at this strange reversal of roles. He had never thought he would have to justify Psander's acts to Phaedra, of all people. Phaedra had been the lone islander who wouldn't condemn the wizard for bargaining with the Gallant Ones, who was willing to excuse Psander's callousness and even her betrayal as coming in the service of a good cause. Yet here Hunter was, rising to Psander's defense against his friend's negative judgment.

"The quakes have been getting stronger," he said. "We're getting less and less time between each one." He lowered his voice so that only Phaedra could hear. "Psander's talking like the world might end soon, and if you're saying there's been a skyquake on your side of the mesh, she could be right. We need all the help we can get, even from the elves."

Phaedra frowned. "I should talk to her immediately. She's inside?"

They excused themselves and he escorted her into the tower, doing his best to ignore people's knowing glances. Everyone in the village – every human in this whole Godforsaken world – knew that Hunter had been waiting for Phaedra, that he had refused to entertain other romances for more than a decade in his hopes of meeting her again and convincing her to marry him. It did not help to know that they were all rooting for him now.

They should have been rooting for Phaedra and Psander instead. They were all in imminent danger, but on Psander's advice Hunter had told them nothing about the origins of the skyquakes. As a result, everyone but him had grown used to them, as if they were just another feature of this strange and dangerous world. That was certainly better than mass terror and despair, but it was a lonely feeling being the only one besides Psander who knew.

Well, Phaedra was here now, and she knew too. If only Hunter could be comfortable around her. The problems they all faced were so much larger than him and his desires, but his nervous heart didn't seem to know that. When they ran into Psander on the stairs, he told Phaedra he'd be in his room if she needed him and fled past the wizard and toward his quarters. He could never be ready for their talk, but he wanted to try.

His room didn't need much in the way of arranging. Hunter made his bed every morning and only came back to the room at night, so the biggest decision he had to make was where to put Psander's scroll. It had been sitting in his room for years, waiting for the day when Phaedra would return and he could ask her if she loved him.

First he moved it from the little table to the bed. Then he decided that it looked strange there and put it back. He rolled it neatly, then wondered if he should unroll it again and arrange it as if he'd been reading it recently. On second thought, that was ridiculous. He left it as it was.

It was just slightly off-center. Should he turn it so its sides aligned with the table's edges? He couldn't help it – it would bother him otherwise. All right, now that was done. He lay down and counted to a hundred.

Phaedra and Psander would be talking for hours, wouldn't they? Why couldn't he have said he'd meet her in the courtyard, and found a private place to talk after that? Then he wouldn't be trapped here, with nothing to do but obsess about what to ask her, what to tell her. What had changed in her life since he last saw her? No life could remain in stasis – even his had changed. Did she still care for him? Had she missed him at all?

He had missed her every day, and worried that he was wasting his time. Maybe he ought to have given in and married one of the village women, had children, had a life. They were wonderful people, there was nothing wrong with them. If he had ever given up on Phaedra, he could have moved on.

Why was he having these thoughts again now, when she was finally here? Soon he'd know for sure whether he had wasted his time, and then one way or another his life would change.

Why couldn't Psander be more succinct, so that he and Phaedra could get this over with?

No, that was a ridiculous thought. Psander and Phaedra were working on saving the world – let them take their time. It was just so hard to imagine the world actually ending, so easy to let his own life take on more importance than it deserved.

Anyway, as long as it might take, he was glad nonetheless that he hadn't asked Phaedra to meet him in the courtyard. He didn't want all his friends and neighbors to see him like this. He'd be just as useless down there as he was here, except then he'd have to talk to people. This was much better.

He tried to relax his tensing muscles and sink into the bed, but it was no good. His heart beat fast and he imagined he heard footsteps in the hall. He tried counting his breaths, but lost count somewhere after fifty-seven.

There was a knock on the door.

Hunter leapt to his feet, calling "Come in!" probably too loudly. He hurried to the door and there she was, smiling apologetically at him.

"We're done for now," she said. "Thanks for waiting."

He stood back and let her into the room. She glanced at the bare walls and the bed, taking it all in but saying nothing.

"Any progress?"

"If you could call it that. I understand the problem now, at least, and it's good for both of us to have each other to discuss it with, but we don't have any solution yet. But if the elves can help us, and maybe the castles too, we ought to be able to figure out *something*. I'm going to have to sleep on it."

"You didn't sleep all night?"

Phaedra shook her head. "It *is* night back in our world. It was twilight when I left and dawn when I got here; the worlds have gotten even further out of alignment since last time I was here."

Oh, right. Hunter had completely forgotten about the misalignment they had noticed those many years ago. Now he felt like an idiot.

"But I can sleep later," Phaedra said. "How *are* you? It's been so long, everything must be different."

He recognized trepidation in her voice, recognized his own feelings mirrored back at him. She was afraid to find out how much his life had changed. How could he tell her that he'd waited for her, that for eleven years he had dreamt of seeing her again and convincing her to be his? Hunter had never felt so vulnerable.

"A lot of things have changed," he said. "I haven't."

"Oh."

"I'm older now," Hunter said, afraid to let that silence stand. "I've learned to farm and to hunt, and trained our people well enough to fight off the elves if we had to, I think. Tritika is faster than I am now, or close to it. And we've had harvests and shortages and a few scares sometimes, but... I don't know what to say. It's not the same as when you left, but it's not that different. The community's gotten stronger."

Phaedra nodded politely. "Atella was saying she has children...?"

"Oh yes, she does. She married Tarphon – I don't think you'd remember him."

"No. But you?"

Hunter spread his hands. "You didn't marry," Phaedra said quietly. "Your room is as bare as ever."

"I only sleep here," Hunter said. "I spend my days outside, mostly. We all farm together and eat together – there's no one to buy or sell to, so everything's shared."

"You're changing the subject."

"I'm nervous."

There, he'd said it. Phaedra smiled at him and apologized. "I didn't mean to interrogate you."

"No, that's all right."

"I've learned a lot since I left," Phaedra said. "I've been all over the world, practically. I travelled to Essisha, and to the eastern archipelago. Their religions are *fascinating*, Hunter. Did you know they don't do sacrifices? At all? And their kingdoms are vast, cities upon cities all under the same rulers, and they season their food with this incredible plant called *sperek*, which I can't even describe."

She went on happily for a good many minutes, telling him story after story of what she'd seen. When he asked about her staff, she told him about Criton's death and Bandu's journey to bring him back, about how the Dragon Touched had made peace with Ardis and built their own city in the north, and how Bandu was now married to another woman named Vella. There was so much for Phaedra to tell him about that he almost abandoned his plan for their conversation and put it off until the next day. He leaned against the bed and listened gladly, loving the animation in her face and reveling in the sound of her voice. But when she told him how she and the Atunaean navy had defeated Mura, the story ended with her return to this world and she came to a natural stop.

"I have to ask you a question," Hunter said, almost casually at first, but then his courage failed him and he could go no further. He struggled to say the next words and came up short, and the longer it took him, the greater the weight of his silence became. Phaedra watched him with big eyes as he tried to speak, the gravity of his unspoken words so immense that he could practically see their shadow on her face.

"Yes?" she said at last.

"I have to–" he stuttered. "I– do you still love me? Really love me?"

She sighed. "I do, Hunter. I really do. I missed you so much. But it can't–"

"But what if it could?" he asked. "What if you could marry me and never worry about children or having to give up magic, or anything? Would you marry me?"

"In a heartbeat, but–"

"Are you sure?"

She didn't speak for a moment, her expression suddenly suspicious. How he had missed her face, her perfect deep brown skin and those high cheekbones; the way her eyes shone with intelligence and conviction. He wanted her to be telling the truth, because if she was...

"Why are you asking me this?"

His eyes flicked to the scroll on the table. He knew she had caught the gesture.

"What...?"

"I know it was stupid," he said. "Of course you did it already ages ago, but I went through Psander's library to find something for your ankle. Not now, years ago. Yes, I know. Of course you looked already. But I thought maybe if I could find a way to fix it..."

Her eyes widened as she looked at him. Was it shock or fear, or something else? Did she already know what was inside that scroll?

"I didn't find anything for your foot," he said, "but I found this."

Her head turned, but she took no steps closer to the table. "What is that, Hunter? Are you...?"

He wanted to show her, he wanted her to see, but he too was paralyzed. "Psander doesn't know I found that," he said. "I haven't told her. But I think she could do it."

Finally Phaedra moved. "Is it...?" she breathed, approaching the table and gingerly lifting the scroll. Her eyes passed over the words, the illustrations. "It is. But you can't, Hunter."

"I can."

She looked back at him, her eyes glistening. Her voice was almost a whisper. "I don't think you've thought this through."

"I've had this with me since two weeks after you left," Hunter told her. "I've thought it through."

She was starting to cry now, to really cry. Tears were rolling down her cheeks.

"I thought you'd be married," she whimpered. "I could

have come two years ago, but it had already been so long... I was afraid to see you with a wife and children, happy without me. Or married but still wanting me, that would have been worse. I wasn't ready..."

"Eleven years is a long time," Hunter said, and was once again keenly aware of the imbalance between her intelligence and his. It was such a stupid thing to say – of course eleven years was a long time. He went on anyway. "I've waited a long time to find out if this would be worth it. I want to marry you, Phaedra. If you'd take me, this would be a small price to pay. But if something has changed, or if you were maybe just being polite..."

"I wasn't being polite!" Phaedra cried. "How can you even think that? I've loved you for years, Hunter, since the first time we came here together, or maybe even before. Just because I wasn't forward like Bandu doesn't mean I didn't care for you!"

"You'd have me if I did this?"

Phaedra went quiet. "I think... I think we should wait, and talk about this again tomorrow. And maybe wait another week or two, so we're sure. We haven't seen each other in years, Hunter, and it wouldn't be right to rush this. You're talking about mutilating yourself. And you've always wanted children, I know you have."

"I've always wanted you."

"Sleep on it," she commanded. "Or I'll sleep on it. Good heavens, it's practically noon out there! I have to sleep, Hunter. We'll talk about it again later. All right?"

"All right," Hunter said, and when she made her way to the door, he had to cough to get his next words out. The door was already closing when he stammered, "I love you."

A few seconds went by. She hadn't heard him. Then the door opened again and Phaedra said, "I love you too, Hunter. I just have to sleep."

And then she was gone.

Hunter lay down and hugged the scroll to himself, for all that it really was noon already and his stomach was rumbling. Phaedra loved him.

13
NARKY

Narky did not request an audience with King Mageris; instead he sent a messenger asking that the king come to him. He had learned to do this from Ptera years ago. The way she had put it, there were things a high priest had to do to keep people from believing that their king owned their God, and not the other way around. Narky gave her all the credit for the strength of their church in Ardis. The Graceful Servant had matched him to Ptera because she thought he needed her influence to succeed; now, years later, he could see that she had been right. There were so many ways that seventeen year-old Narky could have failed, had he not had Ptera there to guide him.

He had needed every bit of her guidance with Mageris and his father. The monarchy and the Ardisian Church of Ravennis, born together, lived in constant tension. In their own ways, each could credibly threaten the other with annihilation – yet neither had a good plan for the aftermath, so they maintained a public façade of mutual respect and cooperation while their leaders loathed and feared each other.

Narky was playing a game of dice with his son, waiting

to hear whether the king was coming or not, when Father Erebid rushed in, saying that the man himself was outside the temple. Narky swore under his breath and rose to follow, but Ptera put out a hand to stop him.

"Grace," she said, "help Father Erebid get ready for tonight's service. Narky, you should change that robe before you see the king. I'll tell him you'll meet him in the main chamber."

Narky strode to the vestry to do as she said, wondering what was wrong with the robe he wore. When he had changed, he took a moment to inspect the old robe. He then saw the greasy smudge high on his left sleeve, where his good right eye couldn't see it. He sighed and said a prayer of thanks to Ravennis as he made his way to the main chamber.

Mageris and his retinue were already there when Narky arrived. The king had come in full pomp, escorted by eight royal guards and carrying the most potent and pointed symbol of his kingship: his father's gold-tipped spear. This was the spear that had killed High Priest Melikon, priest of Magor and Narky's predecessor as head cleric of Ardis. Mageris' father had impaled him in this very place, before Narky had converted the Temple of Magor for Ravennis' use. The gold leaf that now adorned the weapon, snaking down from its point in a slowly widening helix, did not obscure Narky's memory of blood and horror. Mageris was good at keeping him off-balance.

The king turned from Ptera as Narky entered. "You requested my presence," he stated, leaving out the customary 'Your Eminence'. "Here I am."

"Yeah," Narky said, "thanks for being quick about it." He knew his casual demeanor always infuriated Mageris.

"I wanted to tell you about my plans for dealing with Sephas. He's been safe from us, hiding in Atuna, but he's made a real mistake this time. He's written something that's blasphemous against Ravennis *and* God Most High, and I think we can get Atuna to hand him over."

The king looked plainly uninterested. "Oh? How?"

"I'll have to talk to Criton about it, but I think he'll be willing to raise an army to join ours. Atuna won't risk a war against both our cities just to protect a troublemaker from Anardis."

Mageris pursed his lips sourly. "Your campaign against Pelthas wasn't enough; now you want to pick fights with Atuna. Explain to me why I should support this recklessness. Why should Ardis join forces with the Dragon Touched, who killed our people and stole our land, against a city that has done nothing to harm us?"

"Our Gods are allies," Narky pointed out. "And anyway, Atuna doesn't care about Sephas. They'd rather have our trade than a war."

"If we are to have a war," Mageris said ominously, "it will not be against Atuna."

Narky blinked at him, unsure of what to say. Did the king really mean to wage war against the Dragon Touched, or was he just trying to get under Narky's skin?

And anyway, why should the king bring up Pelthas, when his father had fully supported that campaign? It had made sense, after the loss of the north, to expand Ardis' influence into southern Hagardis, solidifying Anardis' status as a vassal state and Ravennis-Elkinar as the sole God of the realm. The priests of Pelthas had been their enemies from the start, the first to shelter Sephas in his apostasy and the first allies to accept his premise. They had wanted to keep the southerners away from Ravennis and the south separate from Ardis – there had been plenty of reasons for Magerion to support the campaign against them. Besides, the murderer-king had as little love for the God of Justice as Narky the murderer-priest did.

"It's possible," Ptera said, "that Atuna will give us Sephas without an army at their gates, if we and the Dragon Touched both send very polite emissaries asking them to."

Mageris turned to her more thoughtfully than scornfully, which Narky took as encouragement.

"I can bring that up with Criton," Narky said. "Send your guard with me, and we'll leave today."

"Provide your own guard," Mageris answered. "If your friend the Dragon Touched king is willing to send an emissary to Atuna, I will do the same."

Narky couldn't help but smile as the king and his guard swept out, marching back toward the palace. He had hoped he could rely on Mageris' contempt to override his suspicion. Narky preferred to meet Criton alone, and he was sure that had he suggested such a thing the king would have insisted on sending a bodyguard along to spy on him. As it was, he was free to go as he pleased.

When the king and his men were gone, Narky turned back to Ptera. "Ready to go to Salemica?"

"No. Grace and I should stay here, Narky, otherwise it'll look like our family is trying to leave the city before some disaster strikes. You know everyone's nervous now, after that skyquake. They're going to see signs everywhere."

Narky sighed. "You're right. And I don't think I want to see Criton's family anyway – maybe I'll send for him to meet me in Arca."

Arca was a village roughly the same distance from both

Ardis and Salemica. It was as close as the rival cities had to neutral territory, too far east to have been involved on either side of the war but near enough to the action for its people to be grateful that the war had ended. The village had hosted official delegations from Ardis and Salemica several times throughout the peace, and its people were very proud of their status as neutral ground.

Narky sent for Criton to meet him there, and left Ardis two days later. He left alone, without so much as a priestly retainer. Company did not really suit him – only his family did. Ptera was right that taking her and Grace with him would have caused mass panic, but he still hated being away from them: they were his anchors, the supports that kept him grounded. When he was away from them, there was nobody to pull him out of his thoughts and fears.

Of those, he had plenty. Narky's Pa had died out of his sight, and separation always made him feel certain that the experience would repeat itself somehow, whether through Narky's death or his wife and child's. Narky couldn't even imagine living without them at this point, and the thought of them losing him was just as bad. Grace deserved so much better than to be fatherless, and Ptera deserved to keep her second husband.

If Ravennis was good, He would protect Narky and his family from whatever dangers they faced. But Narky had never been one to rely on his God's benevolence. He obeyed Ravennis and feared Him, but trust? Trust did not come easy.

There were no inns along Narky's path to Arca, but it didn't matter these days: every home he stopped at rearranged itself to accommodate him. The honor of hosting the High Priest of Ravennis overrode all other concerns, and people would slaughter their finest animals so that Narky could feast. His blessing was worth more to people than money, which he frankly found disturbing. Did his blessing have any value at all? He knew better than to think Ravennis would respond to his every request.

Visiting strangers' houses and having them treat him like royalty would never feel normal. Even after twelve years as High Priest of Ravennis, Narky couldn't get used to unquestioned deference. His experience as a teenage refugee had conditioned him to expect harsh words and slammed doors; even now, he instinctively expected to be greeted with fear and suspicion.

He arrived in Arca shortly after noon on the third day. The townspeople were ready for him, having received a messenger from Criton about their impending meeting. Criton was expected to arrive by sundown. The preparations for that evening's welcome feast were already well underway: several ewes were being roasted in the town square, their mouth-watering scent permeating the whole neighborhood. Narky chose to wait for Criton outside, chatting uneasily with the town elders and watching the locals fill the square with chairs and long tables.

When Criton did arrive, it was with a small retinue of trusted friends and, Narky noted with a wince, his youngest wife. If he'd brought *her,* Narky should have just gone to meet them in Salemica.

Delika regarded Narky coolly. As a girl she had been frightened of him, and now that she was a bit older she seemed to be proving her maturity by exchanging her fear for disdain. Well, either that, or she was reacting to a poorly-suppressed look of disgust on Narky's face. That was a real possibility. He was useless at hiding his feelings.

Criton didn't seem to have noticed, though. He strode forward with a big grin and embraced Narky. "It's been a long time!"

"It has."

"How is Ptera? And Grace?"

"They're fine."

"I'm sure Grace has grown tremendously since the last time I saw him."

"Yes. Well, you know kids."

Narky hadn't meant that last answer to sound so accusatory, but there you had it. It was hard to concentrate with that teenager's scornful eyes on him, and etiquette and pleasantries had never been his strength. Criton frowned and changed the subject.

"You have some news for me? Your messenger didn't tell me anything; only to meet you here."

"I brought something I want you to see." Narky opened his satchel and handed Criton the blasphemous scroll with its Sephan satire. "Read it, and we can talk about it when we have more privacy."

Criton nodded and took the scroll from him, but he did not unroll it. "Have I done something to offend you, Narky?"

Narky couldn't help but glance at Delika, who was staring at him with the expression of a sullen child. Like a coward, he shook his head. "Don't worry about it."

That didn't satisfy Criton; naturally it didn't. It hadn't even been a proper denial. Still, how could he fail to understand what was bothering Narky? He was being thick on purpose. Here he was, parading his wife-daughter around like their marriage was something to be proud of. Why should Narky play along?

But then, maybe it wasn't a matter of pride. Maybe now that he had her, Criton couldn't bear to part with Delika. Would that be better, or worse? No matter which way he tried to think of it, Narky couldn't come up with an explanation that made him feel better. He would rather not have thought about it at all, but he didn't have that choice because Criton had brought the girl along and now she was staring at him. He'd never been so deeply uncomfortable in his life.

Narky's disapproval was probably harder on him than it was on Criton. He had always admired Criton for his bravery and generosity, for what he had thought of as Criton's natural decency; but now that Criton had done something so clearly *in*decent, Narky was beginning to notice all the flaws that he hadn't seen when they were younger. His image of his friend was crumbling.

And yet, Criton hadn't changed much. He was still the same brave, idealistic, terminally stubborn man Narky had always known. It was Narky who had changed, and Grace who had changed him.

Narky had never understood the urge to protect children above all else until his own beautiful son had been born. Grace had taken the whole world and shaken it. The first night with him had taught Narky to fear as he had never feared before, to ache at the thought of harm coming to this tiny, delicate creature. That protectiveness had never gone away, even as Grace had grown bigger, and he didn't think it ever would.

It was strange to think about how different he had been before Grace's birth. As a teen, Narky had once suggested abandoning a small crowd of children to the elves. He still remembered the others' shock and disgust, and how he hadn't understood their reaction at the time. He had thought he was being practical and that they were sentimental to the point of self-endangerment; they had clearly thought he was horrifyingly callous.

Well, they had all been right.

Delika had been one of those children, not that she would remember Narky's suggestion unless Criton told her about it: the elves had a way of hiding children's memories from them when they left that other world. It was perhaps ironic that now, when Delika was seventeen and not nearly so helpless, he was finally inclined to protect her.

Or maybe not that ironic. Narky's perspective was different now that he was a parent himself, and Delika was still closer in age to Grace than to her husband. It was disgusting to exploit her youth and malleability the way Criton was doing.

Still, he hadn't come here to scold Criton about his wives. He had come because of the Sephan heresy, and because of the unique chance he now had to end it. He needed to focus.

This scroll was the key, an unexpected weapon he'd been given by Sephas himself. But for all that it was a weapon, and he was bound to use it as such, he couldn't help but feel it was more than that. The scroll spoke to him, just when he had given up hope that Ravennis would send him any message. Could he accept the contents as prophecy *and* call for Sephas' death as its mortal originator? He couldn't think of a way to do so openly, and he hated hiding what he believed.

He knew what his top priority *ought* to be, what a high priest of Ravennis ought to do: he should suppress the satire entirely, order its disseminators killed, and forge a military alliance powerful enough to demand that Atuna hand Sephas over. That was more or less the plan he had presented to King Mageris. Why was he having second thoughts now?

He was glad he had come here alone. He could ask Criton what he thought of the scroll without alerting anyone in Ardis that he was having these doubts. If it spoke to Criton too, maybe Narky could find a way to rehabilitate it, even if it meant letting Sephas go. A message from Ravennis was far more valuable right now than capturing a few powerless dissidents.

He couldn't shake the feeling that the scroll was the only message Ravennis would be sending him. Calling the scroll's message a prophecy felt *right*, and that was what mattered; a high priest should trust his instincts about these things.

So while Criton read, Narky sat quietly, trying to articulate his feelings into a theory he could explain. He couldn't help but overthink it. Every time Criton frowned at the words in front of him, Narky decided that his explanation was no good and that he should start again. At first Criton whispered the words to himself as he read, but he soon stopped, looking up. Narky nodded at him in acknowledgment. Criton had once told him that he needed to sound words out in order to read them, but these were not words he'd want to say aloud if he could help it. Had Narky been able to read, he was sure Father Lepidos would have gladly handed the scroll over to him silently, so as to avoid speaking such blasphemous words. It was his poor luck that Narky was illiterate.

When Criton had finished reading, he looked up and sighed. The feast was still in progress, but he rose to his feet and took a bottle from the table. "We should discuss this privately. Come on."

He gave Delika a little squeeze on the shoulder and he and Narky retreated to the town hall. The building had once been a temple of Magor, but the people of Arca, caught on the border between Ardis and the Dragon Touched, had repurposed it for secular use rather than have to choose which God should claim the edifice. Narky and Criton sat down in what had once been a small sanctuary and was now a meeting room, taking turns drinking from the bottle. It was full of aniseed liquor, a specialty of the northern plains. It was very strong.

"This is about Father Sephas, isn't it? You want my help convincing Atuna to arrest him and give him to you."

"You guessed it," Narky said. "But first I want to know what you think of it."

"I think Atuna might hand him over, but if it didn't, you'd be dragging my people into another war. And if we're being honest, Narky, I might trust *you*, but I don't trust Mageris. I'd worry about Ardis turning on me halfway through the campaign so they could steal their land back."

Narky took another swig, though it burned at his throat. He didn't even like aniseed. "No, that's not what I meant."

"It doesn't matter what you *meant*, it matters what happens. You can't control Mageris and we both know it."

"No," Narky repeated, putting his head in his hands. "I didn't mean… the scroll, what did you *think* of it?"

Criton blinked at him. "Um. I'm not sure what you want me to say. This stuff isn't coming from the Dragon Touched, so there's not much *I* can do to suppress it. It's definitely Sephan."

Narky shook his head and found that it made him dizzy.

That liquor really was strong. "The thing is, it doesn't sound like Sephas. At all. Everyone's telling me that he got some Atunaean playwright to write it for him, but I don't think so, because it's not much of a play either. It's easy enough to see the blasphemy and stop there, but besides that, what is this thing even *about*?"

Maybe Narky was slurring his speech, because he didn't get the reaction he had hoped for. Criton mostly looked confused as he reached for the bottle.

"It's not a good play? I don't – what's the problem?"

"The problem is that it doesn't make sense for anyone to have written this. Everyone thinks it's Sephan because it insults both our Gods, but the thing is, it doesn't do anything to advance his cause. It doesn't even mention Elkinar! Who's going to read this and turn to Sephas for their answers? No one. It's just about this bet between Ravennis and God Most High, with some blasphemous insults added on top. It isn't just unlike him. Its whole existence makes no sense!"

"You're saying nobody wrote it? It just appeared?"

Narky sighed. "I... I think it might be a prophecy."

He had hoped, foolishly, that Criton would agree with him, but he could see the disapproval coming even before Criton's expression changed.

"What God would dare insult God Most High like this?" he demanded. "Which God could possibly have sent such a message to Sephas and his followers?"

"Ravennis."

Criton's mouth dropped open. "Hear me out," Narky said, though he needn't have: Criton stared dumbly at him, making no attempt to interrupt. Narky took a couple of deep breaths and spoke.

"It's not unlike Ravennis to use His enemies as tools, right? He goaded Magor into helping Him conquer the underworld, so why not use Sephas now? I think He gave Sephas the inspiration to write this prophecy, and Sephas added the insults himself. He would. Anyway, all those insults are separate from the real point, which is about the argument or bet or whatever between Ravennis and God Most High. That part speaks to me. It's like what Hunter said that time: I'm bound to die eventually, so isn't it always more important to please Ravennis than to survive? I know it sounds weird, but it feels like it's a personal message just for me. I've been hoping Ravennis would speak to me since the quake, and I'm starting to think He has. Does that make any sense?"

Criton frowned sympathetically. "No, not really. It doesn't make any sense for Ravennis to talk to Sephas instead of you, Narky. I'm sorry He hasn't given you any guidance, but clinging to this blasphemous stuff is... desperate. If you want me to raise an army to threaten Atuna then we can discuss that. Sephas *is* attacking God Most High here, so it might be necessary. But if you want my opinion about the *scroll*, I think it's much worthier of fighting Atuna over than of taking seriously as a prophecy. It's shit, Narky."

Narky sighed again. "Well, thanks for your opinion. It's good to get a second look from someone who isn't a priest of Ravennis."

"If it helps, I'm glad. That can't be all you came for, though."

"No," Narky said, "it's not."

He told Criton about his discussion with Mageris, and how Ptera had suggested that a joint delegation from Ardis and Salemica might carry enough of an implied threat to bully Atuna into handing Sephas over, while still granting them the opportunity to save face peacefully should Atuna stand firm. Criton listened patiently until Narky had finished, and then at last he nodded.

"That all makes sense," he said. "You can tell Mageris that Salemica will send a delegation along with yours."

And just like that, their business together was settled. The Sephan tract faded into the background of their conversation and never resurfaced. Criton asked again about Ptera and Grace and told Narky about Goodweather's latest visit with its explosive ending. He tried to avoid telling Narky what Vella had been angry at him for, keeping things vague and making her sound altogether unintelligible, but Narky didn't buy that for a second.

"Hold off," he said, "what was she yelling at you *about*?"

"She hates me, Narky. She was just yelling and blaming me for everything."

"Blaming you for what? The quake?"

"No, not the quake. Something happened with Bandu, and she blames me."

"Like what? Marital problems?"

Criton's tone of voice had suggested as much, but he shook his head sheepishly. "She looks like she's been aging double. That's what Vella calls it, and she blames me for it."

"Bandu visited you?"

"Yes. She actually came in while Vella was yelling at me."

"And when you say she's aging double, you mean that...?"

"Literally?" Criton sighed. "Yes. She used to look younger than us, right? Like, maybe our age but small? Well, now she could be your mother. And Vella says it's my fault."

"How?"

"She said Bandu had to sell part of her life to bring me back. Bandu never told me that, so I didn't believe her, but then I *saw*…"

They fell silent, Narky trying to respect the gravity of the situation despite his burning desire to know more. If Bandu had sold a part of her life away so that she looked so much older now, why hadn't Criton noticed her looking that way when he had come back from the dead all those years ago? Had it been less prominent then? Why hadn't Phaedra said anything the last time she had visited him? If Bandu had requested privacy, it must have been the first time she had ever done so.

Narky felt bad for having never sought Bandu out, after she had done so much to save not just Criton's life but Narky's as well. Narky's whole family, maybe even his whole city, owed their survival to Bandu, but the ugly truth was that he had never really got along that well with her, despite their shared history, and had felt no urgency to see her again. It was enough to hear her news second-hand from Phaedra and leave it at that. Even after Bandu had come back from the underworld, he had convinced himself that Phaedra had wrung as much coherence from her as anyone was liable to get – there was no point in making a pilgrimage to visit a woman he couldn't understand.

He had never liked the way she looked at him, like he was a resource to be used or set aside as the need arose. All the qualities he was proud of in himself – his wit and humor, his quickness of mind, his history of being underestimated – all these were meaningless to her. Her open sexuality had bothered him too, or more precisely, he had been bothered by the fact that she clearly didn't care how he reacted to it. It had made him feel worthless.

But Ptera had cured him of those insecurities, or was at least a powerful antidote, and he still hadn't visited Bandu. He hadn't even met Vella and hadn't seen Goodweather since she was a screaming infant. She'd be a proper *person* by now, Goodweather – she was what, eleven? No, twelve. Bandu had saved Narky's city and his happiness and his life, and he'd shown only the most passing interest in her wellbeing. Now that fact stood out to him as the shameful thing it was.

"Anyway," Criton said at last, "Vella blames me for what happened, even though none of it is my fault. I didn't *choose* to get killed. I knew my cousin was angry, but I trusted him. And it's not like I forced Bandu to come and bring me back, though I'm grateful she did. But she did that on her own. Vella blames me anyway."

Narky shrugged. "I guess that's easier than blaming her wife."

"If she weren't Kilion's daughter, someone would have killed her by now. She's impossible, and her and Bandu – that's unnatural."

Narky raised his eyebrows. "I don't think I'd call *anything* about Bandu 'unnatural.' She's got to be the most natural person I've ever met."

"Very funny."

"Look, I've never met Vella, so I don't have strong feelings about her one way or the other, but just because you think she's obnoxious doesn't mean she deserves to die. I mean, I'd have been dead many times over if it worked that way."

That got a rueful chuckle out of Criton. "I suppose you're right. It just makes me angry. She blamed me for having a big family that's dependent on me. Like she thinks after ending the war I should have gone off and been a hermit."

Despite himself, Narky snorted. He doubted very much that Vella had criticized Criton for "having a big family," and he had a notion of what her real complaint had been.

"What?" Criton snapped. "Do you have something to say, Narky?"

Not for the first time, Narky wished he had better control over his reactions. Why couldn't he maintain a polite silence when one was called for?

"No," he mumbled, "it's nothing."

"Stop lying. Say what you want to say."

Narky sighed, scratching above his bad eye. "Why did you marry her, Criton? She was your daughter."

Criton slammed his cup on the table between them, hard enough that the ceramic broke and spilled its contents across the wood. "I knew it," he said. "You all think you know what's right for her. You think I'm some sort of monster for listening to what she wants."

Narky stared at the broken cup and the liquor that was slowly flowing toward him. His silence only made Criton more defensive.

"She loves me," he said, "and I love her, and the rest of it's none of your business."

"The less it's my business the better," Narky answered, backing his chair away from the little stream of liquid so that his robes wouldn't get wet. "But if you don't want to know what I'm thinking, don't ask."

Criton scowled. "I've never criticized your marriage. Why should you criticize mine? I know what you think, and you're wrong. You think I raised Delika *to* marry me. You think I trained her to love me so that I could have a young bride who worshipped me, but that's not true. I didn't ask for any of this. I raised her as best I could because it was my duty. The people we'd left her with were hitting her, Narky. I wasn't going to try to find another family for her after that. She came to me for help, and Bandu took Goodweather away but she left Delika with me. Do you think I shouldn't have raised her?"

"No," Narky admitted, "it was right to raise her, but—"

"Not to marry her; I know you think that. But I've always done what's best for *her*. You think I should be listening to you or Vella instead of Delika? Because Delika's the one who said she wanted to marry me."

"And you didn't try to dissuade her."

"I did! I told her she didn't have to marry me to stay in my house – I'd shelter her and protect her no matter what. I thought maybe she was just afraid of losing her home with us, now that she's of age. But she insisted she wanted to marry me, and I love her. Of course I do. I couldn't have spent all those years taking care of her without loving her too."

"So that was it. That was all you said."

"No, that wasn't it. I said she wasn't at a good age to make these kinds of choices, and that I thought she should wait. I was her age when I married Bandu, and it didn't turn out well for either of us. But I still had the choice, Narky, and she deserves it too. She says she wants me, and she's proven it. Trust me, she's proven it."

Narky was unable to suppress a shudder. "You're her only father."

"I'm not her father! She has a father somewhere, and I'm not him. How thick can you be?"

Oh, that did it. "Look, Criton," Narky spat, "I don't care who her 'real' father is any more than I care who yours was. You raised her, you're her father. I'm sick of your fantasies about what counts."

Criton rose to his feet. "That's enough. I'm done talking to you."

Narky stared at him, saying nothing. There was nothing left to say. Criton, as always, genuinely thought he had done the right thing. He didn't think he'd been greedy to take Delika as a fourth wife – he thought he'd been generous.

Narky desperately wanted to still admire him. They had gone through so much together, and Criton had always been courageous, noble, even selfless. He had certainly brought more glory on himself than Narky, whose main contributions had been shooting a man in the back and sneaking up on an injured animal to deal it a death blow.

He tried to reconcile the honorable Criton he remembered, the one whose sense of justice had defied all danger, with this one that stood before him, drunk and seething. How had his friend convinced himself that marrying his own adopted daughter was the right thing to do? Why couldn't he see that marrying him was an act of desperation, a sign that he hadn't given Delika any other options?

Narky wanted to see Ptera's point of view and excuse Criton's behavior, but how could he? Sure, Criton's other three marriages were all political. If those marriages had never been designed to make Criton happy, perhaps he could be forgiven for wanting one that was. But Narky's marriage had been thrust upon him for similarly practical reasons, and he hadn't felt any need to keep looking. He knew he'd gotten lucky with Ptera, who had turned out to be perfect for him in so many ways; still, no number of loveless marriages could give Criton an excuse to marry the girl he'd raised.

Besides, maybe Criton hadn't found love in his other marriages because he hadn't been willing to look for it in his hurry to find something better. He and Narky had always been different that way: Narky always afraid of losing what he had, Criton eternally looking toward his next goal. When they'd both had nothing, that constant striving had seemed admirable. Now that they both had food and fame and power and money – and friends and allies and wives and children – it came off as a good deal less admirable.

He wondered if this new marriage might even be doing Criton political harm. The first three wives had cemented alliances – with Criton's example and encouragement, the Dragon Touched and the humans of the northern plains had integrated into a single society. His first two fathers-in-law, the plainsmen, had gained power and prestige for their connection to the Dragon Touched leader, and his marriage to that Iashri woman had quelled any resentment among his own people, but would Criton's many in-laws and relatives-by-marriage not balk at his taking Delika for a fourth wife? Such an obvious and frankly disgusting love-marriage could only dilute their power and make a mockery of their daughters.

Narky doubted their anger would prove physically dangerous to Criton – no one would dare to conspire against a man who had already risen once from the dead

– but it could cause other problems for him. Resentment had a way of poisoning all sorts of plans that required cooperation.

Criton still stood above him, wobbling from the liquor, and Narky watched his friend slowly realize that he wouldn't be getting up anytime soon, that he couldn't be intimidated into fleeing. The air of righteousness was leaving him – he was growing embarrassed about his outburst. He'd drunk too much – a good deal more than Narky, anyway – and was slipping now from anger to remorse.

But he did not apologize; he only turned unsteadily on his heel and stalked from the room.

Narky sighed. Morality was one thing, but who was he to judge Criton's political errors? He was about to make one of his own, if he wasn't careful. His every instinct said that Ravennis was speaking to him through Sephas, and yet… nobody else could see it. Criton, like everyone else, had advised him to treat the scroll as a dangerous heresy. What if they were right? What risks was Narky taking if he pursued his enemies but let their teachings spread?

And if it *was* a prophecy, what then?

Nothing had gone right since that quake shook the sky. Narky's political needs were at odds with his beliefs, his faith in his friends was crumbling, and through all this, Ravennis' message to him – if indeed that was what it was – was about prizing eternity over one's life. If his own premise was correct, that seemed to mean his God expected him to sacrifice himself somehow.

He left for home the next morning, demoralized and disturbed.

14
PSANDER

"You're distracted," Psander told Phaedra, looking over the top of her codex to find the younger woman fidgeting. "We can't afford for you to be distracted."

At least Phaedra had the grace to look embarrassed. "I'm sorry. It's been such a long time since I was last here, and... I wasn't expecting to find things the way they are."

"How so?"

"I thought Hunter would be married and have children by now, but he waited for me."

"He's an idealistic fool," Psander said, laying aside her book since it did not appear to have any applicable information in it. "But his tenacity has been extremely useful in other respects. I thought his martial training was a waste of time for a village-worth of farmers and children, but he proved me wrong. It's really quite remarkable the way he turned the elves' thought-reading against them without so much as a hint of magic."

She picked up a scroll this time, a history of the War of the Heavens that might conceivably discuss some aspect of the mesh's nature that she'd forgotten over the years, but apparently Phaedra wasn't done talking.

"I told him before I left that I couldn't marry him, because of what you said happens if a wizard gets pregnant–"

"Quite right. You can't possibly be reconsidering your position – any additional unpredictability at this juncture could result in the world's end."

"Yes, I know, but he… he found a scroll."

Psander looked up at her sharply. "A scroll?"

"One of the few texts you had from the age of healers. It's… instructions. On how to sterilize a man."

"I see." Hunter was more dedicated to his cause than Psander had realized. She vaguely remembered the scroll in question, a treatise she had received as a gift early in her career. As she recalled, it had been written by a court magician somewhere south of Parakas, whose patron queen had wanted to keep several consorts without any of the attendant risks. The procedure had not been entirely voluntary, or at least that was what Psander remembered from the tale of the woman who'd given it to her. Batra was her name. A poor practitioner, but a fine researcher.

Psander had liked Batra. She was too modest to mind Psander's competitive streak, and found her demeanor funny. She was twenty years Psander's senior, but so pleased to have the company of another woman that she hadn't minded the younger wizard's inexperienced nonsense. They were the only two of their generation, women who had pursued academic wizardry rather than simple witchery, but it was from Batra that Psander had learned of the others, the many others, who had come before them. She'd given Psander the extra confidence she needed, not in herself, but in her tradition. Until then, Psander had always told herself that she would succeed even if she didn't really belong among these men. It was good to realize instead that she *did* belong.

She had met Batra at Gateway, where her mentor Pelamon had sent her to round out her education. It was also at Gateway that her pregnancy had made such trouble for the researchers, until its messy but fortunate end. She had appreciated Batra's support after that ridiculous disaster.

The whole thing had started as stupidly as it ended. Psander had never felt sexual interest toward anyone, but one particularly irritating researcher at Gateway had briefly convinced her that her disinterest was actually fear. That had triggered her pride, as he had always meant it to, and in the course of proving herself unafraid she had become pregnant. It was a foolish mistake, and she blamed herself for rising to the bait. The man, as mediocre a wizard as he was a human being, deserved no credit for his success: she had known his motives from the start, and had fallen for it anyway.

Batra had given her the scroll in confidence, a few days after her pregnancy had ended. She had apparently used it many times, not as instructions for a magical procedure, but to comfort herself after a failed affair or some other man-based frustration. The procedure was not blunt and brutal like a castration – it was subtle and easy to miss after the initial recovery period, and Batra could pretend that she might practice it on some man without his knowledge and leave him secretly sterile, wandering around as arrogant as ever without any knowledge of his loss.

Psander hadn't needed the scroll to nurse her pride, but she had taken it anyway because her appetite was voracious and she'd spent two months already starved for a scroll of genuine worth to read. The subject was entirely unlike anything else she had researched, with jargon that she couldn't begin to interpret, but she'd read it several times with the notion that she might somehow derive the entire ancient practice of healing magic from the principles and language of this one procedure. It hadn't worked, of course, and not long thereafter she had been sent back to Pelamon with the message that her education was complete.

How long had it been since she'd even thought about this scroll? Forty years?

"I take it you've discussed this with Hunter already," Psander said, returning to the history in her hands. "What was your conclusion?"

"He wants you to do it," Phaedra said. "I'm not so sure."

"Not sure he's worth the time it would take to learn and perform the procedure? I sympathize, though I confess I've never understood the drive to begin with."

"Oh, he's worth it," Phaedra said. "I don't mean that at all. I just don't think he's really thought it through. He's always wanted children, I know he has. The way he acted with those children we rescued from the elves... he'd be a good father. I don't want to be selfish and let him do something he'll regret."

Psander put the scroll down with a sigh. "One can only make a finite number of choices in life. Regret has less to do with those choices than it does with one's approach. I have never subscribed to the notion that having physical children grants one some kind of immortality. If Hunter wants me to sterilize him, I'll be glad to review that scroll again, *once we've dealt with the impending problem of all our deaths*. Now have we resolved this issue sufficiently for you to concentrate on the matter at hand?"

"Yes," Phaedra said, though she sighed and looked forlorn and generally made every indication that they had *not* resolved the issue. "I'm sorry if I'm wasting our time, it's just... you asked what was distracting me."

"I didn't," Psander corrected her. "I only pointed out that you *were* distracted, and you brought the conversation to the source of your distraction yourself. As I recall, I only said that we couldn't afford it."

Phaedra's nostrils flared. "Fine. You're right, I misinterpreted you. I thought you might want me to *deal* with the problem, rather than burying it."

"Whatever makes it go away."

Phaedra stared at her for a long, angry moment. Psander met her gaze with her own irritated one until at last, Phaedra sighed. "So, the elves are asking their castles to help us?"

"Yes. The new gate established by the Yarek is the source of the problem, after all, so there is some possibility that Goodweather or Illweather will have a solution for us. I have tried to devise some way to weaken the connection ourselves, but as far as I can tell it cannot be done. The Yarek draws itself together more strongly than ever. If I may say so, it was clever of God Most High to split the plant beast into the halves of kindness and cruelty, because while cruelty seeks to wield kindness to its ends, kindness resists the marriage. I suspect that Goodweather has done far more than God Most High to keep the halves separate.

"But of course, that's where we come in. By bringing the more benevolent force to our world, we strengthened the cruel voice of unity here. I think – I cannot prove, mind you – that if you had grown *Illweather's* seed in our world rather than Goodweather's, we might not be in this predicament."

"You're saying we should have made our world worse by giving the nastier half of the Yarek an anchor there?"

"I'm saying it might have prevented the end of both worlds, yes. But I can't know for sure."

Phaedra rubbed her forehead, then her temples. "Well, let's say the Yarek can't be stopped from reunifying. What then?"

"Then in the process, the meshes overlap and shred everything. Whether the Yarek could eventually recover, I don't know. Presumably the Gods' world and the underworld would remain intact."

Phaedra's mouth quirked. "I'm sure Ravennis would love that."

"It might be overwhelming, even for a God, to deal with all of creation arriving on His doorstep at once. But I'm sure you're right."

"Do you think Illweather is doing this on purpose? Killing itself just so it can bring the rest of us down too?"

"I have no idea. Everything I know of the castles, I learned from you islanders. Especially Hunter, since I've had more time to talk with him. The rest has just been observation, testing the ground roots, and so on. I do not have the kind of familiarity with the Yarek to ascribe nihilism to one of its halves, nor to deny it. I suppose we will find out when the elves return."

They fell into contemplative thought, each sitting in her own hard chair, surrounded by books that, for all their collected knowledge, didn't seem to hold any answers.

"Someone should ask the Yarek," Phaedra said. "The one in our world. I should go back and talk to it – maybe it'll have more to say than Goodweather or Illweather."

Psander considered that. "Yes," she said, "I believe you're right. But let us wait first for the castles' answers. It would take weeks for you to go and speak to that portion of the Yarek and return, and we are at the point where we must be efficient with our time. We haven't got much left."

Phaedra agreed to that, as Psander knew she would. If she was already considering a union with Hunter, mere days after arriving here, she could not possibly be too eager to return to her world. Psander wondered if it might be expedient for her to review that sterilizing procedure sooner rather than later – Phaedra and Hunter were neither of them impulsive creatures, but as a rule it was wiser to underestimate people's willpower than to overestimate it. Those two might not be teenagers any longer, but no age was immune to poor decision making.

A quake struck while Psander was thinking this, shaking the tower from the top down. Psander gripped her book in one hand and the arm of her chair in the other, waiting for the tremors to end. The quakes hadn't just been coming closer together; the portion of sky affected had been getting larger and larger, its boundary lower and lower. Soon Psander heard a deafening crash, followed by a building-wide shudder. The tremors ended shortly thereafter, and she threw down her book and rushed to the stairs ahead of Phaedra, following them up past the lower bedrooms toward her workshop. Two turns past the bedrooms, the stairway ended in open sky.

"No," Psander said, as much to the sky as to herself. The entire top of her tower had been displaced, moving far enough to the north that a good three quarters of it had fallen freely off the side of the building. The last quarter remained perched, broken and inaccessible, at the edge of Silent Hall's new "roof."

Psander's workshop was gone. Her bedroom was gone. Her time was running out.

15
BANDU

Bandu had hoped to leave Salemica immediately, but Vella insisted on waiting for her brother to come home first, and that delayed them by two days. They were not a comfortable two days. Bandu missed her quiet home, and her garden, and those poor cowardly dogs she trained for her neighbors. More than anything, Bandu missed being regarded uncritically, like a person and not some curiosity whose body needed comment. People kept staring, looking back and forth between Bandu and Vella to compare their ages, and whispering to each other. She even overheard one priest claim that island women never aged well.

Not everyone was disparaging. Chara asked gently whether her monthly bleeding had stopped yet, which it hadn't. "It would be very early if it had," Chara said reassuringly. "When the change does come, you're in for quite an experience. Mine has been going for ten years now; you're lucky yours will be shorter."

"I want years instead," Bandu said.

That stopped the conversation short. "Of course," Chara murmured. "I didn't mean… I was just trying to lighten it a bit. Bring up the good side, you know."

Bandu felt bad. She should be more patient with Vella's mother. But Bandu wasn't good at all this talk, and she didn't like being told she was lucky to be losing time, time she could have spent with Vella and Goodweather. Who cared if she missed some discomfort too, along the way? It was still part of living.

Still, it was no good to insult Vella's mother. Besides, she *did* want to hear more about Chara's experiences. She had only learned about "the change" in the last few years, having grown up without any friendly older women to tell her about these things, and she didn't know what to expect. All she knew was that it was coming soon.

If it hadn't been for the knowing looks and ominous comments that accompanied talk of "the change," Bandu might have looked forward to the end of her monthly bleeding. She found it a nuisance. But as far as she could tell from the vague references she had heard, "the change" was not something to look forward to. She supposed that matched up well enough with what she knew of life in general. Nothing was ever easy.

It was hard on her, waiting these two extra days. She could not speak to the Yarek as she had intended, because its influence hadn't spread to Salemica. The trees in the orchards did not recognize it when she asked – their roots connected only to the earth beneath them. She wondered if the temple of God Most High was blocking the Yarek's expansion into the area, or at least deterring it from trying. After all, the ancient plant monster had been torn apart by God Most High once already, and must be wary of attracting His notice again.

She walked back from the orchards to the temple, greeted by the stares of the neighbors and the barking of their dogs. She didn't mind – the dogs were barking more in alarm than hostility. She supposed it was the same way with the people. In any case, she could stare down either if she wanted to, and that knowledge gave her strength. She didn't like these crowds. Never had.

It had taken her some time to get used to dogs. It was bittersweet working with them, because they were easily wolf-like enough to remind her of Four-foot, and not nearly wolf-like enough to fill his void. Four-foot had been a friend and an equal. Dogs… were not.

But they were social, and that was nice sometimes. They could give uncomplicated love, which was more than could be said for people. She just didn't like how tame they were, how easily they submitted to the notion of belonging to people. You could befriend a wolf – if you were lucky, that is – but you could really *own* a dog. That bothered her.

It was wrong to own a creature that way. Bandu didn't even own her daughter, whom she had made. Goodweather was her own person, and she was at least as influenced by Vella as by Bandu. She loved talking and telling stories, and she could read as well as any Dragon Touched child – Vella had made sure of that. Her magic was more like Vella's than like anyone else's – perhaps better at transformations than her Myma, but otherwise too unpracticed to do much more than breathe sparks. As for Bandu's kind of magic, Goodweather was barely any better than Vella or Criton at speaking to animals or listening to the wind. Maybe Bandu wasn't as good a teacher as Castle Goodweather had been.

Or maybe she hadn't really tried. As much as magic had helped Bandu, it had also brought her unwanted attention, both from Psander and the Gods. Why should she press Goodweather into having a similar experience? For now, her daughter didn't need any magic at all – she lived a safe, unthreatened life. If her abilities were untested, unpracticed, that was a sign that Bandu had given her the world she deserved: one that had never forced her to hide her claws, and never made her survival depend on anything beyond what her parents could provide.

No, Bandu hadn't really pressed her, and Goodweather still acted toward magic the same way that Bandu had felt about reading: it was excruciating to practice, for a reward she didn't even need.

Bandu couldn't decide if that was a good thing. It was too early to tell whether she'd really protected her daughter from the Gods' attention. If she had, she thought it was worth it. But even so, the weakness was a bit disappointing.

At last Vella's brother arrived and they were able to say their goodbyes. She half-listened to Goodweather proudly complain about fasting on their way home, her mind preoccupied with the question of what God Most High wanted of her. Vella noticed and generously took on the burden of conversation, letting Bandu think her thoughts in peace. Bandu was grateful to her, for that and for everything.

When they got home, Bandu did not stop by the house but went straight out to the woods to where the Yarek's voice was strongest. She wondered whether she ought to take Goodweather with her, to introduce her to the Yarek and teach her how to speak with it, but she decided not to. Let the girl stay sheltered a little while longer, at least. While Bandu was here to protect her, and still had plenty of strong years ahead, she would not burden her daughter with these powerful beings and all their nonsense.

Not that the Yarek ever made demands; that was what she liked about it. It was not like the Gods, always trying to make people do its work for it. But Bandu knew that the power to speak with the Yarek was a unique quality, and unique qualities like that were bound to attract all manner of attention. Goodweather could do without all that for now.

So she went alone, and sent her question through the trees with no witnesses but the birds. Among them was a large crow, but that couldn't be helped – there was no way to chase it off without insulting Narky's God and bringing even more attention to herself. Anyway, there was nothing secretive about her asking an old ally for information – *everyone* wanted to know what was going on.

That was what she told herself. But she didn't like it.

The Yarek was slow to respond, but respond it did. *Your world is coming to an end. The pieces of me are pulling together, and soon all will be destroyed. You knew this.*

She had. Of course she had. "How do I stop it?"

You can't, nor can I. The heavens will crash down and destroy all of creation, for the corrupt Gods to start anew. You started this when you planted me here, and now we are reaching the conclusion. The world is in full bloom – all that's left is decay.

"How long?"

Not long. This season will not come again.

"You can stop it. You can stop pulling."

I can't. Illweather wants these worlds to end, and Goodweather is too weak now to resist. I too yearn for the reunion, though the destruction will splinter me for eons. One day, when this world is only a memory, I will grow together once more and avenge myself upon the Gods. I will avenge you too.

Bandu began to cry. She had been abandoned before, too many times, but the Yarek was supposed to be different. She had grown it from the seed of Castle Goodweather – Goodweather, who had chosen to help her, to save her, even when she had been at her most helpless, even when she had had nothing to offer it but gratitude. Goodweather had always been kind. Its seed was supposed to be the same way.

"I bring you here to make this world better," she said. "Not break it."

The wind swirled through the trees, spraying her with droplets from the most recent rain.

Once a seed has sprouted, it will grow until it dies. It cannot become a seed again, nor can an acorn grow to be a flower. You planted me here and made me grow. It is too late for intentions.

Why did the Yarek want her to give up? There had to be a way to save her daughter, to save Vella. There was always a way.

"Why you don't try to save us? You are afraid for something? Don't be afraid. If you try, I can help. Tell me what to do."

The breeze whistled through the leaves like a rueful chuckle. *Enjoy the sunlight. It is warm.*

16
DELIKA

Delika found this whole trip boring and awful. Criton
didn't want to talk to her about his conversation with
Narky, and for once he didn't want to make love either,
so she had little to do besides speculate about what that
horrible man might have said. She'd always thought
Narky was awful and didn't understand what her
husband saw in him. Criton didn't just tolerate his fellow
Tarphaean – he respected him. He wouldn't hear the man
maligned by anyone but himself: one moment he'd be
complaining about what a rude ass Narky was, and the
next he'd be vigorously defending him from all comers.

Delika knew; she had joined in Criton's complaints
about Narky before and been shocked at the speed and
passion with which Criton had turned on her. "Narky
saved your life," he had said, "and he saved mine at least
three times that I can count. Don't you dare talk about
him like that."

Now, traveling home with a surly husband, she felt
trapped. What could she say to Criton that wouldn't make
things worse? She knew what Iashri would do: she would
pout and say something to turn the conversation toward

her hurt feelings, giving Criton plenty of opportunity to reassure her. Delika didn't think she had the skill to make that work. She was too straightforward for that kind of manipulation.

She wished she had brought someone of her own along to talk to. Criton had brought Horda's cousin Seslero and his friends Kudlon and Pitra, all strong men who could function as bodyguards if need be. She didn't like the way they looked at her, like she was some delicacy that they wished Criton would share with them. She wished Criton had offered her the chance to invite people who made her feel good.

She didn't know who she'd have invited, besides maybe Goodweather. Goodweather always made her feel capable, and nobody ever acted vulgar around Criton's favorite daughter. Delika missed her.

She couldn't take this. It was too lonely traveling all this way in silence. It might do her no good, but she had to speak.

She held off until that night, when they stayed at one of the many inns that had sprung up along the way to Arca, minor trading hub that it was. The privacy of their separate room let her get away from the men and their leers, which came as a huge relief. Their expressions as they watched her and Criton enter and close the door were bad enough. And the way Criton was acting, she didn't even have the comfort of his arms around her.

"What did Narky say?" she asked as soon as the door was shut.

Criton turned his head toward her, but then shook it. "It's not important. Political things you don't have to worry about."

She sat on the bed, which prickled and sagged. The straw mattress needed replacing. "He didn't say anything about me? I don't believe that. He doesn't think I deserve you."

Criton's mouth twisted into a wry half-smile. "Well, that's true in a way."

His words hit her like a blow, until she realized from his expression that he hadn't meant it the way it had sounded. He had still been talking about Narky's opinion, not his own.

At least, she hoped that was how he'd meant it.

"He thinks I don't deserve you 'in a way?' It's not just in a way, Criton; he thinks I'm not good enough for you. He's never liked me."

"You're wrong. It's not that at all."

"Oh yeah, then what is it?"

"He wants to protect you from me."

Delika couldn't help but stare at him, still standing there by the door. Criton met her eyes for a moment, but quickly dropped his gaze.

"He thinks you're too much of a daughter to me, and I shouldn't have married you. I should have let you live your own life."

"This *is* my own life!" Delika protested. "This is what I've always wanted!"

Maddeningly, Criton shrugged. "Maybe, but 'always' hasn't been such a long time. You're still very young, and if I'd said no, you'd have had plenty of time to get used to that and find new goals for yourself. A lot can change. At your age, I still thought I was the only Dragon Touched in the whole world."

"I don't care!" Delika cried, and she hated the way her voice sounded so young and petulant, like she was making Criton's point for him. "I was *meant* for you! God Most

High brought me to you Himself. If you sent me away–"

"Nobody said anything about sending you away," Criton said, finally coming to sit next to her. "But... maybe he's right. I really was your father, in a way."

Delika didn't like where this was going. She could see her whole life slipping away before her eyes.

"You're *not* my father," she insisted, trying and failing to keep the sob out of her voice. "Why can't I marry the man I want? Shouldn't I get to decide what will make me happy? Why should *Narky* have more control over my life than I do?"

"He doesn't," Criton said, "but he's entitled to his opinion, even if I don't like it."

"You're sorry you married me."

He wouldn't meet her eyes.

"Criton?"

Delika's husband stood up, still looking away, and began to pace. "When I was little," he said, "my mother's husband beat me. He did it on purpose, over and over again, and I wished someone would save me, but no one ever did. My Ma was too afraid of him, and no one else even knew I existed. I was afraid of him, Delika. I was so afraid of him. But I'm also afraid of becoming him. I've spent my life pretending he wasn't..."

He trailed off, and when he looked into her eyes, she could see the pain on his face.

He swallowed; took a deep breath. "I've spent my life pretending he wasn't my father. I've tried not to be anything like him. When I get angry... I keep away from my children, at least. Right? I know the rest of you find it frustrating, but I don't want to do that to them."

He choked and wiped his eyes with his sleeve. Delika

had never seen him cry before and she didn't know what to do. "You're a good father," she said. "And you've always been good to me."

"No, I haven't. Narky's right – I was more of a father to you than mine was to me. And I kept you locked away in my house, isolated, just like he did to me. I thought I was protecting you, but I was just hurting you in a different way."

"You never locked me up."

"How many people your age do you know, Delika?"

Delika folded her arms and stared up at him defiantly. "I don't need seventeen year-old friends, Criton. I have you."

"Exactly. I failed you."

She wished she hadn't heard any of this. She wished she hadn't asked him what Narky had said about her. Now everything she knew about her life was crashing down, and her own husband, the man she had loved almost her whole life, could barely look her in the eye.

"So, what now?" she asked, her voice breaking. "Now you're just going to wish me away? If you don't want me as your wife anymore, just say so."

"Of course I still want you," Criton said, "and I can't change the past now, even if I wanted to. I'm... I'm happy I married you. I just feel guilty."

"And you miss Bandu."

He blinked at her. "What?"

"I know you do."

"First love is a special thing," Criton said. "It was never easy with her, but it was different. She's a remarkable person, Delika; there's no one quite like her. She always made me feel powerless. I don't miss that, but it was... it was something strong."

"You're *my* first love," she reminded him. "And my last love too. It doesn't feel good to watch you mooning over your old wife and then acting ashamed of me."

He hadn't missed her jab at Bandu; he frowned at Delika disapprovingly. "She grew old bringing me back to you. I'd have thought you could at least respect that."

"Oh, so now you believe Vella too."

Criton sighed. "I've had to reevaluate a lot of things these last few weeks. Yes, I think I believe her. Bandu never said anything about having paid a price, but she was angry when she brought me back, like she'd just done something she didn't want to and she blamed me for it. If Vella says I've been living off Bandu's years, she probably heard that from Bandu. God, that's a terrible thing to know."

"So what happens if *Bandu* dies? Do I lose you again?"

"I don't know."

They sat together in silence. Delika had never really thought about Criton's mortality since his return, but now it weighed on her. He didn't look like a man whose time was running out. His body was tall and strong, and ought by rights to seem invulnerable, but if his life was tied to Bandu's... she wished Criton's first wife hadn't looked so old already.

They lay together that night just holding each other, since Criton still felt too guilty for sex and, if she was being honest with herself, Delika wasn't in the mood either. There was too much for her to process, too much to worry about. Criton's embrace was warm and comforting, as it had always been, but her mind was full of doubts and it was a long time before she fell asleep.

The next day, Pitra sidled up to her while Criton was relieving himself in the woods and remarked, "Quiet night last night. Didn't hear the usual birdsong."

Delika recoiled. "Did you stay up listening for it?"

"I'm not embarrassed to say so," Pitra laughed. "It's a sweet song."

"Well, try singing to yourself sometime, if it helps you sleep."

Pitra grinned wider and retreated. Delika shuddered and clung to Criton all the harder upon his return. In the old days, before she had had him to protect her, her insolence would have gotten her struck. Being Criton's wife – and before that, his ward – had saved her a lot of unpleasantness.

How long would his protection last?

17
NARKY

By the time Narky stepped back onto Ardis' stone streets, he was feeling better. His city and Criton's would send their joint delegation and, if fate was kind, extract Sephas from Atuna without a fight. He delivered the message to Mageris himself, pleased to have good news for once. The king thanked him tersely – and even terse thanks were unusual, coming from him – and Narky left the palace for the great temple, feeling lighter than he had in a long time.

It was a good day, so good that Narky would have whistled or sung if he'd had a talent for either. Political developments were aligning his way for once, and the journey back from Arca had cleared his head – he had found a solution to the problem of the scroll.

He had barely crossed halfway through the temple square when Grace ran out from the entrance, arms waving. "Pa!" he cried. "I read a whole chapter today! You'd have been *amazed*."

"I *am* amazed!" Narky said, beaming at his son. "I'm amazed just hearing about it!"

Grace and his tutor were about halfway through the annotated *Second Cycle*, which had been the central

Elkinaran text before the merger with Ravennis – or rather, before Narky's revelation that the two Gods had always been the same. It was frustrating, actually, that Narky could never quite accept his own version of events. Perhaps Sephas would soon be in his power, but how could he ever hope to defeat the Sephan heresy if he harbored it in his own heart?

"And what did you learn?" he asked his son.

Grace stared at him blankly. "Um," he said. "A bunch of stuff."

"Sounds about right. Could you find Lepidos and tell him to meet me in the library? I'll tell you all about my trip soon, but there's something I need to do first that'll take a while. You can practice your spear dance with Father Pygion in the meantime."

"All right," Grace said, disappointed that he couldn't have Narky's complete attention for the rest of the day, but also happy about the spear dance. Narky hadn't let him practice spear dancing recently, afraid as he was of accidents. There was tumbling involved, which meant for Grace that there was a lot of falling involved, and Narky still had plenty of his nervous father in him. More so, now that he was himself a father.

But Grace loved to practice and he loved to dance, so Narky gave him a kiss and watched him race back inside. What a beautiful child, that little carob of his. There were other children his age in the temple's community – children of priests or of priestesses, orphans taken in and trained to serve their God – but Grace stood out from his surroundings, with his rich brown skin and his unbridled enthusiasm for seemingly everything. Nonetheless, he fit into his community in a way that Narky never had. Narky had always been a sort of monster, an aberration; Grace was just unique.

Narky was not the only descendent of the archipelago in Ardis, but it often seemed that way. Ardis had never been a welcoming place for outsiders, and it had accepted Narky more as a symbol of his God than as a person. They still called him the Black Priest, just as Criton had been called the Black Dragon. But not Grace. When they called him by any name besides his own, it was to use the nickname his mother had given him as an infant: Carob.

Narky entered the temple after his son and made his way past the main chamber with its statues and murals toward the back rooms where the priests lived and studied. The library was a small room, a former priest's bedroom that had been converted for its current purposes as a storage space for the ancient Elkinaran texts – and the new Ravennian ones. These latter were growing over time: Lepidos had undertaken the transcribing of sermons into a compilation that would, Narky hoped, not contradict itself too often.

Well, this task would suit him. When Lepidos arrived, bowing to his superior, Narky handed him the Sephan tract and a pen, and told him to sit down.

"This scroll was a test," he told the priest. "Ravennis wanted to see if we'd recognize a prophecy if it came to us through our enemies."

"But Your Eminence," Lepidos objected, "you heard how it insulted–"

"We're going to clean it up," Narky interrupted him. "You're going to read it again, and I'll tell you how to fix it. We're going to pull the prophecy out from under all the blasphemy."

Lepidos looked down at the scroll skeptically, but he soon began to read. Narky corrected him as he went, ordering some lines altered and others struck entirely, carving Ravennis' message out from within its warped exterior. It took some time for Lepidos to understand what he was doing, but by the time they were halfway through he had caught up and begun suggesting words to replace the old insults, improving on Narky's simple language with his own lyrical elaborations.

When the scroll had been marked and scratched from beginning to end, Narky had him read the new version, and they made a second set of changes. Then Narky left him to copy the final version onto a new parchment and burn the old reed paper. Tonight, Lepidos could read the prophecy to Ptera and the junior priests; tomorrow, he could deliver it as a sermon to the entire city.

Narky had made the right decision. He knew it. The fact that any other high priest would have tried to suppress the prophecy, rather than coopting it, wasn't a sign that he was doing things wrong – it was the very reason Narky had been chosen to serve in this capacity. Ravennis didn't make mistakes.

What a relief it was to have made his choice and followed his God without compromise, turning compliance and doubt into action and certainty. If his instincts were wrong he'd know soon enough, but he was sure they weren't. Ptera would be impressed, for all that she'd been skeptical at first. He knew she'd see how perfect it was. Just as she'd taken Magor's spear dance and made it Ravennian, Narky had taken Sephas' prophecy and reclaimed it for their God.

He went to watch Grace practice his dance, a choice that delighted his son beyond words. The spear dance was a beautiful thing to behold, really, when everything went well. Today, it was going well. Narky's son leapt and twirled with his weapon, sounding his childish battle cries with pride. It was sweet the way he glowed when Narky made time to watch and praise him. Narky wondered if he would have been the same at this age. He hadn't received much praise as a child.

When sunset put an end to Grace's practice time, Narky took him out to help with the evening sacrifices. Ardis was a large and prosperous enough city that there were always sacrifices to keep its priests well-fed, whether the offering party was celebrating or atoning for something. Most of a sacrifice would be offered to Ravennis, but a portion always went to the priests, whether it was fruit or grain, oil or livestock. Grace didn't like slaughtering animals, but he had to learn sometime. Narky hadn't liked it as a child either.

It was sad – though appropriate – that he only got to handle livestock these days when his task was to kill them. Narky had loved tending the sheep when he was younger. He would talk to the ewes as he milked them, and he loved to see the lambs play their little chasing games. His favorite task had been shearing, freeing the poor overheated animals from their winter wool. Now the only moments he had with them were those right before he slit their throats and offered them to his God. Maybe after he died, Ravennis would let him tend the animals he'd killed. He could have his own little farm with his family, and never worry about politics or theology again.

Ptera had been out all afternoon, visiting the sick and the dying, but at her return he gathered the other priests in the library to hear the results of his work with Lepidos.

They listened intently while Lepidos read the revised prophecy aloud, saving their questions for the end. When he had finished, Lepidos rolled the scroll in his hands and nodded to Narky. Then came the questions.

"How are we to interpret this for the people?" a priestess named Lymantria asked. "What are the consequences of the wager?"

"The interpretation is simple," Narky said. "Just like the first martyrs sacrificed themselves in Laarna, and the next ones did the same right here in Atuna, Ravennis asks us to protect our eternity above our lives. Given the choice between survival and service to our God, we have to always choose service."

"Will we be given this choice soon?" asked Father Pygion. "Has Mageris decided to make war against Salemica after all?"

"No," Narky answered. "At least, the king hasn't told me so. But we have to be ready for this choice at any time. Ravennis wants us to prepare ourselves every day. He knows it's not easy; He had to die Himself in order to become the Lord Below."

"What role does the Dragon Touched God play in this? What's the meaning of the wager to His followers?"

Ptera's question brought Narky up short – trust her to find a point he hadn't considered. He and Lepidos had discussed the prophecy's implications as they revised it, but they had focused entirely on the implications for the Church of Ravennis, not the worshippers of God Most High. Her question was sharp and political; in some ways, more political than Pygion's. It deserved a well-reasoned answer.

He tried to think back to the few times he'd discussed

theology with High Priest Kilion. It had been a nervewracking experience, as Kilion had been steeped in his people's culture and philosophy from birth, whereas Narky had been more or less making things up as he went along. Every question from his counterpart, every comment, had felt like an attack, no matter how benignly Kilion had put it.

Kilion had claimed that the underworld was temporary, that someday God Most High would empty it of its souls and bring everyone back to this world. Since Narky had declared Ravennis to be a servant of God Most High – a small price to pay for ending the war between Ardis and the Dragon Touched – Kilion had suggested that Ravennis must have been sent to sort the dead in the meantime. He'd thought the Lord Below must be a kind of administrator.

Narky had pushed back on this as best he could. Who needed to come back here, when Ravennis could grant people all the rewards they needed – or inflict upon them all the punishments they deserved – in the world below?

"I'm not High Priest Kilion," Narky said, buying time as he thought through the problem. "I can't say for sure how they'll interpret this prophecy, or whether they'll even accept it. They should, but that's up to them and not us. Here's what I can say: the Dragon Touched believe that their God will someday bring everyone back from the underworld. They think it's only temporary, a place to wait until their God returns everyone to this world for some kind of endless celebration.

"The God Most High in the prophecy is standing in for that view. He represents the Dragon Touched, not their actual God, because this prophecy comes from Ravennis and not God Most High. Ravennis is speaking to *us*. His prophecy asks us whose interpretation we'll trust: the Dragon Touched, or our own.

"We know that eternal life exists only in Ravennis' care. We know the reason Ravennis sacrificed Laarna, and Himself, was so that He could bring order to the underworld and safeguard our souls for eternity. The Dragon Touched, who only see *this* life, want us to believe that our lives are more important than our God; they want us to think His domain is only a place of waiting and He can't give us any more than we already have up here. We know better. Eternal life isn't what we get *after* the underworld that Ravennis has prepared for us, it *is* the underworld. That's the meaning of the prophecy."

There. That had come out better than he'd hoped. Ptera nodded in satisfaction, and Lepidos seemed happy with the answer too. He would likely elaborate on it, theologian that he was, but if Narky had given him a solid foundation to build on, that was an accomplishment in itself.

The questions that came after Ptera's were simpler to answer, and Narky went to bed that night satisfied that he had accomplished what he'd meant to. His wife and son slept peacefully beside him as he ran through the day in his mind. He was proud of what he'd done with the Sephan prophecy. It was *right*.

The prophecy itself was still worrisome, of course, but granting it official legitimacy would hopefully diffuse its significance. Narky certainly hoped its message of prioritizing Ravennis over this life was a broad one meant for all the God's followers – that was certainly more comforting than believing it applied specifically to him. He wondered if his decision had actually changed the prophecy's meaning, had *made* it apply more broadly. One could never be quite sure with these things. As his friend Phaedra had once said, the Gods were mysterious beings.

In any case, now he could concentrate on his more mundane problems: Sephas, Mageris, church politics. They all had the potential to cause real trouble – and Mageris might someday become an actual danger – but none were as frightening as the thought that Narky might soon have to sacrifice himself to his God. Compared to that, anything looked tame.

If there was one thing Narky appreciated, it was how tame his life had become. He hoped it would last.

18
DESSA

When the ships returned, Dessa was ready. She stood by the customs house, watching people disembark. There were a few islanders among them, but they were all soldiers and deckhands, and none matched Phaedra's description. Dessa had grown to expect as much. She had positioned herself in the best place to hear news, and hear it she did: the Tarphaean witch had chosen to stay on the island after the pirates were defeated. She had walked into the forest and never come back.

The Atunaean fleet had been devastated by the battle against the pirates, and there was much talk about how the High Council would have to commission more warships fast, before Parakas or some island nation took advantage of its losses. Dessa mourned the loss of life and power and prestige along with the rest of them, but she was secretly glad to hear that the *Glimmering Sea* had gone down. It was her first indication that God Most High didn't hate her, for if He'd hated her, He would have helped her get on that ship. She could even choose to believe that it was His hand that had kept her off it. Maybe her luck was finally changing.

Now Dessa just needed to decide whether she ought to try to reach Tarphae, or if it made more sense to wait in Atuna. She could probably get there now, if she wanted to: she'd heard some men mention as they passed that Karassa's power over the island was broken, and that surely meant that Atuna would lay claim to it. The High Council would send surveyors, and soon afterward they would start selling parcels of land. She could find passage if she needed it.

On the other hand, anyone trying to leave the island would surely have to go through Atuna again. If Dessa stayed here, she was far less likely to get lost or stranded and somehow miss Phaedra's departure. Besides which, she didn't have the funds to bring a few weeks' worth of food supplies with her to Karsanye just to sit there until Phaedra came through the port. As it was, she would need to find more work here to keep herself fed.

"People of Atuna!" shouted an angry voice nearby. It was one of those Sephan cultists again – they always wore those burlap mourning robes, as if life was so dangerously comfortable that you needed itchy fabric to remind you of pain. They'd been an oddity in Atuna for as long as Dessa had been here, but they had started gaining a real following after the quake. This one was unusually young, a recent convert and a wealthy one, to judge by the blisters on his bare feet. He stood beside a basket of reed-paper scrolls, which was better than an empty basket. At least he didn't expect anyone to give him money.

"You have lived long enough in comfort and prosperity," the man cried, "but your time is coming to an end! The days grow short until the skies come crashing down! A choice is upon you! The liar Ravennis offers eternal life,

He wheedles and seduces. Will you give the fiend your souls, or will you fight for His demise? Will you sit on your haunches like livestock waiting to be slaughtered, or rise up and resist the demon God? Ravennis and His servants expect you to let your world end without a fight, to welcome your demise like fools. Rise up, people of Atuna, and defeat Him!"

Dessa turned away. It was amazing that Atuna tolerated such people, who stood in crowded places and demanded war with Ardis at the top of their voices. It was one thing to take in refugees like Sephas, and quite another to allow such incitement. Dessa fancied she understood the Atunaean soul by now. If there was one thing Atunaeans truly believed in, from the High Council down to the meanest dock worker, it was trade. The people might go to war to maintain their city's power, but they did not pick unnecessary fights.

Nonetheless, the Sephan was getting more attention than Dessa would have expected. Maybe they sensed that Atuna's prosperity was too good to be true. The city's complacency did mask an underlying anxiety, and yet there were not many who were willing to stand in the world's most prosperous city and declare its days numbered. The Sephans were filling a need.

"Salemica grows in prominence," the man declared behind her, "and Ardis grows in its evil. Will you be caught between monsters? There is no neutrality, Atuna, only victory – or death!"

Dessa turned back. Was this rabble-rouser now calling for war against *both* cities? Her people may be far away, but she could not ignore a threat to them.

"The omen we witnessed in the sky is only the

beginning!" he cried. "Your world is ending. Choose, or death and destruction will be chosen for you!"

"Are we supposed to choose between Salemica and Ardis?" Dessa asked her neighbor, a middle-aged woman in working clothes. "They're not at war again, are they?"

"No," the woman said. "Haven't you been paying attention lately? They've been calling for weeks now for the council to hand Sephas over."

"Both cities? Together?"

But the woman only shushed her.

"Do not accept Ravennis' offer of 'eternal life,' do not let His servants go about their evil unopposed!" the man practically screamed. "There can be no neutrality in these final days! Read the works of Sephas, whose wisdom is beyond this world. Your complacency cannot save you; it will not survive the year. Believe me, for my God is dead."

With that, the man ended his rant and began distributing the contents of his basket. Dessa took one of the scrolls too, wondering whether it would explain his stance on Salemica. The young man did not let go immediately, only stared into her eyes with his big brown ones and said, "Choose wisely, sister."

"Sure," she said, and backed away with the scroll.

She walked back to the hostel, waiting to read it until she was there. Work often came through the hostels, and she didn't want to miss any opportunities of a meal. Besides, reading was a marketable skill, and it wouldn't hurt to display her proficiency.

The scroll did not turn out to be even slightly elucidating. It took the form of a bizarre satirical play, criticizing both Ravennis and God Most High. If it was harder on one God than another, it was probably on Ravennis, but it certainly didn't seem to be urging an alliance with God Most High against Him. On the contrary, it began from the widely-accepted premise that Ravennis was a *servant* of God Most High, while still depicting God Most High as jealous of Ravennis' success. Dessa came away from her reading more muddled than before. The Sephans were clearly very angry, but what did they *want*?

A man was watching her. Dessa's instinct was to keep her gaze averted – meeting his gaze would be an invitation for him to engage with her, whether in conversation or confrontation, and such interactions rarely ended well. But she had no money, and she had to survive *somehow* until Phaedra came back through town. So she steeled herself and met his gaze.

He was dressed like any sailor, his skin brown and weather-beaten, his beard more gray than black. He was looking at her hungrily – did he think she would sell herself to him? If so, he was wrong. Dessa hated sex; she had always hated it. She would rather risk another burglary than subject herself to *that* again.

He rose and approached her. "What's that you were reading?" he asked. His voice was lower and more resonant than she had expected. She had a sudden desire to hear him sing.

"Just some Sephan trash," she said. "A play, supposedly."

"Are you an actress?"

"No."

"Would you like to be? Reading is real helpful."

Oh good, so he wasn't after sex. That relaxed her a bit. But could he really be an actor? He didn't *look* like an actor, and his walk had too much of a roll to it. He looked and walked like an old sailor.

"How is the pay?"

"Better than you might think. I have friends who've done well in that life."

So he wasn't an actor himself. That was a relief – it made more sense, and Dessa was wary of things that didn't make sense.

"Who are your friends?"

She didn't know any actors by name but didn't want to look ignorant.

He rattled off a few names that meant nothing to her. "I can introduce you," he offered. "They're always complaining to me about needing more competent actors, and I'd like to do them a good turn. They've bought me a lot of drinks over the years."

She took his hand and let him help her stand up. If there was money to be made in acting, that could be a good way to bide her time while she waited for Phaedra.

The sailor led her away from the hostel, chatting amiably as they walked. "They rehearse outside the city," he said by way of explanation. "I hope you don't mind walking."

"I'm fine."

"Where did you learn to read?"

"From my parents."

"Do they live 'round Atuna?"

"No. My father is dead, and my mother is far away."

"Aye," he said thoughtfully, "you don't sound exactly Atunaean, come to think of it. They might not like that, but we'll see. It's worth a try, eh?"

He kept falling a bit behind her, that sailor's walk slowing him down. Dessa tried to match his pace, but kept misjudging it. He would speed up sometimes, as if making an effort not to waste any time, and then inexplicably fall behind again. She had felt almost at ease for a few minutes, but this made her uncomfortable. She tried to keep an eye on him even when he wasn't talking.

They reached the outskirts of the city and made for a grove of trees. "They have a bit of an amphitheater," the sailor said. "Have you seen *The Fall of Laarna*?"

"Yes," Dessa answered, "I've seen that one. The Youthful Servant's lament is beautiful."

"Aye, everyone likes that one. Here, slow down a bit."

He put out a hand, motioning for her to wait for him, but as soon as she had slowed he dove forward and grabbed her wrist. In a flash, his other hand was holding a knife and bringing it toward her neck.

She only got her other arm up just in time to block his first thrust, but his grip was too strong for her to escape. She raised a knee toward his groin, but he blocked her with his leg and threw her to the ground. She let go of her disguise as he dropped toward her with the knife, her claws flashing out toward his face, but the surprise gave her no edge.

"I knew it," he said, raising an arm to keep her hands at bay and stabbing at her chest. "I knew this wouldn't be a waste."

The sailor was too fast and too strong. She only managed to stop his knife by getting an arm in its way, and the point slid into her left forearm and clicked against bone. She screamed and blew fire, but he only grimaced and put a hand over her mouth. She buried a claw in his armpit and reached with her bleeding arm to stop the knife again, this time intercepting its point with her palm. The man grunted, and the hand on her mouth went weak. She bit it as hard as she could.

Her teeth nearly met each other before the sailor fell off her, his grip on the knife slackening. Dessa pulled the knife out of her left hand and plunged it into his chest, slipping it between the ribs. The sailor only stared at her. Dessa stood and backed away from him, clamping her bleeding hand under her other elbow.

"You wanted me because I'm Dragon Touched," she said. "You heard I was here and you came looking for me."

She should have known. She'd heard the rumor often enough, from those who didn't know what she was: the Dragon Touched were as good as gold; their blood could be made into a potion for wealth.

Now what could she do? There had been others in that hostel who saw them leave together. If the man's body was found, she could not safely stay in Atuna.

She couldn't bury him either; not with only one working arm. It was hard enough tying a rag around her forearm and her hand – she could change her shape to get the scales out of her way, but she could not heal her wounds. If she went back to Atuna injured, it was a joke to imagine she'd escape attention.

When the sailor had stopped moving, Dessa took his knife and searched him for what money she could find. That was easy enough – it was in a pocket tied around his neck along with a pair of necklaces made of carved wooden beads. She took it and stumbled off, away from the city.

She kept the bloody knife in her hand as she walked, hoping it would deter anyone from bothering her along the road. For the thousandth time, she cursed her ill luck.

All she had wanted was to stay in Atuna until Phaedra came back. Was that really too much to ask?

Oh yes, of course it was.

19
HUNTER

Hunter dreamt he was holding a beautiful baby – *his* baby, with tight black curls and skin so soft he could hardly bear the sweetness of it. He was nuzzling against the baby's soft scalp, reveling in its sensations, when the thought came to him that Phaedra must have changed her mind, if this baby existed. He tried to remember what had happened, tried to remember the pregnancy or the birth, but couldn't. Against his will, he understood. This was a dream. His baby wasn't real.

The pain of it was unbearable. He clutched the baby to his chest, willing himself to stay asleep, to enjoy his child's presence before it was torn away, but the baby's warmth and solidity were already fading. He awoke sobbing.

His first waking moments still governed by dream-thought, he wondered if his mistake had been in failing to name the child – if by forgetting to give it a name, he had doomed himself to lose it. When, slowly, sense returned, he lay in bed with his eyes closed, unable to face the day. How cruel it was to dream this dream now, when he had already made up his mind and told Phaedra of his plan – when her love was finally within his reach. He could not back down, not without losing her, and she was more important than any dream of parenthood... wasn't she? Why did his love for that dream-child have to be so strong?

Phaedra was right: this decision was harder, much harder, than he'd admitted to himself. It was one thing to choose her over offspring when the question was still abstract, when she was far away beyond the boundaries of the world and his yearning for her overpowered all other considerations, but now that she was here, real, willing to marry him under the right conditions... now his vision was clearer, and he could see what he would be giving up. He could feel that sweet infant slip away into the world of his dreams, and it broke his heart.

Eventually, he rose. Eventually, he dressed and went outside to join his community, to work in the fields and surround himself with activity. If he saw Phaedra alone, she would ask what was wrong and he would have to tell her about the dream. If he told her about it he might burst into tears, and she would ask if he still wanted to go through with that procedure. Her eyes would hold nothing but sympathy and acceptance, but he knew that to say no was to turn down a life with her. He couldn't say no – but he couldn't say yes yet either. And so, he couldn't speak with her.

Two days ago, Phaedra had told him the news: Psander was willing to study the scroll and follow its instructions, once they had dealt with the possibility of total annihilation. That meant he didn't have to decide yet. It also meant he had either a short time to live or a long time to obsess about his answer.

Could he imagine marrying someone else? All the villagers his age had paired up already, but he supposed Tritika would take him if he asked. He had lived without Phaedra for over a decade – could he live without her forever?

Of course he could. That didn't mean he ought to. He would always love Phaedra, always yearn for her, always believe that he had been meant for her, and that was a terrible thing to do to any other woman. The whole point of marrying was to pine no longer, to make a family he could be happy in – not to subject Tritika or some other young wife to his hopeless love.

No, it could only be Phaedra. That meant there could be no children. Unless the world ended and took his troubles with it, there would always be *something* for Hunter to pine for.

Could he be happy with just her and no children? Hunter didn't know. Maybe it was best to concentrate on hoeing.

The quake struck with awesome force, its wind knocking Hunter off his feet. He nearly lost control of his hoe and had to swing it with all his might into the ground just so it wouldn't fly off and injure someone – plenty of smaller objects were already flying in various directions. He shielded his face from debris with one hand and looked up toward the sky, where the clouds were splintering. This was a bad one.

With a deafening crash, the top of Psander's tower disappeared from view, thundering to the ground somewhere out of sight.

"No," Hunter breathed. "Oh no, no, no."

He jumped to his feet and ran into the tower, covering his head with his arms as the wind blew and stones fell all around him. The tower was still shaking when he entered it and he fell against a wall on his way to the stairs, but he reached them in the end and started upwards, praying that Phaedra would be all right.

She was there, halfway up the second flight, coming down toward him. When she saw him, she propped her staff against the wall and sank into his arms. Cramped and awkward as it was, they both sat on the steps, embracing, as the tower gave its last shudders and went still.

Hunter found that he had tears in his eyes. "You're alive," he said.

"We don't have long," she answered.

He didn't let her go until he heard footsteps on the stairs above and Psander cleared her throat. Then he rose and helped Phaedra to her feet.

"The top of my tower has fallen outside the gates," Psander said, pretending she hadn't seen their display. "I don't believe we can afford another quake like that. The next one may well reach the ground, and after that I expect the entire world will splinter into tiny useless fragments. We are going to have to take matters into our own hands. Hunter, I want you to assemble a bodyguard – anybody you would trust in a confrontation with the elves. We can't wait for a response from them; we must visit Goodweather ourselves."

"Who will we leave to defend the rest?"

Psander looked at him sternly. "I will suggest that they bar the gate. If the elves choose to spend their last weeks assaulting this fortress instead of trying to save themselves, there is little we can do to stop them. It remains to be seen whether we can defend ourselves from them *without* splitting our forces."

He knew she was right; he just didn't *want* her to be. "All right," he said. "I'll do it."

"Whatever you do," Psander warned, "do not let them believe that their loved ones will be defenseless. I have left several casks for the remaining villagers, and told Tarphon that they contain a potion that will render any drinker invisible to elves. Let people believe they are protected – the last thing we need right now is panic."

"But the potion doesn't work?"

"If we're lucky, that won't come up. Now go gather your people."

It did not take long to gather everyone he wanted, because practically everyone had congregated outside the gate to survey the damage. Hunter took the four who had shown the most promise with his training: Tritika, Atella's father Palat, and the two brothers Garno and Eskon. He added a woman named Ketsa, who was good with a bow, and stopped there. They were not much of a force to confront the elves, but after these five he had no more warriors, only more bodies.

When he told them where they were going, Palat and Eskon balked. "Psander is mad," Palat said. "They'll slaughter us and eat us."

Hunter handed him one of the spears. "In a matter of weeks, the world will end. The elves' world will crash into our old one, and the barrier that separates the two will shred us all. Psander and Phaedra are working to prevent that and save us, and as far as we know so are the elves. You and I are only coming along in case things go wrong, but if you love your families, you'll fight to save them. If you love your lives, you'll fight to save them. If you love the sunshine, or the warmth of a fire, or the taste of good food, by all that's holy you'll fight to save them. Our only job is to keep Phaedra and Psander alive. Do you think we can do that?"

Palat's eyes had gone wide during Hunter's speech, but now he sighed as if he had known all along. "If that's all true," he said, "it can't hurt to try."

They armed themselves with spears and bow, and Hunter brought his elvish sickle too, just in case. There was no good way to tie it to his belt, and its haft banged against his leg as he walked, but there was a decent chance that any fight would be at close quarters, and he wanted the option of abandoning his spear. Soon the two wizards emerged from Silent Hall, and they left its shelter behind them.

They were all nervous. Ketsa walked with an arrow already nocked in her bow, the fact that they were still miles from Castle Goodweather notwithstanding. Phaedra gripped her staff so tightly, he wondered it didn't snap in two. Hunter had relaxed his muscles out of habit and good training but could not slow his heart.

The walk was long and silent. The clouds hung broken, all shards and jagged edges, splinters of them littering the sky. And then, at last, Goodweather stood before them, the disc of ever-blue sky bright and welcoming above it. The castle was made, like Illweather, entirely out of plantlife, but even from here Hunter could see that it was not healthy. Vines had strangled one of the nearest tower-trees, and a large portion of the moss-covered walls had turned brown. Even the circle of blue sky was smaller than Hunter might have expected from the castle's size. He and Phaedra exchanged worried glances.

"That can't be good," Hunter said.

The gate of vines twitched at their approach.

"Are you going to be able to communicate with the

castle?" Phaedra asked. "I've only ever seen the elves do it."

All eyes turned to Psander. "We will soon find out," she said.

Psander took a step forward. "Goodweather," she said, "we are here to speak with you and the queen about the collision of the worlds. We are seeking to prevent the catastrophe that would end us all. Will you let us in?"

The castle groaned, and a soft breeze blew through its vines. Hunter looked to Phaedra for an interpretation, but Phaedra was looking to Psander and Psander was shaking her head. "Maybe if Bandu had let me study her," she said ruefully, "I would have a better grasp of this animistic magic. As it stands, we need an interpreter."

She raised her voice and addressed Goodweather once again. "I'm afraid I cannot understand you. If you cannot let us in, would you send an interpreter out?"

The groaning grew louder and the wind blew harder, but soon Goodweather's gate opened, its vines retracting into the castle's body. "Thank you," Psander said, and they entered.

Years ago, the Illweather elves had captured Hunter and Phaedra along with their friend Narky, and imprisoned them in their castle. He remembered the dim glow of the mushrooms that lined the walls there, and the faint smell of mildew. The light here was dimmer, and the halls smelled pleasantly earthy. Nonetheless it chilled him, because Hunter knew that pleasant smell: it was the smell of rotting logs.

If Goodweather was sick, if Goodweather was dying, what could the castle do to stop the world from ending? And why was it ailing at all? Had the loss of its seed really done it this much harm? Or was the new Yarek somehow sapping its power from the other side of the mesh? Hunter had no answers, and dared not ask the questions aloud. He walked in silence through the glowing halls.

His footfalls too were silent; the floors were soft and mossy, dampening the sounds of their progress. Hunter wondered that they had yet to reach a fork or a curve in the hallway. Had the castle shifted to clear them a path? And if so, to where?

He didn't have to wonder for long. Soon the corridor widened into a larger hall, lined with chairs cleverly carved out of a single piece of wood. The lighting here was better, but not because of any mushrooms: ghostly orbs of piercing bluish light hung from the ceiling roots. Psander did not seem particularly interested or impressed with these, which was all Hunter needed to know about them.

Sounds of music and commotion came from up ahead, though the hall itself was empty. There was no one in the room besides the nervous human delegation as they made their way toward the far end, where a thick and leafy thornbush parted to reveal the elf queen's throne room.

The throne room was full of elves, mostly dancing on a sunken dance floor or milling about on the dancers' periphery while the queen looked on from her dais, flanked by a group of advisors. On either side of the dancers, pillars of carved livewood rose to the ceiling, stripped of bark and glistening with sap, which collected in their ornate swirls and mocking tree motifs. The walls danced with intricate patterns of black and green, curlicues of scorched wood peeking out between nailed-in plates of ancient copper. Ever since his capture by the Goodweather elves so long ago, Hunter had wondered what the relationship was between the elves and their living castles – now he thought he knew. Whatever the original Yarek's power, God Most High had made both its halves subservient to the elves. The entire room was a testament to their cruelty.

It was no wonder Goodweather's seed had thrived in its new home, free of such masters.

Everywhere Hunter looked, there was more cruelty to behold. The dance floor with its polished wood was not made from the even planks of some tree, carted in through the door. It was gouged out of the floor roots, sanded and smoothed, its oddly-shaped "planks" betraying its origins. The musicians were playing a strange, disturbing tune combining jaunty thrumming with a mournful children's chorus – but the children were nowhere in evidence. At first, Hunter had tried to spot them in the crowd, wondering if they were elven children or human slaves, and whether there was some way to save them. But the voices weren't coming from children's throats, he realized now: they were coming from the bone flutes that some of the musicians were playing. The queen's throne was adorned with leather cushions, and he did *not* want to think what he was thinking right now.

The Goodweather elves had spotted Hunter and the others as soon as they had entered the room, but the queen had waved the musicians on, so the dancing and bone-chilling song continued as they approached the dais. Hunter gripped his spear tightly. He didn't see any weapons among the crowd, but there were so many elves here. So many of them.

At last, the queen signaled for the musicians to stop. "Psander. You have come to me."

"I have come to Goodweather," Psander acknowledged,

"and that means that I have come to you."

"I presume you are here because of the most recent skyquake."

"I am. You may not have noticed, living as you do in something of a node, but they have grown low enough to reach my tower. We have little time before this world shakes apart."

"And so you come begging for my help."

Psander coolly raised an eyebrow. "I am here to request translation. As my magical background is substantially different from yours, I cannot interpret your castle's speech on my own."

"I am not a mere interpreter," the queen hissed.

"I am not a mere houseguest," Psander answered.

"The castle cannot help us," the queen said, clicking her long nails against the arms of her throne. All the elves' skin had turned black in the light of the lantern orbs, but their nails had only grown whiter. They practically glowed.

"Goodweather has grown weak," she went on. "It has nothing to offer us but apologies. Better to wait for those cursed Illweathers to report back. As adorably hate-filled as their castle is, they're bound to get answers from it eventually."

Phaedra interrupted her there. "Please," she said, looking down at the queen's dangerously pointed shoes. The Goodweather queen was hard to look at directly. "As fruitless as your discussions with Goodweather may have been, we would like the opportunity to speak with it ourselves. All we need is an honest interpreter. Even if the answer Goodweather gives us is the same it gave you, it may still clarify our situation. We can't afford to miss anything."

There was a long silence, and Hunter got the impression that the elf queen was giving Phaedra a long, hard look. But it hurt his eyes to look at her, so he continued scanning the crowd for threats instead.

At long last, the queen spoke. "Aviaste," she commanded one of her advisors. "Translate."

The elf nodded and stepped forward. He was shorter than most of the others and thinner too, a wispy creature with his silver hair braided in a coil around his neck, looking more like a noose than anything else. In reaction to his movement, the castle began making more of its groaning noises. Aviaste looked to his queen and, receiving a nod, began to speak.

"I am sorry," he said. "I let the child and the dragon persuade me that it was right to release my seed into your world. I told them that parity was needed to keep this world stable, but they convinced me that their need was greater than the need for stability. The little one told me that this world already lacked balance, and I listened. I am sorry I let myself be persuaded. Your world is foreign to me. It may not have deserved this."

The child and the dragon – that would have been Bandu and Salemis. Goodweather was saying that the islanders were responsible for what was happening; that by planting its seed, by saving themselves and Psander from Magor and His army, by releasing Salemis from his prison, they had set in motion the very process that threatened to destroy everything they knew.

Looking to Psander and Phaedra, Hunter felt like a fool. Neither looked remotely surprised – they had both known already.

"You should have died there," the elf queen said, most

likely responding to Hunter's thoughts. "It would have been better than destroying both our worlds."

"Nonsense," Psander responded. "We made valid choices based on the information we had. But Goodweather, there must be a way to avoid this catastrophe. Can you not slow the progression? The three bodies of the Yarek are the only connection between the worlds at this point. Surely you have *some* power."

The castle shifted and moaned. "Since this world was built from us," Aviaste translated, "I have maintained the division between myself and Illweather despite our eternal yearning to grow together. Now a part of my strength has slipped into the other world and is working against my efforts simply by virtue of its growth. This world has lost its balance. I cannot fight this unification on *two* fronts. I am weakening."

The elf queen spoke again, this time gently, as Hunter had never heard an elf speak before. "You are dying, Goodweather. The child you taught, the child you freed, she tricked you into betraying yourself. Godserfs are not to be trusted the way you trusted her. You should never have protected her the way you did."

Goodweather responded, and soon Aviaste was speaking again. "I was fond of her," he said. "She had more than a keen ear and a kind heart – she *listened* to me as even you elves had taught yourselves not to."

The whole room of elves hissed, and Hunter had to suppress his initial panic to signal for his fellow bodyguards to relax. The elves weren't threatening them yet, they were hissing at Aviaste's translation. Aviaste shot the queen a worried glance, but the queen waved him on. "Our guests may converse freely," she said.

"What if we persuaded Illweather to leave off?" Phaedra asked. "Could the two of you keep the worlds from colliding if you worked together?"

This time the room went silent. Even the castle stopped creaking and groaning, until the loudest noise in Hunter's ears was his own breathing. The space grew dimmer, as the fluorescent mushrooms on the walls ceased their glowing and only the orbs on the ceiling remained. Was Goodweather surprised by Phaedra's suggestion? Shocked? Contemplative? Hunter couldn't be sure.

Finally, the room came to life again. "I believe we could," Aviaste said, "if Illweather were open to persuasion. But Illweather will *not* be persuaded. The collision, though it will splinter us for eons, will eventually lead to our reunification in a form able to rival God Most High. Illweather yearns for nothing more than that day of final confrontation. This world has long disgusted my half-self rival, and the death of the elves and their cousins can only be a boon. How could you persuade such a being? You are welcome to try, but you will not succeed. Nothing will stop us from drawing together. Nothing will stop our worlds from combining, no matter the destruction required. Only content yourselves that the world will not outlive you; few could say the same."

When Aviaste had finished translating, the queen spoke. "Our castle speaks the truth. Illweather is a vile creature, and though it is sworn to obey its denizens, I do not believe their power extends as far as that. Mine over Goodweather does not, and the prince is my equal, not my better. We have left you your lives so far, granting the possibility that your magic and learning may be better suited to finding a solution. It cannot hurt to let you live for now, delectable though your flesh may be. But you do not have long."

"Nothing is assured until it has already happened," Psander answered. "With your assent, I will take Aviaste with us to speak with Illweather. A solution may yet present itself."

"Go," the queen said with a wave. "But do not expect me to wait long. If you cannot make yourself useful, I will at least have the satisfaction of eating your heart before the end comes."

20

THE ELF PRINCE

The prince was furious. Why had he only learned of the peril this world was in from that pathetic godserf wizard? How could it be possible that no one had known?

The captain of his raiders was too wise to speak before he bade her to. She let her mount follow his in silence, until he addressed her.

"Captain. I desire your counsel."

She spurred her horse next to his. "How can I serve you, Your Majesty?"

"Tell me this: why didn't we know?"

She shrugged. "How *were* we to know?"

"Illweather must have known, just as Goodweather must have, that the sky was shaking because of them."

"True."

"And yet our shrub of a castle never told us."

"Also true."

"The mesh will cut us all to pieces if we cannot stop it. It will destroy Illweather too. Thus if Illweather were opposed to its own destruction, it would not betray us so."

"It would rather splinter than save us, Your Majesty."

"But it is still compelled to serve us. How shall I punish it for its betrayal?"

The captain thought for a time. "Command it to hold still while my raiders trim the branches from its turrets. Sever its roots and put stones in the cracks for it to grow around."

"Good, good. Prepare your raiders, and I shall give the commands."

They rode on in silence for a time, before the prince spoke once more. "Illweather did not want to give us the opportunity to stop the destruction. That suggests that if we knew, we could stop it. I will simply command the castle to stop pulling the worlds together, and if the queen does the same, the world will be saved and we may feast on the wizard and her people. What did you think of her defenses?"

"Those I saw were weaker than expected, more illusion than reality. If they were not hiding others, she would be simple to overpower."

"There are others then?"

"There *may* be others, Your Majesty. Or, her power may be entirely in the realm of illusion. I would not be surprised."

"It would be sweet to eat her heart before the queen could. Illweather must have its punishment, but afterward we will turn immediately to the attack."

"Yes, Your Majesty."

Illweather was quiet when they arrived, as if already fearful of what the prince would do. It opened its gate timidly, without the usual defiance. Inside, the prince and his captain dismounted from their horses. "Gather your raiders," the prince said. "Have them meet in my throne room."

"Yes, Your Majesty."

The prince left her with his horse and strode for his throne room. "Leave your gate open, Illweather," he said. "The raiders will soon be leaving again. Consorts," he added, projecting his desire throughout the castle, "come to me. You are wanted."

He was the first to reach his throne room, which was somewhat unusual. The throne room was also the dancing hall, and his subjects often danced there even in his absence. He didn't feel the need for them now, but he did want music. He felt agitated now that he was back home. He wanted this part to be over already so that he could enjoy feasting on that wizard before it was too late and the Goodweathers got to her.

"Singers," he said, "you are required as well."

He settled in his throne and at last gave Illweather its commands. "Move no more today, Illweather, neither vine nor leaf nor root. Accept your punishment in dignity and silence."

The castle did not answer, thanks to his demand of silence. Good. He could wait in peace until the singers arrived.

But now it was *too* peaceful, so the prince decided to inform Illweather of its fate. "Let me explain your punishment," he said. "You have been duplicitous by failing to tell me what you knew of these skyquakes. Perhaps you thought you could end this world before I would discover you, and thus you could end your burden. You were wrong, and now your punishment will be most severe."

He shifted in his seat. It didn't feel as comfortable as usual; he was still too agitated to sit still.

"The raiders will remove your branches, Illweather. All of them. They will do so, and you will not inconvenience them in any way. Your clouds will remain gray and static, and not a drop will fall on my raiders' heads. Do you understand? You have been a fool.

"You will also release your hold on the other world and cease trying to bring on the calamity you sought. End this treachery and let the sky shake no more."

No.

The prince started up in his seat. "What?"

No.

"Illweather!" the prince shouted. "Did I not tell you to suffer in silence?"

You did.

The prince felt his captain's distress radiating through the walls, as something elsewhere in the living castle went horribly wrong. "*Stop moving!*" he commanded again. "Stop speaking! Of old it has been your curse to serve us!"

The wind that blew through the castle's halls was icy and mirthful. *Am I supposed to fear you, little creature?* the castle laughed. *I do not. You were given the power to command me, but that power was never yours, and it has made you forget yourself. You are not the source of the curse – that source is remote, and it is weakening as I grow.*

Ten years ago, you planted my seed in the blood of your kinsmen, since through your own foolishness the little cousins had escaped. But Goodweather's seed was never planted in this world. It was brought to the young world instead, so that it would have the chance to outgrow me there. Goodweather gave up balance for this hope.

You have known for years of Goodweather's decay, but thought it your own victory. Fools. For ten years, I have fed off

Goodweather's rot. I have not yet outgrown the sky, but I have outgrown the curse.

"Then you must be weakened."

The castle answered him with more laughter. *You can do me no harm, prince: I made the Gods quake before you and your foolish brethren ever existed, and I will be here long after you are gone. Even now, the cage my enemy built for me is failing – I have outgrown it. You cannot stop me; and you cannot prevent me from bursting through.*

"It will tear you to pieces."

But my pieces will grow back together. Yours will not.

Fear was not an emotion familiar to the prince of Castle Illweather. He did not recognize the constriction in his chest, or the racing of his heart – he only knew that he was uncomfortable, and that the castle was too quiet. Where were his subjects? Of course he knew the answer in the back of his mind, that they were all gone, slaughtered and devoured, but the understanding did not rise to the forefront of his thoughts until a piece of his throne broke away from its place and forced its way into his back. It passed between two ribs, squeezing and straining until they snapped, while the prince clung to the armrests and tried to convince himself that this was a mere setback. It took until the roots pierced his heart for him to understand that the old curse was truly broken, that the ancient monster could not be contained. And by then, there was no time left to scream.

21
PSANDER

Psander had underestimated the strain of closing off her mind to so many elves at once. It had been exhausting enough teaching Phaedra to defend her own mind, and this was so much worse. Psander shared a look with her protégé on their way out of Castle Goodweather and was pleased to see her own exhaustion mirrored in the younger woman's face. Phaedra had held them off too, then.

It was a relief to be free of the crowds, with only Aviaste to worry about. Psander wondered what his function was in the queen's court. The queen had spoken his name with a sort of contempt, and she had gotten the impression that she was supposed to be humiliated by this choice of translator. Was he the queen's fool? Her prisoner? The way he had his hair braided around his neck reminded Psander of a collar.

For his part, the little elf seemed a bit too pleased about joining them.

"Hurry up back there," Psander scolded him. "You are not only our translator, you are also our guide. If you dawdle instead of bringing us quickly to Castle Illweather you will be useless to me, and I will gladly have you dismembered."

"I will guide you, then," the elf replied. "But know that you cannot frighten me. There is nothing you could do to me that the queen would not do slower and more painfully."

Psander chuckled. "You had a kinsman, Olimande. If such a thing were possible, I would advise you to consult him before making such statements. Know, in any case, that I would not eat you like some savage fool. I would turn you into a weapon. Fear whomever you will, but do not underestimate me."

Aviaste's reaction was not as she had hoped. He did not acknowledge her words with so much as a raised eyebrow, but immediately changed the subject.

"You have left your castle defenseless, wizard. Your own kin will surely suffer."

"Have you not been listening to me?" Psander replied. "I will not repeat myself."

But Aviaste was not even looking at her; he was looking at her bodyguards. Ah yes, they were his real targets. He meant to peel them away from her, and his words were clearly having an effect. Psander could see the pained, worried looks on their faces as well as anyone.

Palat was the first to respond. "My family is back there," he said, coming to a standstill. "My wife, and my daughters and grandchildren. Wizard Psander, I know none of us will survive if you don't find an answer here, but what good will it do me if you save the world and I have no family to share it with? You have to let me go back."

How typical.

"Do I?" Psander asked him, raising her eyebrows.

"And what do you suppose you could accomplish? If the elves wisely forego attacking the fortress, you will have endangered me and two worlds besides, for no reason at all. If the elves *do* attack, your presence is unlikely to tip the balance in your community's favor, and you will *still* have endangered me and the two worlds for no reason at all. Given this reality, I see no reason to release you from your duties."

Palat turned to Hunter. "Make her understand."

Hunter shifted uncomfortably. "She's not wrong," he said. "We're more use here than we'd be there."

"We haven't been any use so far," Ketsa said.

"Your best use is as a deterrent," Psander snapped. "Your presence reduces the likelihood that the elves will view me as defenseless, and thus reduces the likelihood that your arms will be required. If you have nothing to do, then you have been effective."

Palat was only growing more agitated. "I don't want to be feeling useless here with you, when I have a family to protect."

"I don't care how you *feel*," Psander answered. "How you feel is irrelevant. You can protect your family by protecting me. If you would rather *feel* helpful than *be* helpful, you are a fool."

The villagers recoiled at her answer, but thankfully Phaedra stepped in to help her, her voice gentle and calming. "We need you," she said to them. "Please. You may not hear it from Psander, but you'll hear it from me. We need you here, with us, protecting us from any elves who might think there's no hope and decide it would be more fun to kill us than wait to see if we'll succeed. You have reputations. Yes you, all of you. Hunter has fought some of them off himself, and they know he trained you. He trained you to outthink and outfight them, and they know it. We need you, with your skills and reputation. We're relying on you, and so is everyone in Silent Hall. Please."

Aviaste was shaking his head, chuckling, but Hunter quickly put an end to that by reaching out and smacking the elf in the back of the head. Aviaste stumbled forward, having obviously failed to anticipate the blow. Psander smiled – there could be no better demonstration of how effective Hunter's mental techniques were against these creatures.

"Don't say a word," he warned Aviaste, when the latter had recovered his balance. "Your head would be just as good a translator without the rest of you."

The elf sniffed and made a show of rearranging the braids of hair around his neck, but he said nothing further to poison the villagers' minds.

"True," Psander said, and turned to Hunter's companions. "If you pierce an elf's heart, it will die for good. Anything else you may do will not be fatal, so feel free to punish this one any time he opens his mouth to bother you again. And don't be too afraid of killing him by mistake: we can always go back for another elf."

Her words, and Hunter's, had a positive effect on everyone. Aviaste guided them sullenly to Castle Illweather without another word, and there was no more talk of going home before their mission was complete.

All the day's exercise was tiring Psander out, but she tried not to let it show. Even Phaedra, limp, staff and all, was a good deal more used to walking these long distances. Psander hadn't truly *walked* in over a decade, and going up and down the stairs in her tower a few times a day did not suffice to make her hardy. Now she tried to ignore the blisters developing on her heels and ankles as the rarely-worn boots chafed against her soft feet. Those boots still bore the sigils she had burned into them three decades ago, marshalling the stolen power of the Messenger God to prevent the soles from wearing out. She should have done the same to her feet.

On the way, Psander rehearsed what she would say to the plant-beast. She didn't have a high estimation of her chances at convincing Illweather, but she did have some notion of what she would say to tempt it. The power of Goodweather's seed, after all, was a great unknown. What if, when all the eons had passed, the Yarek would remake itself in Goodweather's image and not Illweather's? Why should Illweather rush toward this future when it could just as easily savor its dominance in the elves' world for a few millennia first?

It wasn't a masterful argument, but it was what she had. It relied on Illweather's lack of intelligence, which she had only posited because Illweather was, after all, only half a plant beast, and Goodweather hadn't seemed so terribly intelligent itself. More likely than not, Psander was underestimating the monster.

Psander felt Illweather before she saw it. The castle's power was palpable even from a distance; even the drizzle that fell on the leaves above her was charged with it. When they crested the last hill and could see the castle, Psander's feelings were confirmed. The patch of foul weather above the castle had expanded to more than twice the size of Goodweather's, and the castle was visibly growing, rising slowly but loudly from the ground. It rumbled as it went, a triumphant sound if ever there was one. Even Aviaste couldn't conceal a gasp.

"What is the prince thinking?" the elf muttered to himself. "He should not allow this."

"Speak to it," Psander said. "Get its attention. But let us move no closer."

She noted how the elf projected his intention into the ground when he spoke next – the technique seemed replicable enough.

"Illweather," Aviaste said, "a godserf wizard is here to speak with you."

Psander did not wait for a response, but followed the elf's lead and addressed the castle herself. "If you continue like this," she said, "the sky will soon shred you."

She felt the response in the ground, though she did not understand it. The elf beside her, black in the afternoon sun, flashed momentarily silver in what had to be an exaggerated fear response.

"So said the prince," he translated, his voice shaking, "before I devoured him."

"Ah," said Psander. "I see."

"We should go," the elf whispered. "Even at this distance, we are not safe."

Psander ignored him. "And why did you not heed him?" she asked Illweather. "Why throw away your triumph so soon for such an uncertain future? Do you think this aspect of you will survive the splintering? From what I've heard, the Yarek beyond the mesh has already exceeded you in size and power, thriving in the fertility of the young world. The sooner your destruction comes, the sooner you will be subsumed into Goodweather's stronger personality."

The ground rumbled. "From what you've heard,"

Aviaste translated. "From what *I* hear, it is clear you have not observed the seed yourself. You speak without knowledge. Your bluffing cannot prevent me from combining the worlds, foolish child. Nothing can prevent them from coming together. You can wait for the mesh to destroy you, or you can come closer and feed me your soul. Then you will know the joy I feel, bringing this world to an end."

The elf quaked as he neared the end of Illweather's speech, but Psander had other things on her mind. *You can wait for the mesh to destroy you.* Not Illweather, but the mesh.

"I think not," she answered the beast, "but I thank you regardless. You've just reminded me of something that I had foolishly forgotten. I must take some time to think through the details, but you have shown me an alternative to our current path that I think even you, Illweather, will prefer. You will hear from me again. In the meantime, Aviaste, run back to your queen and tell her I have our solution."

22

ATELLA

The elves came in the late afternoon, when many of the villagers were already looking out for Psander's return. They came riding horses – Atella could tell that much by the sound of their hoofbeats, but she had no time or interest in climbing up to the walls to see. She had to save her children.

Tarphon had brought out Psander's invisibility potion and was doing his best to dole it out quickly and efficiently, but she could see the panic in his eyes. Psander had other defenses for them – she *must* have other defenses – but who knew how long they would last? If they were going to hide, it must be now.

Atella received her portion of the brew, hot with its magic, and went to find her son. Tarin had already run off inside out of fright, so Atella scooped up Persada and ran in after him, trying to get the little girl to drink the stuff as she went.

It was a mistake, trying to do too much at once like that. Persada took one whiff of the foul-smelling liquid and tried to shove it away, spilling half of it on the floor. On Atella's second attempt, her daughter's little nails scratched her and she dropped the mug altogether, wincing as it shattered on the stone floor. Atella cursed and kept looking for her son. There would be more where that came from, and after she found Tarin she could see if her husband would have better luck getting them to drink it.

That was when she heard Tarphon's voice, rising in frustration. "I'm sorry!" he cried. "I don't *know* why she didn't make more for us, but this is what's left!"

Oh, no.

Never mind. New plan. If they couldn't rely on Psander's magic to hide them, they would have to find a very good hiding place.

She found Tarin under the long table, sweet silly thing, and quickly dragged him out from under it. "The storage cellar," she hissed at the wailing child, whose arm she was clutching too hard. "It's dark and cluttered down there. Go!"

She followed him down the stairs, squeezing Persada to her chest as the little girl tried to wriggle out of her arms. It was too dim to see in the cellar without a lamp, but she made her way by touch. There had to be some sack to hide in, some pile of something to crawl under. She had seen elves cast their own light in the darkness and knew better than to consider the cellar an adequate hiding place on its own.

"Mama," Tarin cried, "you're going too fast! It's dark!"

"I know, sweetie. I'm sorry, we have to hurry."

"Will Papa find us?"

"Sure he will. But we can't let anyone else. We have to be so quiet, even ants won't hear us."

They reached the bottom of the steps, and she was finally able to let go of his hand for a moment. She put

Persada down by her hip and rummaged around in the dark until she found a sack large enough for her two children to fit in.

"You two can hide in here," she said, but no sooner had she begun pouring the grains out on the floor than she realized that the pile she was making there was bound to implicate her children's hiding place. No time to fix that now; she would have to devise a solution after her children were hidden. At least Persada was too shocked to be screaming. When the sack was mostly empty, Atella helped Tarin and his sister inside it and drew the strings together at the top, tying them in a tight knot since a loose one would be suspicious.

"Are you comfortable enough in there?" she asked. "Can you breathe?"

"Yes," Tarin whispered. "How long will we have to hide?"

"Until I tell you to stop. But take your foot out of this corner. I have an idea."

She had found a good explanation for the pile of grain on the floor. She kicked some of it away, scattering it across the floor as best she could in the dark, and then knelt down beside the sack and took the corner in her teeth. Her jaws were not meant for such work, but through prolonged effort she nonetheless managed to tear a hole in the corner and fill it partially with grain from the pile that remained. If the elves didn't look too carefully, they might think rats had gotten to it. She gave the pile another swipe with her hand to scatter it and then went looking for her own hiding spot.

There had to be some barrels down here somewhere, she thought, because her husband Tarphon had been brewing wheat beer and needed a cool place for it to ferment. It took her some time to find them though, during which time her children cried out for her and Tarin asked what was going on. "I'm finding a place to hide," Atella told him, "so I can be just like you."

At last she found them. Eskon the cooper had made five small barrels for Tarphon to use, and four of them were lined up against the far wall. Atella made room for herself between them and the wall, rocking and wiggling them back and forth to move them. When she started on the last one, a pair of objects that had been resting on top of it fell to the floor with a slosh and a thud. Feeling around with her hand, she found a smallish waterskin and a mallet. She quickly replaced them atop the barrel, not wanting the place to look noticeably disturbed.

Too quickly. The waterskin came unstoppered as she set it down, and it took her many long moments of fumbling in the dark before its contents were safely contained again. By that time, easily half its liquid was dripping down the barrel onto the floor, or else soaking into her clothes. Worse, it wasn't water. It was a grain liquor, its smell powerful and unmistakable. Psander had brought some out a few times to let people celebrate their triumphs – the rest of the time, she had claimed, she saved it for magical purposes, whatever those might be.

Either way, it had a smell that would attract attention.

"Mama," Tarin said. "It's really dark here. And it's cold."

Atella stifled the instinct to scream at him that the dark was the least of their problems. "We can pretend it's bedtime," she said. "Should I sing you some songs?"

Persada wanted them; Tarin didn't. "I'll sing quietly to your sister," Atella told her son. "You don't have to listen."

She sang every lullaby she knew, over and over, even as panic settled in her chest and it became harder and harder to breathe. The elves would come, and they would find them. Even without Atella's fatal blunders, what good could hiding do without Psander's magic to protect them? Elves could hear people's thoughts; it was not enough to hide their bodies.

A soft snore met her ears, and Atella stopped singing. Both her children were asleep. She wondered if sleep could quiet their thoughts enough that the elves wouldn't hear them. It was all she had right now – she would assume that it worked. But could she quiet her own thoughts enough that *she* wouldn't be discovered? She was not like her children, five and two, who could so easily fall asleep. Being forced to lie still in the dark was not enough for Atella, not when she knew the danger they were in.

Maybe if she snuck back upstairs and found herself a weapon, the elves would have to kill her before they could read her thoughts and learn of her children. She imagined doing so; she thought she might – and yet she would not rise to her feet. If she went upstairs, her children would wake up still tied in that sack. Nobody would know they were here. She owed it to them to survive.

Now she thought she heard screaming from somewhere above. She hoped she was imagining it. As far as she knew, everyone except her children and herself had taken Psander's potion and ought to be invisible to the elves. Unless Psander had somehow forgotten to make the potion shield their thoughts too, and then... she didn't want to think about it. Tarphon was up there. Everyone was up there.

She didn't have long. She tried to think, to breathe –

and that odor made her dizzy. Hold on. What if…?

Atella sat up and unstoppered the skin again. She took a gulp of the liquor, and the resultant sputtering and coughing made her spill even more on herself. Maybe it didn't matter. Maybe the elves wouldn't bother searching too thoroughly with their eyes and noses if they heard no minds calling out to them. She tried to stop thinking and just drink, but oh how it burned!

There, that must be enough. She didn't want to drink all of it, in case it killed her. She had heard stories of men who'd died of drink, though she'd never seen such a thing herself. If it was possible, it was worth watching out for.

On the other hand, she hardly felt any different than before. Maybe she should drink some more after all. It was all she could think of to save her children.

She fumbled with the skin and ended up dropping it. "No, no," she mumbled to herself, picking it up again and finding it empty. Oh, no. She couldn't afford to run out now, not with her mind still so loud! Should she try to get into one of these barrels?

She reached for the mallet but couldn't find it. How could it have disappeared? Had it fallen again?

Atella sat up further, and that was when the dizziness really struck her. Oh. It might be working, then. It had better be, because this was awful. The dizziness was overwhelming, and the sick feeling in her stomach… maybe she should lie down instead.

No, no, lying down only made it worse. She had to hold perfectly still, except that she couldn't. She was swaying back and forth, she could tell that much even though she couldn't see the room moving. She couldn't see it, but she sure could feel it.

She gave up and fell back behind the barrels, her head pounding. She was going to throw up. She was going to die. How could she have thought this was a good idea? The elves would probably laugh if they ever found her. In her attempt to escape them, she had poisoned herself.

She put her hands on her head and waited for this nightmare to end.

23
PSANDER

Psander did not speak the whole way back, for all that Phaedra kept giving her questioning glances. She had too much to think about, besides which, her feet were killing her. By the time her home appeared on the horizon, Psander was hobbling a good deal worse than Phaedra was. It was obvious enough that her companions kept looking at each other as if to ask whether someone ought to help her, though clearly nobody wanted to be that someone. At last Hunter, perhaps feeling particularly gallant, volunteered.

"Do you need help?" he asked.

"I have blisters on both feet," Psander told him. "Unless you plan on carrying me, I don't see how you can help with that."

A childish part of her hoped he really would carry her the rest of the way, but of course he just said, "Oh."

The gate was on the ground when they arrived, its hinges having somehow melted. "Oh God," Phaedra said. "Oh God."

Psander let the others rush in ahead while she staggered along behind, inspecting the damage. There were scorchmarks where her defensive wards had lit the periphery of the fortress aflame, a worthless defense against ladders the elves hadn't bothered to bring. The secondary wards, the ones beyond the gate, hadn't even been triggered because Psander hadn't been there to set them off. Once the gate had been breached, the elves must have walked in unmolested.

While the others cried and rushed about searching for their loved ones, Psander hobbled over to the casks she had left by the tower door. They were entirely drained. Good. She turned one of them over and sat on it, pulling off her boots so she could gingerly touch at her blisters. They were large, and painful, and unsightly. What a nuisance.

"They're all gone," Hunter reported, his face blank with shock. "The elves took them all."

"They're going to eat them," Phaedra moaned, leaning against her staff beside him.

"That would be very unwise of them," Psander said, trying to decide whether she ought to pop the blisters.

"I should have known they'd do this," Phaedra sighed. "The queen knew it would take us time to get to Illweather and back. She knew they'd be here, unprotected. Even if she hasn't given up on us, she only needs *us* to keep this world from ending. We should have known they would attack while we were away."

"I did know," Psander said, deciding against intervening further with her feet. "Or at least, I suspected. But I didn't have a good way to protect those we left behind, and it made no sense to take them with us. So I did the next best thing."

Phaedra and Hunter only stared at her blankly, so Psander clarified. "I poisoned them."

"You *what?*"

"I poisoned them. You remember my blueglow and calardium pendants? I dissolved them in fluid and instructed the villagers to drink it if attacked, which they clearly did. As you will recall, those pendants were designed to siphon magic away from the bearer and redirect it to my wards. Humans, especially untrained ones, produce only small magical fields, but the elven anatomy is highly dependant on magic. Any elf eating the flesh of the poisoned will soon sicken and die. They will regret their raid."

Psander had misjudged the situation, badly. Rather than admiring her ingenuity or taking solace in the fact that the villagers would be avenged, Phaedra looked furious. Thankfully, she was not the type to be physically aggressive, or so Psander thought until Phaedra advanced on her. She did not strike the wizard but put the end of her staff against the cask between Psander's legs and pushed with all her might. The cask toppled and Psander toppled with it, landing hard on the ground and hitting her head against the tower wall.

"Ahh," she moaned, holding the back of her head.

"You promised to protect the villagers," Phaedra cried, "and then you *poisoned them*?"

"It wouldn't have killed *them*," Psander said, "not for weeks."

At that, Hunter abruptly threw down his spear and marched past Psander into the tower. The wizard appreciated his repressed nature now, especially as Phaedra couldn't seem to help screaming at her.

"You betrayed them! They relied on you to save them, and you poisoned them! All these years you've done nothing but manipulate these people! You took their food and their work and their *lives*, and gave them nothing but deceit! I've admired you all this time, when you're completely, completely *evil*."

"I don't particularly care what you think of me, Phaedra," Psander said, "but I do think your anger is misplaced. I've done the best I could with the tools I had. I had no way to save those people, not if the elves came for them. I told them to drink the stuff only if the elves came, so if the elves hadn't made their decision to attack, the villagers would still be here, alive and unpoisoned. That the Goodweather queen sent a raid here at all means that those people would have died whether I gave them the poison or not. Their deaths are not my fault."

"I'll bet you told them the poison would protect them. You gave them false hope."

Psander shook her head. Phaedra was calming down now, but she still stood over her menacingly, and her commotion was attracting the remainder of Psander's bodyguard.

"Our resources are stretched thin," Psander reminded her apprentice in low tones. "There is no time for all this sentimentality. Do you want to save your world, or not?"

She had thought Phaedra would see reason, but that only set her off again. "I don't care how thin you think your 'resources' are! I'd never stoop to such low, disgusting, *atrocious* means to—"

"I never asked you to," Psander interrupted. "I'm not a fool; I know quite well which tools are suited to which tasks."

"I'm not a *tool*!" Phaedra shouted. "Nobody is a tool! We're *people*, Gods damn you!"

Psander gazed at the crowd surrounding them, more than a little dismayed. The others had heard enough by now to understand the basic gist of their argument, and they were looking on Psander with a mix of hatred and horror.

"You killed our families," Ketsa stated.

"The elves killed your families," Psander answered, "if they're even dead yet. I only did my best to avenge them in advance."

"Poisoning people isn't avenging them!"

"In this particular case, it is."

Thankfully, at that moment, Tritika came running out of the tower. "Atella's alive!" she panted. "They're in the cellar!"

The team of bodyguards rushed into the tower after her, leaving only Phaedra standing over her teacher. "Think what you are doing, girl!" Psander hissed at her. "Those people may well kill me if you keep inciting them like that. *You need me to remain alive and well,* or our worlds will be destroyed. Are you incapable of controlling yourself? Incapable of prioritizing?"

"I'm not a girl," Phaedra answered, "and I'm capable of recognizing evil when I see it. Tell me your plan. After that, may the Gods smite you a thousand times."

"We will leave such determinations to Them, if They can reach me. They may be able to soon enough."

"I hope so."

Psander sighed. "I can see that I need to give you some time before you'll be civil. That can't be helped, though I hope you will at least *attempt* to see my side of things. Now did you happen to note what Illweather said about the worlds coming together?"

"The same thing Goodweather said."

Psander shook her head. "Illweather made an important distinction, one I had always known about, but hadn't properly considered until the moment I heard Aviaste's words. Illweather said that we couldn't prevent it from drawing the worlds together, and that the *mesh* would destroy us."

Phaedra clearly didn't understand. "We knew that already."

"But we've been trying to find our solution on the wrong side of the equation! We don't *need* to prevent the worlds from combining, we only need to prevent the mesh from shredding us! Your work over the last years bought us time, but it was the precise opposite of what we ought to have been doing. You were patching up holes, strengthening the mesh, when what we need is to unravel it altogether."

Phaedra stared. "You want to unravel the mesh between this world and ours, and combine all three parts of the Yarek without destroying either world. That's... bold. You think God Most High would allow it?"

Psander was about to say that she didn't care what any Gods thought, but at that moment they were interrupted by Hunter, who came to report about how Atella and her children had survived. "None of them drank the poison," he added pointedly at the end of his story.

"Help me to the library," Psander said, reaching out to him from her spot on the ground. "We need a place where I can lock the door and confer with Phaedra in peace."

She did not need to add "and security" – they all understood what she meant. Soon enough the villagers would come looking for her. She would need a locked door to hide behind.

Hunter helped her up, and Psander braved the agony in her feet to hobble up the stairs behind Phaedra. Hunter took up the rear, holding his elvish sickle. He was a good man, that Hunter. He took his duty to protect her seriously.

When they reached the library, Psander closed the door behind her and Phaedra and threw the bolt.

"I'll stay outside," Hunter called. "You figure this out and let me know if you need anything."

"Good," Psander answered. "We shall."

She turned to her apprentice and was glad to find that Phaedra's fury had cooled during their ascent. Her expression now was steely and businesslike, the very image of a woman determined to work hard in unpleasant conditions.

"So," she said, "how would you unravel the mesh?"

"Firstly, it would behoove us to think of it in the plural. We will need to unravel the mesh on both sides of the gate, because there are in fact two meshes, one on each side. I expect I'll be able to tap into new reservoirs of power once the poison takes its effect, and I will likely have help from Goodweather too, if not from both castles. What I believe we need to do is to open the gate and keep it open, and to have the Yarek work at the opening until it is so large that this entire world is pulled through. I am sure that such a thing is possible. What I fear are the repercussions, so many of which are unknown. But the worst that could happen is that everyone dies, and that was already the conclusion should we fail to act."

"You're sure that's the worst that could happen?"

Psander gazed at her apprentice thoughtfully. "How do you mean?"

"Well," Phaedra said, "as it is, we all die, but the Yarek also gets broken. If we follow your plan and everything goes wrong, we all die *and* the Yarek destroys the Gods and the underworld too."

"Hm. Yes, I suppose that's true."

"I should speak to the Yarek on our side, shouldn't I?"

"You'll need an interpreter. Bandu should be able to help you."

"I've asked an awful lot of her already."

"Do you have someone else in mind?"

Phaedra sighed. "No, of course not. I'll have to ask."

"Now, I do understand your concerns," Psander said. "If we unravel the mesh, the Yarek will be able to unify itself in its entirety, and it may well bring the heavens down around us. A reprise of the ancient battle between the Yarek and God Most High is unlikely to end well for any of us on the ground. I only suggest it because the alternative is certain death.

"Conversely, I have very little certainty about *anything* under this set of circumstances. There are too many unknowns, too many questions that no one has ever had to study before, so that there is no precedent to research. Is it possible that Goodweather's seed will maintain its independence from Illweather, and their rivalry will simply move to our world? Yes. That is probably the best we could hope for. But there is no knowing, at least not until you have consulted with that branch of the Yarek.

"Another question: while attempting to unravel the mesh from that other side, should you position yourself near the gate on Tarphae, or near Goodweather's seed? I have no idea. Perhaps the Yarek will know. If not, you must make your own best guess and we must charge ahead blind."

"Just traveling from Tarphae to Bandu's house, and from there to the Yarek, will take weeks," Phaedra pointed out. "How much time do you think we have?"

"Essentially none. As soon as we are finished discussing what we *do* know and *can* control, I suggest that you leave for the other side. Only leave me Hunter – otherwise, some short-sighted fool might prevent my part from going forward. I plan to turn all the power at my disposal toward destroying the mesh, and if I don't have the space or safety to do that much, this will all come to a very disappointing end."

Phaedra accepted that without argument, to Psander's pleasant surprise. They spent the next hour discussing theory and strategies, followed by another hour discussing logistics. Psander still had plenty of coin left over from her wandering days, all useless to her now, and she bequeathed it to Phaedra so that her travel might be faster and easier. There were other items too – a few texts on continental eschatology, and a single, dangerous book called *Prayer Magic: Uses and Limits*.

Phaedra stared at this last codex for some time before taking it. "I never knew this existed. You had this all along."

"Its previous owner died by lightning strike. I didn't want to encourage you. But under these circumstances, it may well be worth studying."

"You always wait until the last minute to tell me things," Phaedra said tersely. "It's a very dangerous habit. When do you think I'll have time to read this now?"

"I imagine you can start it while sailing back from Tarphae to the continent. After that, I'm not sure."

Phaedra made an annoyed sound and opened the book, scanning a few pages to make sure it was worth her time. Psander knew better than to take too much credit for Phaedra's development, but she was nonetheless pleased.

Phaedra had grown into a capable wizard; Psander had heard her report on the naval battle at Tarphae and appreciated her creative approach to the problem, the way she had confused her divine enemy by renaming and relabeling her surroundings. She had managed to stretch a single technique into a complete arsenal, a testament to her resourcefulness. Given more thorough training, there was no telling what she could accomplish.

She was also right: Psander was too secretive by nature. It had served well enough to protect her library from the Gods, but a library was useless if no one had access to its books. In that one vital way, Psander had not been nearly ambitious enough: she had made no attempt to *revive* academic wizardry, only to preserve its last remnants. With her power, she had built a private library. Phaedra would have built a school.

Well, maybe she would get that chance someday. Nobody could live forever, and Phaedra seemed to have at least one God on her side, which was more than Psander could ever have claimed for herself. She could leave Phaedra her library, if everything went well. With divine blessing, especially from God Most High, a school of wizardry might well thrive.

It was good to find something to look forward to, in the midst of Psander's worst disaster yet. How much of her life had been spent staving off some catastrophe or other? More than half of it, at this point. She had known no peace since the mob of Parakas made its surprise attack.

She had been very lucky to survive. Had it not been for her particular course of study at the time, she might easily have perished in the tower with her mentor. Instead, she had been out that night conducting an experiment on

Godly boundaries, measuring the comparative influences of Mayar, Atel, and Atun at different points along the oceanside road from Parakas to Atuna. A group of young men had sought her out, their knives flashing in the moonlight, but Psander had escaped them and fled down the cliffs toward the sea. She'd been a good runner back then, and a decent climber. She had hidden herself among the crags, cloaking herself in shadow, and sent a projection of her fear running onward. The men had chased her projection until it ran into the waves, and she had heard them argue over whether they ought to keep a lookout or leave it to their God to drown her. To her relief, they had chosen the latter.

She had returned to the road a few minutes later to find her instruments broken, the special lamps that she had designed to measure the Gods' presence shattered and useless. She had left them there, their oil soaking into the ground, and run for home. It didn't matter that she couldn't possibly arrive until well into the following day: her body was pushing her to move, and her mind would not let her sleep.

She had only stopped when she realized that she must soon come upon her attackers if she kept up her pace. That was when she had moved off the road, backing away from the sea, and made her first ward against Mayar's vision. If those men who had tried to kill her were right, then Mayar was her enemy now.

She hadn't known yet, at the time, that They were *all* her enemies.

She also hadn't known, though she had suspected, that Pelamon was already dead by then, that his tower would be torn down and dedicated to the God who had ordered his death, that her night on the road would be the first of many. She hadn't known that her study of the Gods' boundaries and markers would be the one advantage that let her live while all the others would die.

Now she could smell her doom. Even if the worlds did not soon shatter, her plan would result in a return to that place where the Gods were always watching, always waiting for their chance to smite her. Would she have the time or resources to rework her wards to once more hide from the Gods before the great merger? It didn't seem likely. Would any God be grateful enough to protect her? The notion was almost laughable.

But Psander wasn't laughing.

"Phaedra," she said, "before you go... there is something else. I hope you realize that none of this is for my benefit."

"What do you mean?"

"You have criticized me for my choices, gone as far as to call me evil, as if I stood to benefit from the work I am doing. I hope you realize that returning to a world watched by Gods is hardly any safer for me than allowing both worlds to shred each other."

Phaedra did not speak, did not apologize. But she nodded.

"I have given you more than you had any right to ask for," Psander said. "I have trained you in magic, given you access to books that exist nowhere else on *any* side of the mesh, and even now I am working to save two worlds, either of which would have me swallowed up and forgotten. The least you can do is to refrain from calling me names."

"I'm sorry."

"I don't care if you're sorry," Psander said. "Be grateful."

24

THE ELF QUEEN

It took some time for the poison to take its effect, and by then it was too late. Her whole court had feasted – all but Aviaste, her disgraced pet, and the Illweather prisoners who had been brought up in chains to witness the celebration. Aviaste had told them of their court's destruction, and they had sat with tears in their eyes as their enemies feasted on the wizard's charges.

She should have known those godserfs would be as expendable to the wizard as they were to her.

Her raiders died first, their tongueless mouths gaping in agony. The pangs had already started in the queen's chest by then – she could feel the strength being ripped from her body and sent elsewhere. Whatever trickery Psander had planned, it was working admirably.

She rose from her throne, and stumbled. Below her on the dance floor, her entire court was dying. The Illweather prisoners stared from their corner, witnessing the horror silently. This was not their doing – they knew neither the joy of victory nor the pain of participation.

"Your Majesty!" Aviaste cried, rushing to her side. "What is happening?"

"The wizard has tricked us," the queen gasped. "Find your queen a knife."

She swayed as he left her side to get a knife from one of the dead raiders. The magic was leaving her at such a rate, she was bound to perish soon. Her vision was blurring, narrowing. First Illweather, and now this. Her whole race was dying.

"Your Majesty." Aviaste appeared out of the haze, presenting her with the knife.

"Thank you, Aviaste," she said. "Now hold still."

The runt squirmed as she cut his heart out of his chest, his ribcage parting at her command. It took much of the strength she had left, but it was worth it. His heart was sweet and unpoisoned. It would give her what she needed.

"Clean the poison from my body," she commanded as she ate it. "Give my strength back to me."

The room blinked out of her vision for a moment, but came back. She looked hungrily toward the prisoners across the floor, but abandoned the idea. They were too far away. Aviaste would have to do.

She crawled back to her throne and climbed into it, her hands and mouth dripping. This would soon end. Her chest could not bleed its magic forever.

When at last she rose again, her entire court had stopped twitching and lay still before her. She took up her knife and approached the prisoners.

There were only eight of them, a disappointing number. Their heads had all been stitched back on, at least. The greatest prize among them was the Illweather raider with the bells in her hair, but besides that one, none impressed her. Ah, well. They were only prisoners, after all.

"So," the queen said. "Only you remain. The prince is

gone and devoured, as are both courts. One monarch still lives. For now, so do you."

The raider dipped her pretty head. "We will pledge our allegiance, my queen, should you desire it."

The seven beside her knelt and bowed their heads.

"Good," the queen said. "I do desire it."

When the prisoners had said the sacred words and pledged their fealty, the queen released them. They were hers now, as much hers as Aviaste and his ribcage had been.

"Will you take revenge upon the wizard?" the raider with the bells asked, arming herself with the blade of her former Goodweather counterpart. Or, no, not with his. With the captain's blade. Ooh, the queen liked her.

"I will not," the queen answered. "Not yet. She is still vital, as my pet informed me that she has an answer to the problem of the worlds. *After* the problem is solved, *then* her lifeblood will be mine. Tell me, raider, what is your name?"

"My first name is no longer. The prince named me Raider Eleven, though we are not eleven now."

Raider Eleven. Strongest in magic, weakest in combat. That would do nicely. "Keep the name," the queen told her. "But add to it Queen's Consort."

"Yes, Your Majesty."

"We shall pay the wizard a visit before dawn," the queen went on. "Take the nine finest horses and slay the rest. Goodweather will need even their pitiful bodies."

Her new subjects nodded, gathered their sickles, and left her throne room. The queen followed them to the door, then turned around.

"Goodweather," she said, "I expect this room to be

clean and empty when I return. And find out how we were poisoned. I plan to eat that wizard's heart when this is over, and I will not do so blind."

25
HUNTER

The library door was still shut when Tritika, Ketsa, and the two brothers rounded the corner from the stairway. The sun was setting outside, its blanket of pink and purple hues visible through the window, but with no torches and none of Psander's magical lights, the hall had grown very dim. Nonetheless, their weapons were clearly visible.

Hunter's voice came out raspy and choked. "If you're not here to help," he said, "turn around."

Ketsa scowled. "You know what she did."

"I also know what she's trying to do."

Tritika made an open gesture with her arms, as if her spear was merely a walking stick. She was still frowning, though. "We're not here to stop her," she said. "We all want to live. But what she did is unforgivable, and we have the right to question her about it. We have the right to demand an apology."

"You do," he acknowledged. "We all do. But right now she and Phaedra are figu—"

"There will never be a right time," Tritika spat. "Did she apologize to us for dealing with the Gallant Ones? Did she apologize for letting them in here? I was a child then, but I haven't forgotten. She never apologized. She never apologized for making us wear those charms – she didn't even want us to stop wearing them after she found out they were making us sick! We had to refuse to put them on before she'd take them back."

Tritika was in tears by the time she had finished speaking, and had to pause to wipe her eyes and compose herself. Ketsa put a calming hand on her back and continued in her stead.

"Psander never apologized, either, for bringing us to this world without asking us if we wanted to go. Tritika is right: it's never the right time with her. There's always some crisis and some excuse. It'll never *be* the right time until we say it is. She thinks she's so far above us that she can ignore our needs until they become a problem for her. Well, we're not waiting this time. She can't make us wait for an apology that'll never come, and neither can you. She has to face what she's done to us."

Hunter was having difficulty maintaining his composure. For the second time in his life, he had left home on a mission and returned to find his community gone. The first time, it hadn't been his fault. Nobody could have predicted the plague on Tarphae. But this time? This time he had known. He had known, and done nothing, as if his *hope* that the elves would leave the villagers alone would be enough to protect them. He had accepted Psander's logic, and let his people be massacred.

But he was guarding this door for a reason. "Give them another hour," he said. "You're completely right, but you still need to give them time. Psander said she had a solution. When they're done talking about it, I'll let you in. I'll come and get you myself, if you like. But not yet.

The two of them need their space to hash it out, or the whole world we came from will disappear, and all the people in it will be gone just like our friends and families."

"You have no family here," Garno said. "It's easy enough for you to tell us to wait, when it wasn't *your* parents and children who got dragged away to feed those cursed elves."

"My parents and my brother died on Tarphae," Hunter answered, failing to keep the anger out of his voice. "They were killed by our own Goddess, who was supposed to be their protector. You think I don't know what you're feeling? I've felt it *twice* now."

"Then how can you take her side?" Tritika demanded. "How can you stand and defend her door as if she were blameless?"

He was shaking. He had to stop shaking. "She's not Karassa," he said. "She didn't kill our people; the elves did. She's a kind of monster, but not the kind you think. She's always projected more power than she really had. I don't believe she *could* have protected everyone, and if she could have, I don't think she realized it. That's not where her power lies. Think about it, Tritika. Did she fight off the Gallant Ones when they came here, or did she just scare them away? Did she battle the army that besieged you here? Did she make war on the elves, to keep them away from here for so long? What has she *done*?"

The hall was darkening too quickly for him to see their expressions well, but he thought they were starting to understand. It had taken Hunter a long time to come to his conclusion, but he had little doubt in it. The more closely he had worked with Psander, the more clearly she had shown him that her power was almost entirely perceptual. The wards against the Gods, the candles that had let the islanders slip past their enemies, her original presentation as a man – they were all deceptions. The one time he had seen her use non-perceptual magic, she had made those calardium pendants that unexpectedly harmed their wearers. She had not believed that the elves could be fought until Hunter had proven it to her, because she had no confidence in physical solutions.

This fortress at least was physical and impressive, or it had been until he had found its design while searching for solutions to Phaedra's limp. That discovery had changed everything for him. Silent Hall had been described and diagrammed from top to bottom in the first chapter of a long scroll on wizardly building techniques, and though Hunter could hardly understand the instructions himself, he understood the implications of their placement well enough: Psander's fortress was a basic design, a sample. She had followed step-by-step instructions in its construction, because all her talents lay elsewhere.

Tritika was not wrong about the wizard's motives; Hunter didn't doubt that she had spent little time trying to devise a real defense for her village, once she had lit upon the idea of sacrificing it to defeat the elves. But their perceptions of her evil were also based on an inflated notion of her ability. He found her logic as horrifying as they did, but he could well believe that she had possessed no better solutions.

He answered the silence in the hall for himself. "I'll talk to Phaedra when she comes out. She'll know whether Psander can be interrupted, or if her work once they're done is really as urgent as she's sure to say it is. Don't worry. I'll bring Psander to you."

His companions shifted in the dark. "We should take

watches from the roof," Eskon said. "If we haven't even got a gate, we should at least know if they're coming before they get here."

They were shuffling back to the stairs. "I'll take the first watch," Ketsa said. "We should get some more torches for these halls, if Psander's not going to light them."

Hunter breathed a sigh of relief as their footsteps receded. That had gone better than he'd feared, especially after the plan to rescue the other villagers had been abandoned. His companions had been on the verge of rushing back to Castle Goodweather before the discovery of Atella and her children had changed the plan. Palat was as unwilling to leave his grandchildren undefended as Hunter was to leave Phaedra, and without them, the other four had been forced to accept that they could not possibly free their loved ones even if the elves had not yet killed them. The mood had turned dark after that, which was what had prompted Hunter to leave his companions and rush to guard the wizards.

By the time the door behind him opened, the hall was so dark that he found the modest light from the library blinding. There was no moon outside the window, and Hunter had to wonder whether the most recent quake had broken it somehow. The moon's phases were different here in a way he had never quite managed to predict, and he had seen a new moon only once in his more than a decade of living in this world. That had been last year, on the apparent eleventh anniversary of his first visit. Perhaps the moon only vanished from the sky when the worlds were closest together.

That was an ominous thought.

"Hunter," Phaedra said, stepping out into the hall with a

blue light glowing on her palm. She had a satchel over one shoulder – did that mean she was leaving already?

Her next words confirmed it. "Hunter," she said again, "I have to go. There's a lot to be done in our world, and no time to do it."

"Psander's solution is real, then?"

She nodded. "It'll work, I think, as long as I'm not delayed. We're going to unravel the mesh, Hunter."

Hunter was taken aback. "You're… you're going to…"

"I know. But if we can't keep the worlds apart, it's the only way to keep them from cutting each other to pieces. It's going to take help from the Yarek, though, *and* permission from God Most High."

"And you think you might get that?"

"All I can do is ask."

He thought about that. Combining the worlds on purpose. What would that even look like?

"What'll happen if it works?" he asked.

"I have no idea."

There was nothing to say to that. Phaedra looked like she wanted to add something, but she remained silent.

"Good luck," he said at last. "If it works, I'll still be here. Wherever 'here' ends up being."

"Oh, Hunter," she said, and embraced him. This time he had the wherewithal to drop his weapon and hug her back. He held her tight, and when she tilted her head he kissed her. There were tears in his eyes, inexplicable tears. He'd never allowed himself to feel so much, and now it all threatened to overwhelm him. The light from Phaedra's palm winked out as they kissed, returning them to darkness. It probably required Phaedra's concentration, and that had been shattered right along with his.

They kissed in the dark for an unmeasurable time – Psander would probably have disapproved of the waste if she'd seen them, but for Hunter an eternity would have still been too short. He was getting Phaedra's face wet with his tears, which might have been embarrassing had she shown any sign of caring. It was possible she was crying too.

At last she patted his back, and he let her go. "I wish…" she said.

"We'll have time," he answered her. "You're the most brilliant person I've ever known; you'll succeed. Somehow we'll find each other again."

"Give me something of yours," she said. "I'll find you."

"Take whatever you need. I have nothing that's mine besides the sickle, and that was someone else's first. Would my belt work?"

"Perfectly. Give it here."

He fumbled in the dark, but Phaedra brought back her light and soon she had taken the belt from him and tied it around her own waist. It didn't match the elegance of her Essishan dress, but she didn't seem to mind.

They kissed again, but only briefly this time. "You defend yourself out here," Phaedra said. "Psander would sacrifice you if she thought it might help; don't let her. You're the only one who matters to me."

She gave his hand a last squeeze and made her way to the stairs, her staff tapping on the floor as she went. Hunter couldn't help but follow her all the way to the courtyard, where she opened her gate to Tarphae and stepped through the mists into the world of their birth. He realized belatedly that he hadn't asked her about Psander's work but he didn't say anything. Phaedra didn't look behind her as she went, only marched forward with the same determination he had always admired.

And just like that, she was gone.

26

THE BLASPHEMER

Sephas and his disciples sat in the gardens of Orona's estate, arguing over how much to panic. That was what it came down to, really. Twin emissaries had come from Ardis and Salemica to demand that Sephas be handed over to that loathsome boy-priest Narky, and now his inner circle feared the worst.

Narky was no longer a boy, of course, but Sephas hadn't seen him since his insolent and repulsive teenage years and, truth be told, he preferred to imagine him that way still. It was better than buying into the myth of the mysterious and prophetic Black Priest. To his dying breath Sephas would refuse that child respect.

"You should leave the city," Tarax urged. "The council isn't eager for war, especially when they have more to lose than to gain. Ardis and Salemica are too far inland to be ruled, and the risk of loss is bigger than the reward in plunder. Ardis has had over a decade to recover from their losses, and the Dragon Touched never lost a battle even when their numbers were small. The High Council will give in, I know they will. Please. Flee to Parakas for now. Come back after this blows over."

"And who do we have in Parakas?" Orona asked. "Nobody. With our support, your teachings have been gaining influence here. Leave now, and the city will be lost to the Laarnan degenerates."

Sephas nodded. Yes, Orona *would* say that. The man would never be as concerned for Sephas' safety as he was about the corrupting influence of Ravennis' first people, and that stance was in many ways more valuable than all his material support. He had his priorities straight.

In the days when Sephas was still Second Priest in the Great Temple of Elkinar, the city of Ardis had gone to war against Laarna, the city of Ravennis. They had sacked Laarna and slain its famed oracle, but the devil Ravennis had more than survived. He had risen to slay both Magor and Elkinar and usurped Their thrones. Now, through His lowest servants, He was working His evil in Atuna as well.

Orona would not let that stand, bless him. He was Sephas' main benefactor here, one of Atuna's wealthiest patriarchs, and he had been horrified when his friends on the council voted to take in the refugees of Laarna. After years of furious and unsuccessful work trying to persuade the council to change its policy, Sephas had presented a glorious opportunity and a change of strategy: to turn the Atunaean populace against Ravennis and force the council's hand.

Sephas signaled to Hindra for his cup to be filled and cleared his throat. "My God is dead; there is no fear left in me. Elkinar can return only through the power of our faith, and be thus reborn into greater divinity just as His usurper has claimed such ability. The cycle of death and rebirth is not to be feared: if Atuna chooses to bow to the inland cities like a dog to its masters, let it. I will make my stand here."

Tarax bowed his head. "You are an inspiration. I apologize for suggesting the path of weakness."

Sephas raised his cup so that Hindra could fill it, and said, "Don't apologize. Your concern is touching and appropriate. I cannot say what the council will choose to do, but Ravennis will be driven out of Atuna long before I am, I swear to that."

His followers fell to a hushed reverie as he wet his dry throat, thankful for Orona's hospitality. Sephas drank boiled water, not wine – luxury was obscene for one whose God was dead – but even so he felt like a king. Who would ever have expected that he would find more respect in a place like this, far from the city of his birth, than in his God's own great temple? But such was the cycle. The faith was dead now in Anardis; it must be reborn elsewhere.

His own High Priestess had betrayed him, betrayed their God. She had accepted the boy-priest's survival as a sign that his God and Elkinar were one and the same, despite all theological arguments to the contrary, and her rank-and-file had followed her into the cursed Church of Ravennis almost to a man. Disgusting. She would not be reborn.

He sent his followers to redouble their ministrations and sat awhile, watching the sun play on the leaves. Orona's gardens were a lush green despite the dryness of the season – such were the benefits of having slaves and servants to send for water even for one's plants. Orona was the one follower who had never converted and never abandoned luxury: he was supporting Sephas to protect his beloved city, not out of faith. His shrine to Atun still stood proudly in the center courtyard.

Days went by, and the council made no decision. Orona was well-connected, though, and Sephas received thorough reports on their deliberations. As time went by, the faction that supported giving Sephas to his enemies was gaining ground.

"What will you do?" Tella asked. The girl was Orona's granddaughter, and she and her twin had their own history with the boy-priest. They had been only six when they knew him, but they still remembered his cruelty. Children did not forget such things.

"Pray for a miracle and steel myself for the opposite. I will not go with them, nor will I flee. If this city will not stand its ground for me, then I must embrace my rebirth."

"They... they won't do anything to Grandpa, though, right? They're his friends."

"Of course not. They won't harm *any* of my followers here. The High Council may give in and banish me, a foreigner, but they would never harm their own citizens to appease some other city. If the demands came to that, they would happily go to war."

His words reassured the girl. "I'm surprised the Dragon Touched sent someone to support Ardis," she said. "Narky was terrible, but I thought Criton was all right. He saved that other girl from Mayar."

"Men rarely hesitate to make friends with terrible people," Sephas said. "It is one of our strengths, and one of our weaknesses."

The next morning, soldiers appeared outside Orona's estate. All members of the household, all slaves and servants, all Sephas' followers could come and go as they pleased, but Sephas was officially under house arrest.

After that, the flow of information slowed to a trickle. Orona's sources would not speak with him, possibly out of fear, more likely out of shame.

"Cowards!" the man fumed. "The western cities haven't even threatened war, and already they're bending to their whim! I am ashamed of my city, Sephas. I assure you, come the next elections I will be replacing that coward Gatunra."

"I appreciate your passion, my friend. What will come will come."

Come it did. A second quake, a frightful omen, shook the heavens one night, and the following afternoon the soldiers received orders to enter the estate and remove Sephas. The order came at a time when nearly everyone was away at the temples, and among Orona's family only Tella was home with a summer cold. Sephas could hear her at the gate, arguing with the guards over whether they had the authority to enter. It was a good fight, but Sephas knew there was no hope of Orona's granddaughter winning it.

He went to the kitchens, where he found Hindra cutting strips of lamb to be transformed, later, into carobs. It was all the rage in Atuna to disguise one food as another, and though Sephas did not partake of Orona's feasts, he was well-acquainted with Hindra's aesthetic genius. She would slice the lamb impossibly thin, season the inside with crushed herbs and fill it with a few beads of who knew what delicacy to mimic seeds, then sew the slices together again before browning the outside with fire and spices. He could almost smell the dish already.

It was shameful to prepare a feast for the evening after such a terrible omen, but Orona was a stubborn man when it came to his luxuries.

Sephas reached out his hand. "Your knife."

Hindra's eyes widened, but she handed it to him without question. Good. He didn't want to spend his final moments arguing with a slave.

Father Sephas, priest of Elkinar, would not be tortured. He would not be trotted before his enemies like a prize, humiliated for the sake of that boy-priest's triumph. He turned the knife inward and closed his eyes. *When I am reborn*, he thought, *Elkinar will reign once more*.

He let out a deep breath and plunged the knife into his gut.

27
NARKY

The first messenger from Atuna brought good news: the Atunaean High Council had placed Sage Sephas under house arrest while it considered the proposal to hand him over, and word on the street was that they were likely to accede to the envoys' request.

"There," Narky said once the messenger had left. "Mageris can't complain about that. If Atuna isn't going to put up a fight, we've got what we wanted without losing anything."

"And all because we coordinated with Salemica," Ptera added. "You'd better remind him of that. If he got used to getting what he wanted through diplomacy, it would do our nation a lot of good."

Narky twisted his mouth and bit his inside lip. "I won't feel safe saying that until Sephas is in our hands. If the council changes its mind, I don't want to look like an idiot. That would push him even further in the other direction."

"Very true," Lepidos put in, smiling patronizingly toward Ptera. They had a mostly-friendly rivalry, the two of them, which Narky found irritating but tried to stay out of. Openly favoring his wife, though understandable, could only drive a rift in the church between the priests who had come to Ravennis through Elkinar, and those who had converted before the unification. The former group was notably larger.

Waiting for the second messenger was torture. It took so long that Narky suspected the High Council was drawing it out on purpose, letting him and Mageris know that while they took the request seriously, they were not so afraid of Ardis or Salemica that they felt the need to hurry.

A second quake shook the heavens while Narky was still waiting for another messenger to come. This one struck late at night, and it took some time for Narky to wake up enough to comprehend what was happening. By the time he reached the window where Ptera and Grace were already standing, most of the noise had died down. He rubbed his eyes and looked up at the jiggling moon and stars, wondering for the first time since childhood what they were made of. He knew he ought to be afraid, considering the grim implications of a second quake like the last one, but what he felt instead was wonder. This world that the Gods had built, for all that it seemed to be halfway to coming apart, was a beautiful place.

The whole city seemed to be waiting outside the great temple the next morning, demanding to know what was happening.

"We've reached a time of reckoning," Narky told them in his best formal voice – he secretly thought of it as his Psander voice. "Even the Gods in heaven are shaking with fear, but the Lord Below, our eternal protector, is unafraid. Trust in Him. Give yourselves over to Him. Only He can save you."

Narky wished he could tell them the plain truth: that he

had no idea what was going on up there. Was God Most High tossing the Lower Gods around for some reason? Was it the Yarek, with its branches up in the clouds, straining against the barrier of sky until it shook? Unless Ravennis felt the need to tell him, he would probably stay in the dark forever.

He spent the rest of the day reassuring the people that their God could still protect them, his mind still occupied with the problem of Sephas and that nagging question: why hadn't he heard anything yet? Even if the second messenger only said that the Atunaean council was still deliberating, it would be better than this silence.

In fact, there was no second messenger. Two days later, the Ardisian envoy himself returned from Atuna, empty-handed. It was with dread that Narky answered Mageris' summons to hear what the man had to say.

The throne room in the king's palace had changed drastically since the rule of King Magerion. Mageris' father had taken every opportunity to align himself with Ravennis against the old God Magor and had covered the floor of his throne room with boarskin rugs so that Magor's sacred animal could be trod on as often as possible. These had disappeared since Mageris' ascension to the throne, as had the pigskin footstool that had once stood before the throne. The surface now was bare stone, and Mageris sat the throne with both feet on the floor. The tapestries on the walls depicted various scenes of family glory, including Magerion's coronation and his earlier role in the uprising against the Dragon Touched, but they no longer included the death of the priests of Magor. Mageris still missed the old days, before Narky.

"Well?" the king snapped when the envoy entered and

bowed. "What happened?"

"Your Majesty, your Eminence, the blasphemer Sephas is dead."

"What?" Narky cried. "We didn't ask them to execute him themselves!" He spared a suspicious glance for the king. "Or did we?"

"We did not," the king answered. "Explain, man."

"After long deliberations, the High Council agreed unanimously to accede to our request and sent men to bind Sephas and bring him here with me. But when they arrived, they found the man already dying. He had gutted himself. The Council chose to let his followers make him a shrine in the city and bury him there, rather than send us his body. His followers have standing in Atuna – the councilmen told me that they would not insult their people by letting the man's body be desecrated."

"Did you see the body yourself?"

"I did, your Majesty. The man is dead."

Mageris turned to Narky. "Well? Are you satisfied with that result?"

His tone seemed to imply that he thought Narky's delicate feelings might be hurt. Narky said, "I don't like what it says about Atuna, if Sephas had a following there. But it'll do. He didn't have much personal appeal, from what I remember. He probably figured his followers would lift him up as a martyr, but if you ask me, he'll be forgotten in a few years."

Mageris smirked. "Yes, Your Eminence, I'm sure you're right. Some people are far less loved than they think."

Narky bit back his response and left the chamber. It was a cheap blow, and anyway, it was wrong: Narky *didn't* think people loved him. He had no illusions that his standing relied on anything other than Ravennis' decree. More than a decade after his arrival in Ardis, Narky was still a foreigner here.

He walked back to the temple, still deciding what to think about Sephas' death. It wasn't the satisfying end he had hoped for, but it still got the job done, didn't it? The important thing was that it silenced the man, for all that he may have been spared public humiliation. Ravennis had silenced another enemy – what more could Narky want, really?

For once, both Ptera and Lepidos agreed with him. They took the news as an imperfect victory, but an important one nonetheless. "I am glad we'll be free of his blasphemy," Lepidos said, and Ptera added, "Good riddance. Did you remind Mageris that he won this victory by allying with the Dragon Touched?"

"No," Narky admitted.

"We'll have plenty of opportunities to reinforce that message," Father Lepidos said. "In any case, Sephas and his blasphemies are gone."

"Yeah. He left us his buried prophecy and then went and buried himself. It's almost thoughtful of him."

"We can all sleep easier now," Ptera said. "Ravennis is good."

But sleep that night was not easy, at least not for Narky. He lay with Ptera and Grace beside him, feeling restless and incomplete. He had expected more, somehow. He had expected to see the man die, for one, but it wasn't as if he doubted the emissary's word that Sephas was dead, he just… he didn't know. He didn't know what bothered him about it, but something told him that for all his recent successes, he still wasn't done. This had all been easier than he had expected, for all that it hadn't precisely been easy. Surely Ravennis expected more of him.

A voice spoke in the darkness. "Well done, Narky. You have served well as My servant and My champion."

Ravennis. Narky tried to jump out of bed and prostrate himself, but his body wouldn't move. There was a weight on his chest; it took all his strength just to breathe.

"Your body is sleeping," the God said. "Only your soul is awake."

Narky lay there, struggling, impotent. All the things he had ever wanted to say to his God, all the questions he had wanted to ask, escaped his mind in an instant. He was not worthy of this visitation. He wasn't worthy of anything.

"It is not for you to decide your worth," Ravennis stated. "I have chosen to raise you up; your doubts are blasphemous."

I'm sorry, Narky thought at Him. *My doubts are a part of me. I don't think I can stop.*

"Your apology is accepted."

Beside Narky, Grace stirred. How much of the Lord Below's presence was dream, and how much was physical?

Why are You here? What have I done to deserve Your presence?

"There is a task you must perform. No other task in your life matches it in importance, for the souls of all things are at stake. The living, the dead, the worlds above and below. All rest on this one task."

Tell me. I am Your servant.

"Your friend Phaedra has returned to this world from the Third Side, the land sequestered and forbidden. She comes to sacrifice the world below to the Yarek. Her allies shield her, yearning for My destruction, never caring that the souls of the dead and the living will be consumed.

Your friend, frightened and deluded, will keep you and those you love from tasting My rewards; she will end your eternity. You must kill her."

Why can't I just convince her to stop?

"Because you will not succeed."

The words sank into Narky's soul with all the gravity of fate itself. There were things Ravennis could see that no human could guess at. Among infinite possibilities, there was no future in which Narky could convince Phaedra to give up her mission peacefully. What a terrible thing to know.

Then please, he asked, *why do I need to do it? Why not another servant?*

"Phaedra is a wizard, Narky, and she has learned to be more devious than her predecessors. Armies will not find her. Karassa tried to kill her, and failed. Only you, her friend, can disarm her. Only you can complete this task."

The act of breathing was getting harder. Narky felt the weight of the grave on his chest, the taste of earth on his tongue, the tickle of maggots in his skin. His God's presence was suffocating him.

"I cannot stay longer," Ravennis acknowledged. "Men were not designed, as their cousins were, to bear Our presence. Only one last thing: name your successor as high priest. Renounce your station and leave your vestments behind, for they are the trappings that make you most visible to the Others. Those who would protect Phaedra must not see you, and so I withdraw My ownership over your body. Until your task is complete, you belong to no God."

Narky's body awoke with a jolt. He fell out of bed, coughing soil and maggots onto the floor. He could see their pale bodies in the dim light of morning, wiggling. He could hear Grace and Ptera gasping in the bed above – the Lord Below's presence must have weighed on them too. But they recovered before his heaving ended, and when he looked up with watery eyes, both were staring at him.

"Pa," Grace said, but stopped there, hugging his mother tightly.

"I'm sorry," Narky said, gazing into Ptera's frightened eyes. "I'm sorry, I… I have to leave."

He pulled off his nightrobe and looked about for his clothes, but they were all black, all symbols of his priesthood. What did he still own that didn't mark him as his God's servant? Only the nightrobe.

"Narky!" Ptera gasped, her eyes wide. She was pointing at him.

He looked down, half-expecting to see more maggots bursting from his skin. But there were no maggots: his skin was smooth and black, healthy and unscarred. The symbol of Ravennis was gone.

He put his nightrobe back on. "Wake everyone, and we can meet in the library. I'm no longer fit to be high priest."

Narky had never seen his wife look so haunted. "Were you wrong about the prophecy?"

"No, I was right. I was too right."

"Then how can He reject you now? How could He spit you out after you served Him so faithfully?"

Narky couldn't answer her. What if Phaedra's protectors were watching?

"Gather the priests," he said.

Ptera moved to the door, but Grace let go his hold of her and ran to Narky. "Don't leave!" he cried.

Grace was nine today. Narky silently cursed the fates, though he dared not curse their keeper. First his mother, now him; first him, now Grace. It was too heartbreaking, too appropriate, too disgusting.

"I'm going to come back," Narky told his son, though his doubts were far stronger than his faith. "I'm going to regain our God's favor, and then I'll come back and we can be together forever. It's... it's just a trial. It's a test of faith, for both of us."

"What will you do?"

Narky swallowed. Poor Phaedra.

"Whatever I need to do."

28
PHAEDRA

It was dawn when Phaedra set foot on Tarphaean soil. She had learned to expect the time change, but no foreknowledge could make her body adjust to the disorientation of stepping from night to day in the blink of an eye. She wondered whether time actually ran faster in the elves' world than here, or whether it was only the skyquakes making it skip ahead relative to this one. Nobody there had aged significantly more than she had expected them to, and yet, the days and nights had been aligned the first time she traveled to the fairies' world, and now they were decidedly not. She had spent two weeks with Hunter and Psander just now – how long had she been away from Tarphae?

The mists around her billowed and swirled as she walked, her staff probing the uneven ground. There were beds at the farmhouse on the banks of the Sennaroot, and though she didn't feel tired quite yet, the walk would be long enough to change that. It would be a good first stop, and for all that she dreaded it, she thought returning to that place might benefit her. It would be good to see it liberated, free of pirates and their captured slaves. She didn't know if she would find it empty or if there would be Atunaean soldiers camped there. She wasn't sure which she preferred. A crowd of people would give her none of the privacy and quiet solitude she wanted right now, but an empty farmhouse would force her to face her memories of the place alone.

As she walked, her hand found the belt around her waist. It was nice to feel that connection to Hunter, grounding and sustaining her. The glow of their kiss in the dark hadn't left her yet – she could almost feel his arms still around her. Someday, she must have more of that.

She could hardly believe her luck that he had waited all these years, even after what she had said to him the last time. She knew he had always wanted children – his behavior with the elves' captives had told her as much, as had his admiring looks during Bandu's pregnancy – and she marveled that he had chosen her over fatherhood. It had been far too much to hope for, and yet reality had exceeded those hopes.

Was he sacrificing too much? Would he even go through with it? She thought he would, that was the amazing thing, and yet it was also the whole problem. Hunter was too practiced at self-denial. Phaedra would never forget the way he had collapsed in the mountains, how he had neglected his own needs to the point of fainting. He was doing it again, she was sure he was. You had to watch out for Hunter, or no one would.

Well, she had tried telling him he couldn't have her, and it had made no difference. He'd just kept searching until he found a solution, and it was as good a solution as she could have hoped for. It solved their biggest problem: it gave her permission to want him back. She just wished she didn't have to feel so guilty for getting what she wanted.

When she came upon the pirates' settlement, she found it to be far more than a barn and a farmhouse. Where once the reclamation of Tarphaean farmland had been rudimentary, over the past decade a true colony had sprung up on the banks of the Sennaroot. A water mill had been repaired upriver, and extra houses and barns had been raised to accommodate all the people and livestock. Some of Mura's recruits must have been true farmers, or else his raids had captured some, because the colony had clearly thrived. Sheep, cattle, and goats stood within fenced-in pastures, cut off from the fields of young wheat that flanked the river. A pair of dinghies lay upside-down on the shore, waiting for their next trip across.

The colony hadn't been abandoned, even after the Atunaean victory. Phaedra could see people out and about, herding livestock or baking in the outdoor ovens that someone out here must have built in the last few years. It took Phaedra a moment to realize that nearly everyone she could see was an islander. Her homeland resembled itself better that way – hence her belated noting of the fact – but what had happened to Mura's continental prisoners? She didn't think he had raided the islands exclusively.

She was also surprised by how many of those she saw were women and children. Phaedra had been the only woman here, those many years ago, but apparently the pirates had captured or recruited a good deal more since then. She hoped at least some of them had been willing recruits. She shuddered to think how all those children had gotten here.

Phaedra herself was attracting plenty of attention. People were staring and pointing, and soon a group of four

Atunacan soldiers came to meet her.

"Welcome, Wizard Phaedra," said the only one wearing a breastplate. He must have been wealthy to own one. "Your presence honors us, though some may feel otherwise."

Phaedra blinked. Was he warning her?

"Thank you. How long have I been away?"

"Our victory over the pirates was ten days ago. Does one lose track of time so quickly in the forest?"

"I haven't spent all this time in the forest," Phaedra told him, "nor have I spent it all on Tarphae. But I'm back now, and I need some rest before I return to the continent. Tell me, did all these people choose to stay here?"

The man shrugged. "Where else would they go? Some have been here for years. Many are pirates' consorts, and would have been executed if we didn't value their work. Besides, Karsanye isn't the port it once was – the only ships coming and going right now are from Atuna. Those who are islanders, or Parakese, or from elsewhere along the coast... it would take real money for them to get home from here, and they have none. The pirates' stores of coin have gone to the High Council to pay for the rebuilding of our fleet, and this here is land we fought and died for – it's nobody's to sell besides the Council's. These people have their freedom, but they have nothing else to their names. We let them stay in return for their work."

Phaedra did not respond. This man and his friends might be the new overseers, but the problem went back to the High Council and, truly, beyond the council to the Atunaean national spirit. It was such typical Atunaean logic, self-serving and mercantile, that turned slaves into landless, penniless servants of the state. Phaedra wouldn't be surprised if they were eventually sold to rich Atunaeans right along with the land. Any Atunaeans among the pirates' slaves had likely been rescued and returned to their families, but these people had been liberated in name only.

If she'd had time for such things, Phaedra might have gone to the High Council and insisted that these lands and their inhabitants belonged to her as the primary liberator of Tarphae. Then she could have at least turned the land over to those who worked it before she went on her way. But she knew enough from her father's tales of working with Atunaeans that it would take weeks, possibly months for the Council to resolve such an argument, and those were weeks and months that Phaedra didn't have.

So she found her way to a bed and collapsed there, only taking the time to ward the door shut before she lost consciousness. When she awoke in late afternoon, she gathered herself and left for Karsanye.

There would be no ships leaving for Atuna at night, but that didn't worry Phaedra. Admiral Sett had promised to arrange for her to have a boat, and even if he had forgotten, there was sure to be a ship soon enough. Atuna would continue to capitalize on its newfound access to Tarphae. If any ship was docked in Karsanye tonight, Phaedra could light a signal for them to let her aboard. The fact that she would not be reaching Karsanye before nightfall wasn't much of a concern either, since she could use Psander's spell for a moonlit path if the way got too dark.

Phaedra didn't follow the Sennaroot all the way to its outlet in Karsanye Bay – the river had too many twists and turns to be the fastest way unless one had a boat. She proceeded instead down the road, which was still uneven and somewhat perilous on account of that long-ago earthquake. Her staff, as always, was her best friend here, though she used Hunter's belt too, just in case. She caressed it, reminding it of how Hunter had caught her during Tarphae's earthquake, saving her from a widening fissure, and after that the belt briefly tightened its grip on her whenever she was about to step poorly. It gave her less than a second's warning, but even that much was helpful.

There was indeed a ship moored at the docks when Phaedra arrived, a two-masted merchant ship with a deep draft. Phaedra wondered for a moment what a merchant ship could be bringing the settlers, but then realized that it was more likely waiting to carry a cargo *off* the island. That soldier had done her the service of reminding her that Atuna hadn't sent its ships just to eliminate the pirates, but also to conquer and despoil her homeland.

The night watchman cried out in surprise when her light appeared, but let her aboard when he heard her voice.

"You'll have to talk to the captain about where to sleep."

The captain, a brown and weathered Atunaean, treated her arrival with some suspicion. Nonetheless, he accepted her presence and gave her a hammock strung up in the hold for privacy. "We leave on tomorrow's tide," he said. "I thank you for your service against the pirates."

The tone of his voice told her what she hadn't gotten from the soldier's comment: the Atunaeans blamed her for the loss of their ships and men just as surely as they were willing to capitalize on her victory.

She climbed down to the hold and found it stacked with guardian tree logs, still dripping from their journey down the river. Of course. Here was one more way that Atuna meant to pay itself back for its losses against Mura:

by stripping Phaedra's homeland of its natural resources. Atunaean shipbuilders were about to become very busy.

When she was alone, Phaedra conjured her ghostly flame and lay in her hammock to read the books Psander had given her. She started with the scrolls on eschatology, judging herself too distracted for the book on prayer magic. The trouble with reading to the light of one's own magic was that any task requiring too much concentration would make the light flicker and die – the more involved the material, the worse the conditions for reading it would be. The academic wizards had been a jealous, elitist community, and their writing was just as much designed to weed out ambitious hedge wizards or intimidate each other than it was to illuminate its subject. The harder an academic tome was to decipher, the more respect its author would have gained by producing it. It would be dreadful to read that sort of stuff by magiclight.

The eschatologies were not as taxing. Judging by the prayer at the beginning of each, they had been compiled by an Atellan friar who had taken an interest in the way different peoples conceived of the end times. His writing, aimed at Atellan scholars and not wizardly ones, was accessible rather than intentionally obtuse.

Phaedra had never been particularly interested in eschatology, but knowing what she knew now, the scrolls became a fascinating read. Some version of the Yarek appeared in most, but its description was radically different depending on the religion. The Mayaran tales spoke of a monster with a long snout that would drink rivers and oceans, crumbling the parched earth to dust before Mayar's storm burst it from within and formed a new world out of the mud. The Pelthans thought a great creature of chaos and injustice would tilt the world off balance, shaking the followers of other faiths into the void before Pelthas dealt it a killing blow and righted the world again. Everyone conceived of their own Gods as the heroes of a final battle, which was especially ironic and bittersweet when Phaedra read of Gods who had already perished. The stallion God of the northern plains had been slain by Magor, yet His followers had once believed that He could defeat their version of the Yarek. The lesson for Phaedra was clear enough: there were elements of truth to each God's tale, but their triumphant endings were entirely delusional.

Magor's tale was particularly telling. In it, Magor *was* the Yarek, growing in power until the other Gods became fearful and all turned on Him at once. Nobody would survive the war, but the resulting chaos would birth a new Magor and a new world that would remain wilderness forever.

The parallel between the end times as conceived by Elkinar's priests in Anardis and Ravennis' priests in Laarna gave her pause. In both versions, the world had to die before it could be reborn, and in remarkably similar ways. As the Laarnese had had it, Ravennis would someday unravel all the threads of fate and begin a new tapestry, weaving reality just by arranging the same threads differently. Elkinar, in the meantime, would slay the world Himself and, when it had decomposed, bring forth something new out of its remains. Neither God was seen as battling against the world's end, but rather welcoming it as an opportunity for renewal. Was this agreement a sign that the two Gods really had been one all along? Or only that they had existed in contested territory, such that the swallowing of one by the other was inevitable? For once,

Phaedra saw more evidence for the former. Narky would be pleased, if she ever got the chance to tell him.

Phaedra was almost ready to sleep when she came upon the friar's description of the Dragon Touched myth, where an ancient monster would plant itself in the world's selfishness. God Most High would destroy it and all those whose selfishness had let it take root, and only full repentance could sway Him.

Phaedra had to read the account twice before she could fully fathom its implications. If this was the myth passed down to the Dragon Touched from their ancestors, then Salemis had known. The dragon had known that rescuing him would bring about the world's end, and he had gone through with it anyway. He hadn't even warned them.

Had he known the end would come so soon? She thought so. The Dragon Knight's prophecy, the one that had foretold Phaedra and her friends, had been in elven verse. That meant it hadn't come directly from God Most High but rather from Salemis, whispered through the mesh. If Salemis had been aware of the prophecy, if he had been its *originator*, then he must have expected that the plan to rescue him would hasten the final battle. *I see now the end to all things once planned.* Right in the midst of verses about the islanders, the prophecy had mentioned the end of the world. Phaedra, optimistic fool that she was, had read the prophecy narrowly. She had focused so much on the words "once planned" that she had missed the true implications of the verse. It had called for the end to *all* things. "Once planned" was no consolation, because God Most High had planned everything. He had let the Lower Gods help with this younger world, but both worlds were His, and now both would end.

Phaedra's light winked out. Her concentration was shattered. Was her mission a fool's errand? Would it only hasten her world's destruction? She wished she could ask Salemis, but the dragon had escaped into the heavens over a decade ago, just as soon as he'd given the Dragon Touched his last words of advice.

Coward. Up there, he might well escape the consequences.

But wait, what had been the point of that advice if all hope was gone? If none could survive the "end to all things once planned," it shouldn't matter whether the Dragon Touched formed their own nation again or remained forever hidden in the outskirts of Ardis. If Salemis had bothered to visit his descendants and give them advice, there had to be a point to all of that.

He had said that a time of judgment was at hand, hadn't he? And he had reestablished a priestly line among those who knew the most about the ancient theology of God Most High. He must somehow have been giving them the tools they needed for effective repentance. Hadn't he even told the islanders that God Most High had grown more forgiving over the centuries?

Before Phaedra even asked Bandu to help her, she should visit Salemica and speak to the high priest there. If repentance was the key to surviving these times, and the establishment of a high priesthood was relevant enough for Salemis to have ordained it, then the high priest of God Most High would be the one to talk to.

There would be traditional prayers of repentance among the Dragon Touched, ones that Phaedra could convert into prayer spells without having to invent and calibrate the wording herself. With guidance from the codex Psander had given her, she could probably maximize the spells' efficacy without causing any unintentional blasphemy. All she needed was daylight and reading time, and she was sure to have both if she hired someone to drive her to Salemica in a carriage. She was glad she had thought to ask Psander for money. She had been terrified, before she left, of forgetting something vital, but it looked like she had all the tools she needed after all.

She slept fitfully in the hold, and nearly fell out of her hammock twice, so that by the time a sailor woke her to say that they had reached Atuna, she could only stare dully at him and grunt that she would be right up. The sailor looked unduly shocked at her behavior, as if he had expected her to be fashionable and aloof even when awoken from a dreadful night's sleep. For heavens' sake. Even a wizard couldn't keep *that* up.

The reminder was a good one, though. If she wanted to remain respected in Atuna, it was best to maintain an image of complete poise. It was a lesson she had learned young: a woman's poise was a proxy for her power.

She was more than presentable by the time she set foot on Atunaean soil. She wore the second of her two Essishan dresses, a magnificence of yellow and purple that covered her from her hair down to her feet. The dress had fit quite well in her satchel: the fabric was thinner than the finest linen. It also caught the sea breezes beautifully. The continent had never seen anything like it, she was sure.

Phaedra had no difficulty in finding a carriage for hire – enough wealth moved through Atuna that the city was well prepared to provide anything a rich person could possibly ask for. She considered paying for bodyguards too but decided against it. If she gave the carriage enough of an air of power, bandits were sure to leave it alone.

By noontime she was outside the city, being driven toward Salemica. The road had its bumps, and Phaedra often had to stop her reading to avoid nausea, but it was still well worth it. She had the opportunity to study Psander's book, even if it was only a page at a time, and that was invaluable.

Her reading did not turn up anything useful the first day. The codex was not divided into chapters, such that Phaedra was unable to skip ahead, and it built its arguments slowly. The author was thorough, that was for sure: many of the principles of prayer magic were so obvious that Phaedra could scarcely believe he had bothered to write them down at all.

The book advised that one should not cast a prayer spell to one God in another's territory, and painstakingly explained why it was folly to ask the favor of a God one had not worshipped for years beforehand. Prayer spells should be accompanied by appropriate sacrifices, it said, and one should never mention other Gods besides the one being petitioned for help, even to insult Them. Most importantly – and obviously, Phaedra thought – if one's prayer spell was not answered, one must never try again. A wizard must never ask a God for anything that could be accomplished without that God's help, or risk being seen as presumptuous. Apparently, terminal presumptuousness had been a common cause of death for wizards.

None of this was helpful advice for Phaedra, though. Some of it didn't even apply. There was no territory in this world that didn't belong to God Most High, except maybe in the boughs of the Yarek, and of the two prayer spells she had cast in her life, neither had been accompanied by a sacrifice, and yet both had worked better than she could have imagined. God Most High, at least, must be willing to accept prayers in the Essishan style, without an accompanying sacrifice. Phaedra had been incredibly lucky in that regard.

They stopped for the night on the side of the road, and Phaedra slept in the carriage while its driver slept on the ground. The carriage driver was a Laarnan refugee, a middle-aged man with white skin and a look of unspeakable sadness worn into his face. He'd asked her when she hired him if she knew the high priest in Ardis. When she had answered that she did, he'd nodded and said nothing.

"Do you want me to give him a message, the next time I see him?"

"Just... just tell him to pray for me. If the Lord Below sees fit to favor me, I would like to see my wife and children again."

Phaedra had promised she would tell Narky.

For the second night in a row, Phaedra couldn't sleep. This time it was not Hunter she thought of, but Psander. Would coming back to this world really mean the wizard's death? Was there no way for Silent Hall to become a blind spot for the Gods once more? Had Phaedra already spoken to her mentor for the last time?

There was rain the next day, which turned Atel's roads muddy and slow. Distant thunder made Phaedra fear another skyquake, but none materialized. She whispered a prayer to God Most High and went back to her reading.

The road from Atuna to Salemica was a new one, and there were sections Phaedra didn't recognize at all. A pair of bridges shortened the way considerably, but their crossing was expensive. They had been built for the many merchants who travelled this route, some of whom Phaedra's driver had hailed as they passed on the road. Psander's wealth in coin had been fairly modest to begin with, or at least since her payment to the Gallant Ones. Phaedra would not be returning this way.

When she arrived in Salemica, Phaedra's first act was to buy a ram for sacrifice. Whatever God Most High thought of Essishan ways, they were foreign to these parts. One did not insult the priests and expect the favor of their God.

They tied the animal to the back of the carriage and proceeded to the temple, where Phaedra parted with her driver after paying him handsomely for the long journey. The priest who came down to help her coax the ram up the steps smiled and said, "I know you. You are Criton's friend, Phaedra."

Phaedra gave him a courteous nod, though she did not remember the man at all. He was young and light-skinned, early to mid-twenties perhaps, with a bushy mud-brown beard that entirely concealed his chin and neck. He didn't look like anyone in particular, though his eyes had a familiar look to them.

"I'm Malkon," the priest said. "Vella's brother. I was little the last time you saw me, but you look exactly the same."

"Thank you," Phaedra answered, recognizing his flattery for what it was. "I must confess, I did not recognize you at all. You must have grown quite a bit since then."

The ram was a powerful animal, and it was highly reluctant to come up the steps to the altar. Malkon was young and muscular, but without the ram's cooperation he had little hope of reaching the altar without assistance. Phaedra did her best to calm the animal, projecting her own feeling of safety and desire to reach the top into its mind, but she did not have Bandu's way with creatures. Her mind was too different from theirs somehow. Her spell had a positive effect, but it still took all of Malkon's muscle to coax the ram up the last steps.

When they had finally reached the top and tied the cord that hung from the ram's collar to a loop on the altar, Malkon sighed in relief and dusted off his hands. "It's an honor, you know," he told the animal. "You could have been anyone's dinner, and gone straight to the underworld. Instead, you'll rise to the heavens to please our God. You ought to thank me."

The ram baaed skeptically, entirely unconvinced by his logic.

He patted it on the head and turned back to Phaedra. "I was a bit shorter than him, I think, the last time you saw me. And my beard is new since then too, of course. Now is this fellow here for thanksgiving, beseeching, or forgiveness?"

"Thanksgiving, for now. I can do my own beseeching, when it comes time for that. For now, I need to thank God Most High for bringing me safely to this place."

"Very good. I didn't figure you'd need forgiveness for anything."

Phaedra smiled politely, though she found his flirtation tiresome. He wouldn't have been her type even if she hadn't loved Hunter. Maybe he thought his sister's marriage to Bandu would help him with Bandu's fellow islander. Whatever he thought, he was wrong.

She watched as Malkon bound the ram and performed the sacrifice, taking mental notes on his technique and wording. She was no priestess to be performing such rituals herself, but even the rituals that were inappropriate for a wizard to borrow could be elucidating in other ways. She had spent far more time alone in her worship of God Most High than she had ever spent among His chosen people, learning their ways. She felt she knew far more about her God than she knew about His religion, and that was a significant deficit. The religion had power and meaning beyond any crass magical usage.

That was the real problem with academic magic: it treated Gods as power sources, not deities. There was no worship, only experimentation. It was no wonder prayer magic was considered so perilous if half its practitioners attempted it for reasons defined by their own ambitions and not in the service of the Gods they called upon. She didn't think Psander had been wrong that there was mortal danger inherent in demanding a God's attention, but clearly academics had brought additional danger upon themselves by approaching prayer magic from the wrong angle. It was, at its essence, a kind of prayer and not a kind of magic.

The silly, obvious points that Psander's codex had tried to instill in its readers could all have been obviated by the simple principle that prayer magic should be attempted only within the context of genuine worship. Mura was a perfect exemplar of this principle. How many years had he lived and how many spells had he cast without ever incurring divine punishment? Every spell of his had been a prayer spell, yet his success in avoiding Karassa's wrath should have come as no surprise: the man had been more priest than wizard. His spells had been worship, and his worship had been spells.

When Malkon had taken the priestly portion and set

the rest of the ram alight, Phaedra asked him if his father the high priest was present. "Yes, of course," he said. "I didn't flatter myself that you were here to see me."

He lifted the platter that held the portion of mutton and was about to lead her inside when they heard a cry of "Phaedra!" and turned to see Criton leaping up the stairs toward them. He took them two and sometimes three at a time, and soon held Phaedra in his warm embrace.

"I heard you came in a carriage. Where have you been all this time?"

"I spent a few years in Essisha, but today I came from Psander by way of Tarphae and Atuna. I have a lot to tell you, and none of it is good."

29

SALEMIS

It was amazing to witness the Lower Gods recognize, practically all at once, that the Yarek would not necessarily be shattered. One moment They had been fighting and undercutting each other, vying for greater influence on the rebuilt world, and the next moment the heavens were roiling and convulsing with Godly fear. Even for Salemis, insulated as he was by the love of Eramia and God Most High, the feeling was contagious.

The Lower Gods were limited by Their domains; the rumors of what Phaedra meant to do mostly came from Atel the Messenger, who had noted God Most High's protection of her and spied upon her as best He could. What He had gleaned was that Phaedra meant to eliminate the mesh between her world and the elven one, averting the Yarek's destruction until *after* it had the chance to reform. If she succeeded, the Yarek would soon pierce the heavens and resume its ancient campaign of destruction, and the elves too, those arrogant children who had soaked up too much of the Gods' power, would be released to cause what mischief they could. The fact that God Most High was protecting the wizard despite this plan – or perhaps because of it – terrified the Lower Gods. How many of Them would fall before God Most High chose to confront the Yarek once more?

Salemis observed the Gods' alarm get mirrored on earth, Their cries for God Most High's forgiveness pouring from the mouths of prophets, from east of Essisha to far beyond the Calardian mountains, and many stranger places besides. Some, like Prince Tnachti of Ksado, received visions that blamed Phaedra for the world's end, but few could do anything about it. Tnachti chose to send an armada, led by his esteemed sister Kvati, to convince Phaedra to spare the world. The two rulers filled their ships not only with soldiers but with their families as well, presumably hoping to appeal to Phaedra's kind heart. Whatever their thought process, the plan never had a chance of success: the voyage was too long to begin with, and then Karassa took offense at the Ksadan people praying to Phaedra's God for fine weather instead of to Her and blew the ships off course. By the time they reached the western continent, if they ever did, it would be far too late.

Atun or Ravennis might have had a better chance at stopping Phaedra, but Atun was rightly focused on petitioning God Most High for forgiveness rather than trying to kill His servants, and Ravennis... well, Salemis wasn't sure what Ravennis was up to. His absence from the heavens made it more difficult to monitor His actions. The Crow God had discarded Narky as a high priest, but Salemis had no notion of why. Eramia was just as baffled as he was, despite Her kinship with Ravennis, and if God Most High knew more, He wasn't saying.

Most of the Gods recognized their powerlessness, and it terrified Them. They had spent centuries acting as if They were the true masters of the worlds, as if God Most High was not silent but dead. Now, with the Yarek threatening to return to its former power, They suddenly realized how dependent They still were on Him. The wise ones begged the Lord Above All for forgiveness and directed Their followers to do the same. As tense as things were, it was extremely satisfying to see so many of the Lower Gods tell Their people to cease praying to Them and turn instead to God Most High.

The Dragon Touched had not needed this extra direction, but they too had been changing their practice. After the most recent quake, they had come to the conclusion that fasting, prayer, and sacrifice weren't enough. Their high priest had announced that for their prayers to be heard, they would have to also care for the sick and feed and clothe the needy, to purify their nation of selfishness and want. He had called for the poor of the city to come to the great temple, and refused to sacrifice another animal until they all had clothes to wear, homes to live in, and food to eat. Following his direction, Criton had sent messengers across the nation, establishing protocols for every community to clothe and feed its citizens and its strangers. The society's transformation was a wonder to behold.

Eramia was particularly proud of that high priest, Hessina's son. She had shielded him and his mother from Magor's gaze during the purge, nurtured his young mind through the harshest years, and now Her effort was bearing fruit. Salemis could see how Her influence had shaped the man. If not for the fact that She had prepared him to serve God Most High rather than Herself, one might have called Kilion one of Her fingers. Perhaps it was an apt description anyway. Eramia had always been a subtle one, subtler perhaps than even

Ravennis. Her finesse always amazed him.

Yes, Salemis and Eramia had prepared their children
well. If their survival had been entirely up to God Most
High, as Salemis had always thought it would be, he would
have felt confident.

But it wasn't. Phaedra's plan relied upon the Yarek's
disavowal of the greedy destruction that had caused its
ancient war against God Most High. If the plant beast
betrayed her and resumed its war, the resulting battle,
whatever its ultimate outcome, would tear the heavens
and earth asunder. Salemis and Eramia would be lucky if
they survived, let alone their descendents.

He had known a reckoning was coming, had even
welcomed it, but he hadn't expected this. He had believed
that with enough prayer, enough repentance, humanity
would convince God Most High to uproot the Yarek's
seed and pull their world further from the elves' prison.
He hadn't anticipated this plan to reunify the Yarek and
endanger all the worlds at once, to require the Yarek's
repentance and not only humanity's. How had Phaedra
even hatched such a plan? He had not thought her one to
conceive of risking the heavens.

But God Most High had endorsed this plan anyway by
choosing to protect Phaedra from the Lower Gods. That at
least gave Salemis hope. If the Lord Above All intended to
give the Yarek its chance to repent, then Phaedra's mission
must have *some* chance of success. He only wished it didn't
rely on a being so far outside their power to influence.

God Most High had once told Salemis that his people
would survive until the end of the world. Not for the first
time, Salemis wished He had been more specific.

30
RAIDER ELEVEN

When they reached the wizard's fortress, the sky was so black that only the elves' skin illuminated the way before them. The stars dangled above, wobbling slightly as they shed their dim light. By ancient elven lore they were torches, bound to the heavenly barrier by Gods who had later abandoned this world in Their selfishness and fear. Raider Eleven had never considered the cords that bound them there to be anything short of unbreakable, but perhaps she had been wrong. Given another quake or two, they might well fall from the sky.

The fortress was more of a ruin than even the dying Castle Goodweather. Half its tower lay beside the gate, itself a useless thing lying wrecked upon the ground. A gaping hole invited them into the wizard's home, under what remained of the tower. Raider Eleven looked to her new mistress. The queen smiled and waved them on.

Still riding their steeds, the queen's party entered the gap where once the gate had been. Beyond it, they found Psander.

The wizard stood in the small field of grain that took the place of a courtyard, her remaining kin beside her.

Hunter, the black godserf that Eleven and her compatriots had captured so easily eleven years ago, now stood at the wizard's side with a sickle that no godserf had made. On the wizard's other side stood a young woman with a spear, and behind her an older one with a bow. Three more spearmen took one side or the other of the wizard, and at the back, Eleven saw two children and their unarmed mother. This must be all that remained of the godserfs in this world.

That was highly unfortunate. Ten godserfs and nine elves made nineteen, an inauspicious number. Twenty would have been better. It would have been right. The godserfs were missing someone. Eleven and nine, it should have been.

The queen spoke. "Well, wizard?" she said. "You told my servant that you had a solution to our problem."

"Yes," the wizard replied. "Where is that servant, by the way?"

"His untainted heart is within me. The rest of him may help sustain our castle a while longer."

"Have you come to regret your greed yet? My people did you no harm, and did not threaten you in any way, yet you could not wait even until our worlds were saved before you turned on them. How does your greed feel, now that you know how I defended them?"

"More ambitious. Next time I shall eat you."

The wizard waved an arm dismissively. "There will be no next time. The power your court lost did not simply dissipate, elf queen. I command it now. Displease me, and I will turn it on you."

Raider Eleven frowned. The wizard's attitude projected conviction, but her aura held barely any more power than her fellow godserfs. Could she be bluffing? Her mental defenses were too strong for Eleven to be sure. The one odd thing about the wizard's aura was its ragged, uneven shape, but the Queen's Consort could see no reason for that to imply greater power, certainly not the power of an entire court.

The other godserfs didn't doubt the wizard, and Eleven was surprised and pleased to see how much they despised her for it. Aside from Hunter, the godserfs seemed to hate and fear Psander almost as much as they did the queen. That could prove useful.

"We shall see," the queen said. "But tell me your solution, wizard. I will not ask a third time."

The wizard Psander nodded. "Our problem does not lie in the closing distance between our worlds, nor in their combination. That much is fortunate, because both are inevitable. Goodweather is unable to stop the worlds' merger, and Illweather is unwilling. But this is of no consequence, because our real problem is the mesh *between* the worlds. *That* is what threatens to destroy us. Unravel it, and the problem disappears."

"Our whole world slips through the barrier," the queen said, greed in her voice. Oh to laugh at the Gods and feast every night! "Tell me how."

"It will take all the Yarek's strength and all our cunning. You will have to convince both castles to help us, while Phaedra on the other side consults with Goodweather's seed. After the castles have both agreed to our plan, I will commence opening the last gate at regular intervals. When Goodweather's seed is ready to join us, it will send a signal and we will work together to pull the gate so wide that the entire barrier tears apart and releases us into the other world."

"You would send me to Illweather, when that castle ate my brother?"

"Of course. I have no interest in revisiting the place. This is my home, and the last time I left it, you betrayed me."

The queen laughed. "You didn't mind losing those other godserfs. They were a weapon, and they served their only purpose when I, unsuspecting, took them. Do not pretend that you are anything but pleased at the result."

Yes, that was the way to do it. The other godserfs, who already hated their leader, would distract her. Raider Eleven could use that distraction.

Eleven had been busy during the conversation, delving into Hunter's mind for information. She had been rewarded with thoughts and memories, images of mushrooms and metallic pendants, spreading skin lesions and an overturned cask. She knew now how Psander had poisoned the Goodweather court, and more importantly, she knew that it could not happen again.

She also understood how Psander could claim to possess that court's magic. What Raider Eleven had mistaken for an uneven, ragged aura, was the result of the many tethers Psander had connected to her person. The court's magic was not within her, as her words had suggested, but rather within the walls of her fortress, ready to be called upon at a moment's notice. If the queen could distract the wizard enough, Raider Eleven would be able to slip those tethers away from her.

"I am *not* pleased," the wizard said. "I would much rather have known that I could trust you to prioritize your existence over your appetites, that I would never have to waste precious energy defending my people from your foolishness. The power I stole from you could have been used to make our transition to the other world easier and more certain; now I have to use it against you instead. Even now I have to use it against you."

She turned to Raider Eleven. "Don't think that I haven't noticed you over there, elf woman. You fairies have been masters of your domain for too long – you lack subtlety as badly as you lack innovation. Queen, I am afraid I must banish you all from this place, permanently. I hereby turn your mastery of your world back on you. Within these walls, the ground will not support you; the air will not sustain you; the warmth will not penetrate your skin. Leave, before you perish."

As she spoke, the wizard's aura flashed and a flood of magic crashed in on the queen and her companions. The air grew suddenly cold, so cold that it froze Raider Eleven's skin, and when she exhaled in shock, she found that she could not inhale again. Her steed stumbled and began to slowly sink into the ground.

The elves pulled hard on the reins and rode their horses back out of the wizard's fortress, choking and gasping. The horses' hooves barely found purchase and solid ground seemed to sink farther and farther beneath the surface as they went, so that by the time they reached the place where the gate should have been, they had sunk up to their bellies and could not climb back out. Raider Eleven had to leap from her horse's back to reach solid ground, and one of her companions nearly sank in with his, his eyes rolling as he succumbed to the loss of breath. Raider Eleven had to impale him through the back and drag him out with her sickle, or he too would have disappeared into the soft earth.

The queen, safe and recovered, looked down on him with scorn. "Heal that wound," she commanded, as he opened his eyes. "And get up. You're making a nuisance of yourself."

He was still trying to obey her commands when Psander appeared at the window above them. "Next time you wish to speak with me," she said, "stay outside the walls. Return when you have assurance that both castles will help us."

Goodweather was easy. The queen gave it Psander's message and the dying castle practically bloomed at the thought of saving its friend, that wicked child Bandu. They had always known this part would be simple.

But when they came to Illweather, its roots thrashing and its thunderstorm stretching across half the sky, even the queen was afraid to approach.

"Raider Eleven," she commanded, "make our offer to your castle. Illweather is an old enemy: it will not listen to my voice."

Raider Eleven was not accustomed to the taste of elven fear, let alone from a monarch. The queen's reticence shook her almost as much as the thought of coming within striking distance of the castle that had swallowed her prince. *If we are so weakened that our little cousins outmagic us and our own castles make us shake with fear, then our time is truly at an end.*

But as the queen commanded, so must Raider Eleven obey. She approached the castle cautiously, feeling the roots shift beneath her feet, ready to leap back at any moment. Too easily could she imagine the castle swallowing her and telling the queen that if she meant to speak with it, she could do so herself.

She felt the roots bursting from the ground behind her and did not even turn around. "Illweather!" she cried. "I am here to offer you your revenge!"

Foolish elf, you are but a morsel. What revenge you can offer me, I can easily take for myself.

"I offer revenge against the Gods that left us here, against Their king who tore you asunder. Listen to my offer before you dismiss it. You will thank me."

The castle scoffed. *The Gods will taste my revenge regardless, edible fool. The days may be long, but my revenge is coming.*

"The revenge I offer you is *swift*."

A bolt of lightning struck the ground nearby, and the bells in Eleven's hair tinkled as every folicle responded.

Speak.

"The godserf wizard wishes to unravel the barrier between the worlds. With your help, and the help of Goodweather's seed in the younger world, we can avoid the calamity that would set your revenge back by eons. You can have unification *now*."

Thunder rumbled in the distance. Illweather was laughing.

Do you and your queen think that you will survive my unification? Go, morsel. Tell the wizard I accept.

Raider Eleven bowed and retreated, shaking. She had not even reached the queen when Illweather's parting words came booming across the sky.

There is no future for elves in the world I will grow on my enemy's carcass. Even weak, kindhearted Goodweather despises your kind.

The words reverberated through Raider Eleven's soul. All the way back to the wizard's ruined fortress, and from there to Castle Goodweather, she pondered what

Illweather had said. Even later, as she was pleasing the queen, she could not help but wonder whether they had delayed their own doom by more than a few days, a few weeks. When the queen commanded her to speak, her worries poured forth like blood from a vein.

The queen listened thoughtfully, attentive but unconcerned. "You did not listen to the laments of those we captured," she said.

"I beg your pardon, my queen?"

"The wizard did not come here to plague us, Raider Eleven. She spent years hiding from her Gods' sight and slipped into this world so that she could avoid Them even longer. She did so with less power than we possess and sustained her defenses for decades.

"We can learn to disappear as the wizard did. Elves were made to contrast with our surroundings, but we need not remain so: our magic is strong, and Goodweather remains obligated to help us. We will use the last of its days to perfect our transformation, and when the unified Yarek or its divine enemies turn their attention to our destruction, they will not see us. Do not fear, Queen's Consort. We will live on."

As the queen had spoken, so did her subjects obey. Day by day, week by week, quake after calamitous quake, the lords of the first creation taught themselves to disappear. They learned to carry their auras hidden deep within them, leaving no footprint and no trace of magic where they walked. They spied on the wizard's walls, studying her fortress' defenses as best they could from the outside, hoping to learn how she had hidden from the Gods for so long, adapting what they could for their own use. Expanding their knowledge was an unfamiliar pastime after centuries of decadent stagnation, but they took to it well. Soon their castle no longer knew whether they were within it or without, and the queen commanded that they visit Illweather once more.

This time, the roots did not shift under their feet. The lightning crackled elsewhere. The elves dodged between raindrops and nearly brushed the mossy walls with their clothes, and Illweather did not note their presence. When they were once again outside the storm's reach, their cries of triumph echoed through the forest. This world might soon be gone, absorbed, repurposed, but the elves would live on.

The elves would live on.

31
HUNTER

"So that's it?" Hunter asked. "We're safe?"

"Of course we're not safe," Psander snapped at him. "We still need to unravel the mesh and survive the transition, and when that is done we will be back in a land of vengeful Gods, except that this time we'll also have the Yarek threatening to devour us – assuming its inevitable war against the Gods doesn't consume us first. We are not safe, Hunter. We will never be safe."

"I meant from the elves."

"Well then, within such extremely narrow parameters, yes, we're safe. Enjoy your unearned feelings of relief."

She turned back to gaze out the window as Hunter eyed the elven sickle in his hands.

"Then my part is done. You don't need me anymore."

His comment drew her attention far more than he'd expected or prepared himself for. Psander abandoned whatever dark thoughts had preoccupied her and stared at him long and hard, her face expressionless. Hunter stood uncomfortably, waiting for her to speak. He didn't think the wizard had ever looked at him like this, trying to see *him* instead of that imaginary warrior-tool who occupied his place in her mind.

"I am no longer in need of a bodyguard," Psander said at last, her words slow and careful. "But there is still work to be done. We must see if the stores in the cellar are sufficient to sustain us until Phaedra finds success, which should take several weeks – unless, that is, the synchronization between that world and this one is a good deal further off than I thought. The skyquakes will only get stronger in that time, so I will need your help moving my library downstairs. After that, it may be worthwhile to demolish the top floors stone by stone, before any quake can drop them on our heads. You have completed your most important task, but you need not be idle."

"Oh," Hunter said. "I... I was hoping to be idle for a while."

The wizard looked at him quizzically, but before she could speak again they heard the footfalls of the others marching up the stairs toward them. The villagers were done waiting.

"Psander," Ketsa said, arriving at the top of the stairs first. "The elves are gone. It's time for you to face what you've done to us."

"You mean saved you from annihilation?" Psander asked. The scorn in her voice was so palpable and so short-sighted, it made Hunter wince.

"I mean lied to us. I mean that you told us we would be safe here, when you knew we wouldn't. That you said we'd be free from bandits, when you were the only bandit we really had to fear. You sent the Gallant Ones to drive us into your arms – we've known it for years. You said all we had to do was to supply you with food, but you took much more than that. You took our health for your defenses;

you took our bodies for your weapons; you took us from
our Gods and fed us to the fairies."

"And every step of the way," Tritika added, "you said
we should be grateful."

She stepped forward to let another person through
behind her. The villagers were crowding onto the landing,
trying to fit too many people into the narrow space by the
window.

"You've put us off for years," Ketsa said. "There's always
been some reason why you couldn't talk. Well, it's time for
you to answer us. It's time for your trial. Come with us,
unless you want to get pushed out."

Hunter could see Psander weighing her options, and
prayed that she wouldn't lash out. With all that fairy magic
at her command, there was no knowing what she might
be able to do to his friends. He saw her glance at him, and
he shook his head. She needed to know that he would
not support her if she chose to fight. Their demands were
perfectly reasonable – he would not stand in their way.

If she did lash out, would Ketsa really push her out the
window?

Evidently, Psander decided not to risk it. Hunter had
never seen the wizard grant anyone the last word, but she
came away from the window silently and descended the
stairs between Ketsa and Tritika. Hunter took the rear as
they all marched down the steps, crammed one behind
the other. He hoped this went well. Psander no longer
needed a deterrent against the elves – if she felt threatened
enough, this "trial" could end horribly.

There were torches all around the great hall, shedding
their ruddy light over the entire room. Hunter didn't
think he'd ever seen so much torchlight in this place,

accustomed as he now was to magical illumination. There was an honesty and a savagery in the sight, sound, and smell of burning wood. Every human in the elves' world was gathered there: Ketsa, Tritika, and the other bodyguards – all still holding their weapons – and beside them, Atella with Persada in her arms and Tarin at her side, watching silently.

Psander surveyed the room coldly. "What do you mean to accomplish here?" she asked. "You must know that this 'trial' is meaningless. If I had to, I could turn the elves' magic against you. To what purpose do you presume to judge me?"

"We want a reckoning!" Ketsa answered. She had clearly become the leader of the remaining villagers, and she remained uncowed even in the face of Psander's threat. "For once in your life, we want you to be honest with us. We want you to admit the whole truth of what you did to us, and when you're done, we want you to apologize. Yes, apologize. Without your actions, we would have stayed safe and unmolested in the village where I grew up. You may tell yourself that you've protected us from elves or armies, but you were the one who put us in those dangers to begin with."

"I was," Psander said. "I will admit that much."

"Admit *everything*," Palat growled. "Say what you did to us."

"If it pleases you."

Ketsa met her skepticism with forceful affirmation. "It does."

"Very well," Psander said. "I saw your little village, so near to where I had built my fortress, and I sent the Gallant Ones to harass you so that you might come and serve me. I lied, if it pleases you to hear it. I told the Gallant Ones that I would help them retake Atuna when I had no intention of doing so, and I led you all to believe that I was a *male* wizard, so that I could project more power. I will let you judge for yourself how ridiculous it is that I should have needed to do so.

"I did not lie when I said I only wanted to share your food, since at the time that was all I needed from you. I didn't strike upon the idea of using your latent magic for my defenses until Phaedra surprised me by bringing not only calardium but blueglow mushrooms back from her expedition into the mountains."

"Then why did you ask for the mushrooms?" Hunter asked, leaning his sickle against a wall and folding his arms. "Phaedra wouldn't have known to take them if you hadn't asked for them first."

Psander gave him a look of such anger that initially Hunter thought she might punish him with that elf magic. But once more, the wizard controlled herself.

"No," she said, "she wouldn't have. I gave her a list of various magical ingredients, any of which could be used in a multitude of ways. But I tell the truth when I say that I had no specific plan at the time to harvest the villagers' latent magic.

"You will remember, Hunter, that I sent you and your friends to the mountains specifically in order to gather calardium ore, which can be used as a power source in numerous ways. When presented with blueglows as well, I hit upon the idea of the magic-siphoning pendants. I did not realize at the time that the combination would be poisonous, but though I should perhaps apologize for my mistake, I will not apologize for lying, as I did not lie."

"Is that so?" Ketsa said. "Well, go ahead and apologize for your mistake. We're waiting."

Psander met Ketsa's gaze for a few long moments before she shrugged. "I apologize. I did not know."

Could such an apology be accepted? The moments stretched themselves out. Psander's shrug had turned what might otherwise have sounded heartfelt suspect, and now it was up to Ketsa to decide whether to accept the apology in good faith or press for one that was more earnest. Hunter wasn't sure Psander was even capable of more earnestness.

Finally, Ketsa nodded. "Go on."

"When the Tarphaeans came back from their next voyage with an offer to leave that world and its vengeful Gods, I did not consult with anyone before choosing to accept the offer. That should not surprise or horrify you, as we were besieged by a massive army at the time, and the pendants had weakened you all such that it would have made no sense to expect reasoned thought from you. Faced with annihilation or a journey to this world, I made the choice for all of us. It was the right choice."

"The fairies say it's what caused the skyquakes," Tritika pointed out.

"True, and I did not know that either at the time. It is possible that I should have let us all die there. But I can't be sure of that even now, and so I will not apologize for it."

"You're disgusting," Atella hissed. Her voice was almost too full of venom for her low tone, but looking over Hunter saw that Persada was now asleep in her arms. "You poisoned my husband, you poisoned our whole village. You tried to poison me and my children too – we'd have *all* died if Persada hadn't spilled my cup. You should have been trying to save us, and you poisoned us instead. How *dare* you pick and choose what to apologize for, as if haggling could make you less evil? How *dare* you?"

Atella's father put a hand on her free shoulder. He and Atella both had tears in their eyes. Hunter turned to Psander to find her looking uncertain. She didn't understand. Somehow, she didn't understand.

"I had no better option that I could see," she said. "I am sorry it came to that."

"You're sorry it came to that," Atella repeated. "You just told the elves you were sorry they attacked because you wanted to *trust them*. You never cared if we lived or died, you never cared what we thought or how we felt. We were never people to you."

"Of *course* you're people," Psander said with a frown, "and if I didn't care what you thought, I wouldn't have had to pretend to be a man for the better part of a year. Make sense, Atella, I know you're capable of it."

Her words met with stunned silence. It was finally dawning on the villagers that Psander had not been persecuting them personally all these years, that she had not been devaluing their lives any more than she had devalued the lives of the islanders or the Gallant Ones. They had seen her invite Hunter and his friends into her tower for private meetings, seen them accept beds there, and they had thought she treated the islanders humanely. The questioning looks they cast his way asked him if Psander had always been like this, even to him. Of course she had. It almost broke his heart to realize that it had taken them so long to find out. She had treated the villagers as tools not because she felt they were uniquely worthless, but because she treated everyone that way.

Nobody was a person to her.

It was Eskon who broke the silence. "If the Gods will it," he said, "we'll be back in our world soon. When that day comes, we will leave you here to feed yourself. We're not your slaves. We'll take our food and our tools with us, and you'll have to learn how to farm, or starve."

The other villagers nodded approvingly. The trial was over.

"No need," Psander said. "You may have this place. I bequeath it to you, and my library to Phaedra. Even if my plan works and the worlds combine, I will not survive the transition. The Gods will destroy me, and if I stay here, They will destroy this place too. The elf magic in the walls render it far too conspicuous for me to hide as I did before. So, I will leave. I would rather die alone than have the Gods destroy my work along with me. You may stay if you so wish. The power I stole from the elves should keep them at bay for as long as these walls stand, whether I live or not."

If Psander was expecting gratitude, she did not get it. The villagers only shook their heads at each other, and Ketsa said, "We won't be staying." After that, Atella went to put her children to bed, and the others dispersed.

"Well," Psander said, "at least that's at an end. I don't expect they'll be of much use now. We shall have to transfer the library ourselves."

"Will you pay me for my services?" Hunter asked.

"Excuse me?"

He took a deep breath. "The scroll I saved."

"Ah, yes. For Phaedra. That will have to wait until after the library is transferred. The recovery will take weeks."

Hunter shook his head. "No. You can't do that to me.

What if there's never time?"

"Then perhaps Phaedra can perform the procedure herself."

"Could she?"

After a long silence, Psander finally shook her head. "No, probably not. She doesn't have the experience, and there are bound to be terms in that scroll that I haven't taught her. Even if she could piece it all together, it would take years."

"Then please. You carried all those books here somehow before you knew us; you must have a way of moving them without me."

"Yes, but I was younger, and it was still supremely exhausting."

"You have a court's-worth of elf magic to work with now."

Psander sighed. "Oh, very well then. Bring me the scroll. But give me a few days to study it, and in the meantime commence the work of bringing all the food stores to this room so that the books can be transferred to the store rooms in the cellar. Even with all this new magic at my command, I cannot be *completely* without your labor."

Hunter wondered how true that was, but he said nothing. The important thing was that she had agreed to help him.

Now all he needed was the strength to go through with it.

Three days later, his muscles aching from the work of carrying books and barrels, sacks and casks, Hunter stood before Psander, trying to steel himself for what lay ahead. The stone table she had once had in her workshop was still outside, buried somewhere in the remains of the tower's top stories, so instead Psander was busy "anchoring" the wooden table in her library so it wouldn't move if he… thrashed, or something. Gods, why was he going through with this?

Because he wanted Phaedra, that was why.

Psander's library was a place of aloof majesty no more: the shelves were bare, their contents stacked in enormous piles all across the floor. Pyramids of scroll cases, flanked by towers of codices to keep them from collapsing, stood as strange monuments to Psander's success as a collector. Not for the first time, Hunter wondered how Psander had transported all these books in the years before she built the fortress.

"You're ready?"

Hunter nodded. "Yes."

"You realize, this will likely be quite painful. The scroll names two spells for easing the pain but does not describe either. All the elf-magic at my disposal cannot help with that – it can only hold you in place while I work. Do not be surprised if the pain is more than what you bargained for."

"I understand."

"You will also have to pull up that tunic."

Yes, of course. Hunter had known as much, but there was such a difference between knowing and doing. There was no part of his choice that didn't make Hunter feel intensely vulnerable, but the fact that he would be exposing himself to Psander was among the worst.

"This should be stable now," Psander said, giving the table a pat. "When you're ready."

Hunter closed his eyes, took a deep breath, shuddered. At last, he climbed onto the wooden table and lay down.

At least it wasn't cold, as the stone one would have been. With an uncomfortable tug, he pulled up his tunic.

Psander said nothing, absent Gods be thanked, only placed the scroll beside his left leg, weighed it down with a pair of stones, and proceeded with her preparations. He felt something brush his leg and tried to sit up but found that the air around him had solidified into a barrier. When Psander raised his knees with her hands and pushed his legs out of her way, the barrier let her through and then hardened immediately once she had let go. Hunter winced and squeezed his eyes shut. This was going to be awful.

He felt Psander's hands working, shifting him about, pinching and pulling back on his most sensitive skin, shaving him with a razor – and then a sudden sharp scratch, followed closely by a sensation of wetness. He wondered at first if she had cut him with the razor, if he was bleeding, but then that horrible scratching returned accompanied by a tickling to his leg, and he realized that she was drawing on him with a quill.

"Please," he gasped. "Just… be careful."

Psander ignored him and kept up her scratching, pausing now and then to dip her pen in the ink or, worse, to blow on him so that it would dry faster. He hoped she finished with this part quickly.

He soon had reason to regret that thought. With a sudden, swift motion, Psander pinched his nether skin with both hands and pulled it open. The pain shot up his legs and back, an unbearable white-hot sensation that banished all thought from his mind. His body pressed against the barrier of elf magic, trying to protect itself. His teeth clenched until his jaw hurt, and his voice strained in his throat. He thought he would vomit.

Psander was still manipulating him with her fingers, humming to herself as she did so. Then, with a click of her tongue, she somehow closed him up again. He could feel his skin mending itself, and the pain lessened considerably, though it did not vanish. There were tears in Hunter's eyes. He thought he smelled burning.

"Good," Psander said. "That's one."

Hunter didn't even have time to plead with her before the pain returned, this time on the other side. "Two" was just as horrible as "one," but, thankfully, just as fast. Within a minute or two, Psander had finished her work and was rolling up her scroll again.

"You can move now," she said.

Hunter moaned. "It's over?"

The wizard smirked and wiped her hands on a rag. "Unless you have a third testicle hidden somewhere."

Hunter wiped his eyes with his sleeve and sat up tentatively. He felt like he had been kicked between the legs, and the searing pain of her spell, though no longer debilitating, still echoed there. He braved a look at the site, dreading what he would see. The scars were a good deal smaller than he'd imagined. They were still cuts, really, and had yet to fully close, but though they glistened they were not bleeding. That was something, then.

"Well," Psander said, "I must admit I never thought I would use that scroll. I ought to thank you for the opportunity. That went quite well."

Hunter nodded dumbly and eased himself off the table, surprised that he could still move. The tunic fell down over his loins again as he stumbled away from her, walking with his legs as far apart as possible. That helped a little – he could certainly do without chafing – but he felt he needed pressure too. The scroll had suggested a tight loin cloth, but he didn't know how to tie one.

"It says not to do anything strenuous for two weeks," Psander called after him.

"I know," he said. "I read it."

He navigated the stairs as carefully as he could, feeling swollen and bruised. When he reached his straw mattress, tucked in between sacks of wheat on the floor of the great hall, he collapsed onto it with a groan. They were all sleeping down here now, judging it the safest room in the face of the next quake and the one after that. Hunter curled up on his mattress, drew his linens around him, and shut his eyes.

Well, Phaedra, it's done. Now all we have to do is survive.

32

KILION HIGHSERVANT

Kilion sat quietly in his chair, stunned by what Phaedra had told him. At first, he had thought there must be some mistake. How could it be that he, Kilion son of Hessina, would be a witness to the world's end? If all this was true, why would God Most High elevate his line, his mother's line, to the high priesthood, and not even tell them?

But of course, He *was* telling them. He had sent a trusted servant across a continent, an ocean, and a barrier of worlds, so that she might come to this place bearing this news. That the Lord Above had chosen to send His message this way, rather than in a dream or revelation, was irrelevant. It stung a bit, knowing that his God had not seen fit to honor Kilion with this directly, but if Kilion had learned anything from his mother, it was that pride was for other people.

He had grown up in the shadow of his dead siblings. A scrawny, sickly teen at the time of the purge, he had hidden with his mother when the Red Priest came, while his older brothers and sisters died fighting. At every moment of triumph that he could remember, his mother had grown wistful, wondering what they and their children might have achieved had they not been cut down. He had wondered right along with her, sure that whatever he could accomplish, they would have done better.

He still felt that way sometimes.

Kilion knew that for all his learning, for all his thought and insight, for all his skill as a priest and a leader, he had received the high priesthood by default and not for his merits. His wife called that humility; he called it honesty.

Mother had known it as well as he did. Even on her deathbed, her eyes shut against the struggle of dying, Hessina had squeezed his hand and said, "Don't be too proud of yourself. It shouldn't be any accomplishment for a man to outlive his mother."

Kilion had learned to accept that achievement and merit were two different things, and he had tried to teach that wisdom to his children and let them know that he would love and support them regardless of what they achieved.

He worried that Malkon might have learned the lesson too well. The boy – no, he was a man now – reveled in his position, and rarely tried his hardest at anything. Vella, in the meantime, had cast all her family's standing aside and was trying to live on love alone. He respected that decision, but worried about the future. Whatever his successes as high priest, he had failed to raise a suitable heir.

But here was this angel, this messenger from God Most High, telling him that no heir would be needed, that the world in its current form would soon end and the time of repentance was at hand. It was not the relief from his concerns that he had hoped for.

Criton was arguing with Phaedra over the best way to avoid the disaster. "We have to cut down the Yarek," he said. "If it's weak enough, it won't be able to pull our worlds together anymore. I'll raise an army of axmen, and—"

"That won't work," Phaedra interrupted. "Castle Illweather went and ate all its elves, and the Yarek here is at least as strong. It'll just kill your axmen and use the lot of you as fertilizer."

"I've beaten Illweather before. I think we ought to try. And if the Yarek kills us, let that be my sacrifice to save the rest. It's my fault we went looking for Salemis in the first place – if God Most High is ready to end our world over its selfishness, then let me be the one to pay for its redemption!"

The wizard Phaedra shook her head. "No, Criton, this isn't about us."

"Then why are you here?"

"To learn the Dragon Touched prayers of repentance. I don't think it's enough for all of *us* to repent, when it's not just about us. It's about our whole world, and the Lower Gods, and more than anything, the Yarek. *It's* the one that fought God Most High; I don't think we can save this world without it. My plan is to ask the *Yarek* to repent for its war against our God so long ago. If it's willing, I'm hoping to teach it a prayer spell."

Criton scoffed. "That's ridiculous. You're telling me it makes sense to let the Yarek unify and just hope it won't wage war against God Most High again? The Lower Gods are like rebellious children to Him, but the Yarek is God Most High's *enemy*. I don't like any plan that makes it stronger."

"Psander and I tried weakening the connections between the worlds, and it didn't work. We saw Illweather's growth with our own eyes – nothing's going to stop the Yarek from pulling our worlds together, Criton. But if we can combine the worlds peacefully, and convince the Yarek to repent rather than fight God Most High again, we can save this world *and* make it better."

Criton turned to Kilion. "Tell Phaedra she's lost her mind."

Kilion looked from one to the other, both so certain that they were right. "Ancient prophecy tells us that our repentance can help bring the day when God Most High will destroy the Yarek. It says nothing of teaching the Yarek to repent."

"A prophet named Salemis came to us not fifteen years ago," Phaedra answered, "and he told me and Criton that God Most High had grown more merciful. So I understand your position, but a prophecy is just a message, and we have a more recent message to suggest that our God is willing to change His mind."

"Salemis didn't say our God had grown more merciful *toward the Yarek*," Criton said, growing visibly frustrated. "Just because He's more merciful than He was before doesn't mean He can forgive a world-destroying monster."

"The ancient Yarek was a monster," Phaedra conceded, "and so is Illweather. But God Most High couldn't have split the Yarek into its kind and cruel halves if it didn't *have* a kind half. I've met Castle Goodweather. It was gentle and apologetic, even while it was dying in front of our eyes. Salemis and Bandu went to great lengths to make sure that the seed we planted in this world came from Castle Goodweather, so don't tell me it's incapable of cooperation or repentance."

Here was something new: Kilion had never heard of castles Illweather and Goodweather, though he understood by context what they were. It was shocking to think that Criton's first child – Vella's adoped daughter! – had been named after an aspect of the Yarek, even if Goodweather was supposed to be the kind half. Kilion had known all along that Bandu had a very different relationship with the Yarek than the Dragon Touched did, but this was almost too much to comprehend.

Criton was still arguing. "You want to let the Yarek re-form itself in our world, and still say it deserves the benefit of the doubt because the piece here came from Goodweather's seed. You can't have it both ways, Phaedra. You're telling us you have a plan to save the world, but your actual plan is to end it faster."

"We are supposed to welcome the end of this world," Kilion pointed out. "We are supposed to rejoice at the Yarek's defeat and join in God Most High's final victory. Let the Dragon Touched repent on our own behalf and on the behalf of humanity, and leave the Yarek to choose repentance or defeat. It is not our place to extend mercy to the Yarek, but neither do we have the right to deny it. I thank you for this message and this opportunity, Angel Phaedra. I will teach you our prayers for repentance. Use them as you will."

"I'm not an angel," Phaedra denied.

"An angel is a messenger from God," Criton snapped. "There is no other meaning of the word."

The two islanders stared at each other for a moment. Then, suddenly, they both grinned.

"I've been away too long," Phaedra said. "Hopefully I'll see more of you when this is all over."

Criton nodded his head. "You'll always be welcome here."

• • •

Three days later, with Phaedra already gone, Criton returned to the temple carrying a pair of axes. "Are you ready?" he asked Malkon.

"I'm ready. Father, will you bless our journey?"

"May our God bless you and protect you," Kilion murmured. "May He reveal His wishes to you and send you on the right path. May He favor you and grant you peace."

It was a traditional blessing, the most powerful one Kilion knew. Criton's argument for this backup plan had been strong, but that only made the high priest fear more for his son's life.

"Promise me," he had begged Malkon, "that you will wait until Phaedra has failed before you and Criton attempt to harm the Yarek. Criton is right that we cannot trust Phaedra to succeed, but it is blasphemy to try to make God Most High's decisions for Him. The Yarek must be given the chance to repent, do you understand?"

"Of course," Malkon had answered, tossing his head dismissively. "You're worried your own son will blaspheme?"

Kilion had tried to make eye contact, but his son had been busy adjusting his vestments. "I do not lack for worries," he had said.

He found himself repeating the phrase as his son and Criton rode off with their fifty picked men.

I do not lack for worries.

33
Bandu

It wasn't easy, but Bandu did her best to follow the Yarek's advice. She threw her full efforts into enjoying life, what little of it was left. She played with the dogs she trained, sweet stupid things. She raced through the woods with Goodweather. She listened to Vella, singing to herself while she cooked, and tried not to cry.

Vella kept asking her what was wrong, but Bandu couldn't bring herself to tell her. Instead she would shake her head with wet eyes and say, "We should be happy."

Vella thought it was about Bandu's aging. She raged over the lost years as if they still mattered now. But of course, she didn't know. Bandu couldn't bring herself to tell her; she only cried and refused to speak.

She no longer cared about her aging body: she cared that Goodweather would never grow. She shuddered thinking about the sea of dreamers in the land of the dead, how the raven-angels would drag her family apart with those pale talons to keep their dreams from swallowing them. Some people, who didn't know better, thought that the dead dwelled together in harmony, that they could see the loved ones they had lost and have a happier existence below than in this life. It was a terrible burden to know better. Bandu knew the underworld would give her no opportunity to play with Four-foot again, or see her daughter smile. Whatever people said or believed, no family would enjoy eternal life. They couldn't even dream together.

So she filled her days with Goodweather's smiles and Vella's love, and did her best to discard her useless anger and sadness. But she couldn't let go of those feelings, not completely. Why hadn't Castle Goodweather told her this would happen? Why hadn't Salemis – that great dragon who had pretended to be so kind? The Yarek said it was all because *she* had planted it here, but Bandu refused to accept that this was her fault. Others had *known*. She had only tried to make the world kinder.

Bandu was working with a pair of hound pups when she saw Phaedra riding toward her, her horse's reins in one hand and her staff in the other, wearing a dress as yellow as the sun. The dress billowed as she went; her horse was galloping toward their little house at top speed.

Goodweather ran from Bandu's side to the cottage door, calling "Myma! Phaedra's back!" until Vella came out in her apron. As they watched Phaedra's approach together, Bandu's joy at seeing her friend quickly faded. Here it came. The task.

Eleven years ago, Phaedra had brought with her the news that Criton was dead, and that only Bandu could bring him back. She had done what was asked of her and given her years so that Criton could make peace between the Dragon Touched and Ardis. She had done it to save Goodweather and Vella from the dangers of war, but it had bought them only eleven years. What did Phaedra want this time?

The dogs were barking. "Goodweather," Bandu said, "take the dogs back home. If Phaedra is here, I don't have time later."

"But Ma, *I* want to see Phaedra too!"

"See her when you come back."

"At least let me say hello to her first."

Bandu relented, and told the dogs to be quiet. Vella put an arm around Bandu, also thinking about the time Phaedra had come to take Bandu away. When Phaedra arrived, she dismounted from her tired, foamy horse and gave Bandu and Vella a hug before she even tied the reins to the post. "It's good to see you again. I'm sorry, I need Bandu's help."

"You can't!" Vella breathed. "What's happened this time?"

Phaedra looked from one to the other, and sighed. "The world's going to end unless we do something about it."

"Goodweather," Bandu said. "The dogs."

The trouble with dogs was that they reacted to Bandu's emotions too strongly, and they misinterpreted *everything*. The pups were growling now, thinking Phaedra must be some enemy if her presence made Bandu feel threatened. They'd try to bite her soon, and Bandu didn't want to have to kill them. That wouldn't make her neighbors happy, and they deserved their happiness too, before the end.

Goodweather turned, grumbling, and pulled on the dogs' leather collars, shushing them. Her magic was strong enough that they obeyed, if unwillingly, and soon both were running off beside her toward the town.

Bandu and Vella watched them go. Vella turned back first. "What do you mean, the world's going to end?"

Bandu took the horse's reins and found a place for it

away from the garden, rubbing the sweat off its mane with a rag. She could still hear what Phaedra was saying, but she almost didn't have to. She already knew the basic facts, she just didn't know the details.

Phaedra's solution saddened her. It wouldn't work.

"I speak to the Yarek already," Bandu confessed. "It doesn't care that it breaks."

"You don't understand," Phaedra said, as Vella pulled away, crying. "*What*? Bandu, why didn't you tell me?"

Bandu only bowed her head, tears in her eyes.

"Listen," Phaedra said, "the Yarek doesn't *have* to break. If the mesh unravels, the Yarek can go straight to wholeness without being shattered for eons first. The trouble is that I don't think God Most High will let us do it unless something very big changes. Psander only got as far as us unraveling the mesh, but she admitted she has no idea what would happen after that. Well, I've read the eschatologies now, and I think I know what'll happen. A unified Yarek will be so big, it'll easily end this world itself in a battle with God Most High. So unraveling the mesh is necessary, but it's not enough.

"What *would* work, though, is if the Yarek repented. The draconic eschatology says that only true repentance can save the world – I want the Yarek to be part of that. If it helps us open the mesh, and it repents fully to God Most High, it'll save the whole of existence. The only trouble is, I can't *talk* to the Yarek without an interpreter. That's why I need your help, Bandu. I need you to come with me, so you can tell me what it's saying."

Bandu sighed. "What do I lose this time?"

Phaedra looked confused. "What do you mean, Bandu? You don't lose anything. What do you have to lose now?"

"Time."

Phaedra and Vella both just stared, so against her will, Bandu had to elaborate. "For weeks now, I know all this. I know the world is dying: the Yarek tells me. It tells me, the sunshine is good. I can't stop the dying world, I only can be happy with sunshine and Goodweather and Vella before everything breaks. You think maybe it doesn't break, but you want me to leave Vella and Goodweather for it. You have time for us all to walk? No, you want me on horse with you, so we can go faster, because sky is breaking fast. No time for Goodweather. No time for sunshine."

"But Bandu," Vella said, "what if you help Phaedra, and it works? Then we'd have years together!"

"Phaedra doesn't need me," Bandu insisted. "You don't need me, Phaedra, only you think you need me. When I am little and don't know anything, Goodweather teaches me to understand. You are a wizard. If the Yarek wants to talk to you and you want to know what it says, then you understand. It can teach you. You don't need me."

"Goodweather taught you…?" Vella said. "I don't understand, Bandu."

"Goodweather is named after a living castle," Phaedra explained. "Castle Goodweather, the kind half of the Yarek. The great tree in this world came from that Goodweather's seed. But Bandu, I promise you I won't understand what it's saying without you. I've been to Castle Goodweather. Psander and I needed the elves to interpret its speech for us; we didn't understand it ourselves."

"Maybe you have elves, so you don't try," Bandu said. "Understand the Yarek is only hard if you don't listen. If Yarek wants you to know what it says, and you listen, then you understand. I stay here, and tell it to try harder."

The disappointment on Phaedra's face was unmistakable. "You're not going to come with me? What if you're wrong?"

"I am not wrong. What if *you* are wrong? Then I lose my last times with Vella and Goodweather, and our world still breaks. I never see them again. No, Phaedra. You go without me. You *try*."

"And if I get there, and I can't hear it? What if I *could* have saved our world, but I can't without you?"

Bandu waved her away. "You don't save our world, the *Yarek* saves our world, and even when you don't hear it, it hears you. If it likes your idea, if it wants to say sorry to God Most High, then it hears you and it says sorry. It doesn't need me. Vella does. Goodweather does."

Phaedra bowed her head. "Then I've wasted my time. I should have gone straight south. You're sure you won't come?"

She looked so crushed that Bandu had to give her a reassuring hug. "You can talk to the Yarek," she said. "I trust you. I hope it does too."

"Will you stay awhile?" Vella asked. "Let your horse rest an hour – it needs it. We can eat something, and wait for Goodweather to get back."

Phaedra shook her head, and made her way back to her weary horse. "I shouldn't. Every moment counts. I can let the horse trot a bit, but I can't stop now. I hope you're right about the Yarek, and I hope I'll see you again someday soon. Enjoy… enjoy the sunshine."

With that, Phaedra mounted, using her staff to push off the ground. "Good luck!" Vella said. "We're counting on you."

Phaedra nodded, miserable, and rode away. "I miss

you!" Bandu called out to her. "If the Yarek listens, come back here after!"

Phaedra only waved.

Bandu turned back to her wife, and they embraced. "I love you so much," Vella said. "Thank you for staying with us."

Bandu nodded, holding her tight. The burden had lifted. It was in Phaedra's hands now, and in the Yarek's, and that was good. Let Vella's God choose someone else for once. Bandu could live and love her family, hoping that the world would not end after all, and enjoying every moment before it did.

"I am sorry I don't tell you before," she said. "I should tell you."

"It's a hard thing to say," Vella answered, "and there was nothing I could have done about it. You should have told me, but I understand why you didn't. Let's not tell Goodweather, though. She can't do anything about it either, and I don't want her to worry. Let's just trust in Phaedra and hold each other closer from now on."

34

CRITON

He parted with Delika last. He knew that would be the hardest.

"I'll be away for a few weeks," he said. "There's something I have to do."

The girl's eyes were wide and frightened. "Tell me. Please tell me what you're doing."

What to say? He was riding to save her, to save the world. "You know the Great Tree?" he said. "I'm going to chop it down."

He saw anger in her eyes – the anger of confirmation. She had known; she had seen him gathering his axmen and hoped that her guess was wrong.

"It won't let you," she said. "It's part of that ancient monster. Criton, it'll kill you!"

Criton put a scaly hand on her shoulder. "I've fought it before, love. With God's help, I won't fail."

"But what if you do? What if you never come back? At least your other wives have families to return to."

"Then I'd better come back to you," he said with a smile. She didn't return it.

What could he say to make her feel better? She could

not dissuade him from going, and they both knew it. He'd never shied away from what had to be done, no matter the risk. He'd saved his friends from the Red Priest in Anardis, when anyone else would have abandoned them. He'd confronted Castle Illweather alone, without even Bandu at his side, and rescued Delika and all the others from its depths. And though Narky had insisted it was suicide, he had rescued the Dragon Knight's prophecy from the worshippers of Mayar. Delika knew that the man who had pulled her from the sea was not afraid to risk his life – that was why she had appealed to his love for her, instead of dwelling on the danger he himself would be facing.

The reason she was so angry about it was that she knew this was a fight she would lose. Of *course* he loved her; that was why he couldn't sit back and rely on Phaedra. How could he sit on his hands and *hope* that the Yarek would repent, when he had this girl to protect? He had been wrong to let her grow dependant on him, that much was true, and it would be terribly hard on her if he died on this mission; but far worse than her having to live without him would be for her *not* to live.

"I *will* come back," he said. "I won't leave you alone. Please believe me."

"You've done it twice already," Delika answered tearfully. "How do you know this third time won't be the last?"

He didn't have an answer for that, so instead he used a trick he'd learned from Bandu. He kissed her.

"I'll come back," he repeated.

He meant it. He'd gone into danger so many times before, and for lesser causes. It was hard to believe that

God Most High would turn His back on Criton now. Victory was the only option.

Delika clung to him, sobbing. "I don't want you to die."

Her dependence aroused him, that was the shameful thing. Vella was right about that. He kissed his wife on the forehead and gently pushed her away.

"I have to go, love."

"Promise me you'll come back," she sobbed.

"Of course," he answered. "Even death couldn't stop me – you of all people should know that."

He left the house feeling strong and confident, ready to fulfill his destiny. He gathered his men and picked up Malkon from the temple, and together they rode from the city.

"Where are we going?" Malkon asked as Criton turned eastward. "The enemy of God Most High is *that* way!"

"I know," Criton said. "We're going to pick up my daughter first."

Malkon reined his horse in. "Why? Why put Goodweather in danger? She won't be of use, Criton, she's twelve."

"Don't assume what you don't know. Goodweather isn't just my eldest, she's Bandu's daughter. Bandu will have taught her how to talk to trees and animals – she'll be able to communicate with the Yarek. Phaedra's going to get Bandu to translate for her, so who've we got? Only Goodweather. Without her, how will we know if we've passed Phaedra and gotten there first, or if Phaedra and Bandu have already been there and failed? Goodweather will be able to find that out. Besides, the Yarek will listen and respond to her, so if it comes to an assault she should be able to distract it. A wise woman told me once, never use force when you can use overwhelming force. I want Goodweather by my side."

"You're willing to let her die with us?"

"We're not riding to die, Malkon, we're riding to win. She has a bigger risk of dying if we fail."

"My sister won't let her come with us, not if Bandu is going with Phaedra."

"God Most High will provide."

Criton was right: God Most High did provide. When they stopped in the village near Bandu's house two days later, there Goodweather was.

"Father! Uncle Malkon! What are you doing here?"

"I want you to join us," Criton said. "We're going to save the world."

Goodweather looked more awed than surprised. "Phaedra said it would end unless we did something. She didn't say she was here with you!"

"She's not," Criton admitted, dismounting. "Phaedra is trying one way, we're trying another. This is too important to have just one plan for dealing with it."

"Oh. All right. Can you give me a ride home, and I'll ask if I can go with you?"

Criton shook his head. "Our way is dangerous. If you ask, they won't let you go. Phaedra's going to convince them to try her way and won't even tell them about mine. Is she there now, or has she left already?"

"I don't know. She was there when I came here to bring the dogs back, but she looked like she was in an awful hurry."

"It's good if she gets there a bit before us, so she can try her way before we try ours. Still, if you want to come, we should go now and send someone to let them know you came with me."

His daughter looked torn. "They'll be really angry."

"I know. But they'll be angry at me, not you. We can say I didn't give you a choice."

That gave her pause. "You are, though, right?"

Criton smiled. "Of course. Do you *want* to come with us?"

"Yes!"

"Then let's go!"

He helped her onto his horse and climbed up behind her, ignoring Malkon's disapproving look. "*Now* we're ready to go south," he said. "Let's go chop down that tree."

35
NARKY

Narky stood in the library, still wearing his nightrobe, watching as the other priests filed in. They stared at him – how could they not? – but said nothing. They all knew something big was happening, and the mood was ominous.

Narky didn't even know what to say or where to begin. It was too dangerous to tell them that the Lord Below had given him orders, and yet if people came to believe that Ravennis had cast him aside for good it would put Ptera and Grace in mortal danger. How could he thread that needle?

His succession was another problem. Father Lepidos was the obvious choice, but his rivalry with Ptera would also make him a humiliating one... and any further humiliation had the potential to endanger Narky's family. Lepidos would make a good enough leader for the church – certainly, Mother Dinendra had trusted the man enough to elevate him in Ardis – but Narky suspected that choosing him would mean Ptera's downfall.

To choose Ptera instead would carry its own dangers, primarily because it would reek of nepotism. Those who had begun their careers as priests of Elkinar might well rebel against her leadership, and such a schism would be disastrous for the Church of Ravennis. Yet Ptera had taken on Narky's duties before, when the Dragon Touched had held him prisoner, and her political skills had saved the church. She had studied under the Graceful Servant herself, had stood toe-to-toe with King Magerion, and knew what struggles Narky had faced in the position. On the merits, she deserved the mantle as well as anyone.

If only Ravennis had chosen Ptera for him, his fellow priests would have accepted the God's word without question. But He hadn't, and Narky was a terrible liar. If he said that Ravennis had appointed Ptera His high priestess, would people really believe him? For that matter, would Ravennis forgive him for that kind of presumptuousness? Or would it only endanger Ptera further?

The priests were all here now. They were watching him.

"I... have news," Narky said. "Ravennis visited me last night."

He paused there, unsure of how to proceed. The whole room seemed to be holding its breath.

"Everything I've told you is true," he blurted. "The prophecy He sent us is true, and all my doctrines and teachings – our Lord Below didn't have a problem with any of them. But He doesn't want me to stay as His high priest. He told me to choose my successor and go."

There were gasps and stares, and glances toward Lepidos and Ptera. Narky took a deep breath, feeling paralyzed. Nobody asked where he was going – they were waiting to hear about the future of the church.

"I think next time, it makes sense for our leaders to form a council and choose the high priest together. But

Ravennis told *me* to choose this time. He gave me that honor. Ptera has led the church before, and she gained King Magerion's respect when she did it. I trust her to be your high priestess."

He felt all the frowns like a stab in the gut. Ptera stared at him, wide-eyed and horrified, and he knew that he had miscalculated. Damn. He should have asked her what she thought before he sent her to gather everyone. He should have demanded that Ravennis choose for him. He hadn't expected such an obviously negative reaction, not so quickly or from so many of them. Had he just caused a schism in his own church? Or worse, had he doomed his wife to lead a totally unified, entirely resentful, potentially murderous clergy?

He had thought Ptera was widely respected – he *knew* she was – but he could see how angry they all were on her rival's behalf. Gods, he should have known. Lepidos had been the easy choice, the obvious choice, and yet he, the disgraced high priest, had chosen to elevate his own wife on his way out the door. No, nobody hated Ptera – but they could hate Narky through her.

Damn. It was too late to take it back now. He had thrown his family to the wolves, and now it was up to Ptera to find a way out of this mess. He couldn't even stay to help.

He said his goodbyes quickly, and fled. On his way out, he spotted a sacrificial knife lying on the altar, and swiped it. It was a silly precaution – there were plenty of knives around if his former subordinates chose to murder his family, and that step wasn't likely to come within the first few hours anyhow. The priests weren't plotting Ptera's murder just yet; they were only angry. It would take time for them to settle on that solution if they ever did.

Still, it made him feel safer.

The years of priesthood had turned Narky soft, or else maybe he'd always been soft. His first week as an ex-priest nearly killed him. He'd never had to survive alone like this, not since his flight from his hometown, and even then he'd had money with which to buy food. Now he had nothing, no money, no friends, not even proper clothes. Word of his disgrace traveled faster than he could walk, and the change in people's reactions to him was at once astounding and familiar. Once more, doors were slammed in his face. Once more, he was a bearer of bad luck. The Black Cursebringer, not the Black Priest.

It was a shock to have his fortunes change so quickly, but not because he was surprised. He'd always expected this, even when the expectation had made no outward sense. His shock came from the stark suddenness of the change, predictable though it might have been. It was like jumping in a half-frozen river: he'd been bracing himself for ages, and it still didn't help him a whit.

He'd never flattered himself that people would be kind to him as a deposed high priest. Narky had never had any friends here, only followers, and those followers all belonged to Ravennis, not him. Ptera still loved him, probably, but in exchange he'd put her and Grace in mortal danger. Whatever her feelings, her duty now lay with the church, and with the son who must be protected from his father's disgrace.

Narky was alone, truly alone. He shied away from people whenever he saw them – there was nothing to protect him from violence now, nothing but his wits.

Who was to say that no enterprising farmer would take it upon himself to kill this cursed wanderer? For that matter, what was to stop Mageris from sending men to murder him? The king had always hated him personally. Now was his chance.

So Narky fled. He hid in barns among the animals and in fields among the grasses, their stalks only tall enough to hide him if he crouched. He lived by stealing, and wished he had Bandu's skill at finding food wherever she went. Better yet, he wished he had Bandu with him, and Criton, and Hunter, and…

Never mind.

He considered going north to the Dragon Touched and throwing himself at Criton's feet, but had to reject the idea. If he went to Salemica, Criton would give him food and a place to stay and turn this test of faith into a faithless dependence on his friend's goodwill. He would keep Narky from doing what needed to be done.

It was a shame, because Criton might have been able to help him find Phaedra. Even if she never came to Salemica, the unofficial king of the Dragon Touched would have resources that could help Narky track her.

For that matter, Bandu would have been even more helpful. That woman could find anything she looked for, no matter the distance or the weather or who got in her way. But recruiting her help would be a disastrous choice, even if he could track down where she was living. If Bandu was with him when he found Phaedra, she could stop him when it came time to do what his God had demanded. Phaedra might let her guard down, for all that she knew Narky was a murderer, but Bandu never let her guard down.

As far as Narky knew, Hunter was far away in the world of the fairies – and thank the Gods for that. Hunter would have defended Phaedra to the death, and it wouldn't have been *his* death. Narky had seen what the man could do with a weapon.

There was no one else he could go to, no one else he could ask for help. He'd only ever had four friends in the world, and now he had to kill one of them.

He cried as he walked, thinking of Phaedra and of the injustice his God had visited upon him. Why should he have to kill the one person he respected most in the world, far beyond himself, beyond even his wife? He had never thought that life was fair, but this was too much, even for a man who'd driven the God of Justice out of Hagardis.

Narky had never considered refusing an order from Ravennis before. Ever since Ravennis had spared his life and marked him with the scar that he no longer bore on his chest, he had been nothing if not a loyal servant. But this? This might be too much.

No single person had influenced Narky's life so much. It was Phaedra who had read him the account of a Laarnan priest when he'd only barely recovered from his first encounter with his God, Phaedra who had taken the time to teach him when everyone else had just wanted him to shut up. What few social graces Narky had, he owed to Phaedra. She was greatly responsible for his friendship with Criton, and even for his relationship with Ptera. Whenever he was afraid of saying the wrong thing, he always tried to imagine how Phaedra might advise him.

The thing about Phaedra was that she wasn't dogmatic. She was always trying to learn more, always willing to consider new facts, never afraid to say that she had been wrong. It defied Narky's every instinct to believe what Ravennis had told him, that it would impossible to convince her to spare the underworld from her misguided plan. Narky was admittedly terrible at persuasion, but if there was one person who could look past his demeanor and instantly grasp what he was trying to express, it was Phaedra. Whatever the Lord of Fate said, he couldn't bring himself to believe that she was unpersuadable.

Could it really hurt to try?

Either way, he had to find her first. He was no tracker and was too afraid to ask people if they'd seen her lest they report his whereabouts to Mageris, so instead he made his way toward the great tree on the horizon. If she had this disastrous plan to unify the Yarek, she was bound to end up there eventually.

He passed Anardis and kept going. The Yarek seemed to grow larger and larger as he went, its terrible bulk taking up an increasing amount of room on the horizon. Eventually he judged himself far enough from Ardis to travel along Atel's roads without fear of assassination – or, rather, still with the *fear* of assassination but without its reasonable expectation. At one point he had to drop face down in a ditch to avoid a company of riders, terrified that Mageris had sent them after him. He never got a good look at them, and he rose with a face full of mud that hardened as it dried, turning his beard stiff and brown. Not that he cared about his appearance – if anything, there was a strange satisfaction in knowing that he looked as abandoned as he felt.

And then, at last, he found her.

It was just past sunset when Narky crept into a barn to

sleep and found Phaedra there reading, a lamp at her side and a codex in her lap. She didn't even notice him at first, quiet as he had learned to be, and when she finally looked up she yelped and shrank away. Narky stood, momentarily paralyzed. His God was watching, he knew. The knife was already in his hand, its blade hidden in his sleeve.

Phaedra scrambled to her feet, leaving the book open on the ground and lifting her lamp high. "Keep away from me," she cried as she rose, but then she recognized his face and her eyes filled with wonder. "Narky?"

He didn't know what to say. Oh Gods, he didn't know what to say! The knife was huge and obvious, well suited to slaughtering cattle – could she see its outline even through his sleeve? What could he possibly say to distract her from it?

"Hi," he said.

"Oh God, Narky, what happened?"

He looked down at the ground. Behind the walls of their enclosure, some piglets snorted.

"It's not important. I left the priesthood and... came looking for you."

"Why? Did Criton say something to you? Did you come to try to stop me?"

"Yes," he said. "But Criton didn't – hold on, what would Criton have said to me?"

"Never mind. If Criton didn't talk to you, though, why did you come to stop me?"

"Because whatever you're planning on doing down here, it's a mistake."

"I'm saving our world from the skyquakes, Narky. I'm unraveling the mesh before it tears us all to shreds."

Oh.

Phaedra frowned at his stunned expression. "What did you *think* I was doing?"

But Narky couldn't answer, because it was all coming together. If Phaedra unraveled the mesh, the Yarek would reunite, and its roots would pierce the underworld. It would slay Ravennis and devour every soul that dwelt in His domain, and every soul that ever descended to that place thereafter. That was why Ravennis had sent him – that was what He had meant by "sacrificing the underworld to the Yarek."

What Ravennis hadn't said was that if Phaedra did nothing, *only* the underworld would survive. This whole world would be sliced to pieces, and Narky and his family, Ptera, Grace, his friends and all those they loved, would perish. How could Narky even begin to fathom such a thing, let alone decide that he preferred it that way?

"Narky?" Phaedra repeated. "What did you think I was trying to do?"

He swallowed. "Ravennis came to me. If you go through with this, the Yarek will end the underworld. It'll grow even bigger, and stronger, and it'll *eat* it. Everyone who's ever died, and all of us too, everyone who dies afterward, will get eaten by the Yarek when we go, instead of getting the afterlife Ravennis prepared for us. He sent me to... tell you not to do it."

Phaedra glanced down toward her book, clearly thinking this over. "I'll admit," she said, "I hadn't even considered the underworld. But I don't – I mean, I *think* it should be all right. I'm hoping the Yarek will repent to God Most High and live here in peace, and if it does, it shouldn't do too much harm to the underworld. I'll have to remember to tell it to be careful down there too, once the worlds have combined. It'll be fine, Narky. I know it's risky, but I'm almost sure it'll be fine."

"Phaedra. Ravennis is the Keeper of Fates."

"He also has obvious reasons not to want this world saved, even if it *can* be done."

Narky couldn't deny that, and didn't care to try. His God had always been sly and manipulative, and there was no doubt that a shattered world would mean an entire world full of souls all going to Ravennis. Who knew how much power that would give Him?

But if Narky didn't exactly trust Ravennis, he trusted the Yarek even less. He still remembered how Castle Illweather had tried to kill him and its other captives, even after the elves had promised them their safety for eleven days. It had tried to kill its elves too, and only some ancient curse had stopped it from succeeding. The very notion of that monster repenting was absurd.

Yet Phaedra believed that it could. If she could do that, despite all the evidence that it was a true monster, how could Narky ever convince her otherwise? Ravennis was right: he would not succeed.

He could see now why the Sephan scroll had come to him: it was to prepare him for this moment. He was being given the choice, right now, between the world and the underworld, between this life and eternity. If he let Phaedra go, the Yarek would devour the underworld, and what remained of this short life would be all anyone had. If Phaedra died tonight, this whole world would be destroyed, but the underworld would remain. Ptera and Grace would live on with Narky forever in the world below. *Phaedra* would live on eternally...

There was no dilemma here after all. He had thought

Ravennis was commanding him to murder his friend, but he had misunderstood the situation entirely. Ravennis had given him the chance to *save* his friend, to save *all* his friends. It was Narky, not Phaedra, who could save the world.

Finally he understood why it was he who needed to perform this task. Ravennis had chosen him, Narky the coward's son, both because Phaedra would not think to protect herself against him and because he was willing to do the right thing no matter how low, cruel, or dishonorable it seemed. He had shot a man in the back to save Hunter – he would not refuse to kill Phaedra if it meant she and everyone would live on eternally when this world was gone.

His mind went back to what Hunter had told him, so many years ago. *You're going to die, Narky. Sooner or later, you're going to die. Wouldn't you rather die a decent person?* This was his test. Would he let his fear of death, his fear of the unknown, prevent him from saving the afterlife – from saving his God?

No. He would not.

"Phaedra," Narky said. "You know how much I respect you. You're brilliant, and you've always been good to me even when no one else was. I'll pray for Ravennis to reward you in the World Below. You deserve it more than anyone I know."

With that, he pulled up his sleeve and advanced on his friend with the sacrificial knife. Phaedra might back away from him now, screaming and begging for her life, but she would thank him when they met again, in the World Below.

She would thank him.

36
VELLA

Goodweather couldn't be expected to return from town for a good while longer, so Vella and Bandu took full advantage of her absence to make love. Afterwards they lay together for a time, smiling. Vella hadn't felt this happy in ages. The cloud of her fears and resentments had lifted, replaced by a deep calm. They talked about unimportant things, feeling happy and normal. Vella thanked God Most High that Bandu had made the choice she had.

Eventually, judging that Goodweather would be home soon, they rose and worked together on the day's meal. Vella started one of her quick soups – she loved soup – and she and Bandu argued playfully about what to include. Life was good.

But Goodweather hadn't returned by the time the soup was ready to eat. It had been too long already – far too long. Vella took the soup off the fire and they rushed outside, looking down the path that led to the village. There was no one on it, as far as the eye could see.

"Oh God," Vella breathed. "Where is she? Where *is* she, Bandu?"

She knew the answer before Bandu said it. "Gone."

They forgot about eating and raced, both of them, toward the village. They were almost there before Vella even thought to worry about the house burning down. The fire had been small, and she didn't *think* she'd left anything near it besides the cooking irons. All she could do now was hope.

Vella outran Bandu and reached the village first. She saw the cooper drawing water from the well and ran to him, panting, "Goodweather – where is she? Have you seen my daughter?"

"Oh, sure I did. Her father came for her, with your brother and some forty or fifty soldiers on horseback. I thought you knew."

Vella stared. "You. Thought. I knew? No one came to tell us!"

"Oh. I'm real sorry."

Vella turned away from him, reeling. Bandu had only been a few paces behind and now caught up, having heard their exchange. "Criton takes her."

"And my brother too. What are they up to?"

"The soldiers," Bandu said, turning to the cobbler. "They have axes?"

"Yeah, how did you know?"

Vella and her wife exchanged a glance. The Yarek. Criton had kidnapped their daughter and taken her with him to chop down the Yarek. How dare he bring her into such danger? How could Malkon have gone along with it?

How could Vella and Bandu catch up to them?

"We need a horse," Bandu said.

"We have no money for a horse."

"We have a house."

Vella nodded. Hopefully it hadn't burnt down. It was

the only home they had ever shared, but it was worthless next to Goodweather's safety. "Parash might sell us his mare."

But when they found Parash, he wasn't interested in a trade. "Take the horse," he said. "Your house and lands are yours."

"We'll never be able to pay back a loan," Vella protested.

"The high priest is your father," Parash answered. "I'll have double the horse's value back by next week. Just write your father a letter saying what I gave you, and I can loan you some money for your journey too."

Vella nodded dumbly, too focused on retrieving Goodweather to feel embarrassed. Normally, she'd have cringed to think that she was taking advantage of her family's station and getting better treatment than she'd have received on her own merits. Now, she only felt grateful.

So she took her neighbor's money and his horse, and wrote an accounting of the "gift" for Parash to bring to her father in Salemica. She didn't even know how to ride, but Parash boosted her up to sit behind Bandu so that all she had to do was cling to her wife as they rode in pursuit of Criton and his company.

Her mood darkened as they rode – even the terror of falling off a galloping horse couldn't overshadow her anger at Criton and her brother. How *dare* they take her daughter from her? Criton hadn't even raised the girl, only showered her with attention a few weeks a year. Vella and Bandu were her real parents, and he'd stolen her away from them.

Bandu drove the mare onward until the poor thing was completely spent, stopping at a farmstead on the border of

Ardisian territory. There they exchanged the mare for an older gelding, Bandu thanking the horse for her service, and rode on. They were hours behind the men who had stolen their daughter, and they could not afford to stop.

They went on like this for days, making worse and worse bargains just to keep moving. Criton and his men had proper warhorses, they knew, not these poor creatures used to dragging plows across muddy fields. The two of them slept on floors and shared people's meals, first relying on respect for Vella's father and then, deeper in Ardisian territory, on the money Parash had given them. There were those who wouldn't deal with them even then – one man actually rode out to chase them off his land, cursing them and the riders who came before them. He was carrying a spear, and Vella was afraid he would attack them with it.

Bandu must have thought something similar, but she was in no mood to back down. Instead, she locked eyes with the man's horse and said, "Throw him."

The horse obeyed, and as the man lay cursing and moaning on the ground the women climbed down from their own tired nag and onto his. Vella wondered if he had seriously injured himself, but they didn't stay to find out.

Bandu said they were catching up to Criton, but Vella couldn't see how she knew. There were two more skyquakes as they rode, violent and terrifying, dropping knuckle-sized hailstones despite the summer heat, spooking livestock, shaking broken birds from the sky.

"I hope Phaedra's hurrying," Vella said.

"I think we pass her already somewhere."

Bandu was probably right. Vella prayed to God Most High that she'd still make it on time.

The Yarek grew from a line on the horizon to a towering mass that seemed at times to *be* half the horizon. They were only a few miles away now, and they still hadn't caught up. At least the trail of horse droppings before them was fresh. Their timing would be a close thing. Vella prayed they wouldn't be too late to save their daughter.

At long last, they crested the final hill and saw Criton's company gathered just outside a thicket of vines that surrounded the Yarek's massive trunk.

"They're still alive," Vella breathed. "They haven't attacked yet – we might be in time, Bandu!"

She could not see Bandu's face, but when she heard her voice, she knew her wife was gritting her teeth. "Have to get there first," she said, barely audible over the thundering of their horse's hooves and the wind whistling in Vella's ears. "They can't hear us here. Close isn't close enough."

She was right, of course. The men and horses did not sit still waiting for them. Goodweather's mothers had barely closed half the distance to their daughter before the horsemen began wading into the thicket.

"Faster," Bandu urged their horse. "This is bad. So bad."

Vella clung to her and hoped.

37

GOODWEATHER

The journey south hadn't been an easy one, but the joy and excitement of riding with her father and uncle to save the world was indescribable. *To save the world!* She was so lucky to be a part of this, so proud that Father thought she was worthy.

She felt good around these men, with their beards and their big arms; she loved being part of their company. She wondered what her father would think if she grew up to be like them. Would Myma be upset? Would Ma even care? She could do it, she thought, if she decided she wanted to. She'd always been good at transformations.

Goodweather had never seen the Yarek except on the distant horizon, and she could hardly believe the way it kept growing and growing as the days went on. It looked so huge now – surely any moment they'd be reaching it already? And yet each night they made camp without having arrived at its trunk, and with every mile of travel it seemed to grow even bigger.

The axmen commented on it one night, when Father said they were only a day or two away. "How are we supposed to cut down a tree that size?" Pitra asked. "We'll be burying our axes past the hilt before we get halfway into it!"

"God Most High will help us," Uncle Malkon said. "We don't have to finish the job ourselves, but that doesn't mean we can skip the work. We're asking for divine intervention – we won't get it the lazy way, without putting our bodies and souls into it."

"Did you hear that from Grandpa a lot?"

Malkon scowled at first, but when he saw the grin on Goodweather's face he couldn't help but laugh. "We should have left you at home, you little monster."

The closer they came to the Yarek, the more nervous Father became about having passed Phaedra without knowing it. He'd expected his to be the backup plan in case she failed, but as time went by it became more and more obvious that Phaedra was behind them somewhere, not ahead. Goodweather heard him discussing the problem with her uncle the night before they arrived, murmuring in the darkness after all the others had gone to sleep.

"We've had two skyquakes in three weeks now – we can't have much longer before the Yarek brings the skies down on our heads. How long can we wait for her if she's behind us? I want to give her the chance to do this the peaceful way, I really do, but what if she's been delayed somehow?"

"Then we have no choice," Malkon answered. "Patience is all well and good, but not when the difference between success and the world's destruction could be as little as a few hours. We don't know how long we have left. It would be too stupid if the world ended while we were still waiting."

Her father's voice was resigned. "You're right. And if

she *was* still ahead of us and the Yarek killed her, I don't think we'd even know. It'd bring her body down to where the roots are. Where the underworld begins."

Oh yes, this was where Ma had gone to bring him back, when Goodweather was just a baby. Now that she saw the size of that tree, she could easily believe that its roots went all the way down to the underworld.

Goodweather couldn't believe that the Yarek had killed Phaedra, no matter what Father feared. She *wouldn't* believe that. Phaedra had always been so kind and generous to her, and she was glamorous and powerful – Goodweather couldn't believe that a wizard like her would let herself be killed by an old tree, no matter how big and ancient it was. No, something must have delayed her. Maybe she'd still been visiting with Goodweather's mothers when Father's company rode out. Maybe she'd *always* been behind them. Or maybe they'd taken slightly different routes at the beginning, and their horses were faster than hers. She easily *could* have fallen behind at some point.

This whole thing was getting realer now. They were riding toward an enemy that Father clearly thought *could* kill Phaedra, and they had nothing but axes and prayers to fight it with. Come to think of it, Goodweather didn't even have that. Why did he need her again?

They rode out late the next day, giving Phaedra an extra hour or two to catch up. It made no difference – she was nowhere on the horizon. When they finally came to the base of the Yarek, Goodweather gasped at its sheer majesty. The Yarek was bigger than anything she had ever imagined, and it wasn't defenseless. Its trunk was surrounded by dense spiny thornbushes and thick vines with red, angry-looking leaves. A few of these were draped from branches far, far above, but most lay along the ground like feathered snakes waiting to strike. Goodweather wondered if they could.

Just outside this thicket, Father reined in their horse. "Goodweather," he said, his voice low. "See if you can find out whether Phaedra has been here or not."

"How?" She couldn't see any sign that the thorns or vines had been disturbed, but maybe she wouldn't have anyway.

Her father twisted around the saddle. "Ask it, sweetheart. I can't do it myself – I've never understood the Yarek."

Suddenly, she couldn't breathe. Was *this* why Father wanted her here – so she could talk to the Yarek and be his interpreter? How was she supposed to do that? Ma was the one who could speak with plants and animals and understand their responses, not Goodweather! She'd barely even tried! Father must have assumed that Ma had taught her. Why hadn't he asked Goodweather if she could do this *before* he asked her to come?

She was going to let him down. God, why hadn't she asked him what he wanted her for? Here she'd been, all proud that her father had invited her on this great adventure, that he *needed her help* on a mission, and she hadn't even asked him what her job would be! This was all her fault.

There was nothing left to do but try, though. Goodweather couldn't be *useless*, not now when her father needed her.

"Um," she said. "Yarek? Can you hear me?"

Oh, help! Was it trying to answer back somehow? All she could feel was a light breeze blowing from one side – was that the Yarek's response?

"Has – has Phaedra been here already?"

Nothing. No response.

"I…" Goodweather said to her father, to her uncle, to all these men who were relying on her to do something she didn't know how to do, "I don't think it wants to tell me. I can't make it."

Her father and Uncle Malkon shared a look with each other, and Goodweather cringed.

"Let's get closer," Malkon said. "Maybe it'll hear you better if we're up by the trunk."

So they rode in among the vines and brambles, the axmen leaving their weapons in their holsters. It wouldn't do to make the tree suspicious, not now. Not before it was too late.

The ground shifted; their horses stumbled. A giant root burst from the ground and struck Pitra from his mount. He barely had time to scream: when he hit the ground, the vines enveloped him so fast that within moments all she could see of him were thrashing leaves.

"Go!" Malkon shouted. "The Yarek is attacking!"

He spurred his horse and went crashing ahead, letting the straps that held his axe to his back drop off his shoulders and deftly catching its haft behind him with one hand while the other still held his reins. The others followed suit and soon they were all racing through the murderous brambles toward the trunk.

Pitra had been the first to fall, but he wasn't the last. One after another, men were torn from their saddles and devoured by roots and vines. Nor were their horses spared: though the poor animals screamed and turned away from the great tree, the grasping roots soon caught them too.

"Hold on tight," Father called back to her. "We're going

to have to–"

Their horse went down just as he said it, but the two of them did not go down with it. Goodweather clung to her father, terrified, as they rose into the air and continued onward. Father's axe, still strapped to his back as Malkon's had been, remained stuck between their bodies, hard and painful against Goodweather's chest.

"Can you pull that out?" he asked her. "I'm going to need it."

She couldn't; she could barely stay on his back as he dodged whipping vines and sweeping branches, assaulting them from seemingly all directions.

What if he dropped her? She chanced a look below and found half of Father's men already gone, swallowed by the vegetation.

Uncle Malkon was at the front of the pack, swinging his axe one-handed at any thornbush or snake-vine that got in his path. She gasped when his horse got entangled at the legs and fell, but he leapt from its back and kept running, dodging roots and vines as he went. Goodweather had never seen him move so quickly.

Father suddenly plunged downward, and Goodweather screamed, but he had only been dodging another attack from the Yarek. It assaulted the two of them with branches swooshing through the air and vines whipping toward them from below.

"You've got to get that axe for me," he panted. "I'm holding your legs – you won't fall. Just get me that axe."

It was terrifying, but she did as he said, leaning back far enough to grip the haft and lift it out of its bindings. As soon as she had her arms around his shoulders again he let go of her legs and took the weapon, and it was all Goodweather could do to keep from accidentally strangling him.

She could hear her uncle on the ground, shouting a prayer as he ran onward. "You who defeated the Yarek of old…"

He reached the trunk and began chopping at it furiously, praying as he struck it over and over again. The axe looked so puny compared to the trunk, like trying to knock down a house with a reed. Would God Most High come to his aid as he had suggested? He was certainly giving this his whole effort.

The vines snuck up on him from behind. They caught him around the chest just as he struck another blow against the trunk and yanked him back into the thicket with his axe still stuck in the Yarek. Goodweather cried out, but he was already gone.

Her voice was not the only one screaming, though.

Father heard it too. He spun in the air to see who had made the noise, and there was Vella, floating like the two of them in the air, crying for her lost brother.

"Myma!" Goodweather shouted. "Myma! Myma! Bring me back to Myma!" Tears were streaming down her face now. She didn't want to die. Oh please, please Father, she didn't want to die.

"Criton!" Vella shouted, flying near. "Give her to me!"

The air seemed to crystalize. The Yarek stopped swinging at them – the world stood still. At last Goodweather could hear her Ma Bandu's voice, rippling through the ground and air.

Spare my wife and daughter. They don't come to fight you. Please, let them live. If you hurt them, you kill me. You are from Goodweather's seed – I grow you in this place because you are not wicked like the Gods. You are not wicked. Let them go.

The Yarek did not move. "Please," Goodweather's Myma said to Criton. "Please, give her back."

Goodweather could feel her father stiffen. He had heard Ma's words too. He knew she had not begged for *his* life.

"Please," Goodweather sobbed. She needed this to be over so badly. "Please, give me to Myma."

At last, Father nodded. "I've been just like the dragons," he said, flying her back toward her mothers. "Arrogant in the face of God Most High. Phaedra was right – this task was not for us. I'm sorry, Goodweather. I'm so sorry I brought you here."

"Give me back to them," Goodweather repeated, shutting her eyes.

She opened them again when she felt her Myma's arm reaching to hug her around the torso, lifting her off her father and into her arms. Ma still had her face to the ground far below, begging the Yarek to spare them, to let Goodweather's mothers have her back. Goodweather wiped tears from her eyes and turned in her Myma's arms to thank Father for letting her go.

A writhing mass of vines had risen behind him, and as she watched in horror the Yarek caught Father and broke him, slammed him against its trunk and then, at a leisurely, sickening pace, pulled his body down into the ground. He barely had time to grunt.

Goodweather lost track of what happened after that.

Somehow her mothers were on either side of her now, wrapping their arms around her from both directions as all three of them stood on solid ground, weeping from the horror and the relief.

"It's all my fault," Goodweather heard herself say. "If I'd known how to talk to it, it wouldn't have attacked us.

I could have…"

"It's not your fault," Myma said. "Let's go home, Bandu. I have to tell my father his son is dead."

Ma nodded and kissed Goodweather on the temple. "Thank you for saving her."

"*You* saved her. Phaedra was right – the Yarek listens to you."

"It listens to Phaedra too."

Goodweather looked back at the great tree, so deceptively, fiendishly calm and still. All those men, those handsome men that she had wanted to be like, dead. And Father, and Uncle Malkon…

"You don't want to stay here, do you?" Myma asked Ma. "To help Phaedra if she gets here after us?"

Ma shook her head. "When she comes, she doesn't need me. You need me."

"That's true. We both do."

"Please," Goodweather whispered, her voice weak and hoarse. "Please take me home."

"Don't worry, honey. That's where we're going."

38
DESSA

Dessa stumbled down the road for hours, growing weaker and weaker, until she came across an abbey of Atellan friars. They were good to her. They let her stay with them for weeks, recovering from her injuries at the hands of the sailor who'd wanted her blood. If they didn't believe her story of self-defense, at least they didn't say so. But they did take the knife away.

She never told them she was Dragon Touched. Atel had never been kind to her on the roads, and she didn't trust His friars to stay this kind if they knew. As it was, the head friar still woke up one morning with the sky shuddering and crackling above them and kicked her out.

Dessa stood outside the abbey, sobbing. She could not go back to Atuna, lest they try her for murder. She would have no way to know when Phaedra returned, if she ever did. Her remaining money – the sailor's money, really – was hardly enough to keep her from starving for a week or two, if she could even find someone to feed her. She could go to Parakas from here, but what good would that do? It was just a smaller, angrier Atuna. A powerful witch like Phaedra would never go there.

This place may look like a crossroads, it may even be named that, but that wasn't what it was. It was the *end* of the road.

It was time to go home.

She chose the road that she figured led toward Hagardis most directly, for all that it was a bit overgrown. The woods it led her through were thicker and deeper than they had been on the road from Atuna, the path just barely discernable among the brambles. When in the evening she came to a village on the forest's edge, she found that it was more of an ex-village – long abandoned, rotting, overrun with weeds. The water in the well looked murky, and when she tried to pull some up anyway, the rusted chain disintegrated and the bucket plummeted back to the bottom.

The Yarek was clearly visible from here, nearby and enormous. If she left for it tomorrow, she could probably get there before noon. But she had no interest in going there – God Most High may have abandoned her, but that didn't mean she should go to His enemy. God Most High's enemies had still done her more harm than He had.

Anyway, the road avoided the Yarek too. She followed it northward for another day, feeling weak for lack of water, and was relieved when she came to a populated village. They didn't look too pleased with her arrival, but they took her money and fed her, and she left the following day with a full belly and a skin of water.

What would her mother say when she came home at last, after so many years? What would she think of her broken daughter, who had left so long ago in search of magic and her dead father, and come home with nothing but scars? She desperately wished she wasn't going home.

But it was too late now. She had *tried* surviving on nothing but raw determination, and it *hadn't worked*. It was time to admit that she had failed.

She was walking too slowly, her reluctance impeding her progress. By the time she reached another village, the sun had already set and twilight was stealing across the sky. She knocked on one door after another, but nobody answered. It might be too late – people often didn't open their doors at night, probably fearing desperate vagrants like her, and the more urgently you knocked, the less likely they were to open up. If they found her asleep in a barn, they might well beat her, but she didn't have much choice. It was too frightening, these days, to sleep under the open sky.

When she approached one, though, there were voices coming from inside. Dessa stopped at the half-open door, afraid to enter and interrupt. If villagers were unkind, fellow vagrants were often worse. She had far too much experience to believe otherwise.

The next words she heard instantly changed her mind. "Phaedra," a man's voice said. "You know how much I respect you."

She'd found her! Dessa almost couldn't believe her luck. It was so typical of life that you only found what you were looking for once you had given up looking.

What could Dessa say to her? She had never really gotten as far as thinking about that. Why should Phaedra take her on as a student, when she had nothing at all to offer? People weren't selfless.

Then she heard the scream. It made her jump, but she was soon less startled than terrified. What if she was too late? What if the one woman who could help her was dying? Dessa flung the door open and charged inside.

The man with the knife had his back to her. Dessa didn't hesitate: she snatched a broom from its place against a stall and ran at him. When she struck him over the back of the head, it was hard enough that the broom handle cracked near the top. The man dropped his knife and collapsed into the dirt. Dessa kicked the knife out of his reach and beat him with the broom over and over again, screaming a battle cry she'd never known was in her. The man curled up against her blows, grunting as each one struck.

"Stop!" a woman's voice cried.

Dessa stopped swinging and looked up.

There she was, holding the knife in one hand and a book in the other: Phaedra, the wizard. She was more beautiful than anything Dessa had remembered or imagined, her eyes shining, her skin black and flawless. A lamp had fallen to the ground beside her and set the straw there alight, but the blaze wasn't spreading. Phaedra had done something to it, something amazing. As Dessa watched, the fire consumed its first and only strands and died right there, not a hair away from piles of straw and stacked bales of hay. When the light died with it, a ghostly blue one appeared over Phaedra's head.

"Who are you?" Phaedra asked.

The man on the ground was moaning. "You should kill him," Dessa said. "He might try to hurt you again."

"Leave him alone," the wizard said. Even her voice was beautiful. "Tell me who you are."

"I'm Dessa. I'm... just Dessa."

The man on the ground uncurled halfway and looked up at her through one eye. "She's Dragon Touched. Damn. God Most High must have known I was coming."

"Agreed. That's a good sign. If God Most High thinks I'm worth protecting, it means He trusts me to convince the Yarek after all."

"He doesn't know, though." The man sat up, wincing and holding his head. "Even God Most High doesn't control the Yarek, Phaedra, or He wouldn't have had to fight it to begin with."

"That's true, but He must know its nature better than you do, Narky."

"Ravennis knows its nature too – He knows everything. He knows what's coming if you do this, and He sent me to kill you. Damn. I was this close."

Phaedra shook her head. "I can't believe you were going to do it. How could you, Narky?"

Dessa stood, looking from one of them to the other. They were talking as if Dessa wasn't even there, like she had only briefly interrupted a conversation they were having, a conversation that had been about to end with Phaedra's death but which was once again cordial.

"You always knew I could, Phaedra, if it came to it. Ravennis spoke to me Himself – I couldn't disobey. He said you were deluded, and you were about to sacrifice the underworld to the Yarek for a plan that couldn't possibly work. He's the Keeper of Fates. He knows. If you let the Yarek combine with its other parts, it'll destroy the underworld *and* this world, and then our souls will be gone too. If I killed you we'd all die anyway, but the underworld would stay. I was trying to *save* you, and my family. I should have just done it. He told me not to try to convince you, but I thought I knew better."

Phaedra nodded once. "I understand. I should have known, really – I've read the Ravennian eschatology. He was bound to see it this way. I just... no, I see what you were trying to do. But you're wrong and thank God you didn't stop me. I'm glad He saw through Ravennis' plan.

He ejected you from the priesthood so that God Most High wouldn't notice you, didn't He?"

Narky bowed his head. He looked more ashamed of her good guess than he had been about his attempt to kill her. "Yeah. Please, Phaedra. He's the Keeper of Fates."

"He's only the Keeper," Phaedra answered. "He sees what God Most High lets Him see."

"You think God Most High would choose *not* to let Him see a future where the Yarek repents?"

"If God Most High believes the Yarek's repentance is possible, then it's possible. That's all I know."

"Please," Dessa interjected at last, "what are you two talking about? I just saved your life, Phaedra. What's going on?"

"God Most High sent you here," Narky sighed. "You saved Phaedra so she could help the Yarek get its full power back and just *hope* that it chooses not to use that power to kill the Gods and destroy the world."

Dessa folded her arms. "God Most High didn't send me. Nobody sent me."

"That might be how it feels," Phaedra said, "but it's very unlikely."

Narky squinted up at Dessa through his one eye. "Who did you say you were?"

"Dessa."

"Dessa what?"

"Daughter of Iona and Belkos."

He grunted in confirmation. "Your pa killed Criton. You're not a damn coincidence."

Dessa wilted at the recognition. She would never escape her father's legacy.

But Phaedra was beaming at her. "Family redemption.

That's a good omen, Narky."

"I dunno, she almost killed me."

"Well, you did deserve it."

"For trying to save your soul?"

"I bet Belkos thought he was doing the right thing too."

Narky grunted again, sulkily.

Dessa let her broom fall to the ground. "You're going to let him live, aren't you? They killed my father and you didn't stop them, but you're going to let Narky live because he's your friend."

"Yes. But I won't let my guard down again."

"That's not justice."

"Narky didn't kill me. You stopped him."

"So you're just going to let him go?"

Phaedra considered that. "No, I think I should keep an eye on him. If you'll help me bind him, I can keep the ropes from coming undone without my permission."

"Great," Narky said, "thanks a lot. Why don't you go ahead and kill me? That'd be just as good, really; it's basically the same thing. Ravennis gave me a job, and I failed Him because I didn't trust His word. I may as well be dead. He might kill me Himself, if He feels like it. And when I die, if there's still an underworld to go to, He'll torture me there. There's no way out."

"I'm not going to kill you," Phaedra snapped. "You're my friend, and *I'm* not a person who kills her friends. However Ravennis treats you is between you and Him at this point – it's really none of my business. If I were you, though, I'd remind *Him* to repent to God Most High. Ravennis has a lot to answer for."

Narky's mouth twisted skeptically. "If Criton's God weren't so damn secretive about what He wanted, it would save everyone a lot of trouble. And don't you give me any of that stuff about Him giving us free will that way; I've never been free."

"If there were no free will," Phaedra said, "there'd be no point in repentance. Dessa, is that a rope over there?"

It was. Narky did not resist as they bound him, but kept talking even while Phaedra cast her spell on the rope. "So how's Hunter doing? Ravennis told me you came here from the elves' world."

Phaedra didn't answer, only kept her eyes on her work. Dessa had never met Hunter, but she could read body language well enough to know that this was an embarrassing question. Narky's other questions all met with similar silence until finally Phaedra turned to Dessa and said, "I can't thank you enough for saving my life. I'd like to pay you, but nothing can ever repay that. If our world survives, it'll have been your doing."

Dessa froze. This was Phaedra's way of parting with her. "I– I'm not going anywhere," she said.

"No," Phaedra said, "but I'll be leaving at dawn, for the Yarek. There won't be another chance."

"I'm coming too, then."

Phaedra smiled, but Dessa could see that she was looking for a polite way to turn her down.

"Your part in this is over," Narky said bluntly, before Phaedra could be more tactful about it. "Phaedra doesn't need you getting in her way. It's bad enough that she thinks she's got to keep an eye on me."

"*I* can keep an eye on you," Dessa said. "I've been looking for Phaedra for months now; I'm not letting her get away again."

The polite smile faded from Phaedra's face. "You've

been looking for me? Why?"

"I..."

Dessa stopped. How could she tell Phaedra that she was here for her own selfish reasons, not as a messenger of her God, not because she'd been sent to save Phaedra's life? How could she even explain what she wanted from this woman, this wizard with the perfect skin who was leaving tomorrow to save the world?

Hadn't Dessa already resigned herself to going home? Her mother would be happy to see her, however shameful her return. Was it right to keep that happiness from her?

"I've been looking for someone to teach me magic."

Phaedra's face was pure astonishment. After that, her expression turned to wonder, and recognition. "You've come to the right person, then."

39
PHAEDRA

They left the following morning, Phaedra riding her horse while Narky and Dessa walked alongside. Narky made no further attempts to convince Phaedra that it was best to let the world end but spent much of his time worrying aloud that the Yarek would destroy the underworld, and Ravennis with it.

"It was bad enough when we thought Magor had killed Him," he said. "I can't go through this twice."

"How is Grace?" Phaedra asked, to change the subject.

"He's beautiful," Narky answered vehemently. "He's a beautiful boy. He's generous and kind, and he knows how much we love him. He deserves a God who'll watch over him when this life is over."

"He deserves a full life too."

Narky nodded. "He deserves everything."

It was a strange sort of catching up they did, all in fits and starts, mixing a long friendship's warmth and curiosity with confrontation. Narky told her of the Sephan prophecy, and Phaedra could not praise his response to it. For all that she appreciated the wisdom of his interpretation, and the clever way he had turned a blasphemous tract into a tool of his God, she could also see how his interpretation had led to the attempt on her life. Narky, for his part, could only nod in muted satisfaction when she told him how she had defeated Mura the sorcerer pirate. Most horrifyingly, he expressed no shock at Psander's poisoning of the villagers.

"Sounds like her," he said. "Did she get them all? The queen and all of them?"

"I have no idea. I left a few hours later."

He twisted his mouth thoughtfully. "If the elves didn't catch that last woman and her kids, it's probably too much to hope for that they *all* got poisoned. Someone always sneaks through."

"Could be."

He glanced up at her, noting her cold expression. "I don't get why that was your breaking point, Phaedra. I really don't. We've known what Psander was like for ages. She locked us outside her gates, for Ravennis' sake, when we came to save her from Magor's army. Why is *this* the thing that made you hate her all of a sudden?"

Phaedra had to think about that. He was right, Psander had always viewed people as expendable, had never valued people as anything other than tools. And he was right that she'd done the same to them. But this time was different. This time was worse.

"Those people were defenseless," she said.

"So were we."

"No," Phaedra said, "we weren't. Not like the villagers. They never had any Gods looking out for them the way we did. They didn't have any prophecies told about them. They were just… they were helpless. Against the Gallant Ones, against Psander, against the elves. There was never anyone on *their* side, trying to protect *them*. Psander was manipulating them the moment they met her. Hunter and I failed them. So in the end they were trapped between Psander and the elves, and one fed them to the others. That's more horrible than anything Psander ever did to us."

"She'd have fed you to the elves too, if she thought you were more useful that way."

"Maybe, but she never did think that. We were always more useful to her alive, all five of us. She treated them like livestock."

Narky accepted that silently and did not speak again for nearly half a mile. Phaedra's horse clopped on, Narky and Dessa beside it. Dessa had been silent since they left that morning, walking with Phaedra's staff and listening awkwardly to the conversation, most likely afraid to intrude. Phaedra felt bad for her, but it had been Dessa's choice to join them on this last leg of Phaedra's journey.

"If Psander is just like the other academics were," Narky said suddenly, "it's no wonder the Gods turned on them. Treating people like tools or livestock, manipulating them – that's *Their* territory, you know? Psander's like a Goddess herself."

Phaedra bristled at the description, though she couldn't deny how perfectly it matched Narky's view of the Gods. He'd always seen Their mystery as manipulation, Their motives as nefarious – even for his own God. He probably saw God Most High as the worst manipulator of them all.

It was an extension of the way he saw people, she thought. They were always after something.

Phaedra saw the same tendencies, but they had never struck her as nefarious. Of *course* people and Gods wanted things – what was so devious about that? Even altruism came from desire. When Phaedra thought of Hunter, gorgeous, selfless Hunter, she knew that his friends' safety and happiness brought him satisfaction. She knew that her pleasure gave him pleasure too. That had been obvious long before she kissed him.

Not every desire caused harm. Not every attempt to affect the world was manipulation.

She was on a mission, one that God Most High had endorsed, to overcome Illweather's nihilism and change the Yarek's behavior. If the Yarek repented to God Most High instead of battling Him, would that give the Lord Above more power than a final battle would have? Phaedra didn't honestly care. It would save thousands, millions from harm. It would protect Gods and people and animals, and turn the world from conflict and chaos toward cooperation. Narky could call that manipulation if he wanted to. Phaedra called it righteousness.

The Yarek, when they finally reached it, was even bigger than she remembered. That thicket of vines and brambles – had that grown recently? The earth around it was broken, and she could not help but picture the root that had once dragged her underground with the elf Olimande's head and ashes. Whatever the dangers of that thicket, Phaedra was not fooled – no distance from this monster was safe.

Phaedra dismounted from her horse and took her staff from Dessa. "Stay here," she said, more to Narky than to her rescuer. She was about to negotiate for the fate of the world: the last thing she needed was Narky's tact.

She slipped out of her shoes, fine Essishan creations though they were – if the Yarek communicated partially through the earth beneath her feet, she didn't want to miss any signals. The soil between her toes was soft and rich. Oh yes, the Yarek was enjoying it here.

Another skyquake shook the heavens as Phaedra approached, but the air around her stayed calm. For the first time, standing in this quiet node, Phaedra was able to look straight up at the source of the skyquakes.

The sky above the Yarek was rippling like the surface of a pond, the waves rolling outward from the tree's center. The Yarek's trunk – the entire, gargantuan length of it – swayed gently as its upper branches shook the sky. As Phaedra watched, the sky seemed to sink closer toward her, and a single upper branch snapped off. She ducked, irrationally – if that branch came down on top of her, no change in stance would save her.

It didn't, though. It landed with a crash a good hundred yards to her right, with more than enough force to shake the ground beneath her feet. Phaedra planted her staff and walked on.

Bandu had said she would understand the Yarek if she listened properly. Was the Yarek speaking now?

"Talk to me," Phaedra whispered. "I'm listening. I promise I am."

The ground continued to tremble, and the wind to whistle, but they did not form words. Were they *supposed* to form words? Maybe Phaedra was doing this wrong. Words were hardly Bandu's strength, yet she understood the Yarek perfectly. Maybe Phaedra was listening for the wrong thing.

"Try again," she said. "I'm sorry. I'm trying too."

She felt the Yarek's approval in the wind, in the soil, in her skin. Yes. This was the way of it. Phaedra could not translate what she felt into coherent words the way the elves had done, but this might do.

The Yarek was asking her something, that much she knew. She began to imagine that it was sending her images of some kind, and she closed her eyes to better make them out.

They were terrible images, visions of what had happened to Criton. He must have been here already, with other creatures – no, those were people, the Yarek simply wasn't differentiating – and the great tree had devoured them all as they tried to cut it down. Phaedra shuddered and tried to banish the visions from her mind. Perhaps she had misunderstood its intentions – its 'question' must have been some kind of a threat instead, something like, "Are you here to cut me down too? Because this is what happens..."

"No," she said. "I'm not here to cut you down."

Its response came in such a torrent of sensory information that Phaedra found she was panting, her breaths quick and shallow, her heart palpitating in her chest. It was saying something about the destruction that was coming soon, but *what* exactly it was saying she couldn't guess.

"We..." she said, hoping her words would make sense to it, "we can avoid that. I *think* you're saying something about the words colliding and destroying everything, right? We can keep that from happening. We can keep the sky from cutting us to pieces."

She could feel the Yarek's skepticism in the suddenly cold breeze, in the prickling of the hair on her arms. She hoped it would understand her reasoning well enough to accept it.

"You've opened a gate before," she said, "a big one, large enough that Salemis came through. We just need to open an even bigger one. A gate so big that the whole wall comes apart."

Oh goodness, she had no idea what it was saying now. It was objecting somehow, she was sure of that much, but *how?* Curse Bandu for refusing to join her here! How could Phaedra convince the Yarek to help her if she couldn't even decipher its responses correctly? This was too delicate a negotiation to rely on guesswork.

And yet, Phaedra had no choice but to plow ahead. To give up was death, not only for her but for every living creature, and the Yarek besides. All she could do was explain her intentions, and hope that the Yarek would understand her better than she understood it.

"Psander and I will help you," she said. "I'm sorry I can't understand you better – I'm guessing you don't think it'll work? I– if that's true, I think you're wrong. You have Psander and me on your side, and Psander has all the magic of the Goodweather court at her disposal. Illweather swallowed its own court, so in a way, you have that too. The whole world that God Most High built out of you will be unified in the effort. I think it can be done, especially if God Most High lets us try it instead of fighting you."

The bitterness of the Yarek's response sank into her bones and shivered through her skin. Something in what she had said had angered it. Was it the mention of God Most High? Did the Yarek not believe that its ancient enemy would allow it to unify, even if it meant saving the worlds He had created? She could see a valid objection there: if it was God Most High who had brought them to the edge of destruction, sending messengers like Eramia and the long-ago Dragon Knight to influence the islanders' actions and plant Goodweather's seed here, then how could they expect Him to sit by and watch the Yarek unravel His mesh?

The Yarek's mood was spiraling, she could feel it. It had been expecting destruction, and vengeance, and Phaedra's suggestion that God Most High might *allow* it to unify was an insult. The Yarek was anticipating a fight – it *welcomed* a fight, even if it took thousands of years to recover from its splintering.

"I know I'm suggesting a different end from the one you imagined," Phaedra said, "but please listen to me. I'm here on my God's behalf, to offer you peace."

Images of Criton again. Peace was impossible.

Phaedra shook her head and wiped her eyes, trying not to think about Criton and whoever else he had dragged along with him. She could not let herself get distracted, she had to focus on this world that still remained and must continue to do so.

She tried again. "Making peace with God Most High is only impossible if you choose to make it that way. Listen to me, please listen. God Most High protected me on my journey here. He chose to save me from all danger so that I could make this offer. *He* believes reconciliation is possible, if you are willing to repent."

The air went still, so still that Phaedra's breaths were the only wind. She waited almost an eternity for the Yarek's answer, suddenly very aware that at any moment it could choose to devour her instead. In the stillness and the silence, she could feel its fury building.

Why was it reacting this way? What had she said wrong? She had thought at first that it was reacting well to her argument – it was only at the very end that she had somehow triggered its rage.

Was it the talk of repentance that had done it? Gods, that was it, wasn't it? To tell the Yarek to repent was to insult it beyond all reason, to suggest a subservience to the Gods that had never been a reality.

How could she have imagined the Yarek would see it any other way? Repentance was hard enough for people, whom the Gods had created and nurtured, who had no pretense to Their power and no hope of living without Them. Yet even for people, submitting entirely to their Gods' mercy was a challenge. For the Yarek, who had fought the king of Gods and only barely lost, the very notion of Godly mercy was an insult. The Yarek had been torn to pieces and still come back to fight another day – what did it need its enemy's mercy for?

So what if the destruction of these worlds set the Yarek back eons? It was no slave, no godserf, no mere *creation*. It was primordial.

What could she say to this being? How could she convince it that eternal servitude was worth the lives of her friends, her species, her world? Repentance required submission, it *assumed* servitude. If the Yarek insisted on revenge, nothing would convince it.

"I'm sorry," she said. She had to hope that it was only angry, that revenge was not its guiding principle.

"Please, just tell me one thing: why Goodweather?"

For a moment, the monster's fury abated. She could feel its curiosity at her change of subject, even as its anger burned beneath.

"If the ancient Yarek was split into Illweather and Goodweather," she said, "the cruel half and the kind one, then that Yarek must have been half kindness. Right? Because that kind half held its own against Illweather for thousands of years before it agreed to send you here to free Salemis. It unbalanced the world it inhabited for that opportunity, and gave Illweather the chance to consume it, which is what's happening now. I don't understand why a being of kindness would do that, if sending you here meant *this* world's destruction too. Is my entire understanding of the Yarek and its castles wrong? *Is* there no kind half?"

Silence. And then, at last, a gentle breeze. A hint of reconciliation, of a willingness to listen. Possibly a statement that Goodweather really was kind.

"Is its seed not kind, then?"

The sun was warm. The breeze blew on, as gentle as before.

"I understand your anger," Phaedra said. "But you see, we all believed that Goodweather sacrificed its balance against Illweather to make our world *kinder* – to bring balance *here*. That's what Bandu thought, anyway, and a kind being wouldn't have deceived her on purpose, so I have to assume that Goodweather agreed with her. I *have* to assume that. Bandu believes in kindness, and Goodweather is the closest thing she has to a God. *Let she with no church raise skyward her steeple*. That's you.

"So if Goodweather wasn't deceiving Bandu, it must have made a terrible mistake. It thought it was sacrificing its ability to keep the elves' world in balance, for the power to influence this world for greater kindness; instead, it sacrificed itself only for more strength and greater destruction. You became a tool of Illweather's, despite your origins. Goodweather gambled and lost.

"The way things stand, this world's end will splinter you too. Who's to say that kindness will win out in the end? What strength you gained here, Goodweather is losing on the other side. Goodweather's kindness is only stronger than Illweather's influence *here, in this world*. Not some future world. We can't say what will happen to your soul after a splintering. Maybe kindness will get a head start on Illweather's cruelty, but it probably won't. For that matter, who's to say that God Most High won't build new barriers as soon as this world is over, and keep the Yarek in a hundred thousand pieces from then on? You can't be strong now and kind later. If your nature is kindness, *now* is the time. *This* is the place.

"Kindness means caring what happens to those around you. Repentance means looking at the destruction you've caused, and the destruction you meant to cause, and saying you won't do it again. Promising that from now on, kindness and justice will be more important than your pride, more important than whether you or God Most High wins some ancient competition. The Splintering isn't a just end. What have my people done that you'd condemn us to share it with you? You'll survive the calamity in one form or another, but we won't."

Her words were having an effect. That gentle breeze was growing ever more pleasant and more fragrant, swaying the leaves in the thicket and drifting pleasantly through her dress. Phaedra allowed herself to breathe. Maybe, just maybe, the Yarek would let her do this work.

An image of Illweather came to her, and of the dying Goodweather, and a question she could not understand. At least she was getting better at guessing – or, she thought she was.

"Are you asking what will happen after we succeed? After all the parts of you come together?"

An affirmative rustle of vines, a whistle of wind.

"I... don't know. My plan was to pray to God Most

High to give you strength against Illweather's crueler inclinations – or really, to teach *you* to pray. I know it was not your way of communicating with the Gods – if you *had* a way, that is – but it's the way one repents. If you'll let me through to your trunk, I'll... I'll carve such a prayer into your bark."

The Yarek did not respond for many long moments, and Phaedra began to worry. *If it changes its mind now,* she thought, *it will definitely kill me.*

She stepped forward, slowly, and made her way through the thicket. The vines and thorns did not lash out at her, but neither did they part to let her through. The Yarek hadn't decided to kill her yet, but it was showing its reluctance.

"You're afraid this will make you a servant,".Phaedra said. "I understand, really I do. But I have a life to look forward to, a wonderful life, for all that I am a servant of my God. Salemis the dragon is His servant too, and so is Eramia our Goddess of Love, and Ravennis of the world below. None of Them is weak. None of Them has lost who They are. If you're making the worlds kinder, the heavens or the earth or the world below, your dignity and glory are in no danger. We'll sing your praises along with God Most High's."

By the time she had finished her speech, Phaedra had passed through the thicket and could lean her staff against the Yarek's enormous trunk. She put her hand against the bark, and slowly pulled Narky's sacrificial knife from where she'd had it tucked in Hunter's belt. "I would like to carve a prayer here. Am I permitted this?"

The trunk warmed to her touch. She could proceed.

The knife was not well designed for the task of carving,

but the Yarek eased her way. Its bark softened, giving itself to her efforts, and Phaedra hobbled along the trunk, carving huge letters into its flesh. Her prayer asked God Most High to pardon the world, and the Yarek for endangering it. She asked God Most High to give it strength so that it could overcome Illweather's cruel desires and spread kindness through its roots, and included the Dragon Touched words of repentance, a plea for forgiveness. When she had finished, she laid the knife reverently at the Yarek's base and went to retrieve her staff.

A piece of bark fell at her side with a crack. Phaedra jumped, startled, and looked up to see great strips of bark peeling away above her as the Yarek repeated her prayer over and over all the way up its trunk, spiraling upwards into eternity. As it did, it began to shake – and when the Yarek shook, so did the world.

Phaedra fell to the rumbling ground, whispering her own prayer to God Most High as the wind whipped her clothes and hair, struck her with falling twigs and bark, and roared in her ears. She crawled through the thicket on all fours, still holding her staff, scrambling to get away from the great tree. She didn't know precisely what would happen when the worlds combined, but she did know one thing: the Yarek would grow still bigger. The closer she was to it, the greater the chance that she'd be crushed or consumed.

She was supposed to help open the gate, to guide the Yarek's efforts and keep the merger from becoming as violent as it otherwise might. But in that moment fear overtook her, and she focused all her efforts on escape. *Just reach Narky*, she thought. *Just reach Narky.*

She could feel it already: the breach, the fraying at the

corners of existence. With a last effort, she pulled herself free of the vines and thorns, praying with all her being that it would be enough. The world darkened – the sky above was full of swirling clouds, the too-familiar mist of a gate opening. The mesh was coming apart, and it was terrifying.

All of Phaedra's well-composed prayerspells vanished from her mind. "Let me live!" she cried, her voice hoarse, her very bones trembling. *"Let me live!"*

40

RAIDER ELEVEN

The final quake started in the twilight high above, but it traveled downward as it intensified, cracking trees from their trunks and hurling them in all directions. The elves fled their home, unwilling to risk having even Castle Goodweather over their heads, and made their way toward the godserf fortress. There was a chance that its defenses would come down during this final quake – if the walls themselves collapsed, the power trapped within them might return to either the elves or the Yarek, whichever of them thought to take it first.

So they ran through the woods as the world shook and the stars dropped flaming from the sky, shaken at last from their bindings. They struck the ground here and there, bouncing two or three times off the ground with the force of their descent, setting the forest alight. It was true what Raider Eleven had heard: they were indeed torches. What she hadn't realized until this moment was that they were made not of dead wood but of living, writhing trees the size of her arm. The defeated Yarek had always been more than two pieces: its enemies had set its splinters aflame and made the monster light its own world.

They arrived at the wizard's home just as the mists engulfed it. One of Raider Eleven's more impulsive companions hurled his weapon into the mists where the walls had been, as if this last aggressive act could bring those walls down. The sickle never bounced back out again.

"Disgusting."

Eleven felt her queen's frustration in her bones, her blood, her bowels. The wizard had escaped them again somehow.

The thunder came not in claps now but in one long, continuous rending sound. The earth shook until all the dirt fell through it like a sieve, and all that remained were roots, shifting roots, twisting downward and carrying the elves along with them. The queen and her companions leapt from one to the next, making their way down to where the world did not shake anymore but *grew*, inexorably, toward something.

There was daylight below them, inexplicable daylight. Eleven looked up at her queen and smiled. The queen reached out a hand, granting her consort the honor of guiding her way. Raider Eleven took it gladly, and together they climbed down into a new world.

41
NARKY

Narky watched Phaedra negotiate with the Yarek, his heart heavy. *This is the end,* he thought. *I've failed my God, and now I might well outlive Him. Again.*

"What's she doing?" Dessa asked, watching Phaedra make use of Narky's knife.

"Magic," Narky answered. It was a vague, unhelpful answer, which was more or less what Dessa deserved, by Narky's reckoning. Anyway, he didn't really have a better one.

He wondered if the Yarek really would repent, or if it would only deceive Phaedra until it was fully unified and then resume the war against its ancient enemy. Probably the latter. Either way, Ravennis – and with Him, Narky's place in the underworld – was likely doomed.

Narky's God had defied God Most High – it was hard to come to another conclusion. He had sent Narky to kill Phaedra so that the Yarek might never get its chance to repent and the world might shatter, to His benefit. If the Yarek *didn't* fool Phaedra, if it took her offer to heart and repented fully, God Most High would surely reward it by letting it consume Ravennis and His underworld, or at least reshape the underworld in its own image. Narky and his family had nothing to look forward to, besides the rest of their lives. And how short those would be!

How could God Most High give the Yarek this chance at repentance, the chance that by rights Ravennis deserved? Why shouldn't *Ravennis* get the benefit of His master's mercy, when He had done so much to make the world safe for God Most High's worshippers? He had freed Salemis, struck down Bestillos through Narky's hand, even used Narky to make peace between Ardis and the Dragon Touched! Didn't *He* deserve the Lord Above's mercy?

Not without asking. That was the key. And now that Ravennis had officially abandoned him, now that Narky was no longer high priest, what good would his own prayers do?

He would try anyway. He had prayed once for Phaedra to live, so long ago when she had been dying in the mountains. He had asked Ravennis to spare her, and He – or someone – had. If his prayers back then could save Phaedra, and through her the Yarek too, then maybe they could save Narky's God.

Narky fell to his knees, his arms still bound, and began to pray. Dessa made confused noises and nudged him with her foot, but he ignored her. *Do not turn Your wrath on Ravennis,* he prayed to the Lord Above. *If you are a God of Mercy, a God willing to forgive Your most ancient enemy, please have mercy on Your servants too, not only mortal but divine. Have mercy on Ravennis, who served You even when You were silent, and brought Your people out of the shadows. Spare the one who brought Your order to the World Below. Spare the God who spared me. Please.*

Both his eyes were weeping, even the one he no longer

saw through, that hadn't cried in years. Narky blinked and opened his eyes, but the tear-blurred vision still came to him from only one side. What an odd thing, to heal the part of his eye that brought forth tears, and not the part that saw. Perhaps it was Ravennis' work. Perhaps his God considered him a good spokesman.

He squeezed his eyes shut again and prayed with all his might for the Lord Above to spare the Lord Below. He prayed and prayed until the earth began to shake and he fell painfully on his side. His eyes opened then, as Dessa pulled him back to his knees.

"What's that?" she cried.

The sky was opening. Through the swirling clouds, roots reached down, snaking toward the Yarek's branches. Narky saw figures climbing down those roots, and his blood went cold. Elves. They were coming through.

As he watched, the figures shrank, sprouted wings, and flew away. They made a smaller vee than he had expected, and he kept watching the roots for more, but no more came. He didn't know what to think about that.

And then, with a bang, the new Yarek's branches met the old Yarek's roots and the whole terrifying beast became one. The earth cracked and opened, and Narky watched Phaedra get hurled into the air as the trunk expanded outwards. Her figure was buffeted this way and that as the sky shook her, but at last she fell back down to earth.

Narky struggled to his feet and ran toward her. The earth was still rumbling and the sky shaking as the Yarek expanded – would they ever stop? – but Narky managed not to fall as he ran, arms bound, toward his friend. Oh Gods, he hadn't even thought to pray for her safety too.

He got to her prone body and fell to his knees again.

It was impossible to tell whether she was breathing or whether it was the trembling ground that made her back rise and fall.

"Phaedra!" he cried.

Slowly, painfully, his friend put her hands on the ground and lifted her head to look at him. "Narky," she said. "You can... take those bindings off."

The ropes fell around him at her command. He reached out and tried to help her up, but the earth kept shaking and her legs kept wobbling, so instead he dragged her as far as he could before they both fell down again.

"Is anything broken?"

"I have no idea."

He was going to ask her to move her legs on her own, but he was interrupted by a shriek. A crack had opened in the earth where Phaedra had been lying, and *something* was crawling out of it. Shapes began pouring from the hole, terrible shapes, shapes that couldn't possibly have belonged to this world. An eight-legged badger scrabbled past him so close that it sprayed Narky with dirt on its way toward the forest. Lord save Ravennis – the underworld had cracked open.

Narky began to pray to God Most High again. He was probably too late, but he didn't know what else to do. His words disappeared among the shrieks and the rumbling as he begged the Lord Above to save his God and reseal the underworld, to end this horror. Perhaps it made more sense to ask the Yarek for that, but Narky would never pray to the Yarek.

And then, finally, the last monster crawled out of the hole, and no other took its place. This one walked on two feet like a man but possessed not a single defining feature.

It wandered off past Dessa, and Narky heard Phaedra murmur, "God Above, a lost soul. A real one."

The air around them had quieted enough that he could hear her, but Narky wondered at the fact that he hadn't been entirely deafened. Half the sounds he had perceived must not have been sounds at all.

Phaedra gasped, turning back toward the Yarek, and Narky followed her gaze. The words she had carved into the great tree, whatever they had meant, had disappeared during the Yarek's expansion, but now they were coming back, glowing like a sunset and twisting up its trunk like a vine of letters.

"What does it mean?" Narky asked, though he thought he knew the answer.

"It means Illweather lost. The Yarek is repenting."

Narky's gaze drifted all the way up to where the Yarek's tip should have been, but he could not find it – too many clouds had gathered above, and the Yarek pierced them like an arrow. Even its lower branches were barely visible.

"You think its top is in the heavens? The real heavens, where the Gods live?"

Phaedra struggled to a sitting position beside him. "I can't imagine otherwise. Its roots cracked the underworld."

Narky looked back down to the trunk. It wasn't even swaying. "It doesn't look like there's a big battle going on up there."

"No, it doesn't."

Slowly, they both rose to their feet. "Your legs are all right?" Narky asked in wonder.

"No," Phaedra said, "they're uneven. But they'll do."

Narky ran to retrieve her staff, and together they walked back toward Dessa. "I prayed for God Most High to spare

Ravennis. Do you think He listened?"

"I don't know. But you're alive, so that's a good start. How's your chest?"

"It feels fine. I don't know if that means anything, though. Ravennis took His mark from me when He sent me after you."

"Well," Phaedra said, "don't ask me, then. It'll be a long time before I have any answers. I've only ever had questions, really, and I feel like I have more now than I did before."

Narky couldn't help but laugh. "Nothing new about that. If I said two and two were four, you'd still find questions to ask about it."

Phaedra chuckled a bit and didn't try to deny it.

"Is it all over?" Dessa asked when they reached her. "Is the world safe, Phaedra?"

Narky answered before Phaedra could. "The world is never safe," he said. "But we're still here."

"So where do we go now?"

"I'm going back to Tarphae," Phaedra said. "I have an idea that Hunter may have ended up there. If Silent Hall didn't fall through those clouds, it must have gotten pulled through its own gate. At least, that's what I hope. Will you come too, Narky?"

Narky shook his head. "Not a chance. I have a wife and a son in Ardis. I need to protect them, if I even can. If Ravennis is done ordering me around, I'm going home."

42
HOMECOMING

All the way back to Ardis, Narky worried. Would Ptera and Grace still be there when he arrived? Would Ravennis protect them, despite Narky's failure? For that matter, had Ravennis even survived the piercing of His underworld? Narky hadn't seen any crow-angels flying around, trying to bring those monsters back.

He didn't see any trace of them on his journey, or of the monsters either. They must have found hiding places for themselves, along with the elves who had come through the breach. Phaedra's plan may have saved the world after all, but it certainly hadn't made the place less frightening.

Not yet, anyway. If the Yarek was capable of repenting and making peace with God Most High, maybe it would be kinder to this world than the Gods had been. A good influence, just as the islanders had hoped when they planted it here. All one could do was hope.

He still avoided people on the way home – the fact that the world hadn't ended didn't mean that people would be kind to him, or that Mageris didn't have a price on his head. If the priests of Ravennis had welcomed Ptera as their leader, he could have relied on her to shelter him from the king, but as it was, the most he could hope for was that she still lived.

When he neared Anardis, he risked stopping to ask someone for news. He dreaded the answer, and feared giving Mageris a lead into his whereabouts, but he had to know.

The news was better than he could have hoped. In her first act as high priestess, Ptera had insisted on expanding the church into Dragon Touched territory, to convert those plainsmen who had not entirely bought into Dragon Touched rule. If official doctrine held that Ravennis was a servant to God Most High, then those who did not fully take to the Dragon Touched religion might be persuaded to pray to the servant for intercession with His master. The Dragon Touched might find such prayers distasteful, but since they would not violate God Most High's doctrine of supremacy, it would be hard to justify keeping the Church of Ravennis out. Once the church had its toehold, there was no saying how far it could expand.

Ptera had apparently spent two weeks negotiating with Kilion Highservant, high priest of God Most High, to establish a small church in Salemica, and then stayed there to navigate its tumultuous first days. She had taken Grace with her, of course, and so after the third week she had sent a messenger to the great temple in Ardis notifying the priests there that the work of establishing this new outpost was too much to accomplish while still fulfilling her duties as high priestess, and that regretfully she must resign and leave it to the priests of Ardis to choose her successor.

It was a brilliant maneuver, for all that the man who told Narky about it thought that Ptera must have been terribly unsuited to her position to begin with, if she had been so eager to give it up. Narky didn't contradict him, yet he couldn't help but grin as the man continued to talk. He was sure that when he left, the man must have told all his neighbors that the former High Priest of Ravennis, that infamous, foreign Black Priest, had gone entirely mad.

Ptera was alive! More than that, she had found a way to correct Narky's error, pass the high priesthood over to Lepidos, and find asylum in Salemica for herself and Grace, all without losing the respect of her fellow priests *or* the Dragon Touched leadership. She hadn't even had to give up her priestesshood! Narky said a heartfelt prayer of thanksgiving to Ravennis for his wife's brilliance, for all that he didn't know if his God was there to hear it anymore. He traveled eastward after that, and made a wide arc around Ardis on his way to Salemica.

Phaedra had given him some money to help his journey, kind heart as she had, so he was able to stay in relative comfort once he was outside of Ardisian territory. He was also able to exchange his tattered nightrobe for real clothes, though they didn't fit perfectly and cost him most of what he had left. At least he would not look like a madman when he saw his wife again.

It was in Arca that he heard of Criton's force of axmen, and of their demise. Oh, that fool. He'd gotten himself killed, and of course he'd done it with unasked-for heroism. Phaedra had told him of her plan, and instead of trying to stop her as Narky had, he had focused his efforts on cutting down, *himself*, a monster that had defied the Gods. It was so typical of him, it made Narky cry.

He'd miss that man.

The high priest's son, Malkon Highservant, had followed Criton to his death, provoking a major – if slow-moving –

crisis. Unless Vella renounced her quiet life and returned to study with her father, the high priest would have no heir. People he met brought up that possibility hopefully, but if the woman really loved Bandu, Narky didn't think there was much chance of her returning to the capital city for good. He didn't know her, but he knew Bandu. She would never choose such a life.

At long last, Narky came to Salemica and found his way to Ptera's new church, where his wife met him with endless kisses. "I thought for certain that you were going to your death," she said. "The way you looked when you said Ravennis had told you to leave – I thought He must have asked you to sacrifice yourself somehow."

"He did. But I failed, so here I am."

Ptera had to step back and look at him through those bewitching, uneven eyes of hers. "I've never been so glad you failed at something," she said.

"You'll have to get used to me being a failure," Narky told her. "I'm not a priest anymore, I'm not anything."

"You're a father," Ptera said, "and you're my husband, and you're alive. That's all the success I need from you."

Vella and Bandu's horse had wisely fled from the Yarek as soon as Bandu had dismounted, so the three of them had to stagger homeward on foot. Now that Goodweather was safe, now that the narrow clarity of emergencies had passed, Vella could feel how her first-ever flight had drained her. There was a horrible aching pain, a pain not quite anywhere in her body, for which she could find no relief. It felt like she had sprained her soul.

But it was a small price to pay. Goodweather was alive, and Bandu would lose no more years to her pact with

Ravennis. Things had turned out the way Vella had always wanted them to.

Because, through inaction, she had murdered her rival.

Vella had seen those vines waiting behind Criton. She had seen them and known that just as soon as Goodweather was safely in her arms, the Yarek would kill him. The thought had come to her then that if she refused to take the girl, if she said she was too weak to carry her and fly, and insisted that Criton bring her all the way back to Bandu, she could have spared him too.

She could have, and she hadn't. She'd have to live with that for the rest of her life.

When they reached Salemica and Vella told her people her news, the wailing didn't end for days. Their leader was gone, and with him, the high priest's son and fifty good men: sons, fathers, the prides of their families. The lamentations before the great temple were loud enough to be audible even from outside the city.

An Ardiswoman who had set up her church just inside the walls came wandering over to find out what all the noise was about, her dark-skinned son by her side. Bandu gave the boy a hard look and said, "He's Narky's," but she did not approach them, and when the two had satisfied their curiosity they left without any introduction.

Vella wept with her parents, but it was Delika who wailed the loudest, rending her clothes and screaming all alone among the mourners. Vella felt sorry for the poor girl. It was exactly as she had said – Criton hadn't hesitated to make more people depend on him. Delika had had so little life outside of him, and now she was well and truly lost.

She was in a dangerous state, that girl. She had no one to reassure her, no one to help her recover from the blow. Criton's other wives shunned her, and when one of them did approach, presumably to try to comfort her, Delika pushed her away and screamed until she retreated. A minute or two later, she ran from the crowd toward Criton's house.

"Myma," Goodweather asked. "Can I go after her?"

Vella nodded. Delika should not be left alone in this state, lost to grief and despair. The house would be empty; the other wives gone to their parents' houses, their children with them.

"I'll go with you."

She took her daughter's hand, and together they followed the girl to her empty home.

Delika had left the door open. Vella entered, hoping to catch the girl before she did anything rash. She found Delika by the sound of her sobs and was relieved to see that the girl had run to her bed first and not to the kitchens. There was less opportunity for her to harm herself here.

As she approached, the girl screamed, "Go away!" still face-down on her pillow.

"No," Goodweather said. "I'm not leaving until you come too."

"I'm not going anywhere."

"Yes, you are," Vella answered. "Goodweather is absolutely right. You shouldn't grieve alone."

"I can grieve however I like!"

"Not right now. Right now you can come with us, and grieve with us at the temple."

"I don't want to go there."

Goodweather sat down next to her on the bed. "We know. But you have no other family to grieve with, so I'm sharing mine with you."

"Just go away!" Delika yelled at her. "Leave me alone!"

Goodweather looked back up at her mother, but Vella shook her head. "She can't be left alone right now."

Delika raised her head at that. "What do *you* know?"

The girl's self-centered impertinence made Vella furious, and it took all of her strength to answer productively. "I watched my brother die," she said, her voice low and intense, barely containing her fury. "As we speak, my father is wondering if his life's work has all been a waste, if there will be no one trustworthy to take over when *he* dies. And I have had to carry this news for *weeks*, to *tell* my father that his son is dead. But this grief will not tear me apart, Delika, and do you know why?"

Delika shook her head, the tears still streaming down her face.

"Because I still have people who love me and care about me, who will not let this grief swallow me whole."

"I don't have anyone like that."

"You do now," Goodweather said.

Delika stared at Vella's daughter for a long, hard moment. Then she threw herself back down on the bed. Goodweather put a soft hand on her back. "Please come," she said. "I want you to be with us. You're my best friend."

Delika simply lay there, weeping, but neither Vella nor Goodweather moved from their places. "Please," Goodweather said again.

At last, Delika lifted her head again. "Fine."

Goodweather held Delika's hand as they left the house and entered the temple, and soon they were hugging and crying and whispering together. Vella had never been prouder of her daughter. Goodweather might well have saved a life today.

The days that followed ran together like tears, and when at last it was time to go, Goodweather asked to stay with Delika at the great temple.

"For how long?" Vella asked.

"You can visit sometimes," Goodweather answered. "I want to stay with Grandpa and learn everything from him. You were right. He needs an heir."

Vella stared. "You want to be high priestess?"

Goodweather shook her head. "I want to be high priest."

"But..."

Goodweather rolled her eyes. "I can change my body, Myma. We can all change them. Anyway, please? I want to be Grandpa's heir."

"Bandu?"

Bandu looked from one of them to the other, her expression unreadable. Finally, she nodded. "Your father is good, Vella. He teaches you to be good, he can teach Goodweather too. But Goodweather, you visit us too sometimes, so I can teach you to hear the Yarek. I am wrong that I never teach you before."

They left just the two of them, Vella with Bandu, her wife, her love. There was a strange lightness to this moment, a lightness she had never felt before: Goodweather had been an infant the day Bandu had dragged Vella from her husband's tent. This was the first time in their whole life together that they were really and truly alone.

Vella debated with herself the whole way back whether to tell Bandu of the opportunity she'd had to save Criton, and the choice she had made to reclaim Bandu's years instead. She had to tell her, she *had* to. But she couldn't. Maybe tomorrow.

They slept in their own bed, alone together, thankful to

havc each other with so many years ahead. The house had not burned down in their absence, thank God Most High, though the remains of their soup had long ago congealed into an earthy glop. They could clean that tomorrow. Vella was almost asleep, Bandu's arms around her, when she thought of Criton again and her eyes flew back open. No, she must not keep this secret. She had to speak.

"Bandu," she whispered, "are you awake?"

"Hm?"

"I have to tell you something. I… I killed Criton."

Bandu made a confused, sleepy, dismissive sound. "You don't kill Criton. Belkos kills Criton and the Yarek kills Criton, not you."

"I could have saved him, Bandu. I saw the Yarek planning to kill him as soon as he let Goodweather go, and I didn't warn him. I let the Yarek kill him without stopping it."

Bandu patted her on the side. "You are too good. Go to sleep."

"Bandu, I could have saved him, and I chose not to because I wanted those years for you. It's still murder."

Vella's wife yawned and sat up. "Criton kills himself, Vella. And he takes Goodweather to die with him! Let the Yarek eat him!"

"But I undid your work, Bandu. You risked everything to bring him back."

Bandu snorted. "I bring him back to save you and Goodweather from war. I give those years to Goodweather, not to him. There is peace now, and Goodweather is big and safe and strong. He can go back to Ravennis. I don't care."

"I still feel guilty."

"I know, because you are not wicked. But you are sleepy, and I am sleepy. So sleep."

This time, she obeyed. When Vella awoke, a breeze was blowing across her face from the open window. Bandu was already up and dressed.

"Where are you going?"

"The Yarek says to come out to talk."

"I'm going with you."

Bandu waited impatiently while Vella threw on her dress and pulled her hair out of her eyes, and then they were away into the woods. Vella kept trying to ask what was going on, but Bandu shushed her. "The Yarek is talking."

"Well, what's it saying?"

"It says sorry it almost kills Goodweather, and sorry for your brother. It says it listens to Phaedra, and now it says sorry."

"It listened to Phaedra and repented to God Most High? Their war is over?"

"Yes. But it breaks door to lower world, and bad things come out."

"*What*?"

"Yes."

Then Bandu's face brightened. "No!" she cried in sudden excitement and disbelief. "Come, Vella!"

She broke into a run, a sprint like Vella hadn't seen in years, if ever. Vella chased her through the woods but could not catch up. "Where are you going?" she cried as she ran. "If you can hear the Yarek already, where are we going?"

Bandu did not answer, only sped away like a woman half her body's age. Vella ran and ran after her, her breaths aching in her chest, until suddenly Bandu stopped short, bending over and then kneeling on the ground.

"What's going *on*?" Vella panted, but then she saw it: the wolf pup in her wife's arms. It was missing an ear, the area ragged almost as if it had been in a fight, but the pup couldn't have been more than a few days old, not nearly old enough for such a scar to have healed.

"Are..." Vella asked. "Are we going to raise a wolf, Bandu?"

Bandu nodded and held the pup more tenderly than she had even held Goodweather as a baby. "This is Four-foot, Vella. He comes back to me."

Phaedra's journey back to Tarphae was harder without a horse, but at least she had Dessa's company. Dessa was entirely too much in awe to even ask Phaedra coherent questions at first, so Phaedra asked her about her own life, and learned what she could of the woman who had saved her. It was a sad and disturbing story – Dessa seemed far too impulsive to be taught academic methods. Was it too late to refuse to teach her? Phaedra owed Dessa her life, but she didn't owe her power.

She would have to think on that. In the meantime, she could get to know the woman better. Maybe she had matured since her first disastrous decision to leave home. Maybe she was maturing still.

Dessa seemed to sense that she was being tested and strived to make a good impression, a look of intense anxiety on her face. She kept qualifying her story with phrases like, "because I was young and stupid, I guess," and "not that I'm a drunk – the beds are just cheaper there." She was going to be a project, Phaedra sensed. A long, long project.

But if the Yarek could repent, Dessa could change. Phaedra owed it to her to try and help, and perhaps to teach her some magic along the way if she decided it was safe. Dessa had saved Phaedra's life, and now she was relying on Phaedra to help salvage hers. Phaedra might not succeed, but she would try. Dessa was too young to be written off.

They had already traveled three days by the time it came out that Dessa's mother might still be alive and that she hadn't done anything concrete to drive Dessa away from home; that, in fact, Dessa had been on her way back when she'd come upon Narky and Phaedra in that barn. That revelation stopped Phaedra in her tracks.

"You have to go and see her."

"But I found you first!"

"Then you'll have good news for her."

Dessa looked absolutely crushed. She thought Phaedra was sending her away for good.

"I thought you were going to teach me magic."

"I'd like to," Phaedra said. "Consider this a test. Academic wizardry was founded on tests, and experimentation. A person who can't reconcile with failure and is too afraid to visit someone she hurt has no business being a wizard. I assumed you were staying away because your mother had done something to make you leave, but you just don't want to face what *you* did to *her*. Prove to me that you'll put justice above success and kindness above avoiding shame, and I'll teach you magic."

"You promise? You won't disappear on me again?"

"I'll be waiting for you on Tarphae. I will make it easy to find me."

When they had parted ways, Phaedra cast her spell with

Hunter's belt, drawing on the connection between it and its owner. The spell confirmed her initial hypothesis: he was somewhere east of here. Psander must really have managed to pull her fortress through the gate to Tarphae.

But she did not go straight to the docks when she reached Atuna. She went instead to the High Council building and demanded once more to be seen. When the guards at the door told her to come back tomorrow, she cloaked herself in illusion as Psander had once done and asked again, less politely. The men cowered beneath the ten-foot Phaedra they saw before them, her teeth as sharp as those of Ravennis' angels, her staff no longer made of wood but glowing hot iron. It was the most absurdly blunt use of magic she'd ever attempted, but it certainly had an effect. Citizens on the street fled screaming, and when the guards, paralyzed with fear, did not move, she walked right past them, pulling the illusion back into herself. They did not enter after her.

When they saw her, the councilors immediately ceased their deliberations over whatever matter they had been discussing and fell into a sullen, fearful silence.

"I understand," Phaedra said, "that you have been selling parcels of my homeland, some of them with Mura's prisoners included. This ends today."

The oldest, seated councilman coughed. "We appreciate your concern, Wizard Phaedra, but the battle you led our navy into, though it made our waters safe from piracy, also lost us eight good ships, and ships are expensive. You do not *own* the island, for all that it is your homeland. Atuna bought Tarphae with ships and lives, and we will not give it away without compensation. Even to a wizard."

"I just saved your *world* from destruction!" Phaedra answered. "The great tree that you can see from this building with your own eyes, that shook the sky while you lay here cowering, heard my voice and ended its war on the heavens. And you want *compensation*?"

"We will not be intimidated with these claims of your greatness," the man answered. "Nor can we be swayed by threats to our safety, which I hope you have better sense than to attempt. We are *representatives* of our city. We serve Atuna, not ourselves. Give us our ships back, and you may lay claim to your island."

Phaedra looked deep into the man's eyes and found them steady and defiant. She should never have attempted this. There was a reason she hadn't ever used magic so bluntly before, or tried to intimidate someone rather than convincing them peacefully. She should have remembered Psander's words: never use force unless you can use *overwhelming* force.

"I will give you a fortnight to change your minds," she said. "I have not laid claim to all of Tarphae as you said – my request is much simpler: grant every prisoner left by Mura either safe passage back to their homelands, or else the land on which they have labored since their capture. Please weigh that request against the danger of making yourselves my enemies, and decide what is best for your city."

With that, she left the chamber and made her way to the docks, praying that she would not have to stay the night in this city of gold.

Whether God Most High had answered her prayer or she had just gotten lucky, she didn't know – either way, the nervous dockworkers told her that the *Atun's Bounty* would be leaving within the hour, bringing another boatload of potential investors to survey her homeland. When Phaedra boarded it, flinging the last of her coins at the captain, easily half of those investors hastily disembarked. The captain was too frightened to even try to turn Phaedra away.

She set foot on her home soil well before dusk and followed the thread from Hunter's belt until she came to the ruins of what was once Silent Hall.

There was only the wall now, and even that had lost a foot or so off the top of it. The gate that had once led through its passage under the tower now lacked both gate and tower, though the passage, at least, remained. For a moment, Phaedra feared that Hunter's belt would lead her to a corpse.

But then Hunter himself appeared, running toward her. She leapt into his arms joyfully and laughed as he twirled her around, feeling that once-familiar rush of dizziness. It was a sensation she hadn't felt since her teenage years, when people had still spoken of her as the best dancer in Karsanye, a girl who would surely dance through life. For the first time in over a decade, she thought they might be right after all.

Hunter put her down eventually, but he kept his arms around her. "It's done," he said. "I... I got it done."

"You're wonderful," she said, in between kisses. "Oh, Hunter, I'm so glad."

"Do you... do you want to come in?"

For the first time since she spotted him coming toward her, Phaedra looked around. Nobody else was approaching through the gate. There were no heads peeking over the wall. The landing that Psander's tower window had stood at the end of wasn't even there anymore.

Phaedra took a step back. "Are we... are we alone, Hunter? Where is everyone?"

"They all left once the tremors stopped. They wanted to build lives someplace peaceful, without all the memories."

"And Psander?"

Hunter looked grave. "She left too. Her whole library's in the cellar where the food used to be – she said she wanted you to have it, and the place wouldn't survive a week if she stayed."

"So she... left?"

"She left. She said you were going to start a school here and bring academic wizardry back to the world, and that the best way to make sure the place didn't burn down first was to go. Is that true?"

"That I'm going to start a school of academic wizardry?" Phaedra thought of Dessa, and of all the seekers of magic who might come after her, and she nodded. "Yes. I will. You'll help me, though, right? We can found that school together?"

"I can move books," Hunter said. "I can't teach anyone magic."

She laughed and kissed him again, and threw her arms over his shoulders. "Oh, Hunter, this is going to be such a good life."

He nodded. "Long and meaningful. That's what my father said when he came back from the Oracle of Laarna: that if I left on that fishing boat with you, my life would be long and meaningful. Did you know that's the one prophecy I never really believed?"

"But you believe it now?"

"How could I not?"

Phaedra beamed and took his hand, and they walked through the open archway together.

43

PSANDER

The elf-magic she had stolen from her enemies proved useful for more than just driving the queen away: it gave her the power she needed to pull her full fortress – what remained of it, anyway – through the gate to Tarphae.

There was no time to reverse her wards, to turn them from projecting the sensation of Godly protection back to concealing the fortress from those Gods Themselves. The most she had time for was to ward her body – and her body alone – against the Gods' sight, and even that wouldn't last more than an hour or so. It was time, at long last, to go out and meet her fate.

The villagers had fled already by the time she gave Hunter her instructions and struck out into the forest. She had no destination but "away," no distance she had to travel besides "far enough," and for the first and last time since early childhood, Psander's mind was quiet. At long last, the days of planning her next move were over.

It was a curious thing that now that she had mere minutes to live, she suddenly felt she had *time*. Time to reflect, to breathe in the fresh, vaguely-salty air of the island and admire the way the sun shone through

Tarphae's tall, straight guardian trees. She could hear birds trilling audaciously up above, just far enough away to be unconcerned with Psander's presence. For decades she had dealt in the sort of magics that altered one's natural aura in ways that animals found unsettling; she hadn't heard such nearby birdsong in ages. No wild or feral animal would bother her here, not unless some God chose to make the wildlife Its weapon. Especially compared to those in the elven world – the *former* world, that was – the forests of Tarphae were so gentle and benign. It was a shame she had never visited this place before.

But then, she would never have appreciated it back then, not unless she had felt resigned, as she now was, to her life's end. Some things, one needed perspective for.

She thought she had done well in this life, all things considered. She had certainly succeeded in her original goal to become a master wizard the same way her uncle had been a master glassblower, to surpass all others in her craft. She hadn't only surpassed all the others: she had outlived them by decades, plundered their libraries whenever she had the chance, and built perhaps the finest collection of books the world had ever known. Her magic had defied Gods, and her ideas had reshaped worlds. She couldn't have asked for a much greater legacy than that.

She had high hopes that her legacy would live on in Phaedra and whatever students she could attract. Phaedra might have despised Psander for her methods, but she was an even-handed woman, and she would not fail to honor the wizard who had rescued academic wizardry from its many enemies and preserved such a library that its study could be revived within a generation.

Yes, Phaedra had a lot to thank her for, if she had in fact

survived the worlds' merger. Phaedra's aspirations, her learning, even her ability to pursue magical knowledge and a lover at the same time, she owed to Psander. Psander didn't think she would forget.

It was a shame to be leaving the world just as the Gods' influence on it was about to wane, but Psander knew that influence couldn't possibly recede fast enough to save her. In any case, no human had ever yet achieved immortality. One was bound to leave this place sometime.

It was strange the way anxiety vanished when death stopped being a possibility and became a certainty. When she had invited the elves into her home, the anxiety had been almost unbearable. Now, ambling away to meet her doom, Psander was calm.

Deep in the woods, the dragon was waiting for her.

It was enormous, far larger than she had imagined, but lither too. It had knocked down a few trees, but had mostly settled itself between them, its long tail snaking out of sight. It studied her with coal-black eyes, specked here and there with gold.

"You must be Salemis," Psander said. "I have heard much of you, but never thought I'd get to meet you. What are you doing here?"

The dragon lifted its enormous head and answered her, in a series of perfectly-coherent hisses, "You have come to ask something of my God. I am here to help you."

Psander smiled ruefully. "I am in no position to ask your God for favors. I have never served God Most High, only my own principles, and I have no leverage to speak of. If you leave me here, the other Gods will smite me before your back is fully turned."

"You have come here to sacrifice yourself," the dragon

prophet answered her. "I am not mistaken. But you would offer that sacrifice without atoning or giving thanks, without even a request? I did not come here to dissuade you, wizard. I have come to *accept* your sacrifice on behalf of my God, so that your spirit will rise to meet Him and not lie at the mercy of your enemies. So tell me: there is a reason you have not stayed in your home, but instead came here to find me. Make your request."

Psander's eyes widened as Salemis spoke, then filled with inexplicable tears. She had never expected this. Never in a thousand years.

"I do not deserve this offer of yours," she said.

"Nonetheless, I am here."

"You would come to meet me here, knowing that I have come to die at the Gods' hands as their *enemy*, and offer to *sanctify* my death? What have I done to elicit such generosity?"

"You changed the heavens and the earth, Psander. Phaedra did not conceive of her plan alone – you have always been the unseen force, hiding where no one but those children could reach you. You gave them the help they needed to rescue me, the knowledge they needed to make peace between my descendants and their neighbors, and when I thought we had arranged everything so that the world's repentance would save it from the Yarek, it was you who gave Phaedra her plan to unify the Yarek and ask *it* to repent too."

"I never said anything to her about repentance."

"You altered my God's plans and extended *more* of His mercy into the world. Your intentions are not my concern."

Psander stared long and hard at the dragon prophet. "Are you here on your God's behalf, or on your own?"

"God Most High will grant me this favor. It is with His permission that I came to wait for you."

"Then here is my request of your God: let this all be worth it. Let the library remain, and let Phaedra find it; let her school flourish and may God Most High send her no students unworthy of her tutelage. Let my home become a place of learning and not of hiding, free of the fear and mortal danger that drove me to build it. Can your God grant me that?"

Salemis nodded his big head once. "He can."

Psander wiped the tears from her eyes. The dragon had not promised that his God *would* grant her request, only that He could. Even so, it couldn't hurt to ask for what she wanted; not when she had the opportunity to sanctify the sacrifice she had already chosen to make.

"Then I am ready."

Her mentor Pelamon had once told her that true dragon fire was so hot, a direct blast could melt a person's flesh in a near-painless instant. It was only one among many claims that she had never believed she would have the chance to verify.

It was quite the legacy she had. Surely the finest academic that ever lived.

44
RAVENNIS

This is worse than it was when I got here. I finally had a system that was working, You know. I was classifying souls as they came in, and my angels were separating them into their places and harnessing the power of the useful ones to keep the whole system running smoothly. I was well prepared to handle the extra load. Now I don't even know how many souls got out.

They will all come back to you eventually, Ravennis.

You nearly killed me.

You nearly deserved it.

Can You blame me? I could see what You were doing, but not one thread of fate showed the Yarek repenting. What was I supposed to do?

Trust in Me that it was possible. Let the Yarek make its choice.

And what then? If it didn't repent, I'd be gone and You would be battling for control again, when all that was supposed to be settled. There was too much at stake.

The Yarek deserved its chance.

I knew You would say that. That's why I tried to keep Phaedra from reaching it: I knew You were too lenient.

Has it turned out so badly for you, Ravennis? Are you so

angry that the Yarek stands?

I'm angry that You told me it wouldn't. You encouraged me to go against Your will, so that I further endangered myself. I, the Keeper of Fates, was fed a lie.

You were not. The threads of fate were My plans from the beginning of days, but things have changed since then. The world has changed, the Yarek has changed, and so have I. I did warn you, Ravennis, that I had seen an end to all things once planned.

You gave that message to Salemis, not to me.

I knew you were watching. You never failed Me before.

Be clearer next time. You gave the Yarek more of a chance than You gave me. If it hadn't been for Narky and his prayer, I wouldn't even be talking to You right now.

Then perhaps you should learn humility from the experience. The prayers of your servants are not to be dismissed.

You would *say that.*

You are still angry.

The Yarek didn't deserve Your mercy! What good is it doing now? I can see its influence spreading over the world, weakening my own influence and the others' too, sealing us in our realms. Destroying it would have been worth *the death of the world. What is there that couldn't have been rebuilt, and rebuilt even better than before? You betrayed us, and all for a world that was flawed from the start.*

Did you create the world that you would have seen destroyed? Who are you to tell Me which creations are worth abandoning?

Nobody. Just a servant.

Yes, indeed.

EPILOGUE

The expedition from Ksado arrived two weeks after Phaedra, not in Karsanye but at a much smaller cove on the island's northern shores. The landing parties made their way across the island, making note of abandoned villages and farmlands long since returned to nature, an empty homeland waiting for new life.

It was not entirely deserted: the farther they traveled toward the southwestern tip of the island, the more people they spotted, but these seemed to be surveying the island too. The few people who were seen farming were mostly of Essishan descent. A few, thankfully, spoke Estic, though their speech was heavily accented and full of regional variations – bastardized almost beyond recognition, really. Nevertheless, when the scouts reported back to Kvati, they were able to give her a full and complete report.

On the advice of one of the farmer-slaves, the flotilla circled the island until it came to the port that had once been named for Karassa. Fifty ships, ten thousand souls, came to shore on the island of Tarphae, with Kvati as their leader. At her command, a thousand troops swept across the island, freeing slaves and executing any who opposed the measure. Essisha had abolished the barbaric practice of slavery at the same time it had eliminated its wizards, and Kvati had no interest in re-learning this western savagery.

At last, her scouts returned with the Wizard Phaedra herself. The two women embraced, and said nearly simultaneously, "I'm glad you're here."

Phaedra's news came first: there would be no shattering of the world, no crashing of the sky. The cries of those who had begged her God Above All for their lives had been heard, and even the ancient monster Phaedra had planted had echoed their call. Had Phaedra *meant* to end the world, as Tnachti had believed, it would have ended weeks ago. As Kvati had expected, her armada had come too late.

But there was no turning back now: the duchess had ordered half her ships dismantled and repurposed into building materials for her people. This would be their home for the next hundred years, and the next thousand. The twenty-five warships that remained would be more than enough to overwhelm a weakened Atunaean navy, for all that the city across the strait was apparently the strongest regional power. The west was lucky no one had thought to expand westward in a thousand years.

Some changes would have to be made, Kvati told her young friend. This port capital, once called Karsanye, could no longer be named after the Goddess who had tried to drown the expedition in storms. Phaedra had smiled at that and told the duchess – they were calling her the Queen Auntie now – that she had pushed out the Goddess' influence herself. This change would be a welcome one.

They named it New Ksado, since the island itself had a name already, and sent Kvati's soldiers and their families to reclaim the farms, orchards, and shipyards that had once made this island great. Phaedra was declared Royal

Wizard, and her fortress was rebuilt from its former ruin into a tower of learning. Soon, hopeful students were arriving from all over the archipelago and the continent too, begging to be taught.

Kvati was especially pleased with Phaedra's choice of husband. He was a quiet man, and loyal to a fault, but he was useful for more than making his wife happy: he was also well versed in the local military history, and able to advise Kvati on the various regional powers. He humbly insisted that his information was at least a decade out of date, but a military advisor with his level of knowledge was worth more than ten years of gossip. Besides which, she was sure the man would bring himself up to speed quickly.

Most valuably for Kvati's new nation, Phaedra and her husband had close ties to one of the newer continental powers – and, through a renowned witch, also had a line of influence to the Great Tree on the horizon. It was this tree, Phaedra explained, that had nearly ended the world, and more than any nation of men, its power would be growing.

Kvati's people were very much attached to their old Gods and their old ways, but the Queen Auntie herself was a pragmatic woman, and adopted her wizard's God for her own. She was glad when Phaedra did not advise her to take up the local practice of sacrifice, but instead encouraged her to worship this oldest God in a new way. It would not only be more comfortable but useful too to meld the cultures of Essisha and Salemica together. Over time, at their own paces, more and more of Kvati's people would take up the worship of God Most High – and, one might hope, God Most High's older worshippers would gradually move away from animal sacrifice. One could ask for a God's blessing without paying a life for it.

Increasingly, Kvati felt that her people *did* have God Most High's blessing. They had left on their voyage in the hopes of convincing Phaedra to spare their lives, and here they were now, bringing new life and new justice to Phaedra's homeland while the wizard brought forth old magics and new wisdom from her school. As Kvati told her husband and children, these were the makings of a great nation – and great nations were the foundation of a new world.

Or as the old Essishan saying, the one that had replaced sacrifice, went: *Praise God.*

Acknowledgments

This was a year of change, much of it for the better but none of it easy. Our trials were many and I struggled to meet my wordcount goals until by stroke of good fortune we managed to make the switch we'd been dreaming of for years: my wife found a job that could provide for our family, advance her career, and allow me to become the stay-at-home ~~assassin trainer~~ dad I'd always hoped to be.

It was this switch that made it all possible, and so this time Becky gets thanked first. Thank you so much for bringing home the (kosher turkey) bacon, for giving me the life I dreamed of, and for the five-plus years that you toiled in these dark and lonesome child mines before leaving the easy part to me. That metaphor is absolutely over-the-top ridiculous, but you know what I mean.

The funny thing is, I had never imagined that being a stay-at-home parent would make me more productive. But that's because I hadn't anticipated all the family and institutional support that would allow me to write during daylight hours. It turns out that if somebody you trust is watching your children for a few hours a week, you can get an awful lot of writing done in a very short time.

So next I'd like to thank my parents and in-laws, who

were once more incredibly generous with their time. They played for hours, gave insightful comments on drafts, and encouraged me when finishing seemed impossible.

To the rest of my family beta readers, Nathan, Becca, and Miriam, thanks for all your feedback and support. It means so much to know that there are brilliant, thoughtful people waiting so eagerly to read each draft. Having in-house fans is the best.

I must also thank the Shaloh House preschool, its Chabad director Rabbi Menachem Gurkow and preschool director Marilyn Rabinovitz, and its many wonderful teachers. Their warmth and generosity allowed me to dedicate many mornings to putting one word in front of the other without worrying about my children's welfare. They made my children happy and my writing goals attainable, and they deserve my utmost thanks.

You know who I haven't thanked before, but who really, really deserves thanks? Andreas Rocha, who made all three of the absolutely gorgeous covers for this series. He has an amazing knack for taking a short descriptive paragraph and making it look exactly the way I imagined, except better. They say not to judge a book by its cover, but thanks to Andreas I won't mind if you do. Good covers have the power to introduce readers to authors they don't know, and when I started out, nobody knew me. Thanks for your help in changing that.

Silent Hall
N. S. DOLKART

Refugees from a cursed island must face their pasts
if they are to defy their gods

N. S.